HARLEQUIN SUPERROMANCE
Celebrates its 20th Anniversary

*Two decades of bringing you the very best
in romance reading.*

*To recognize this important milestone,
we've invited six very
special authors—whose names you're sure to recognize—
to tell us how they feel about Superromance.
Each title this month has a letter
from one of these authors.*

**Sandra Field, whose foreword you'll read in this
book, was one of the first authors approached to
write for Superromance. Her compelling and
dramatic stories, filled with very real and very
interesting characters, were perfectly suited
to the series—then and now.**

***Homecoming* is Laura Abbot's seventh Superromance.
This former English teacher from the Midwest
creates wonderfully appealing,
true-to-life characters and puts them in
complete and familiar worlds—
both hallmarks of Harlequin Superromance.**

D06683989

Dear Reader,

What a powerful, compelling concept "home" is! For some, alas, it is a painful word, reflecting disappointment, failed expectations, even loneliness. For others, the mere word itself evokes rich memories, nostalgic emotions and a sense of belonging.

Homecoming was a project that moved me in many ways, not only because it was my privilege to work with some truly wonderful authors, but because through Tom Baines and Lynn Kendall I could explore to my heart's content some of the many connotations of "home."

One of the most important "homes" in this book, however, is Meacham House, a program for disadvantaged young people, "homeless" by virtue of the fact that they lack stable families, guidance and a place where they know they are accepted and loved. If your community has turned a blind eye to these rootless adolescents, I hope the fictional Meacham House will inspire you to take steps to make such a "home" a reality for them.

Finally, a generous thank-you to our wonderful new Hoosier friends who made my husband and me feel so "at home" as we toured Indiana while researching this book. You are special!

Happy homecomings!

Laura Abbot

P.S. I'd love to hear from you.
Please write me at P.O. Box 2105, Eureka Springs, AR 72632 or at LauraAbbot@msn.com. I also invite you to check out these Web sites: www.nettrends.com/lauraabbot and www.superauthors.com.

FOREWORD BY SANDRA FIELD

Homecoming
Laura Abbot

HARLEQUIN®

TORONTO • NEW YORK • LONDON
AMSTERDAM • PARIS • SYDNEY • HAMBURG
STOCKHOLM • ATHENS • TOKYO • MILAN • MADRID
PRAGUE • WARSAW • BUDAPEST • AUCKLAND

To my fellow Riverbend authors whose talent and generosity of spirit have won my heartfelt appreciation and respect.

And to the special young people and dedicated adults of Lane House who furnished part of the inspiration for this book.

ISBN 0-373-70937-4

HOMECOMING

Visit us at www.eHarlequin.com

Printed in U.S.A.

FOREWORD BY SANDRA FIELD

In the late seventies, I'd mapped out a clear course of action: move to Nova Scotia's Annapolis Valley with my two children and embark on a master's degree in psychology at Acadia University. I'd been writing for both Harlequin Romance and Harlequin Presents for a few years; this would furnish me with an income. Simple! And then George Glay, a Toronto-based editor with Harlequin, got in touch with me, asking if I would consider writing for a new series called Superromance, and I had to rethink my plans. I knew very little about the book industry, but I suspected it wasn't every day of the week that editors approached writers; the reverse, in my experience, was far more often true.

In those days, Superromances were 95,000 words in length, as opposed to the 50-55,000 words of the shorter series. A subplot was essential. So I invented another writing persona called Jocelyn Haley and went to work, and I never did do the master's in psychology. We did, however, move to the valley, where we rented an old farmhouse outside Wolfville. Flanked by barns and orchards, the house overlooked 3000 acres of farmland reclaimed from the Fundy tides by early French settlers called Acadians. Flat and fertile farmland, with a wide expanse of sky. Hawks, eagles, gulls and the waving grasses of summer.

For me, writing Superromances had something of the quality of that place. There was a spaciousness that enabled me to contemplate the joys and vicissitudes of love. There was room for my characters to develop, for the intricacies of personality and motivation to lead the hero and heroine in whichever direction they wished to go, and minor characters appeared as unexpectedly as the small, short-eared owls that would materialize at dusk over the ditches and dirt roads behind the house. There was ample time to play.

And isn't that, in the end, what writing is all about? About abundance. About enjoying the process. And, of course, about passing on the pleasures of that process to you, the reader of Superromances.

CAST OF CHARACTERS

Tom Baines: Prize-winning journalist, estranged father and River Rat

Lynn Kendall: Minister and newcomer to Riverbend

Ruth and Rachel Steele: Tom's twin maiden aunts, operators of Steele's Books

Kate McMann: Manager of Steele's Books and Lynn's best friend

Pete Baines: Tom's fifteen-year-old son

Libby Baines: Tom's thirteen-year-old daughter

Abraham Steele: Town patriarch and bank president, recently deceased

Prentice Jewett: Influential property owner and town curmudgeon

Charlie Callahan: Contractor, temporary guardian and River Rat

Beth Pennington: Physician's assistant, athletic trainer and Charlie's ex-wife

Aaron Mazerik: Former bad boy, current basketball coach and counselor at Riverbend High

Lily Bennett Holden: Golden girl, widow, artist and River Rat

PROLOGUE

Dublin, Ireland
Spring 1999

IT WAS AN ORDINARY MORNING, another routine assignment. Dense clouds hung oppressively over the city, and for the fourth straight day rain fell. Drenched pedestrians hurried to their destinations, heads lowered, black umbrellas offering scant protection. Automobiles, buses and lorries careered through the crowded streets, honking, vying for position and heedlessly splashing those on the sidewalks unlucky enough to be near the gutter.

Tom Baines leaned wearily against the seat of the press syndicate's staff car. The driver was skillful and, despite the heavy traffic, would get him and his photographer, Gordy Maxwell, to the assignment on time. With luck, the event would go off according to schedule, and he could return to the hotel, close the drapes and nurse the hellacious hangover thudding like thunderbolts against his skull.

"You want the standard stuff?" Beside him, Gordy fidgeted with the leather strap of his camera case.

Opening his eyes to a slit, Tom replied in a low growl, "Yeah, the diplomatic greeting at curbside, the politicians' handshake—you know the drill."

"That doesn't make the front page." Gordy, who

had a gift for stating the obvious, had been with Tom
for eight years and, like Tom, chafed at routine assignments. The Scot's prize-winning photographs and
Tom's incisive news dispatches and columns had established them as one of the premier partnerships in
print journalism. Their success was the result of ini-
tiative, courage, even recklessness, and a bit of luck.
By contrast, today's assignment was a no-brainer.

"You got that right, pal." Ever since the uneasy
peace agreement between the warring factions in
Northern Ireland, this posting had offered few big stories. "We'll do a quick in and out and be back at the
hotel in time for lunch."

The driver swerved, and the movement increased
the pain in Tom's head. He never should have had
that final double scotch at the pub last night.

"Here we are, gents." The driver maneuvered the
car near the spot where the press pool was setting up
under an awning. Tom glanced at his watch. Five
minutes to show time. According to protocol, the
United Nations ambassador would be greeted curbside
by the mayor. Despite the rain, onlookers had gathered, including a group of children wearing uniform
blue jackets sporting their school insignia. Bloody
Irish were accustomed to this nasty weather. Or else,
as Gordy would put it, they were just plain daft.

Tom pulled a ball cap low over his forehead, buttoned his thigh-length raincoat and immediately
stepped into a puddle. *Damn.* Gordy scurried alongside, his red hair already soaked.

Just as Gordy and Tom reached the shelter of the
press tent, the rain slackened to a drizzle. The assembled journalists studied the motorcade's progress on a
TV monitor. While Gordy pulled his camera out of

its case and began adjusting lenses and settings, Tom watched as the police escort, several blocks away, led the limousine, UN flags on the hood fluttering in the breeze. The picture then panned to the functionaries huddled in the entrance to the government office building, including the mayor.

Members of the press pool surged nearer the site where the limousine would dispatch its eminent passenger. As usual, Tom and Gordy avoided the others clustering like a multilimbed journalistic beast on a feeding frenzy and, instead, walked partway down the sidewalk, past the reserved parking place. In the distance the limo appeared. The schoolchildren on the opposite curb pressed forward, even as their teacher admonished them to stay well back.

Perfunctorily Tom pulled out his small leather-bound notebook and pen and began jotting a few notes. Suddenly Gordy grabbed him by the elbow, his voice low and urgent.

"See that?" He jerked Tom's arm slightly and nodded to the left. Coming up the street, traveling in the opposite direction from the limousine, was a lone motorcyclist in a bedraggled green wool sweater and a newsboy's cap, with a large pack slung over his shoulders. The other members of the press, their backs turned, eyes trained on the mayor, failed to notice. However, two or three of the schoolboys, perhaps entranced with the motorcycle, stepped into the street. The hum of the limousine engine sounded in Tom's ears. One moment the scene was benign. The next he heard Gordy yell, "My God, the children!" and, beside him was a vacant spot where his friend had stood.

With dawning horror, Tom took in a series of nearly simultaneous images. Unaware of the two lads approaching him, the cyclist had paused, his machine idling beside the school group. Slowly, surreptitiously, he reached into his backpack. The limousine purred the last few yards before coming to a stop. Down the red-carpeted steps came the mayor and his entourage, welcoming smiles sprouting on their media-conscious faces. And Gordy was running toward the cyclist, whose mouth had contorted in a malevolent sneer.

"Gor-dy!" Tom's scream sounded in his ears alone, because at that moment, the cyclist retrieved something from his backpack and hurled it with unerring accuracy at the very spot where the envoy was emerging from the limousine, his right hand extended toward the beaming mayor. The earsplitting explosion knocked the two men to the ground and rocked the limousine, which then itself exploded, sending shards of flying metal and pieces of bodies into the air.

Tom ran forward through the dense, noxious-smelling smoke, headed toward the spot where he'd last seen Gordy. A piece of flying metal glanced off his shoulder, his shoes crunched against slivers of glass, and wails of fear and pain pierced his eardrums. His lungs, seared with the fumes of gasoline and high explosives, struggled for oxygen.

Gordy! God! Let him be all right!

Oblivious to the rain, now intensifying again and sizzling on the burning metal, Tom groped through the debris, his hand coming to rest on a motorcycle fender. Ignoring the heat searing his palm, he struggled on, his eyes burning and streaming.

A gust of wind swept down the street, and the smoke dissipated momentarily. Directly in front of him lay a mangled camera, the lens shattered, and there, just beyond was Gordy, his body flung, ragdoll-like, facedown, head bent grotesquely to one side, red hair matted with the darker red of blood spewing from a gaping wound.

Tom knelt beside his friend, and a howl erupted from his laboring lungs, through his parched throat and into the smoke-filled air, just as, far in the distance came the insistent sound of klaxons.

Gently Tom rolled Gordy over, the lifeless arms dangling across Tom's thighs. He intended to carry his friend away from this unspeakable place, to lay him to rest where soft rain would cleanse the familiar but now blood-soaked body, where the scent of lilacs would wash away the stench of evil, where nothing could ever hurt him again.

But as he gathered Gordy's body in his arms, he saw crumpled under it a much smaller figure, a boy whose thin legs were covered with the thick knee socks worn by Irish schoolchildren. That was what Gordy had been doing—racing to save this child from the terrorist's fury. Then Tom noticed something miraculous—the boy's bony chest was rising and falling, rising and falling.

Swiping a hand down over Gordy's eyes, Tom moved his friend's body to one side, pausing to rest his hand briefly on Gordy's shoulder in farewell.

Then Tom scooped the unconscious child into his arms, struggled to his feet and bore the young victim through the pelting rain and human confusion to one of the ambulances choking the street, now strewn with debris…and the dead.

CHAPTER ONE

Riverbend, Indiana
August 2000

No WAY. Life couldn't be this serene, this simple, this innocent. Tom stood on the shady front porch of Uncle Abe's farmhouse surveying the scene before him. Neat fields of corn—broad green shoots reaching toward the azure sky, tassels spreading a gold blanket to the horizon—freshly painted barns and in the distance the meandering river glinting in the morning sun. A pastoral picture, even accompanied by a chorus of songbirds. So here he was, back home in Indiana. For whatever good that might do him.

He patted his shirt pocket, searching for a cigarette, before muttering a low curse. He'd given the damn things up. Old habits died hard.

But cigarettes weren't the answer any more than booze and women were. In the past year, God knows he'd tried to lose himself in both. To forget. Nothing had worked. The restlessness, the discontent persisted. Last winter, after abruptly abandoning his life as a foreign correspondent, the drifting had been welcome. At first. For a while.

Rocking back on his heels, he stuck his hands in the pockets of his rumpled khaki shorts. And now this. He looked around—at the large stone barbecue pit in the side yard, at the weathered chairs lining the porch and at the house itself, site of the raucous, male-only rites of long-ago hunting seasons—all of it now Uncle Abe's legacy to him.

Uncle Abe. Abraham Steele, Riverbend patriarch and benefactor. Admired, respected, sometimes loved and sometimes feared. Standing here after so many years was unsettling. Echoes of the shouts and laughter of his cousin Jacob and the rest of his group of friends, who had called themselves the River Rats because of their penchant for hanging out by the river, seemed borne on the breeze now feathering his face. He sighed. A long time ago. Another lifetime.

And now Jacob had up and disappeared, Uncle Abe was dead, and as for himself...well, who the hell knew?

He'd returned only once since his kids, Pete, fifteen, and Libby, thirteen, were born. And that was years ago. He'd wanted to show them off to their great-uncle. Show them the one place as a boy where he'd felt welcome. Now with his marriage long over and his son and daughter disenchanted with him, no place felt like home. But then, what did he expect?

Maybe it had been ungracious of him, but he'd written to his aunts, twin sisters Ruth and Rachel Steele, to request they give him some time by himself when he first arrived. He figured he might as well try solitude. Nothing else had worked. Besides, after only a few days in Indiana, he knew he wasn't quite ready for Riverbend.

As his gaze lifted to the tops of the century-old trees that sheltered the home, he had the disturbing sense that, for better or worse, this was the end of the line for him.

ON THE CARTERS' flower-bedecked screened-in porch, Lynn Kendall laid down her pen, set aside the journal in which she'd been writing and rocked quietly, hands folded in her lap. The faint squeak of the wicker chair, the rhythmic thump of the rockers on the wooden floorboards and the cheery song of a nearby wren filled her with contentment. At the edge of the lawn, the Sycamore River meandered in its timeless fashion.

She wiggled her toes in her comfy slippers. When was the last time she'd indulged herself like this? Here she was, at eight-thirty in the morning, still in her robe, and she didn't feel remotely guilty. Why should she? This was her vacation. Four glorious weeks!

She'd spent the first few days in Illinois visiting her mother and married sister. Rockford had been a good place to grow up in, and the house still evoked fond memories of coming of age under the watchful eyes of both her widowed mother and Nana, her grandmother. Nana. A smile hovered on her lips. What a lady! How thankful she was for her influence. One of Nana's favorite admonishments had been, "Take care of yourself first, sweetie, because you have to be all right before you can take care of anybody else."

Words Lynn was taking to heart here in this delightful sanctuary near Riverbend, which her friends Seth and Mary Carter had generously made available while they toured Australia. Without their kindness, she could never have afforded such a complete and restful getaway.

Granted, she was only a few miles from all her responsibilities, but no one except her good friend Kate McMann, who occasionally brought her supplies, and her secretary knew exactly where she was vacationing. Rest, relaxation, study, meditation, exercise, fresh air, no alarm clock. What more could a woman ask?

As if challenging her complacency, Benedict, her enormous black tomcat, jumped into her lap and began kneading her chest. "You think I could use more, fella? Like what?"

Benedict drew back, cocked his head as if assessing her sanity, then, with a swish of his tail, settled in her lap, emitting a single ragged purr. "Maybe you're right. Maybe there *is* something else." Lynn ran her fingers absently along the cat's soft coat. If she couldn't fool one savvy feline, how could she hope to fool herself? She tried to be satisfied with her life. She'd known the path she'd chosen wouldn't be easy, and it hadn't been. But it had offered rewards beyond any she could've imagined. Even after only a year and a half in Riverbend, she had come to understand some of the pleasant implications of the expression "God works in mysterious ways."

She stopped rocking and watched a canoe, propelled by two teenagers, glide down the river. Yes, a difficult path, but one that would be even more fulfilling if it could be shared. Shared with a mate, one who would come to know and love *all* of her, not just the part she showed to the world. And one who could accept who she needed to be, who she'd been *called* to be.

She leaned over, burying her nose in Benedict's fur. Then she straightened. "Mysterious ways? I could sure use some now, Sir, if it's not too much trouble."

LATER THAT DAY, Lynn dragged her bicycle from the garage. She needed regular rides to get herself into condition for the charity biking event in which she was to participate in the fall. She was probably nuts to go out on such a hot, steamy afternoon, but the nearby country roads were ideal for cycling.

At the far end of her route, she stopped, her attention arrested by an untended country cemetery at the top of a rise. She wheeled her bike up the hill, noticing that from here she could see the river in the distance. Then she propped her bicycle against the stone wall, entered through the rusty gate and hunkered before the first of several stones. "Ebenezer Vale, Faithful Husband, Father, and Friend, 1809-1878." Awed by the dates, she brushed back the weeds from an adjacent marker. "Letitia Vale, Rose of Heaven, 1815-1871." Curious, she pondered their lives. What had it been like more than a hundred years ago, alongside the river? Had Ebenezer Vale been a farmer? A canal man? Perhaps a blacksmith?

As Lynn stood up to leave, she tripped over a small flat stone, almost completely covered with weeds. Kneeling, she plucked away the vegetation until she could make out the simple but heartbreaking epitaph. "Baby died."

A sudden breeze raised bumps along her arms, and tears obscured the etched letters. Gently she laid her palm on the stone and spoke quietly. "Rest in peace, little one." In that moment she felt a pervading calm before being pulled back into the present by the chirp of grasshoppers and the hum of a distant tractor.

Sighing, she rubbed her hands down her spandex cycling tights, then slowly rose to her feet, vowing to return and explore the cemetery. Maybe she'd bring garden tools and attempt to restore some order to this sacred place.

Feeling renewed, she returned to the road, hopped on her bicycle and started off, mentally contemplating what plants she might place in the graveyard next spring to honor those long-dead. She was coasting happily along a level stretch when suddenly her bike jerked, barely giving her time to brake with one foot. She saved herself from being sent sprawling, but one of the pedals scraped her shin, leaving a long painful abrasion.

Standing on the roadside staring at the broken chain, she chastised herself for riding this far from home alone. She knew better. Frustrated, she studied her surroundings. Across the road she spied a dirt driveway that disappeared into a tunnel of eight-foot-high corn stalks. In the distance she made out the top of a steep-hipped roof. Surely it would be safer to take her chances with a resident of the area than with a passing motorist.

Hooking her helmet over the handlebars and rolling the bicycle along, she started up the driveway. The breeze had died and the air was stifling. She knew her face was a mottled crimson and her hair damp with perspiration. And the abrasion on her leg was starting to bleed. Surely some kindly maternal type lived in the house, which she could now make out completely as the cornfield gave way to a clearing. It was a white two-story with a stone chimney and a deep full-length porch. Even though there was no sign of life, the front door stood open.

Lynn laid the bike on the ground, pushed back the limp strands of hair hanging in her face and climbed the porch steps.

''Who's there?'' The voice was neither kindly nor maternal. Instead, it was gruff, unwelcoming—and distinctly male. A tall, broad-shouldered man with a short black crewcut graying at the temples, a two-or three-day growth of beard and a scowl on his face stepped out onto the porch. From the looks of him, he'd slept in his khaki shorts, and his wild Hawaiian shirt could have been previously owned by the proprietor of a dockside tattoo parlor. Her eyes drifted down hairy legs to the well-worn, water-spotted sandals on his feet. Whoever he was, he was no one's idea of a Norman Rockwell Hoosier. He eyed her. "You lost in the forest, Goldilocks?"

Biting back a grin and at the same time wondering what on earth possessed her, she decided two could play this game. "Granny, your eyes are failing. Don't you know Little Red Riding Hood when you see her?"

"Little Red Riding Hood, huh?" He stood, legs apart, arms folded over his chest. "Well, whoever, we don't want any."

"Any what?" She continued up the steps until she stood level with him, though several feet away.

"Of what you're selling."

"I'm not selling anything. I'm—"

"Furthermore, I'm a committed member of the Church of Perpetual Hedonism." He reached behind him and hooked his fingers through the screen-door handle. "Now, if you'll excuse me—"

Lynn took two steps forward. The arm with which she'd reached out to detain him fell uselessly to her side. "Wait. Please." The very least the man could do was let her use his phone. She could call Kate. "I've had some difficulty. See?" She pointed to her bike. "The chain broke, and I'm, well, stranded."

The man emitted an enormous sigh. "So you're...what? Looking for a Good Samaritan?"

Aptly put. "As a matter of fact, yes. And would that be...you?" She hoped she hadn't laid on too much sarcasm. Just enough to shame him into agreeing to help.

His brown eyes raked her body from top to toe. "You're bleeding."

She glanced at her shin. A trickle of blood was running down it to pool in the top of her sock. "So it seems."

He opened the door and stood aside to allow her to pass. "Come in. I'll get you something to put on the leg."

She stood her ground. "How do I know you're harmless?"

For the first time in their cautious exchange, she thought he might smile. "You don't." He shrugged. "For all you know, I could be the Big Bad Wolf." His eyes had a definite teasing glint.

"That's always a possibility." She studied him warily. He was not unattractive if you went for that Bruce Willis look. In fairness, cleaned up, he might even be...presentable.

"The question is, can you repair a bicycle?"

"We'll see. But not until after we look at that leg." He placed a hand behind her back and propelled her forward. "C'mon. We're letting flies in."

She stepped tentatively over the threshold. "You're sure I'm not disturbing your nap?"

"As a matter of fact, you are."

As her eyes adjusted to the dim light of the large high-ceilinged room, she noted that, indeed, a bed pillow with a dent in it lay on the large brown leather sofa. Mounted game birds and sepia-toned ancestors stared down at her from the cream-yellow walls. The massive mahogany furniture was definitely dated. But interesting. Even the most cursory inspection suggested that no one had run a vacuum or dust rag around the place lately. "Perhaps your wife could help me, and we can let you get back to your siesta."

"Fortunately that's one problem I don't have."

"What? A wife or getting back to your nap?"

"A wife."

Why was she not surprised? He hadn't moved from the doorway and, in fact, was continuing to give her a somewhat embarrassing once-over. "The alcohol? The bandages?" she prompted.

"Oh, sure. Sit down." He gestured at an over-stuffed armchair. "I'll be right back."

Perching on the edge of the chair, she tucked her hair behind her ears and looked around. A fireplace and ornately carved oak mantel dominated one wall. From the entry hall a set of stairs rose to the second story. Behind her, she could see an ample modernized kitchen. Her Good Samaritan had disappeared upstairs where, she supposed, the bedrooms and bath were located. Should she even be here? This man was a total stranger.

While she briefly considered fleeing—where? how?—he returned, his arms laden with washcloth, bandages, cotton balls and alcohol. He knelt beside her and set the supplies on the floor. "Here. Let me look." Before she could protest, he'd grabbed her leg and was swabbing the wound with the damp wash-cloth. Something about the cool cloth felt very pleas-ant but, she realized to her chagrin, not nearly as pleasant as the feel of his warm hand cupping the back of her calf. Her focus narrowed to the infinitesimal shifting of pressure of his fingers against her skin.

"Ouch!" She jerked away. "You might tell a girl when you're getting ready to apply alcohol to an open wound."

Expertly he stripped the backing off the bandage. "And a girl might pay attention, instead of closing her eyes and smiling that sappy grin."

She stared at him, lost for a comeback. Had she really behaved so transparently? And worse yet, so uncharacteristically? She nodded at the neat binding of the wound. "You've done this before."

He paused, then responded dryly, "I have."

He was still holding her leg, now with both hands. Wasn't he finished? She moved to stand up. "Thank you, Mr....er..."

He put his hands on her shoulders and pushed her back into the seat. "Sit still. I'll get you something cool to drink."

She exhaled. "I'd like that." And she realized she would. She was parched, tired and unaccountably curious about this man.

He returned shortly with two glasses of ice water. He pulled up a stool, sat in front of her and raised his glass. "Here's to little girls wandering in the woods."

She smiled, then gulped down a third of the liquid. "Since you're definitely not Granny, perhaps you could tell me who you really are."

He stuck out a hand. "Tom Baines."

She clasped his hand, then uttered a tiny cry of recognition. "*You're* Tom Baines?" She knew from her friend Kate that one of Riverbend's claims to fame was the Pulitzer prize-winning journalist's connection to the Steele family.

A soft smile crossed his lips. "I'm that former newspaperman in the flesh."

"Former?" When she questioned him, she noticed the smile fade, replaced by a look she could only define as guarded.

"It's not much of a life for an older guy. It's a young man's game."

"You don't look so old to me." In fact, he looked pretty darn virile.

"Thirty-six. That's over the hump."

"No way is thirty-six over the hump." What she'd intended as a riposte came out, instead, as a serious challenge. He stilled for a moment and she could see his jaw working.

He rose to his feet. "Believe it." He carried his empty glass to the kitchen, then stood by the door. "Ready to deal with your bike?"

Had she offended him? "Sure. I mean, thanks." She stumbled down the porch steps after him. "Really, I could call a friend."

"Not necessary." He hunkered down to look at the bike.

Did he always talk like this? As if he was barking orders? Maybe it was a journalistic occupational hazard—expending your store of words on paper, not in conversation.

After studying the chain-and-sprocket mechanism, he turned to her. "I have an extra chain, but it won't fit your bike. Sorry."

"Are you a cyclist?"

He picked up the bike and started around the house. "Not hardly. But I've found it's a cheap, efficient mode of transportation in places like Bangkok."

She trailed after him, wondering how many exotic

locales he had temporarily called home and what in the world he was doing at this isolated house. Surely if you retired from a career as a foreign correspondent, you wouldn't be satisfied in rural Indiana.

In the large detached garage were a sleek Chrysler convertible and an old red pickup truck. He hoisted the bicycle into the truck bed and laid it on its side. "Get in. I'll take you home."

Another barked order. She had to bite her tongue to prevent a sharp retort. After all, he *was* helping her. And he wasn't exactly a stranger, if reading his columns for years counted as acquaintance. She directed him to the Carters' house.

When they arrived, he lifted the bike out of the truck and propped it against the carport wall. In the gathering twilight he seemed to look at her appraisingly once more, then he ran his hands up and down her arms. She knew she should move, but she might as well have been carved in stone, for all the will she possessed. Next he did a curious thing. He stepped closer, gently brushed his knuckles across her cheek, then said, "Don't be too sure you didn't meet the wolf."

Abruptly he turned, strode to his truck and drove off, leaving Lynn leaning weakly against the wall, wondering why his words had set her heart racing. Wondering if God didn't have a particularly mischievous sense of humor. "Mysterious ways, indeed," she murmured.

AFTER A SUPPER of cold leftover pizza, a peanut-butter-and-banana sandwich and a wizened apple, Tom found himself back where he'd started the day—on the front porch, brooding. He'd kill for a cigarette.

He tilted his chair back on its rear legs, his feet propped on the railing, his fingers laced behind his head. Why did that woman have to come along to disturb his much-prized isolation? More baffling, why had he even let her in the door? Stupid question. He wasn't, yet, so much of a jerk as to turn away a damsel in distress. Besides, she'd looked awfully appealing.

Another enigma. Appealing? With that flushed face, those limp hanks of strawberry-blond hair, that determined set to her jaw and a leg dripping blood? About as appealing as… Words failed him, which was practically a first.

Because although the truth was she looked like the "before" model in a beauty makeover, something about her had nevertheless twisted his gut. Maybe the wide smiling mouth or the flirtatious twinkle in those soft gray eyes. Or the sprinkling of pale freckles across her nose and on her high forehead. Or perhaps it was something more elemental—like the way those tights clung to her nicely rounded bottom or the feel of her shapely calf in his hand or the pert breasts concealed by—

He was suddenly reminded of an article he'd read somewhere that suggested a man could tell within the first five minutes of being with a woman whether or not he wanted to go to bed with her. He hadn't believed it. Then.

He allowed the front legs of the chair to come down with a thump, then stood up. He'd diverted himself with women in France, Sweden and the Orient. But he'd never been so immediately or viscerally aroused on first sight by even the most glamorous or seductive of them as he'd been by... He slapped the railing. Hell! He didn't even know her name.

Under other circumstances, such an oversight would make him the laughingstock of the newsroom. Tom Baines, author of the internationally syndicated column "Hot Spots" and ace reporter who'd covered uprisings, pestilences, revolutions and disasters from Africa to Japan hadn't had the wits to ask the one vital question. Her name, for crying out loud!

He sat back down, but after a few seconds he uttered a triumphant "Hah!"

Because he *did* know all he needed to. He knew exactly where she lived.

CHAPTER TWO

LYNN RUBBED THE SLEEP out of her eyes, wiped her face gently with a damp washcloth, then brushed her teeth. Unbelievable. She couldn't remember the last time she'd slept until eight. Sighing with pleasure, she smeared lotion on her cheeks and forehead, soothing the sunburn her fair skin had suffered yesterday.

She examined her face in the mirror. She never wore much makeup, only enough to bring out her pale eyes and moisten her lips. On vacation, though, she was doing without, even if she did look a bit washed-out.

"Washed-out" was nothing, though, compared to how she must've looked to Tom Baines. Hot and sweaty, hair hanging in her face, thoroughly unfeminine. She grimaced at her reflection. What did she care? He had been rude and downright boorish.

And handsome as all get-out! Overnight she'd had to reassess her opinions of the Bruce Willis bad-boy look. And what had that final gesture been about? She'd expected irritation from him. Justifiable. She'd definitely inconvenienced him. Heaven forbid, she'd interrupted his nap! And yet... She remembered with vivid clarity the way his hands had skimmed her arms, the sweetness of that whisper of his knuckles across her sunburned cheek. There had been an unexpected, even incongruous gentleness in his leave-taking. Along with the decidedly suggestive growl in his parting comment.

She'd never imagined such a fleeting touch and so few words could cause the kind of seismic reaction she'd experienced as she'd watched him climb into the truck and drive away.

Enough. She gathered her hair into a ponytail, pulled her pink cotton batiste robe over her shorty pajamas and padded barefoot into the kitchen, heading straight for the coffee canister.

Benedict brushed across her bare legs, rubbing against the bandage, still neatly in place, despite the shower she'd had last night. "You sly kitty. You know how to wangle your breakfast, don't you?" She flipped on the coffeemaker, then, trailing the meowing cat, entered the utility room where she poured food into his dish. "Are you satisfied now, big man?" Contented chomping was her answer until suddenly the cat froze, ears forward in listening mode.

Then Lynn heard something, too—the sound of a car door slamming close by. Maybe even in the driveway. Before she could get to a window to investigate, there was an insistent pounding on the door. She couldn't imagine who'd be here at eight-fifteen in the morning.

She smoothed her robe, retied the sash, tiptoed to the kitchen window and peered out. The knocking resumed. There, parked big as life in front of the carport, was a battered red pickup. A familiar battered red pickup. Her mouth went dry. Tom? One thing was for sure. His manners hadn't improved overnight. The crack of dawn was no time for social calls. What could he possibly want?

Benedict was already in the front hallway in his guard-cat pose. She opened the door and stared at Tom. He wore a different pair of rumpled shorts—navy blue this time—and a white T-shirt. His hair was still damp from what she assumed had been a morning shower and he was clean-shaven.

"Ms. Carter?"

"No."

He looked puzzled. "That's the name on the mailbox."

"Yes."

"But that's not your name?"

"No." She, who'd spent her life helping others, couldn't resist the impulse to string him along. He brought out in her an impish, playful side that wouldn't be denied.

"Well, let me start over." He turned away, looking heavenward, as if seeking guidance, then faced her again. "Ms. R. R. Hood, I presume?"

She bit the corner of her lip to keep from laughing. "No."

He cocked an eyebrow. "You're not going to make this easy for me, are you?"

She shook her head.

"I must be rusty. Usually my interviewing technique is more productive."

"Interviewing technique? Pardon me if I'm misinformed, but doesn't interviewing usually involve, um, asking questions, rather than presuming?" She hugged herself. She shouldn't be enjoying this so much.

"Touché." He took a step forward, forcing her to retreat into the hall. As he advanced, she caught a whiff of some fresh-smelling soap, and it was enough to almost buckle her knees. Dear heaven, he was attractive! "So exactly what *is* your name?"

By now he had cupped her chin in his hand and was probing her eyes with his. Her mouth was mere inches from his. She mustered her voice. "Lynn Kendall," she said a bit too loudly.

"Lynn Kendall?" he repeated slowly, as if savoring the name on his tongue. His hand strayed to her shoulder. She was determined not to give ground, but the fierce fluttering of her heart alarmed her. Benedict tried to help by insinuating himself between their legs. Tom's gaze locked on her face. Finally he said, "Could a man get a cup of coffee here this morning, Ms. Kendall, especially since he's come to pick up a bicycle to be fixed?"

"He has? You are?" Lynn stumbled, then gathered her wits. "Coffee? Sure." Relieved to have an excuse to move, Lynn edged toward the kitchen, but somehow couldn't summon the will to stop looking at him. Then she nearly tripped over Benedict, loyally sticking to her side. Before she could regain her balance, Tom had grabbed her by the elbow, his arm snaking around her waist.

"You okay?"

Okay? Did "flustered" qualify? "Fine, thanks." She stepped out of his grasp, calling over her shoulder, "Black or polluted?"

"I like mine neat." He followed her into the kitchen, then sat on a stool and folded his arms on the countertop. *Neat,* she thought. He probably arranged his life like that, as well. No frills, no complications. She poured two mugs of coffee, shoved one across the counter toward him, then stood inhaling the rich aroma, grateful for the barrier the counter provided.

"So, Lynn Kendall, why isn't your name on the mailbox?"

"I don't live here."

"Oh?"

"I'm on vacation. The Carters were kind enough to let me use their place. I needed some peace and solitude."

"Is that a pointed remark?" He eyed her over the rim of his coffee mug.

She considered her answer. "It would be ungracious of me to provoke my Good Samaritan. I'm grateful to you for helping me yesterday."

"What about today?" He took a sip of coffee. "Have truck, will travel. To the bicycle-repair shop."

She wavered. With his pickup, it would be much simpler for him than for her to haul the bike. Then she made a reluctant admission. Accepting his offer would ensure that she would have one more encounter with him. Shameless, that was what she was. She ran her finger around the rim of her mug, then lifted her eyes. "Thank you. That would be most helpful. Maybe with my endorsement, you could start your own business. The Traveling Samaritan."

"I'm not always so generous." His mouth quirked and his eyes teased. "Only certain people qualify."

"Like hot, bedraggled roadside victims who stumble into your lair?"

He set his mug down and began rounding the

counter. "No, like certain females with mischievous streaks who aren't afraid of big bad wolves." He'd reached her and put his hands on her waist, pinning her to the spot. He lowered his voice. "You're not afraid, are you?"

Afraid? Terrified, maybe. "Of course not."

"Good," he whispered, and then his mouth closed over hers in a gentle, yet searing kiss. For support, she gripped the counter at her back. This couldn't be happening. But in spite of herself, she liked it.

He pulled away first and in his face was mirrored her own surprise. And something else. A fleeting seriousness, as if he'd overstepped a self-imposed boundary. He appeared to search for a means to defuse his impetuosity and finally said in an even voice, "Lynn Kendall? That's a nice, solid name." With that, he started toward the door, but then turned and added, "I'll let you know when the bike will be ready. In the meantime, don't befriend any other strangers."

And he left. Just like that.

Lynn blinked. What on earth had possessed the man? Or more to the point, what on earth had possessed her? He had walked into the house, taken her by storm and walked out, a man obviously accustomed to getting his own way. And the worst of it was, she'd liked it. She liked *him*.

But this was vacation. This wasn't her world, her real life. She couldn't be sure how she'd feel if it was. She only knew she wouldn't be able to live with herself if he ever came to believe she was toying with him.

Yet in his dark eyes, beyond the surface humor, she read wariness. Down that path, she suspected, lay trouble for him. And if she became involved, perhaps trouble for her, too.

For that had not been an idle kiss.

She scooped up Benedict and wandered toward the screened-in porch, speaking in a quiet voice. "Surely, Sir, *this* isn't what You had in mind, is it?"

RUTH STEELE bustled around the kitchen, clearing the dishes, rinsing them and loading them into the dishwasher, all while maintaining a running monologue. "I don't know what's the matter with that nephew of ours. I know he asked us to give him some time when he got back, but I thought he'd have called by now. Something's peculiar. He's not himself. Aloof. Distant. Like Heathcliff."

Rachel Steele arched her eyebrows as her sister scrubbed the chrome of the sink faucets. "Easy, dear. You're going to take the finish off." She sat at the kitchen table quietly going through the newspaper, scissors in her hand, while her twin rambled on. Snipping out a column, she said, "Here's a good recipe for creamed spinach."

"Are you listening to me at all?" Ruth folded a tea towel over the drying rack and faced her sister. "Or don't you care about the boy?"

Her lips pursed, Rachel set down the scissors and looked up. "What a ridiculous question! Of course I care about Tom, but in case you haven't noticed, he's hardly a boy. And if he needs time and space, the least we can do is give it to him."

"I suppose. But we're going to have to tell him about Aaron soon. Before he hears it somewhere else."

Rachel considered Ruth's statement. She agreed with her and was, in some ways, just as disturbed by recent events. Ever since their brother Abraham's death and his son Jacob's mysterious failure to return home for the memorial service, things had been out of kilter. "Tom was mighty fond of his uncle. The news of Abraham's death must have hit him hard." She pressed a hand to her chest, massaging a dull ache. "And now we have to burden him with more when we tell him Abraham had an illegitimate son living here in Riverbend all these years. And that it's Aaron Mazerik. A new cousin from out of the blue."

Ruth sighed. "He won't like Abraham's harboring such a secret clear to the grave."

Both sisters had been thrown by the revelation about Aaron. But Rachel knew that Ruth had a difficult time realizing that Tom was a fully grown functioning individual who had been satisfactorily running his own life for years without her direct intervention. Although neither of the sisters was particularly bothered by the fact that they had never married, it was second nature to take family members under their wings. And sometimes even outsiders like Kate McMann—whom they'd hired to manage their bookstore—and her adorable twin daughters.

When Rachel fell silent, Ruth crossed the room and stood over her, frowning. "What can Tom possibly be doing out there at Abe's old farmhouse by himself?"

"After the frantic schedule he's kept during all those years abroad, maybe solitude is just what he needs."

Ruth scoffed. "Solitude? That's not what he needs."

"Oh?" Rachel waited. She always knew when her twin had a pronouncement to make.

"No. He needs a good woman. Not a stay-at-home like his first wife and certainly not one of those empty-headed jet-setters." She untied her apron and carefully folded it before facing her sister again. "No, ma'am. I'm talking about a truly good woman who will settle that boy down, bring out the best in him."

"Man," Rachel automatically corrected. That was, however, her only criticism of her sister's remarks. A good woman was exactly what their battle-scarred, rootless nephew needed, especially now.

WHEN TOM TOOK Lynn's bicycle to the repair shop, he briefly considered dropping in on his aunts at their bookstore just off the Courthouse Square. But he decided against it. As soon as he set those wheels in motion, he'd be inviting family involvement in his life, and he wasn't ready yet for their solicitude, their questions. Especially when he could provide no answers. Nor was he ready to get sucked into Riverbend's stifling social scene.

As he drove home, he pondered, as he often did, the direction his life had taken since the bombing. After Gordy's death, he'd handled his assignments perfunctorily, merely going through the motions until one day he had up and quit, rationalizing that a complete break would give him the chance to deal with his emotions. But in these past few months no amount of traveling—to Waikiki, San Francisco, Vancouver, New York City—no well-intentioned interventions of friends and colleagues, had insulated him from his darkest thoughts. On top of everything else he was now suffering from writer's block. In fact, his aimless searching had seemed increasingly meaningless. He couldn't even identify what he was seeking.

The only certainty was that the answer wouldn't be found in violence and death. Not anymore. He'd made his living—a damned lucrative one—capitalizing on the events that tore apart the lives of others. As long as he'd remained uninvolved, he'd been good at it, even relishing the adrenaline rushes. But after that awful day in Dublin, he'd known. Immediately. He no longer had the stomach for it.

Gordy had been too young, too full of life, too good to die. Tom regretted he hadn't told Gordy before it was too late just how true and loyal a friend he'd been and how much he, Tom, had relied on him to make the unbearable bearable.

As his mind roamed all the futile ways he'd tried to escape from himself this past year, he kept returning to a single image. The beautifully natural, trusting face of Lynn Kendall. He couldn't put his finger on exactly what it was that so compelled his attention. But he knew it wasn't so much his physical attraction to her—although that was powerful—as the quality of light—he could think of no better word—she had about her. Pure, joyful, serene.

Had he come on too strong with her? Frightened her? His impulsive behavior had surprised even him, as if he had fallen under some kind of arcadian spell woven by his renewed sense of home. But that was too simplistic an explanation. Unknowingly she had broken through years of carefully constructed defenses where the opposite sex was concerned. She was different from those women with whom he'd had fleeting relationships ever since the breakup of his marriage. What was there about her, anyway?

He veered into his driveway, pulled behind the house and shut off the engine. But he didn't make a move to get out of the cab, dumbstruck by the realization that she had something he wanted. Something tenuous, elusive. Something he wasn't sure he'd ever experienced.

Peace.

LYNN WIPED her damp forehead with her arm, then bent again to the task of pulling weeds from around the headstones. She had the Vale-family plot nearly cleared. The afternoon was muggy and overcast, but every so often there was a refreshing breeze. She liked working the earth and making orderly again that which had been long neglected. Levering the trowel beneath a particularly stubborn root system, she quietly hummed to herself. Much contentment arose from simple things like earth and wind and flowers.

Why, she wondered, do we humans complicate our world, almost as if we deliberately and willfully set out to do so? Take this morning, for instance. She didn't have to let Tom in. She didn't have to serve him coffee. Most assuredly, she didn't have to permit him to kiss her. And worst of all, she needn't have responded so enthusiastically! But she had. Deliberately and willfully.

She stopped humming. This simple, carefree vacation away from all the demands of her work had become anything but simple. On the surface she'd gone about her business since this morning, but on a deeper level she'd been counting the hours until she would see Tom Baines again.

If she chose to let anyone in Riverbend know her whereabouts, she could probably glean all kinds of information about him. Perhaps discover why he seemed, well, mysterious. But she didn't want to compromise her vacation. Besides, she preferred to judge people on their own merits, not on hearsay.

A fluttering of leaves in the nearby sycamore tree caused her to look up. The wind was shifting, coming now from the east, ruffling the dried stalks of wildflowers in the cemetery. When she glanced toward the road where her car was parked, she was surprised to see a lone figure jogging toward her, his white T-shirt and navy shorts all too familiar.

Tom. He lifted a hand in greeting, then negotiated the rise of the hill from which the cemetery had an unimpeded view of the river.

Lynn shaded her eyes and watched until he sank, breathless, on the ground beside her, a lopsided grin on his face. "You really didn't need to run all this way to tell me my bicycle is fixed," she said.

He pulled a red bandanna from his pocket and wiped the beads of sweat from his forehead. "The bike won't be ready until the end of the week. I'm out for my daily run."

Lynn gestured at the graveyard. "Do you come here often?"

"Actually I haven't been out here in years." He nodded toward a large marker topped by a Celtic cross. "That's my great-grandfather's resting place. Several members of my father's family are buried here. When I was a little kid, we used to come here sometimes on Memorial Day. But once Dad joined the State Department, my family rarely came back.''

"Why is that?''

"My father was in the diplomatic service. We lived all over the world.''

"That must've been interesting. Educational, too. No wonder you became a foreign correspondent.''

He leaned against an adjacent headstone, knees bent, his hands dangling between them. "I suppose.''

"Wow. Such enthusiasm.'' She shook her head and grinned.

In response he smiled ruefully. "Look, I saw stuff like the Taj Mahal and the pyramids at an early age. But I think I'd have traded all the nannies, the sights and the European boarding schools for a normal upbringing in Riverbend.''

"But your roots are here. Did you come often?''

He nodded. "I spent most school holidays and every summer here visiting my uncle Abe. In fact, it's his farmhouse I'm living in now. As a kid, I looked forward to those times with him and couldn't wait to get back. However, I probably acted like a jerk. It wasn't easy for me to let on that this place was so important to me. I had a reputation to protect as a worldly sophisticated—'' he grinned wryly "—spoiled brat.''

Although he was trying to pass his behavior off as youthful insensitivity, Lynn heard in his words the yearning of a lonely boy shuttled from place to place, not feeling wanted anywhere.

She glanced at him. "Where are your parents now?''

"They retired to the south of France in the early nineties, then died within months of each other about five years ago."

"I'm sorry."

He said nothing, seemingly lost in his thoughts. Picking up her trowel, she resumed working the earth. She sensed Tom needed space. Overhead, dark clouds were gathering and the air smelled of approaching rain. She quickened her efforts to complete her task. Tom remained where he was. At last Lynn said, "What brings you to Indiana now?"

He sighed. "That's a good question. Maybe because it's all I have left."

She sat back on her heels. "What do you mean?"

He sat cross-legged and leaned forward. "I've been all over the globe, Lynn. I've seen things I don't even want to think about." He paused. "Look around here. Death seems deceptively pleasant in a setting like this. There could be a lot of worse fates than spending eternity high on an Indiana hillside. Worse fates like starving to death, or being swept away along with your entire village by a typhoon, or having your head blown off in a border skirmish. When you've been where I've been, *seen* what I've seen, maybe a small town in Indiana is what you need to restore your faith in humanity."

Lynn laid aside her trowel and covered his hand with hers. "Riverbend is a step, then. A good one." She searched his jaded weary eyes. "I hope you find what you're looking for." She hesitated before squeezing his hand, then resumed weeding.

"I didn't mean to burden you with all that."

"No, please. It's another side of you, one I'm glad

you could share.'' Lynn could sense him struggling to dispel his somber mood.

Finally he shrugged, grinned abashedly and said, ''I wanted you to see I'm more than just a good kisser.''

She couldn't help herself. She blushed. The curse of the fair-skinned. ''Pretty high on yourself, aren't you?''

''C'mon, give me your honest opinion. On a scale of one to ten.''

Just then a huge raindrop fell on her head, followed by another and another. ''It's raining.'' She gathered up her tools.

He took hold of her arm. ''So?''

''We'd better get to the car.'' A clap of thunder underlined the urgency she felt.

He stood up, pulling her to her feet. ''I wasn't asking you about the weather.''

Rain fell softly all around them and the now-cooler air raised gooseflesh on her arms. Or was that because he was still holding her, grinning down at her? ''You're not going anyplace until I get my answer.''

''Answer?''

''Don't hold back. Probably at least an eight, huh?''

''Tom, I—''

He gave a mock sigh while the rain intensified, soaking through her T-shirt. ''Maybe I better demonstrate again.'' His lips closed over hers at the same time his arms came around her, and as he pulled her toward him, she could've been anywhere, so centered was she in the moment. When she let herself lean into him, when she moved her palms against his chest, she couldn't have said whether the accompanying lightning bolt across the river was a signal of approval or disapproval. And she didn't care.

Slowly, teasingly, he pulled his lips a bare half-inch from hers and looked deeply into her eyes. "Well?"

She breathed out her answer spontaneously. "A nine-point-five, I think."

"You think? *Think?*" He laughed huskily. "Let's make sure." And to the accompaniment of another crack of lightning, he convinced her that his kisses were worthy of a ten.

LYNN STOOD in the middle of Tom's bedroom listening to the raging thunderstorm. She had done the polite thing, of course, and given him a ride home from the cemetery. And it did make sense to follow his suggestion of changing out of her sodden T-shirt into a dry one of his, even if the faint lemony fragrance of freshly laundered cotton stimulated thoughts that would make for one heck of a detergent commercial. His shirt hung nearly to the hem of her shorts, and even though she'd toweled off, her wet hair was plastered to her head. She glanced at her reflection in the mirror over the dresser and rolled her eyes. Charming. Again.

A tap sounded on the door. "You ready for a cup of coffee?" Tom asked.

"In a minute." His footsteps retreated, and Lynn hesitated, her attention drawn to three photographs on the dresser top. The first one showed a thin-faced boy of ten or so with intense dark eyes, wearing a heavy sweater over a shirt and tie. Scrawled in the corner in childish cursive was an inscription. She picked up the frame and held it nearer to the light. "Tom, thank you, and God bless you always.'' It was signed ''Terence Coyne.'' Curious. Setting that photo aside, she studied the remaining two—one of a ruddy-cheeked, unsmiling teenager in tennis whites, a racket cradled in his arms, and the other of a girl of twelve or thirteen, smiling shyly, her mouth revealing a full set of braces.

What did these youngsters have to do with Tom? He didn't strike her as the sentimental type who would collect pictures of children he encountered in his work. This was just another reminder how little she knew about this man, an insight that made her instinctive positive reactions to him all the more reckless, even irresponsible.

Making one last halfhearted attempt to fix her hair, she wandered downstairs, drawn by the aroma of coffee. Tom sat on the sofa beneath the ceiling fan, waiting. He held up her mug and motioned for her to join him. She took the coffee from him and curled up on one end of the sofa. Outside she could hear wind lashing the trees as rain pelted the large windows. Light from the lone lamp flickered, then flared, and the ceiling-fan motor sputtered before resuming its steady hum.

''Power surge,'' Tom muttered. ''One of the hazards of country living.''

''How's your candle supply?''

''Good question. I'm hoping we won't have to find out.'' He sent her a mischievous grin. ''On the other hand, candlelight can be pretty romantic.'' Setting his coffee on the table, he faced her.

''Maybe, but electric light makes me downright sensible. And 'sensible' in this context means drinking up, retrieving my T-shirt and driving home as soon as the rain lets up.''

He leaned back, draping one arm along the sofa back. ''Forgive me, then, if I hope for an all-night deluge.''

Something about the wicked gleam in his eye and the *all night* flustered her. Calm, dignity, control. That was what she needed. ''You know those kisses at the cemetery?''

''The nine-point-five and the ten?''

Smugness was written all over him. She could've handled this issue more objectively had he not reminded her of the scorching ratings. ''Yes. Let's put this into perspective. I only met you yesterday—''

''Is that right?''

Was he playing with her? ''And you need to know, I don't usually act like this.''

''There's always a first time.''

''Tom, really. This is serious.''

He folded his arms across his chest. ''Okay. Serious. What do you mean you 'don't usually act like this'?''

''With men.''

''I can tell.''

''You can? How?''

''You lack…artifice.''

''Artifice?''

''Believe me, I've had plenty of practice recognizing it. Decoding feminine wiles is something of a specialty of mine.''

''Aha! The worldly journalist?''

''Your words, not mine.''

"You're saying, by contrast, that I'm a babe in the woods?"

"Something like that."

She didn't know whether to feel shame or pride. He had nailed her, though. Artifice wasn't part of her arsenal. Nor was this flirtatious conversation. The only face-saving way out was to get up and leave.

No sooner had she made that decision than the lamp flickered again, went out and stayed out. Overhead the fan blades slowed to a stop. Tom leaped to his feet. "My prayers have been answered. Candlelight it is."

His prayers. What about hers for a timely exit, an escape from the danger presented by proximity to him? Darn. The rain sounded harder than ever. She couldn't drive in that. She clenched and unclenched her fingers as she listened to him rifling through the cupboard drawers.

"Beautiful," he murmured. The next thing she heard was a match striking, and then he was back, setting two candlesticks on the coffee table. The flames illuminated his face—firm jaw, aquiline nose, deep-set dark eyes.

He sat down beside her, not touching her, watching the candles, letting the silence between them lengthen. Finally he settled an arm around her shoulders. "You think I'm just another guy on the make, don't you?"

She raised an eyebrow. "Aren't you?"

He gave a sardonic chuckle. "Ordinarily you'd be justified in coming to that conclusion, but—" he tilted her chin so she couldn't avoid looking at him "—not tonight." His fingers wound through the hair at her temple while he traced her forehead with the pad of his thumb. "Not tonight," he repeated with a sense of wonder. "There's something about you. You're...different. Not like other women at all."

Little did he know how close to the mark he was, she thought with irony. She *was* different, as several men in whom she'd been interested had been painfully quick to point out. She didn't want to be perceived as different, at least not in situations like this when, despite all logic, she found herself genuinely and powerfully drawn to someone. "No, I don't suppose I am."

With his forefinger he caressed away the vertical frown lines between her eyes. "Are you afraid?"

She drew his hand into her lap, holding it still. "Afraid?" She pondered the question. "Not for the reasons you might think. I do have to say, though, that our brief relationship seems backward to me. Usually you start by getting to know a person, then come the kisses. Not the other way around."

"Call me unconventional."

"And call me foolish."

"Foolish?" He squared his shoulders. "You poor misguided thing. Why would I call you that?"

She shot him a skeptical look, then saw how his grin faded and his eyes sobered, hauntingly so.

"Lynn—" he faltered before continuing "—you are special. Corny as it sounds, you're *not* like any woman I've ever known. And I like that. A lot." The sound of rain on the roof filled the brief silence. He leaned forward and brushed her cheek with his lips. "So before we go any further, maybe you're right. We should get better acquainted."

Her initial reaction, relief tinged with disappointment, faded in the hope of a deepening relationship.

But it would have to be an honest one, right from the beginning. On both their parts. That meant soon, very soon, she would have to tell him. And run the risk again. No man thus far had been willing to share with her the life she'd chosen. No one had even come close.

Why should Tom Baines be any different?

HE WAS ACTUALLY going to do it. Something he scrupulously avoided. Talk about himself. Why? Because of some mysterious hold this woman had over him. Bottom line—he didn't want her to leave. Was he really that lonely? Or was she really that special?

He thought he knew the answer, and it scared him. She *was* that special, and he found himself helpless to fight his need to be with her. Yet he had no right to involve another person in his private hell. Even one that, for some peculiar reason, he sensed might understand.

Lynn picked up her mug and stretched out her legs on the sofa. "Okay," she said. "Let's get started. You first. You must have quite a few friends in Riverbend."

He locked his hands behind his head and scrutinized the ceiling. Where to begin? "Once I did. There was a bunch of us that used to run around together. Or I should say, *they* used to. Because my cousin was involved, they included me whenever I visited." He couldn't let on to anyone, even Lynn, how much it had meant to him as a kid to be accepted by the River Rats gang, to feel as if he was genuinely liked just for himself. A far cry from the insidious pecking order of boarding school. "Some of them still live in the area, but I haven't looked them up yet."

"Why not?"

Why not, indeed. "I'm not ready."

"For what?"

"The demands. Country-club functions, Rotary Club speeches, family dinners."

"Family?"

"Yeah. I still have two aunts here. They own a bookstore."

"Of course, Ruth and Rachel Steele." A broad grin lit her face.

He looked puzzled. "Yes. How do you know them? I thought you were vacationing here?"

"I am. But I'm familiar with Riverbend and I love to read." He had the distinct impression she was concealing something, but before he could pursue that train of thought, she went on, "They're delightful, well-informed women." Her next question caught him with his guard down. "Who are the children in the photographs on your dresser?"

His gut tightened. The children. A decidedly difficult subject. It wasn't a part of his history he relished sharing. "The tennis player is my son Pete, and the girl is my daughter Libby."

Her breath caught. "I had no idea you were married."

"I'm not. Haven't been for a long time." He watched guiltily as her respiration returned to normal. He could have told her sooner.

"Oh." She pulled up her knees and hugged them. "Do the children live with their mother?"

He nodded. "In Chicago."

"Tell me about them."

"Pete just finished his sophomore year in high school, and Libby will be a freshman this fall." He groped for more. "Pete's the jock. Libby's more musical."

"Will they be coming to visit you this summer?"

Not if they could help it. "I don't think so."

"Are you disappointed?"

Disappointed? It was hard to be disappointed about something you'd never taken the time to know you'd miss. "They have their own friends, lots of summer activities at home."

Resting her chin on her knees, she eyed him. "None of that replaces a father."

Her tone struck him as disapproving. Well, so be it. There was no point in bucking the stone wall Pete and Libby had thrown up to insulate themselves, not that he blamed them. The list of birthday parties, school programs, holidays, sporting events, recitals he'd missed rivaled the daily market quotations for length. After all, hadn't he been doing something "important"? Covering assassinations, purges, explosions, all in the name of putting bread on the table? He looked up at Lynn, hating himself for the egocentric, insensitive bastard he was. "In this case, I'm not so sure about that. I wasn't around enough to be much of a role model."

"What do you mean *wasn't*?"

He let out a long sigh. "I might as well get this over with. Lynn, I haven't seen my children in over six months."

The shock on her face burned itself into his retinas. He'd blown it. She wasn't a woman who would understand a man's estrangement from his children. She was a woman worthy of the truth. He didn't know how he knew, but he was convinced she saw straight into his heart. The question was, would that insight disgust her, drive her away?

The shock in her eyes faded to a compassion that, if anything, was more difficult to bear than disapproval. "Tom, I'm so sorry. Something must be terribly wrong. How painful for you!"

She'd misunderstood. It was Pete and Libby who'd endured his neglect, until finally they'd more or less suggested he butt out of their lives completely. It had seemed the kindest thing to do. And if he was honest with himself, he'd kept so busy with his work he hadn't had time to miss them all that much. Ever since Dublin, though, he'd been having second thoughts. And he didn't like what he saw. Who he'd been. Was.

He was about to request a change of subject when a loud knocking at the front door saved him. He jumped to his feet. "Excuse me."

Lynn, too, rose, picked up one of the candles and followed him. When he pulled the door open, a gust of wind nearly tore it from his hand, and he saw rain coursing from the hat brim of the familiar figure of the farm manager standing outside. "Shep, c'mon in, man. You're drenched." He ushered him into the hallway.

"Thought I'd better check on you, Tom. Let you know a big maple's down across the highway. It took out the phone and power lines." He wiped his feet on the rug in the entryway, and when he took off his hat, water dripped to the floor. "Sorry." He looked around uncertainly. Then his glance fell on Lynn, who stood quietly nearby, a sheepish smile on her face.

"Let me introduce Lynn—"

"Not necessary, son. I know this pretty gal." He walked past Tom and stuck out his hand. "I thought that was your car outside. How you doin', Reverend?"

Tom blinked. He couldn't have heard right. He could've sworn Shep called Lynn "Reverend." That plain didn't make sense. "Do you know Ms. Kendall?"

Still holding Lynn's hand, Shep put his other arm around her in a protective embrace. "Know her? Son, 'course I do. She's the pastor at the Riverbend Community Church."

Lynn, her eyes shimmering like pools of rainwater, looked at Tom, then nodded tentatively as if seeking his forgiveness. "It wasn't my turn yet. I was going to tell you."

For the second time in slightly more than twenty-four hours, Tom was utterly speechless.

CHAPTER THREE

IT WAS ONLY LATER that night after Lynn and Shep had left and Tom was cleaning up the kitchen that he vented his anger. A minister? He threw the sponge against the backsplash. He'd bared his soul, for Pete's sake! And that compassionate look that had melted his heart? Chalk it up to professional concern. He supposed he should be grateful to Shep for preventing him from making a greater fool of himself. For one crazy moment this afternoon he'd even entertained the notion that this was a woman he could make a life with!

Shep, apparently oblivious to the tension in the room, had, thank God, made small talk with them until the rain stopped and they heard on the radio that the highway had been cleared. Good old Shep. He and his wife, Dorrie, had been taking care of the farm for as long as he could remember. He'd cut his teeth on Dorrie's oatmeal-raisin cookies and, as a boy, he'd found few places as comfortable as their warm, cheery kitchen.

In the minutes following Shep's revelation, it seemed to Tom that Lynn had avoided him, preferring to listen to Shep's account of the storm damage than to make eye contact with him. Why would she have wanted to look at him, anyway? She'd been caught red-handed in a monumental evasion. His jaw had ached from biting back his questions. He didn't understand. Had she lied about being on vacation? What were those responsive kisses all about? Riverbend Community Church had been his family's church for generations. His aunt Rachel even played the organ there. Why hadn't anyone told him about a lady minister?

He dumped the coffee grounds into the wastebasket, straightened, then slumped over the counter. It wasn't his aunts' fault. When had they had a chance to tell him anything? He'd made it clear that he didn't want family members disturbing him. The lifelong loner, true to form.

He flipped off the lights, which had come back on shortly after Shep's arrival, and climbed the stairs to his bedroom, stripping off his shirt as he went. What had Lynn said? "It wasn't my turn yet. I was going to tell you." Would she have? Maybe. But why had she waited at all?

Finally, just before she left to drive home, she'd laid her hand softly on his arm and sought his eyes. "I'm sorry, Tom," she'd murmured. "I'd hoped it wouldn't make a difference."

How could it not? He was barely ready to have any kind of relationship with a woman, much less with one who had other, vastly more significant…allegiances.

Without bothering to brush his teeth, he fell, exhausted, onto his bed where he lay on his back staring at the ceiling and calling himself all kinds of names until finally, more than an hour later, he fell into a restless slumber.

AFTER BREAKFAST the next morning, Lynn prowled around the house, unable to sit still long enough to read or work on her cross-stitch project. Meditation was out of the question, though that was probably what she most needed. Benedict had curled up for a snooze in the porch rocker. Why couldn't she find herself a peaceful perch, too? Someplace where she could blot out last night. Lose the disturbing memories.

She was furious with herself. When would she ever learn? Where men were concerned, it was folly to get her hopes up. Tom's reaction had been typical. What was it about her vocation that threatened them? Scared them off?

Or were most men simply unwilling to share their woman with others? With God?

From his own experience, Uncle Will, her role model and mentor, had warned her there would be times like this during her ministry. He'd also emphasized it was not only permissible but essential to be human, to question, to hurt.

Shaking her head in self-reproach, she decided she might as well do something useful. She picked up a dust cloth and began polishing the living-room furniture. If confession was good for the soul, she'd better come clean. She hadn't been forthright with Tom. She'd held back. She'd been enjoying him. She was attracted to him. She'd hoped this once…

She dabbed furiously at a water spot on top of the bookcase. Yes, she was a minister and couldn't imagine doing anything else with her life. But doctors, nurses, teachers, others were called to their vocations, too. Why should it be any different for her? She'd been created a woman, just as a female neurosurgeon or school guidance counselor is a woman. And as a woman, she had normal needs and desires—to be loved, to marry, to give birth, to nurture a family, and to love in return.

She wandered onto the porch and knelt beside the rocker, her fingers stroking Benedict's sleek fur. Sighing heavily, she laid her head against the wicker of the chair. After several moments she whispered, "Tell me, is it too much to want it all?"

WHEN TOM CAME THROUGH the door of the bookstore, Aunt Ruth looked up from the display table where she was arranging the latest shipment of bestsellers, a knowing smile crinkling the skin at the corners of her eyes. "About time. We've been wondering when you were going to show yourself. You know, Penelope only had to wait ten years for Odysseus."

Tom skirted the table and grabbed his buxom aunt in a warm hug, remembering how much he enjoyed her quick wit. "This old bear decided hibernation had to come to an end."

His aunt pulled back and studied him. "At least you haven't grown one of those scraggly beards. Rachel and I knew you'd rejoin the human race when you were darned good and ready."

Tom glanced around the shop. "Where's Aunt Rachel?"

"Over at the church practicing."

He winced at the word *church*. Then he compounded his discomfort by asking, "How *are* things at the church?"

If his aunt found his question out of character, she

didn't let on. "Simply dandy. The choir has almost as many men as women, the ladies' circle solved the problem of whose recipes to use for the annual picnic, and the next battle is heating up. Our perennial gadfly, Prentice Jewett, is agitating to keep Reverend Lynn from using the Meacham House as a community youth center. In other words, it's business as usual."

He didn't miss the acerbic tone of her last remark. "I gather you and Mr. Jewett don't see eye to eye."

She raked him with an incredulous look. "That jackass? He wouldn't know the Lord if He sat down beside him and offered him a free pass through the pearly gates."

"Sounds like trouble waiting to happen."

"Sure is. But we'll get through it. We always do."

He laughed. "As I've often said, the trouble with churches is they're full of hypocrites."

His aunt punched him playfully on the arm. "And as I've often said, what better place for them than church?"

"This new minister…Reverend Lynn…?"

"Kendall. She's a crackerjack. Best we've had in a while. 'Course, chauvinistic fools like Prentice and others had to be convinced that a woman could do the job. But Lynn's smart. She took her time. Impressed them with her efficiency, charmed them with her warmth, and preached and pastored her way into the hearts of most." She cocked her head. "I don't imagine you've darkened the door of a church lately. Why are you so curious?"

He shifted his weight to his other foot. "I'm not, really. It just seemed polite to inquire."

In a blessedly abrupt change of subject, Ruth linked

her arm through his and led him to the rear of the bookstore. "There's somebody I want you to meet." She paused at the door to the back room and looked around. "Kate, are you in here?"

An attractive young woman with a smudge of dirt on her face came out from behind a column of stacked packing boxes. "Yes, Ruth. Just doing an inventory of the delivery."

"This is Kate McMann, our indispensable manager." Ruth gestured toward Tom. "My nephew Tom Baines."

"Oh, I know Tom Baines," the young woman responded, nodding at him. "Your fame precedes you."

Kate looked faintly familiar, but Tom couldn't quite place her. "I guess you were a 'Hot Spots' reader," he said.

She grinned. "Well, that, too. No, I remember you from a long time ago."

"I'm sorry, I—"

"You wouldn't remember me. I was one of the pesky junior-high kids who thought you older kids were the gods and goddesses of Riverbend. My—" she fluttered her eyelashes teasingly "—the stories they told about you."

"Oh, puh-leeze," Ruth interjected. "No more black-sheep tales. I keep hoping my wayward nephew here has reformed."

Tom drew up to his full height. "Reformed? Who? Me?" He paused. "Be careful, Aunt Ruth. I know all about your wild youth. It must be in the genes. Besides, you wouldn't like me nearly as much if I changed my evil ways."

Ruth snorted. "I've been found out."

"Found out? About what?" Rachel breezed in the back door, stopped, did a double take, then crossed the room toward Tom, her arms outflung. "Tom!"

"Hi, Auntie. Give me a hug."

Rachel held him at arm's length. "Not until you tell me why you've been such a hermit the past week."

Ruth took a step forward. "Now, Rachel—"

"Don't 'Now, Rachel' me. Just tell me, Tom. Are you out of your self-indulgent funk yet?"

No way could he confess that not only was he not out of his funk, if anything, thanks to the Reverend Lynn Kendall, he'd sunk in deeper. "Yes, Aunt Rachel. Tom Baines has returned to life as we know it in Riverbend, Indiana."

"Praise be," Rachel intoned before giving him the postponed hug. When she drew back, she held him by the shoulders and studied him. "You look good. Rested. Maybe even ready for a serious talk with your aunts."

Something in her expression registered concern beyond the state of his health. "Sounds ominous."

She dropped her hands, averted her eyes and fidgeted with the pin on her lapel. "Not really. But Ruth and I would like you to stop by the house at your earliest convenience."

"I'll call you."

"Make it soon," both twins said at once, their synchronicity of expression causing the group to dissolve in laughter and dispelling Tom's momentary uneasiness.

"HI, GARBO. It's Kate. Do you still 'vant to be alone,' or could you stand some company?"

Lynn cradled the phone closer to her ear. "I'd love some." And who better than a best friend? Maybe Kate could help her make some sense out of her confused emotional state. "What do you have in mind?"

"The aunts are taking my twins to the carnival over in the next county and have invited them to spend the night. So...I'll bring some of my famous chicken and fixings—you know, a kind of movable feast—and we can pig out at your place. After all, I don't want to blow your cover by asking you to come to town."

"I can't think of anything I'd like better than your cooking, except your company, of course. Besides, there's something I need your counsel about."

"Oh?"

Lynn could hear curiosity in her friend's tone. "When you get here."

"Aha. The plot thickens. I can't wait."

A few hours later Kate breezed into the house bearing containers with enough food to feed six. "A hex on calories tonight," she declared as she laid out the supper.

Lynn stared at the dishes. "Are we expecting company?"

"Would I reveal the whereabouts of your hermitage?" She drew an *X* across her heart. "I promise I was not followed."

Lynn laughed, and the two women began to eat. After Kate regaled her with the latest antics of her twins, Lynn ventured a confession. "I'm trying hard not to feel guilty about being here near Riverbend, yet not being here, if you know what I mean."

"It wouldn't be much of an escape if you were on call. For all anybody knows, you could be in Anchorage." Kate jabbed a chicken leg in her direction. "Give yourself a break. Remember the night you stayed in the hospital until dawn keeping vigil over Iris Templeton, or the youth-group camp-out at Turkey Run State Park when it poured rain? Or how about the trip you made with the Hurtles when their daughter was arrested for—"

"Okay, okay. I get the picture."

"You won't be worth much to all those people who depend on you if you're a basket case yourself. So, my child, go in peace and enjoy your vacation."

Lynn smiled at this friend who knew her so well. For whatever reason, she had needed validation that it was permissible to spend these few weeks away. Common sense told her this was necessary R and R, but her involvement with the people of Riverbend made it difficult to turn her back, even for so short a time. Thank goodness for Kate, who brooked no nonsense. "Remember when we first met?"

"Do I? I'd never seen anybody spend as much time in both the philosophy/religion and fiction sections of the store or converse more knowledgeably about the books."

"And you guessed who I was even though I was just in town for an interview." Lynn chuckled. "I was so scared. I'll never forget Prentice Jewett saying, 'If God had intended women to be ministers, He'd never have converted Paul.' It's still a mystery to me why I was called to the church."

Kate smiled knowingly. "First, never sell yourself short. Second, never underestimate the power of people like the aunts to influence public opinion. They liked you from the first.''

''And I liked them, too. How are they, by the way?''

''Wonderful, as always. Especially after today's return of the native.''

''What are you talking about?'' Lynn forked up some creamy cole slaw and awaited Kate's answer.

''Their nephew Tom Baines is back.''

With difficulty Lynn chewed and swallowed. ''I know.''

''Lynn?'' Kate leaned forward across the table and was looking at her with keen interest. ''How do you know? He's been incommunicado ever since he returned. Wait a minute, wait a minute.'' Kate waved her fingers back and forward in front of her face. ''Don't tell me. Tom Baines is what, or rather who, you wanted to talk about tonight.''

Lynn nodded miserably. ''Dead on, Sherlock.''

''Well, you've come to the right person. I can tell you stories about Tom Baines, all right.''

''Such as?'' Lynn tried to keep the eagerness out of her voice.

''He taught all the River Rats to smoke.''

''River Rats?''

''Yeah. The gang of older kids who always ran around together. They were five or six years older than my friends and I, and we all thought they were so cool. We spent several summers being total pests, spying on them. You know some of them—Lily Holden, Charlie Callahan, Mitch Sterling, among others. But Tom was by far the most sophisticated. He'd lived in places with foreign-sounding names and went to

European boarding schools and could whip any of the others at poker. The girls were all in love with him. He was, you know, the dangerous type.''

"You don't need to limit it to past tense," Lynn volunteered quietly.

Kate raised an eyebrow. "Oho. I do believe you're blushing." She paused, her eyes locked on Lynn's. "How dangerous?"

"Very dangerous." Lynn had the distinct sensation she'd crawled far out on a particularly fragile limb.

"Start at the beginning. How did you meet Tom?"

Lynn carefully reconstructed the encounters, omitting only accurate descriptions of the—yes, there was the word again—"dangerous" kisses. She concluded by describing the stunned look on Tom's face when Shep had called her Reverend.

She paused, watching Benedict creep closer to the table, his nose twitching. "No chicken for you," she said, shooing him away before she turned back to Kate. "I should have told Tom earlier. But the chance never seemed to come up. And although I'm not proud of it, I have an increasingly difficult time revealing my work to men. Interesting men."

"Why is that?"

"Because the response is inevitable. They stop seeing me as a woman and start viewing me as some kind of saint. Unapproachable. Untouchable."

"Men!" Kate snorted in disbelief. "Insecure little boys."

"One of the fellows I dated while I was in seminary came right out and told me he couldn't commit to any woman who was going to be at the beck and call of a congregation twenty-four hours a day. He expected his wife to be home, period.''

"Tiny minds," Kate muttered. "You just haven't met the right guy.''

"Be that as it may, I need to reconcile myself to the fact it might never happen.''

"And if it doesn't?''

"I can be okay with that, even if it's not my preference.''

"So Tom Baines lit your fire?''

"Kate, really. That's putting it rather crudely.''

Kate bobbed her head. "Oh, yeah. He did. You're pretty transparent, Rev.'' She leaned over and picked up both Lynn's hands. "Give Tom a chance. Based on what I know about him, I think you could be very important in his life.'' Her expression was sober, serious. "Very important.''

"But he looked so shocked when he found out.''

"Of course he did. You have to admit yours is not exactly a typical female profession. He needs time to get used to the idea.''

"I suppose you're right.''

"Just because you've been burned in the past doesn't mean you have to carry that baggage into every new relationship.''

Her friend's words struck home, and Lynn managed a wan grin. "You mean my expectations get in the way of possibility?''

Kate smiled knowingly. "Elementary, my dear Watson.''

THE NEXT AFTERNOON Tom set about his task with a vengeance. What the hell was he doing here at the cemetery, of all places? He made several passes with the gas-powered lawn trimmer, ruthlessly clearing the weeds beside the crumbling stone wall. After only a few minutes he'd worked up a sweat, but the exercise proved no more successful than had his other futile attempts to divert himself. Nothing was working. Why not? Because, if he was honest, he was cleaning up this place for Lynn.

And being here only served as a vivid reminder of her gentleness, sunny laughter and guileless eyes.

A minister.

That revelation had nearly choked him. It was one thing for her not to be his customary type of woman, but quite another for her to so completely shake his confidence in his ability to read people. The implications were clear. Adios, Ms. Kendall. He wasn't going to change his lifestyle for anyone.

He continued attacking the weeds, all the while thanking his lucky stars for the close call. Very cautiously, very carefully and very precipitately, he would back away from the trap into which, heaven help him, he'd nearly fallen.

He hacked and chopped until finally he turned the trimmer off and set it aside, then slumped against the wall. Unaccountably, it seemed vital to him to create order in this overgrown burial site. Lynn's weeding had been a start. But much more remained to be done. Something about the years of neglect made him infinitely sad. These souls deserved a better resting place.

He closed his eyes, unable to stem the onslaught of gut-wrenching images—mangled bodies lying in a rain-filled ditch, the bloated stomachs of starving infants and, despite his efforts to will it away, Gordy's blood-spattered body, sprawled on the dark, unyielding pavement.

Tom was only vaguely aware of the breeze ruffling his hair. Not much he could do for any of them, victims of man's unspeakable inhumanity to man.

But there was something he could do here, insignificant a gesture as it might be.

He grabbed the handle of the trimmer again and hoisted himself to his feet. Insignificant, but maybe, just maybe, a small step toward filling the dark void within him, healing his pain.

DURING THE NEXT FEW DAYS, Lynn found peace in taking long walks along the river, weeding the Carters' flower beds, trying a new recipe for dill bread, jotting down ideas for sermons and trying, sometimes almost successfully, to forget Tom Baines.

Late one evening she sat rocking on the screened-in porch watching the moonlight shimmering on the river, listening to the soft cello sonata emanating from the stereo and stroking the contented Benedict. She hadn't heard from Tom. Not that she'd really expected to. She'd just hoped. She had, however, come to a decision.

When he brought back her bicycle, as he'd said he would, she would take the first step. Kate had been right about her self-destructive tendencies. She set herself up with men, giving neither them nor herself a chance. It was unrealistic to expect a man, any man, to fall in with her life's plan, without allowing time for the in-depth, revealing communication upon which a solid relationship depended.

She was great at counseling others. Why was she

so blind, even pigheaded, where she herself was concerned?

Yet there were things about Tom that disturbed her. Why he preferred solitude, instead of getting in touch with his old friends. Especially the River Rats. And why he seemed evasive when she'd asked about the photographs of his children. Most men would've been boastful, but Tom had seemed somehow pained by her questions. And there was another puzzling thing. He had never mentioned the third child, the one who'd signed his photograph ''Terence Coyne.'' In fairness, she acknowledged that Shep had interrupted their discussion. Yet she couldn't shake the feeling that, in any event, Tom wouldn't have volunteered anything about the boy.

The mournful cello vibrato pierced her awareness, emphasizing the ephemeral quality of life. Time slipped by so quickly, yet she'd been waiting for life to happen to her, expecting others to understand her and surmount her defenses.

As baffling and unnerving as it was, she had the profound sense that Tom wasn't the big bad wolf. That he was worth the risk.

THE LATE-AFTERNOON SUN filtered through leafy branches, dappling Riverbend's manicured lawns with light and shadow, as Tom drove his truck with Lynn's newly repaired bicycle in the bed. Should he call in advance, warn her he was coming over? Nah. She might interpret that as a deliberate move to see her again when, in fact, all he wanted was to deliver the bike, beat a hasty retreat and consign Reverend Lynn Kendall to the remotest corner of his memory. The last thing he needed was to imply he might have some interest in her.

He flat out didn't understand the hold she seemed to have on him. What was it about her that made it so difficult to walk away? She wasn't sophisticated or classically beautiful, and her sights were clearly fixed on a realm beyond his. Tom muttered a curse under his breath. He wasn't accustomed to things that didn't make sense. His job, hell, his entire training, was to take the nonsensical, the incomprehensible, the bizarre, and explain it, even justify it to the masses.

Almost too late he saw a collie amble out into the street. He slammed on the brakes, then sat shaking his head, his nerves jangling. Cocking his ears at him, the dog wagged his feathery tail, then ambled on. Damn. A bad day was getting worse. It had started this morning when he'd steeled himself to phone Pete and Libby. He hadn't expected the call to be any more cordial than the past ones, and it wasn't. Libby's curt response was typical.

"Can't talk, Dad. I'm on my way to swim-team practice.... Pete? He slept over at Cory's.... Gotta run." The click of the receiver and the subsequent hum on the line sent a powerful message. He was persona non grata.

If that wasn't enough, he'd had yet another call from his former editor, who was pressuring him to write a book detailing the atrocities of the final decades of the twentieth century. A cheery subject if he'd ever heard one. Now the fool dog and, next, his upcoming awkward conversation with Lynn.

All in all, he was in a foul mood. So what else was new? Even before Dublin, he'd been aware of a sense of cynicism and ennui, but during this past year, he took the prize for being a surly bastard.

Maybe that was part of Lynn's attraction. When he was with her, he almost forgot what a jerk he was. As he drove past the outskirts of town and tooled down the two-lane highway, he rehearsed his speech. "Got caught up in the moment...nothing in common...don't want to compromise your job..." *Job?* That was a lame word, surely, to describe what she did with her life.

By the time he turned onto River Road, his frown was so intense his jaw ached. Short and sweet. No prolonged explanations, no rationalizations. Shouldn't be a problem. Not that much had happened between them.

He blew out an exasperated sigh. And now nothing was going to. He rebelled against the wave of regret that swept over him.

By the time he reached the Carters' drive, he was ready, the words poised on his lips. He drew the truck up to the carport, lifted out the bike and leaned it against the side of the house. Before he reached the front door, it opened and Lynn stepped onto the porch, a smile illuminating her entire face.

Her hair was caught up with one of those scrunchy things, but tendrils of reddish gold curled beside her ears and at the nape of her neck. She wore a sleeveless navy blue blouse and one of those gauzy skirts. He swallowed hard. The way the sun was shining through the wispy material, he had no trouble making out her well-shaped legs.

But it was the killer smile that drew his eyes to

hers, bright and eager. Almost expectant. As if she had a surprise for him.

She took a step toward him. "Tom, how kind of you to return the bike."

He stood his ground. "I always finish what I begin. Besides, the truck makes it a lot easier."

"I appreciate your thoughtfulness. How much do I owe you?"

"Not a thing. It was no big deal." Was it his imagination or was this conversation stilted? Well, what else could it be, since all his senses were geared up to cut off a relationship that had never really gotten started?

"Are you sure?"

"I'm sure."

"Well, thank you very much then. Please come inside and let me fix you some iced tea by way of thanks."

He didn't want to go inside and he didn't want any iced tea. He wanted out of here. But the only way that was going to happen with any degree of grace was to follow her inside and wait for his opening. "I'll come inside for a few minutes, but I don't care for anything to drink."

He couldn't help noticing that the smile had faded from her lips, and the eyes fixed on him were puzzled. "If you have something else to do…"

"It's not that." Damn, this was uncomfortable.

"Maybe you'd rather take a walk. It's beautiful this time of the evening." She held out her hand, and the now-hopeful expression in her eyes doomed him.

"Sounds good." He took her hand, trying not to notice how perfectly her fingers entwined with his, and walked beside her through a gap in the bushes until they reached a narrow path along the river. The breeze off the water's surface and the shade from the trees lining the bank made the air here feel ten degrees cooler.

They walked quietly for perhaps a quarter of a mile, his thoughts focused on finding the right words. Yet at the same time, he felt an incongruous calm. She said nothing, but the silence between them wasn't awkward. Rather, she seemed to anticipate and accept that something was forthcoming from him, and was giving him the gift of time.

When the incessant chirping of tree frogs finally penetrated his brain, he stopped, then turned toward her, now taking both her hands in his. Looking at her, he felt like a trusted shepherd ready to butcher the spring lamb. "Lynn, I'm afraid I've done you a grave disservice, and I want you to know how sorry I am."

"A disservice?" She looked baffled.

"I took advantage of a situation. It was selfish. I like you, but I—" he could feel himself fumbling "—never should have presumed to kiss you."

"More than once I believe," she murmured, her eyes not leaving his.

"Somehow I just thought…"

"You thought I was an ordinary warm-blooded woman who enjoyed that expert nine-point-five performance."

"I guess I did."

"But now you think I'm not an ordinary woman, right?"

He stared at the ground between them, at the rich soil, at the weeds bordering the path, at the beetle emerging from under a nearby rock. He owed her the truth. Reluctantly he looked up. "You're a minister!" he blurted, inwardly cursing his tactlessness.

She clutched his hands, but said nothing for several seconds. "It doesn't have to be an obstacle, you know."

"An obstacle?"

"To our feelings."

Whoa! Where was this going? Who was in charge here? "Feelings?"

With the toe of her sandal, she made a small swirl in the dirt. "Forgive me if this sounds too forward, but I like you, Tom. And the nine-point-five?" Her face turned rosy in the twilight. "I lied. It was always a ten."

"Lynn, I—"

"Let me finish before I totally lose my nerve. I am asking you to give us a chance. Always before, I've caved in when a man has opted out of a relationship with me. I'm well aware my being a minister poses problems. And I know it's hard for you. How many men want to share a woman with an entire congregation? What kind of man is willing to take a supportive role, even a backseat, in his wife's career?" She hurtled on, while his heart thudded in concert. "Then there's the mysterious part. You know, the fact that I've been 'called.' Some men find that somehow…threatening."

Even in the cool of the evening, he was aware he was sweating. He'd had no idea this would be so difficult. He read the plea in her eyes, heard the huskiness in her voice. He felt like a cad. In the midst of his confusion of feelings, he barely registered her next question. And when he did, his breath caught in his throat.

"Tom, do you find it threatening?"

He swallowed. "Yes." He had no answer that would satisfy her, let her down easily. "Because I can't understand it."

She dropped his hands and turned away, studying the eddies in the river. "Is it necessary to understand everything? All at once?"

"I suppose not. But in my business I try."

Her voice sounded small. "Do you think you'd be willing to try in this case?"

He stared at one stray curl, lying vulnerable and exposed on her bare neck, and imagined planting his lips in that tender spot. "Try?" What was she suggesting?

She hugged her arms around her slender waist. "This is difficult for me. But I promised myself I wouldn't pretend or fool myself." He moved behind her in order to hear her. "I'm a woman, Tom, but I'm not accustomed to...coming on to a man like this, but please be honest with me. Are you attracted to me?"

Hell. He might be a cad, but he'd never lie to this woman. "Yes."

"I'm attracted to you, too. *Very* attracted."

Without thinking, he slipped his arms around her and captured her hands. "What are you saying?"

"I sense you're ready to cut and run. It's too troublesome and demanding to get involved with the Reverend Lynn Kendall." Slowly she pivoted in his arms and the invitation in her eyes and the trembling of her lips rattled him to the core. "But could you consider getting involved with Lynn, the woman?"

"It's complicated. I…"

She lowered her eyes. "That wasn't fair of me to ask. You take me, you take the whole package."

A fish leaped near the bank, falling with a loud slap back into the water. Upriver the sound of a motorboat matched the hum in his brain. "It's not you. You're a beautiful, desirable woman."

"But?" When she looked up, her expression was unflinching.

"But…I'm not a good person, Lynn."

"I don't believe that." She hesitated. "But I believe you believe it."

"You don't know where I've been, what I've seen." His stomach roiled. Death houses in Calcutta, orphanages in Romania, executions in Afghanistan. "And you don't want to know."

"Are you blaming yourself?"

The question rocked him. He knew he couldn't have stopped the carnage, the crime, the destruction. Yet he'd preyed upon it, fed off it. Could he somehow have been more compassionate? Or had he found it easier, more comfortable, to remain detached, impassive? *Was* guilt part of his problem? Part of this inertia he felt?

Slowly he became aware that her hands were resting on his shoulders, which were tensed both with anger at a universe he couldn't control and with unbridled longing for this woman who saw into the depths of his being. "Lynn, you don't understand. It's a dirty world out there."

Her eyes filled as, deliberately and tenderly, she moved her right hand and laid it over his pounding heart. "But it doesn't have to be a dirty world in here.'' Her palm warmed his entire chest and he found he had no response for her. "Will you trust me? Give us a chance?"

No man in his right mind could have resisted. Acting against every rational fiber of his being, he pulled her tight against him and buried his face in her hair. "You don't know what you're asking," he whispered raggedly.

He felt her lips moving against his ear. "I know exactly what I'm asking. More than I've ever asked of anyone."

He was helpless. "What if…"

She stepped back and looked directly at him, her eyes dark with…fear? "No *what ifs*. Just tell me I haven't made a complete fool of myself."

His last resolve crumpled, and just before he crushed her mouth with his, he managed to murmur, "You a fool? Hardly."

CHAPTER FOUR

TOM COULDN'T GET enough—the softness, the yielding, the sheer femininity of her. When he finally pulled his mouth away, he held her tight, his eyes closed against the outer world and the inevitable questions. Moist smells from the river mingled with the flowery fragrance of her hair as he drew her head into the crook of his neck and felt the warmth of her breath against his skin. Why her? Why now?

The only answer that occurred to him was that, for whatever reasons, fate had tilted his world on its axis.

They stood, wrapped in each other's arms for what seemed a very long time, the only sounds the lapping of the river against the bank, the buzz of locusts, the faint rustle of the cottonwoods. Slowly, deliberately, Tom stepped back, cupping her face in his hands. "Whew. Looks as if we've taken this relationship to the next level."

Her luminous eyes betrayed a spark of humor. "'We'? You're sure I didn't push you into this?"

He gave a low laugh. "Fat chance. No wolf worth his sheep's clothing gives in that easily." He kissed her lightly. "No, I exercised my own free will."

She reached up and cupped his hands, then spoke quietly. "I'm glad, Tom. Really glad." Then she stepped away and, still holding one of his hands, began walking toward the house.

He followed, realizing he wanted her in the most elemental way, but also in another, more unfamiliar way, one separate and apart from his sexual longing.

"I SHOULD HAVE TOLD YOU earlier," Lynn said later as they lay snuggling in the Carters' hammock, "about being a minister."

"I'm glad you didn't."

"Why?"

She heard the low chuckle rumble out of his chest. "Because if I'd known, I'd have run like hell."

She moved her head, the better to see his eyes. "And now?"

The lone light from inside the house cast a glow over his face, and she could read the momentary hesitation. "Honestly, Lynn? I don't know."

Although she'd expected as much, she wasn't prepared for her surge of disappointment. This wasn't going to be easy. Much more was at stake than simple attraction. "That's fair," she whispered. "In truth, you haven't yet met the real me."

He trailed a finger over her cheek. "Who have I met, then?"

"The vacation me."

"I like the vacation you."

"But will you like the real-world me?"

He tapped her nose. "We'll have to see, won't we?"

Lynn relaxed. He was going to give them a chance. "You should know what you're getting into."

"Like?"

"Like being with someone who has irregular hours, who works on weekends, who gets her fair share of criticism..."

He smiled. "So far you're describing a foreign correspondent."

She put a finger on his lips. "Wait, I'm not finished." She paused, considering how to articulate the rest. "Who needs quiet time to prime her spiritual pump, who must love the unlovable, respond day or night to others and keep herself attuned to a higher power."

She watched him struggle for an answer. "Now we're onto shakier ground."

"So?" Her heart shriveled in anticipation of rejection.

"I've never run from new experiences. I'm not going to start now."

She could barely breathe. "But?"

"I can't make any promises. It's not just you. God and I have had no more than a nodding acquaintance for quite a few years. So I'm not exactly a churchgoer."

"That's your journey, Tom. Not one I'd try to influence—at least not directly. Let's see how things unfold. No expectations. Okay?"

He pulled her close again and his lips caressed her temple. "I can live with that if you can."

She stared dreamily at the canopy of leaves overhead, wondering if she'd made the right choice. Could Tom be the one to care enough to embrace the whole of her? Or were the obstacles too formidable?

His words came out of the night and took aim at her heart. "Hey, Rev, isn't this about faith? About stepping into unfamiliar territory?"

She relaxed into a giggle. "You *do* have a way with words."

"You know we may surprise some people."

"The aunts, for example?"

"Yeah, for starters."

It seemed like a good opening to bring up the rest of his family. "Did you know I officiated at your uncle's memorial service?"

"I figured as much."

"I'm sorry you couldn't be there."

"I was overseas when I got the word, and like I said, I'm not much for church. I prefer remembering Uncle Abe out on the farm in his baggy old clothes."

"I've never heard anyone else call him Abe."

Tom smiled fondly. "No one else did. It was just one of the ways he made me feel special."

"You must miss him."

"I do. Even though he did a lot for Riverbend, he could be a difficult person. Regrettably very few saw the mellow side of him. For instance, taking an interest in his knockabout nephew, leaving me this farm."

"Weren't you one of the River Rats?"

"A sort of honorary summer member." He shook his head. "Those were the days. It's a wonder our parents didn't disown us."

"You were *that* bad?"

"Not all of us. I was the worst, always trying to prove something. For me, it boiled down to the friendships. Something I needed then."

She bit back the obvious "Only then?" and, instead, said, "I understand from Kate McMann that several of you still live in Riverbend." She waited for him to respond. When he didn't, she went on, "Have you seen any of them?"

Shifting her so that she nestled against his shoulder, he rested his chin on her head. "No." The hammock ropes squeaked in rhythm with the swaying motion.

"As you said, I've met the vacation you. Well, you've met the hermit me, not the Riverbend me."

"So we're both in for some surprises?"

"Lynn, I don't know where I fit anymore. If I fit."

She was instantly alert to the self-doubt and vulnerability in his voice. Her heart troubled, she laid a hand on his chest. "You'll find the way home, Tom. I know it."

Just before kissing her again, he breathed out the words, "I have to, Lynn. I have to."

THE NEXT MORNING Lynn couldn't afford the luxury of basking in the shimmering, though tenuous first flush of what she dared to call love, though she had no doubt that word would inspire the same fear in Tom as it did in her. Not after Marilyn Rasmusson's call.

Her secretary apologized for disturbing her vacation, but as Lynn was quick to assure her after hearing her message, she'd had no choice. Lynn hung up the phone and emitted an exasperated sigh. Prentice Jewett, the same Prentice Jewett who had tried to block her call to Riverbend Community Church, was at it again. This time the target was the Meacham House project.

Lynn glanced at Benedict, eyeing her from the window ledge where he was sunning. "Kitty, looks like our vacation is over." Resignedly she rose and walked into Seth Carter's den, booted up the computer and accessed the e-mail server in preparation for receiving from Marilyn the text of a letter Prentice was circulating to prominent Riverbend citizens and all church members.

Why now? They'd been over this ground. Initial

objections to using Meacham House, a Victorian downtown residence adjacent to the church property and recently bequeathed to the church, as a teen outreach center had been discussed and, she'd thought, overcome. The staff was in place and a series of kickoff events was scheduled to coincide with the beginning of school only a few weeks away.

Benedict hopped onto the desk and sat on his haunches watching the screen intently as the message line scrolled up. Lynn scanned the letter and groaned. Sometimes it was darn difficult to understand human nature. She hated these "little tests," as Uncle Will called them, but accepted them as part of the challenge of working with all different kinds of people.

She hit "print" and waited. A few seconds later she held the offending page in her hand.

Dear Friends of Riverbend:
As you are aware, there are plans to use historic Meacham House as a teen outreach center. However, it is not too late to reverse that decision. I appeal to you as citizens interested in keeping our downtown viable to register your feelings immediately with the Chamber of Commerce, board members of the Riverbend Community Church and the Reverend Lynn Kendall, who has been the spearhead of this ill-conceived venture.

The young persons toward whom the program is directed are not apt to reflect the standards of public decency consistent with the positive image Riverbend businessmen work hard to project, nor is the church likely to reap any benefits from investing in such an endeavor. To the contrary, maintaining the Meacham House property, especially given the wear and tear the teen program undoubtedly will inflict, will drain funds better spent on programs with measurable, observable results.

One can only suppose what Frederick Meacham and his descendants would make of the desecration of the home on Bridge Street they so lovingly cared for and long enjoyed! Time is of the essence.

Act now!

Yours in concern,
Prentice T. Jewett

Lynn's shoulders sagged. The attack was even worse than she'd anticipated. Last spring the board had attempted to identify and deflect the objections, which stemmed mainly from those intimidated by and fearful of teenagers, particularly the teenagers whose apparel, tattoos and body piercings seemed to demonstrate a flouting of convention. However, Ed Pennington, the treasurer, had carefully worked out the figures to demonstrate the church could well afford to support the much-needed program.

It required only a cursory tour of Riverbend to see that there were few safe places for young people, particularly those economically disadvantaged. After interviewing some of the teens, Lynn had come away with the distinct impression they felt alienated by the adult community, and as she well knew, alienation was a breeding ground for trouble.

Benedict leaped into her lap and kneaded her chest with his clawless paws. ''It's the pits, Ben. But you and I know those kids are worth saving.'' The cat nudged his nose between her neck and shoulder. "So settle down while I make this phone call."

Reluctantly Lynn picked up the phone and dialed Prentice Jewett's office. When she was connected to him, she identified herself, then got right to the point. "I understand you are the author of a letter objecting to the Meacham House project."

If he was startled to hear from her, he didn't let on. "Shouldn't come as any surprise to you. I told you last spring that you hadn't seen the end of me. You bleeding-heart women are all alike. It's unconscionable to sacrifice perfectly fine church property in the unlikely event of helping a few scraggly kids."

"I'm sorry you feel that way."

"You can be sorry all you want, but I'm putting a stop to this nonsense."

Lynn marshaled her compelling arguments, but the man wouldn't budge. Before hanging up, she asked him to discontinue circulating the letter.

His terse response was, "The die's cast. Goodbye."

After disconnecting, Lynn wilted. She felt very alone. But lifting her eyes to gaze out the window at the slow-moving river, she was encouraged by remembering the support already in place for Meacham House—Ed and Grace Pennington, Aaron Mazerik, Lily Holden, Kate McMann and, of course, the Steele sisters, who had been publicly and vocally enthusiastic. The opening would occur, with or without Prentice Jewett's blessing. But at the same time she couldn't help being disappointed that people like Prentice had such difficulty embracing those in the world unlike themselves.

The vacation had been restful, but this development meant she would have to return to Riverbend sooner than planned. She couldn't leave it to Molly Linden, the Meacham House director, to fight the battle alone. She needed to be there, too.

She shrugged in resignation. She would return in the morning after she kept her afternoon date with Tom to put the finishing touches on their cleanup efforts at the cemetery. One more day surely wasn't asking too much.

She thumbed through the church directory, then began making calls to rally support.

TOM'S JAW DROPPED. "Whoa. Wait a minute. You're telling me Aaron's my—"

"Cousin. Abraham's son."

Tom gripped the wooden arms of the antique rocker and looked in desperation from Aunt Ruth on the sofa to Aunt Rachel in the wing chair she favored for her back. The familiarity of the aunts' music room brought no comfort. It was inconceivable they were sitting here calmly saying that his uncle had had an illegitimate son. Especially not Aaron Mazerik.

"We know how upsetting this must be for you," Rachel said.

"Upsetting?" Tom launched out of the rocker and paced to the bookcase and back to the piano. "I find it inconceivable Uncle Abe would do something like that."

"That's what we thought, too," Ruth said quietly.

"My God, what will Jacob think? That makes Aaron his…half brother!"

Ruth's face fell. "I only wish we knew where Jacob was. At least we'd all be in this together."

Tom stopped in his tracks and studied his aunts, then fell on one knee beside Rachel's chair. "Oh, hell.

On top of Jacob's disappearance and Uncle Abe's death, the news you have a nephew you never knew about must've hit the two of you like a ton of bricks."

Rachel folded and refolded the handkerchief in her lap. "It did," she said quietly.

Ruth leaned forward. "But shocking as it is, I'm grateful Abraham didn't abandon Aaron and his mother."

His mother. Jeez, Tom hadn't even stopped to consider the full ramifications. "You mean Evie?" How many times had she waited on him through the years at the Sunnyside Café?

"She never said a word." Ruth nodded in grudging admiration.

"And she could have created a scandal," Rachel added.

Tom sat back against the sofa, trying to digest all the information, process all the questions. Had Uncle Abe carried on an affair under their very noses? For how long? Had he supported Evie and Aaron? Aaron. My God, how must he feel? Had he known all those years? Harbored resentment?

"What about Aaron?" Tom asked.

"Aaron only found out after Abraham died."

"This has to be tough on him, too."

"I can't begin to imagine," Ruth said softly.

"What's he doing now?"

Rachel smiled. "That young man did a complete turnaround—went from being the town bad boy to becoming a truly fine coach and counselor at the high school. He genuinely cares for the youngsters."

"He probably knows firsthand about having a rough time growing up," Tom said grimly.

Ruth sighed. "I'm afraid so."

"What do we do now?"

Rachel looked directly at him. "We've been to see him. We assured him we consider him one of us—a Steele."

"Does he want to be?"

"Time will tell," Ruth said.

"I need a few days to come to grips with this." Tom rose to his feet. "Then I'll go talk with him."

"Thank you, dear." Rachel picked up the handkerchief and dabbed her eyes.

"Tom," Ruth pleaded, "please remember how much your uncle Abraham loved you. He had his faults, but he was a good man."

Faults? Keeping a son a secret was more than that. Sin seemed a better word. But surely, Tom thought, his uncle had had his reasons. *Let there be reasons.* "I'm grateful to you both for telling me. It can't have been easy for you. Until Jacob comes home, *if* he comes home, I'll represent the family with Aaron."

On the way back to the farm the full impact of his promise hit him. Aaron might be a high-school counselor, but that didn't mean he'd forget or forgive the injustice done him. Worse yet, what might he want from the Steeles?

Tom drew in a deep breath. God, he missed Jacob. Why had his cousin left Riverbend suddenly all those years ago, dropping totally out of sight? And where the hell was he, anyway?

ALTHOUGH TOM HAD GREETED HER that afternoon with a genuine smile and a warm hug when he'd picked her up to go to the cemetery, he seemed preoccupied as he drove. Lynn afforded him quiet by concentrating on the profusion of colors outside the window—the vivid blue of cornflowers, the cash-green of the soybean fields, the pristine white of well-maintained farmhouses. The premature end to her vacation had precipitated a chaotic morning—packing, cleaning the Carters' house, checking in again with Marilyn at the church office.

Now, however, she relished the restful steady motion of the truck, determined to milk the last few hours of pleasure from this special time with Tom before she returned to Riverbend. She turned slightly to look at him. His jaw was set, his eyes indecipherable behind his dark glasses, and his mouth, in profile, a grim line. He was a thousand miles away, but instinctively she knew his absorption had nothing to do with her.

When they reached the cemetery, he parked alongside the road, then shut off the engine and rolled down the windows. The incessant scritching of insects filled the silence. Lynn waited. As if collecting himself, Tom squeezed her hand and said, "Ready? I'll get the stuff out of the back."

Lynn watched as he collected the tools, then she grabbed the cooler and followed him up the rise to the stone wall. He hitched the lawn trimmer over his shoulder and began working on the far wall. She drew on her gardener's gloves and squatted beside a family plot in a still-overgrown corner of the graveyard and began weeding. She enjoyed the mindless repetition of pulling a handful of roots from the ground and the satisfaction of observable progress.

She glanced at Tom, moving steadily around the exterior of the wall, sweat glistening on his tanned, bare arms. The slight frown was a dead giveaway. It wasn't her imagination. Something was troubling him. She ached to soothe it away.

After an hour and a half, she sat back on her heels, surveying with satisfaction the restored order. She prayed those long gone did, indeed, rest in peace here. She stood up, putting her hands in the small of her back to ease the crick there, and watched while Tom returned the tools to the truck. A faint breeze lifted tendrils of hair off her forehead. When he returned, he carried a faded quilt under one arm, which he spread on the shorn grass. He sat, leaning his back against the wall, his legs extended, his feet crossed at the ankles. He patted the space beside him, then adopted a falsetto voice. "Come in, Little Red Riding Hood. It's only your granny."

Lynn shot him a skeptical look. "Granny, my foot!"

"Do you prefer wolves?"

She sank down beside him, kissed him on the cheek and whispered in his ear, "Infinitely."

He put his arm around her and she rested her head against his shoulder. Light from the setting sun glinted off the surface of the distant river, turning the molasses-brown water to shimmering silver. Fields dense with golden-tasseled corn surrounded them. Lynn sighed contentedly.

Tom played with her hair. Still he said nothing. Again she resisted the impulse to speak. Finally his hand dropped back to her shoulder and he said, "Ironic, isn't it? All that beauty, all that fecundity, yet in another place, another time, that scene could just as easily be a killing field."

Lynn stifled a gasp and sat very still. Finally she trusted her voice. "Tom?"

He laughed hollowly. "Sorry. I don't know where that came from."

"I think you do." When she laid her hand on his thigh, she could feel the twitch in the ridge of muscle beneath the denim of his jeans. "I'm a good listener."

"I'll bet you are. It's part of the job description." He shook his head. "Hell, I didn't mean that the way it came out. Sarcastic."

She ignored the slight. "Is it something about this place? Does it remind you of something?"

He reached up and fumbled at his shirt pocket. "Damn. I keep forgetting. I don't smoke anymore." He tilted back his head. "Does it remind me of something? Yeah. It reminds me that things are seldom what they seem. Rice paddies, mountain resorts and outdoor markets can all appear picturesque." He practically spit out the word *appear*.

"But?"

"In the blink of an eye, they can become scenes of senseless bloodshed." He removed his arm from her shoulder, got to his feet, then stood, hands in his pockets, staring at the grave markers.

"Is that what you see here?"

"Stupid, isn't it?"

His loneliness and alienation were almost palpable. She closed her eyes briefly before responding. "No. In fact, it's understandable, given what you've witnessed as a journalist. Detachment must be difficult to come by."

He shifted his weight from one foot to the other. "Impossible. That's why all this—" he waved his arm in a gesture that encompassed the cemetery and the fields beyond "—seems…phony. Superficial."

Lynn pushed herself up and sat on the wall. She raised her eyes to his, still obscured behind the dark glasses. "Trusting is that hard?"

"Especially when much of what you think is true turns out to be a lie."

"Such as?"

He turned away. "Never mind."

She stared at her lap where, in the course of the conversation, she'd clasped her hands in a death grip. This was a man with heavy burdens. A man who needed to talk. A man who couldn't be hurried.

And a man she desperately wanted to help. To love.

He turned back to her, extending a hand. She reached out and let herself be pulled into his arms. He nestled her against his chest. "I'm sorry. I didn't mean to be such poor company. My mood has nothing to do with you."

"I know that. What *does* it have to do with?"

She waited, aware of his breathing, of his hand tracing the contours of her shoulder blades. "Death."

The one syllable reverberated in her ears—bleak, ugly, final. She pulled back, still in his loose embrace, reached up and slowly removed his sunglasses. Then she sought his eyes, plumbing their depths. Cynicism, yes. But far more important—pain and confusion. "Is it anything you can share?"

He studied her for a moment, then barely shook his head. "No. Nobody who hasn't been there could understand."

"I haven't been where you've been—" she spaced out her words "—but I do know firsthand about death."

He adjusted his expression, but not before she'd seen the flicker of disbelief. With his index finger he traced down her forehead, then her nose, until, when he reached her lips, he paused as if to say, *Shh.* Then he smiled regretfully. "This is the last evening of your vacation. I don't want to ruin it. Quite the contrary." He nuzzled her neck. "I want to take you home, cook you a decadently large steak and ply you with sweet talk."

She knew better than to press him. Instead, she fell in with his change of mood by clutching both his hands in hers and drawing their locked fists to her chest. "Why, Granny, you've made me an offer I can't refuse." She lowered her lashes and gave him a calculated sultry look. "I take mine medium rare."

WITH HIS BARBECUE FORK, Tom distributed the hot coals before slapping two huge T-bones on the grill with more force than he'd intended. Damn. He was a self-absorbed ass! The worst of it was, he'd almost spilled his guts to her. Almost told her about being rejected by two children who hardly claimed him as a father. About the uncle whose recently revealed secret life made a mockery of Tom's memories. And…about Gordy.

But he wouldn't sully her idealized view of the world with his problems. It bugged him that she seemed to have all the answers, yet he recognized he needed some of her certitude, her optimism. He stopped short of calling it faith. Why was she even putting up with him? They had nothing in common.

And then he saw her. Coming down the steps, her body silhouetted in the last rays of the sun, her hair floating around her face, her smile warm, genuine, accepting. It made no sense, this tremor in his chest, this powerful need. Hell. He could no more walk away from her than fly. He held out his arms. Her smile grew more intimate and she walked without hesitation into his embrace.

"Any chance," he said, "I could talk you into bypassing dinner and settling for this?" He lowered his lips to hers and spent a long minute exploring her mouth and pulling her heated body closer to his.

When he drew away, she looked up at him with shining eyes. "It's tempting. Very tempting."

"So?" He gave her another sample kiss.

"Mmm," she hummed against his ear. "I'm a greedy woman. I want both." She nipped his earlobe. "Starting with the steak." Then she grabbed his hands playfully and leaned back, only his grip preventing her from falling. She arched her neck and laughed, a melodious tinkling sound in the twilight.

Hell, he didn't care how different they were. He didn't understand how it had happened or what he would do about it, but this woman was becoming indispensable to him. She almost made him believe in light and life.

And laughter. Over dinner, she regaled him with stories of her parishioners—the curly-headed preschooler who always called her "Mrs. God," the octogenarian notorious for the mystery meat loaf she insisted on preparing for Meals on Wheels, the church treasurer so painstaking that he spent an entire week tracking down a single unaccounted-for penny. With her flair for the dramatic, Lynn brought the characters to life for him. But it wasn't only her mimicry that made the individuals so vivid. It was the obvious love she felt for them. "And so," she concluded, "my days are never dull."

He chuckled appreciatively. "I imagine not." He toyed with his fork, aware that, with his next comment, he'd reveal his trademark cynicism. "Surely not everyone is so quaint or amusing."

She leveled a look at him. "I didn't fool you, huh?" Her lips quirked in a rueful smile. "No, some are real...challenges. People have a heavy emotional investment in institutions like schools and churches, and sometimes they can be territorial, self-righteous and judgmental. That's why I have to try to be open and, when necessary, forgiving." She picked up her napkin and wiped up imaginary crumbs. Something was troubling her.

"Like when?"

She looked up at him. "Like now."

"Trouble in paradise?"

"I'll overlook the sarcasm. Yes, trouble. Have you heard about the Meacham House project?"

"Only what I read in the newspaper. An after-school program for at-risk kids involving classes, tutoring, counseling. Does that about cover it?"

"Yes. It's desperately needed. Too many kids with absentee parents are hanging out on the streets just looking for trouble. The church will provide the facility and some volunteers, although we hope others from the community will become involved, as well. We thought we'd addressed all possible objections, but apparently not."

"Oh?"

"Prentice Jewett, who owns several downtown buildings, is launching another protest."

"And you're his number-one target."

She smiled regretfully. "How perceptive of you."

"What happens now?"

"When I go home tomorrow, I'll continue talking with supporters and we'll try to pacify Mr. Jewett. But somehow I don't see that happening."

He reached across the table and grasped her hand. "You're stepping into the lion's den, huh?"

"It's part of the job."

He rubbed a thumb over her knuckles, considering his next words. "You'll be in the public eye much more, Lynn. Have you considered the impact of that?"

"What do you mean?"

"Is it wise for you to be seen with the prodigal black sheep?"

"Who? You? I'm not worried about your past." She sighed. "But you're right. I do have to be concerned about people's perception. Are you willing to dive into my fishbowl?"

Was he? If they were publicly linked, what would that mean for her? For him? "Honestly? I don't know."

He'd expected her to be disappointed, but instead, she squeezed his fingers and said, "That's a fair answer, Tom. This is not your cause. It's mine and I'll deal with it." She hesitated, biting her lower lip. "But I need to say this. I care about you. I want to continue seeing you. If we don't do anything to raise eyebrows…"

He stood, rounded the table and pulled her up into his arms. "Like this, you mean?" Taut with desire, he sought her parted lips, felt the curves of her body melt into the planes of his. When he ended the kiss, he waited, holding her, searching her eyes.

She sagged against him. "Yes, that would do it."

The kiss had played hell with his concentration. "What?"

"Raise eyebrows." She straightened and held him by the arms. "Tom, I've told you how I feel. Now it's up to you to decide whether you can deal with the complications of my public visibility. Either way, I'll understand.''

She paused a beat as if expecting him to say something, but he was mute from the obligation not to kid himself—or her. In the uncomfortable silence, she began clearing the cutlery, stacking the dishes. ''Lynn, I—''

She turned toward him. ''I don't expect an answer tonight. This is too important for both of us. Let's take the future a day at a time. But I promise you one thing. I won't ask more from you than you're able to give.''

And what might that be? Hell if he knew. But she'd given him space. Space and time. It would take both—and more—to heal that deeper, unidentifiable need crowding his heart. He picked up the salad and followed her into the brightly lit kitchen. He set the bowl carefully on the counter, then turned to face her. ''You seem to know me better than I know myself. I don't usually let people get this close.''

She cocked her head, studying him, then said quietly, ''I know. Take your time.''

He breathed a relieved sigh. ''Thank you.'' He took the plates from her hands, set them in the sink, then led her to the front porch where, for a long time, they sat holding hands, each lost in their thoughts.

As was her custom after rehearsing the hymns and choral accompaniment for Sunday, Rachel Steele let her hands and feet automatically play over the organ keys and pedals, finding, almost by second nature, the notes of some of her favorites—''Sheep May Safely Graze,'' ''My Faith Looks up to Thee,'' ''Jesu, Joy of Man's Desiring.'' As she hummed and sang along, she found her glance straying repeatedly to the pulpit. Oh, the substitute clergyman's sermons had been adequate, but none had touched her the way Lynn's usually did. She'd missed Lynn and hoped her vacation had been restful. Lord knows, that young woman was a tireless worker.

As her fingers drifted over the keys, gradually her thoughts centered on Tom. She'd always worried about him. Even though Celia had been her sister, rest in peace, Rachel couldn't approve of the way she'd reared that boy. Toting him all over the globe, never settling down long enough for him to form lasting friendships. Say what you would about Abraham, beneath that gruffness, he'd always had a soft spot for his nephew and had offered the boy the only home he knew. Now Tom was back in Riverbend. Why? She and Ruth had puzzled over the question. He'd apparently walked away from a lucrative, high-profile job. And when he'd finally stopped by the other day, she and Ruth had both noticed a sadness about him. Hard to put a finger on it. Disillusionment, maybe. Ruth was right. He needed quite a few things, not the least of which was a good woman.

As Rachel swung into ''Rock of Ages,'' a shaft of light speared its way across the sanctuary and rested on the pulpit. In that moment, the tiniest seedling of a notion took root in her mind. Ever so slowly her voice died out, her hands stilled, and she did something quite out of character. She quit playing in midsong. Overwhelming in its simplicity and aptness, the idea grew in the silence until Rachel couldn't sit there any longer. Hastily she put her music away, turned off the organ, locked the church and hurried down Bridge Street.

Arriving breathless at the bookstore, she scurried to the office where she found her sister poring over publishers' catalogs. "Ruth, I've just had a brainstorm!"

Ruth peered over the top of her spectacles. "Dare I ask?"

Ruth, the impetuous sister, had always teased her about being the thinker of the two. But this, Rachel knew, was a good idea. Too good to keep to herself. Besides, she'd need Ruth's cooperation. "How would you like to be involved in a little matchmaking scheme?"

Ruth slowly removed her glasses and smiled suspiciously. "What are you up to now?"

"Solving our problem."

"Which problem might that be?"

"Why, a good woman for Tom, of course," Rachel said with satisfaction. "All we need to do is get them together."

"May I be so bold as to ask who 'them' might be?"

Rachel leaned on the desk, the better to observe her twin's reaction. "Why, Reverend Lynn and Tom, of course."

She was rewarded by Ruth's indrawn breath. "Have you taken leave of your senses? What would our sweet Lynn want with that brooding nephew of ours?"

"Whose side are you on, anyway?"

"Tom's naturally," Ruth sputtered.

"Then you'll see why my idea is perfect." Rachel plopped down in a chair. "She's just what he needs. Warm, optimistic, unselfish, intelligent, gregarious."

Ruth started to speak and then stopped, as if beginning to consider the idea, rather than refute it. "They're as different as night and day."

"You know the old saying that opposites attract." Rachel waited. Ruth didn't disappoint her.

"I suppose we could find a way to get them together. They could take it from there." Ruth studied her sister. "Would you do me the favor of wiping that smug smile off your face?"

"Why? I feel good."

"All right, then, gloat. See if I care." Ruth picked up an envelope from the desk and, after turning it in her fingers for a few seconds, laid it on the edge of the desk. "When you *do* feel like getting rid of that silly grin, this'll do the trick."

Puzzled, Rachel picked up the envelope and extracted the letter. As she read, she could feel a frown replacing the smile. Finally she slapped the letter down and stared, dumbfounded, at her sister. "That jackass. Prentice Jewett gives a bad name to everyone over sixty."

"My sentiments exactly."

"So what are we going to do?"

"Cook his goose, sister. Cook his goose."

CHAPTER FIVE

FROM THE MOMENT Lynn's return to Riverbend became general knowledge, she'd been overwhelmed with phone calls, paperwork and the inevitable crises. From replacing the veteran Sunday-school superintendent to reassuring Maude Haley that memorial funds would not be spent on utilities, she'd been kept on the run. And thanks to the furor generated by Prentice, she'd spent more time than she would've liked soliciting renewed support for Meacham House. However, she was cautiously optimistic their early September kickoff event would go smoothly.

Early this Tuesday morning, as was her custom each workday, she sat in a pew near the back of the sanctuary, inhaling the comforting aromas of lemon oil, candle wax and faded roses. This hushed time tended to center her for the day's demands. Today's demands, however, had begun at 4 a.m. when a hospice volunteer had called her to the Murray home where, amid his children and grandchildren, dear old Phineas Murray had left this life.

Lynn inhaled deeply, then slowly let out her breath. In. Out. In. Out. "We are but dust and to dust we shall return." The words came unbidden. Death—as complex and varied as any human event. The memory of the cemetery and Tom's haunted eyes floated into her awareness. In her heart she knew he would never be at peace until he'd overcome his demons. She also knew that helping him would require a deft and delicate touch.

She closed her eyes, concentrating on her breathing. But insistent questions pecked at her repose. Why did she feel so strongly that her destiny was linked with his? He was a most unlikely answer to her prayers. Could they find their way together? Would he ever be able to understand and embrace her calling? What could she offer him?

She sat a few more minutes before sensing someone's presence. When she opened her eyes, Marilyn Rasmusson was waiting at the side door. "I'm sorry to disturb you, Lynn, but Prentice Jewett is here. I told him he didn't have an appointment, but—"

"It's all right. This was bound to happen sometime. Tell him I'll be there shortly."

After Marilyn left, Lynn took time to formulate her approach, suspecting nothing she said would make a dent. She rose to her feet, then paused, running her hand over the smooth wooden back of the pew in front of her. "Dear Lord," she whispered, "it may be a very long day."

TOM GATHERED the sheet around him, buried his head beneath the pillow and tried—unsuccessfully—to shut out the shrill ringing. Who the hell was calling him at this ungodly hour? If he'd purchased an answering machine, there would at least be an end to the clamor. Whoever this caller was, he was determined. On the fifth ring, Tom reluctantly rolled over, sat up and swung his legs over the side of the bed. Stifling a yawn, he fumbled for the phone, noting that the bedside alarm read 7:22 a.m. "What?" he barked.

"And top of the morning to you, too. Are you hung over?"

So much for amenities. But then, Harry Milstein hadn't made a bundle in the publishing business because of his bedside manner. "Jeez, Harry, did you ever consider that some of us actually sleep?"

"Hell of a way to spend time when you could be writing."

Slumping over his knees, Tom put a hand to his forehead. A hangover would be a relief compared to sidestepping an insistent editor. "What do you want, Harry?"

"I wanna know how far along you are on the book."

"The book? What part of *no* don't you New York types understand?"

"Tommy, Tommy, listen to me. It's a natural. Who else is better equipped to write the definitive volume about the last quarter of the twentieth century? 'Hot Spots' in depth. Eyewitness history."

"No."

"No? I've got a sweetheart of a contract here you can't refuse."

"Watch me." Tom swallowed the sourness in his mouth. There wasn't enough money in the world to induce him to catalog those heinous scenes or revisit the rapacious acts of power-hungry despots. But therein lay his problem. He was a journalist. A reporter of events. He corrected himself. *Had been.* Now he was merely a writer with no material. *Nada.*

"Listen, I'm gonna send you the contract. Won't hurt ya to look at it. You're my man, Tommy. It's got *New York Times* bestseller written all over it. I'll check with you later."

Tom stared at the dead phone. A wake-up call in more ways than one. How long could he avoid examining his future? What the hell *was* he going to do? Money wasn't the problem. He'd socked plenty away in sound investments during his overseas stints, and he took care of his kids generously. But a man had to have worthwhile work. He wasn't such a deadbeat that he didn't understand that. Trouble was, he no longer had a clue what *worthwhile* meant for him.

He set the receiver in the cradle, struggled to his feet and headed for the shower. Not an auspicious beginning for the day he'd set aside to go see Aaron Mazerik.

Soaping up under the steady stream of hot water, he tried to project the meeting. The last encounter he remembered with Aaron was one summer in high school when they'd had a knock-down-drag-out fight over some girl whose name he couldn't recall but whose claim to fame was a figure made to drive adolescent boys wild. Aaron, cocky and defensive, never took guff from anybody. Tom winced. The characterization sounded remarkably like himself. What had the intervening years done to the two of them? And, in light of Aaron's newly revealed parentage, where did they go from here? Damned if he knew.

He drained the mug, then set it on the counter before moving decisively to the wall phone. As long as he was doing something about Aaron, maybe today was the day to do something more about his kids. Deep down he admitted he didn't like the wad of guilt he carried around. He didn't want to be the kind of father who ignores his children.

He dialed the kids' number and listened to the ring, trying to ignore the beating of his heart.

"Hello." Libby. Her voice sounded faint, petulant.

He glanced at his watch. Eight-forty-five. "Did I wake you?"

"Who's this?"

"Your dad."

"Why are you calling so early?"

"I *did* wake you."

"Duh."

He worked hard to keep his irritation in check. "We haven't talked in a while. I wanted to see how you were doing."

"Now?"

"Is something wrong with now?"

"Dad, it's the crack of dawn."

"I guess I'd forgotten how teenagers sleep in, especially in the summer." He paused, groping for a topic. "How's the swim team doing?"

"Fine."

No old-time prospector ever had more trouble locating the mother lode. "I thought I'd come see one of your meets soon."

"You're kidding, right?"

"Why would I be kidding?"

"Like you've been so interested before?"

He guessed he had that coming. "You're right. I haven't been much of a father." He paused uncomfortably. "But I want to do something about that."

"What?"

"Maybe I could come visit, and you and Pete and I could spend some time together. What do you think?"

"When?"

"How does next weekend sound?"

"So soon?"

"Libby, are you trying to avoid me?"

"I thought it was the other way around."

The arrow found its target. "Hey, I know it must have seemed that way. But I'd like to try to change things. I'm asking you to give me a chance."

No answer. He waited. "Okay," Libby said in a tight voice.

"Is Pete there?"

"No. He's gone to the lake with a friend."

"Would you tell him I called? Tell him I'm coming?"

"Yeah. Sure."

"Great. I'll talk with your mother about all this."

"Okay. Bye."

"Libby? Wait." He closed his eyes, aware his fingers had tightened around the phone. "I love you, honey."

After a long interval, he heard her say, "Yeah, well, see ya."

Slowly he hung up and stood listening to the quiet. In the past he'd have been discouraged and given up. But today something was different. Today he was determined to give his kids his best shot. And today at the very end of the conversation, he was nearly positive he'd heard his daughter choke back a sob.

TOM STOOD on the sidewalk early that afternoon studying the Riverbend High School gymnasium, hearing in his memory the rabid fans stomping and cheering as Jacob and Mitch Sterling helped put the town on the map in the only way that counted in rural Indiana—basketball. When he used to visit his uncle for winter break, Tom envied Jacob not only his star quality, but the solid security of attending the same school, growing up with the same friends, being accepted, no questions asked. Of course he hadn't articulated it that way then. Rather, those feelings had found expression in a gnawing hurt he'd tried desperately to mask by spouting off about his adolescent adventures and conquests. And that obnoxiousness was exactly what Aaron would remember about him.

Tom started up the walk toward the gym. Well, that was okay. Aaron hadn't exactly been a Dale Carnegie clone himself with that giant chip on his shoulder. Entering the lobby, Tom paused, letting his eyes adjust to the dimness. Trophies crowded in the glass case reflected dull points of light. Tom made a frame of his hands and peered through the panes in the locked doors to the basketball court. Championship banners hung from the walls, and it took little imagination to conjure up the blare of a pep band and the *thump-swish* of basketballs.

How could it have been over fifteen years ago? Tom shrugged, then started down the corridor toward the offices. He didn't even know if Aaron would be here. He'd thought about calling ahead of time, but had rejected the idea. This was awkward enough without having the initial encounter take place over the phone. He stepped around textbook cartons stacked in the office entryway and nodded at the receptionist. "Aaron Mazerik in?"

"He's with a student. Have a seat. He'll be with you shortly." She resumed the filing he'd interrupted. Tom sat on the bench she'd indicated and waited, resenting his uncle's secret indiscretion and wondering how the hell he would begin this conversation.

Before he could script the encounter, a tall, lithe, dark-haired man emerged from the office, an arm around the shoulders of a scrawny, pimple-faced teen. "Remember, Josh, if you want to take physics, you're going to have to do your best in that advanced math class whether or not you're crazy about Mr. Zachary."

"Okay, Coach. I understand." The boy nudged his glasses up on his nose. "Thanks."

Tom rose to his feet as the boy turned to leave. Which was when Aaron, with a lift of an eyebrow acknowledged him. "Aaron." Tom nodded his head in greeting.

"Ruth Steele said you were back in Riverbend." That was it. No word of greeting whatsoever.

"In a funny kind of way, it's always been home."

"You've been gone a long time." Aaron, his weight balanced on the balls of his feet, hadn't moved. "Seen the world, I guess."

"Some of it I'd rather not have seen."

"I made it as far as Indianapolis," Aaron said tonelessly.

Tom could feel the sweat gathering in his armpits. His cousin wasn't making this easy. "Is there, er, someplace we could talk?"

Aaron handed the receptionist a manila folder, then glanced at Tom's feet. "I see you're wearing running shoes. How about we toss the ball around a little in the gym?"

Was this the modern-day equivalent of throwing down the gauntlet? Tom hadn't picked up a basketball since boring stretches on assignment in Saudi during the midnineties. "Sure."

Their footsteps echoing in the eerily empty corridor, Aaron led the way back to the gym, where he unlocked a door, then retrieved a basketball from an equipment closet. "Here." He rifled the ball to Tom, who made a head feint, dribbled around Aaron and went in for a layup. Muscles he hadn't used in months protested. Aaron grabbed the ball, jumped, then floated a two-handed overhead shot into the basket.

For the next five minutes they grunted, dribbled, pivoted, jockeyed for position and tacitly competed in a grueling game of one-on-one. Finally Tom, panting, held up his hands in surrender. "Time-out."

Aaron tucked the ball into the crook of his arm. "You're not bad. With a little coaching, we'll get you there."

Tom plucked his handkerchief from his jeans pocket and wiped his forehead. "I'm way out of shape."

"I didn't mean to take advantage of you."

Something in Aaron's voice caused Tom to look at him closely. The man was giving no quarter. "Didn't you?" Tom inquired mildly.

Aaron bounced the basketball twice. "Maybe," he conceded. "I don't give in easily."

"Are we still talking about basketball?"

"Probably not." Aaron gestured to the one section of bleachers pulled out from the wall. "Okay, let's get this over with." Aaron rolled the ball in the general direction of the closet and walked toward the seats.

Tom sat lounging back, his elbows resting on the row behind the one where he was sitting. Aaron straddled the seat. Only the hum of a distant floor polisher somewhere in an exterior hallway broke the silence. "So did you ever get into Rhonda Marley's pants?" The shadow of a smile played over Aaron's lips.

"She of the 42 D's? Nah." Tom chuckled. "Thanks, I've been trying for years to remember her name."

"But you obviously didn't have any trouble remembering the equipment."

"Endowments like that are unforgettable." Tom paused, looking intently at Aaron. "Seems like you beat me then, too."

"Probably."

Tom moistened his lips. "If Jacob were here..."

"Yeah, I know. He'd be the family representative, coming to see how the bastard son is taking the news."

"So? How *are* you taking it?"

Aaron placed a hand on each knee and arched his back, then stared over Tom's head. "How do you think? Out of the clear blue sky I discover that the wealthy, beloved town patriarch never had the guts to acknowledge he fathered a second son, a son whose mother worked her fingers to the bone as a waitress and still lives in a dump. That all the clothes, golf clubs, tennis rackets, boats and cars I coveted could have been mine." He lowered his head and looked straight at Tom, his jaws clenched. "That instead of being Aaron Mazerik—punk, misfit, outsider—I could have been Aaron Steele—privileged, admired, accepted." He rolled his tongue around inside his mouth. "How do I feel about all this? It's a helluva jolt, that's what."

Tom waited, sensing Aaron needed to say more.

He did. "And you know what? Here's the irony. Even if I could, I wouldn't change a damn thing. I love my mother, and although I don't understand it, I admire her for what she's been willing to endure. I've learned a lot from butting my head up against life, and I know that things are just that. Things. And in the big scheme, they don't matter.''

Aaron stood up and began pacing in front of the bleachers. "But I've got to tell you, Tom, I'm angry. I'm angry that my mother had to raise me by herself, I'm angry that she had to struggle for so long, and I'm angry that, instead of continuing to be Aaron Mazerik, good-guy counselor and coach—a position I've worked damned hard to achieve—for the moment the only way this town views me is as Aaron Mazerik, bastard son of Abraham Steele." He stopped and looked down at Tom. "Put yourself in my position. Hell, how do you think I feel?"

Tom eased forward, considering his words. "I've got no argument with you. You're entitled to all those feelings." He leaned over, his elbows on his knees, his head hanging, wondering how to ask the next question. Finally he straightened. "Did my uncle help you at all?" he asked, hating the raw edge of pain in his voice.

Aaron slumped down beside him. "He tried, I guess."

"In what way?"

Aaron, his voice expressionless, told Tom how Abraham had used Dr. Julian Bennett as an emissary to help Evie and Aaron financially and to keep tabs on them, and how Abraham had always treated him with interest, even kindness, right up until he died. "But under the circumstances, that's small consolation."

"He robbed you of a father, didn't he?" His stomach lurched. For all intents and purposes, he hadn't had a father, either. Nor did his own kids.

Aaron gave him a puzzled sidelong glance, apparently hearing something different, mellower in Tom's voice. "Yes, he did."

"So where do we go from here?"

"Damned if I know." After an awkward silence, Aaron abruptly stood. "If you don't mind, I've had enough for one day." They started walking toward the door. Pausing to lock up, Aaron spoke again. "Your aunts have been decent about this. Please thank them for me."

"I will." Tom hated to end the conversation negatively, but it was his responsibility to say the rest. "Aaron, if there are any legalities we need to discuss—"

Aaron wheeled around and faced him. "Like what?" he demanded.

"Claims or—"

Aaron's eyes narrowed and his words came out in a hiss. "There is nothing the Steeles can give me that I don't already have. What kind of man do you think I am, anyway?"

Beneath the anger, Tom recognized a sudden kinship in Aaron that had nothing to do with bloodlines, but rather with life experience. "I think," he said slowly, "you're a man I would very much like to get to know."

PETE BAINES threw his gym bag in the general direction of the closet and slumped down at his desk. He knew he should unpack his wet swimsuit before his mother threw a hissy fit, but that could wait. Here he'd had a great time at the lake with his buddies and had even succeeded in getting better acquainted with Polly Bridges, to the point where she'd let him kiss her

Saturday night. He grew hot just thinking about her in that skimpy bikini of hers.

And then Libby had to ruin it all. He'd been all set to ask Polly out for next weekend. But no. His absentee father was actually going to put in an appearance, and they were expected to drop all their plans and do what? Act like it was a big deal? Pretend they were a regular family?

Fat chance! He was getting along very well, thank you, without the interference of his father, whose rare visits simply served to screw up his life. Maybe it had been different when he was a dumb little kid and a trip to the zoo with his dad seemed like a really neat idea. He knew better now.

He brushed his hand across the globe sitting on his desk and set it rotating, frowning at the colored pins he'd stuck in it—back when his mother had suggested he could keep track of his dad that way. Sure enough. A red pin in Afghanistan, a blue one in Singapore, a green one in Croatia, a yellow one in Iraq, along with several others. Like a friggin' pin would somehow make up for always having to tell his friends his father was on assignment and couldn't come to—you name it—the Webelos ceremony, his eighth-grade graduation, the club tennis tournament.

Abruptly he knocked the spinning globe onto the floor. He was tired of all this! Either he had a father or he didn't. And at this point, it would be easier just to forget him. His dad had this weird habit of showing up every time Pete started to feel good about his life. Like this upcoming weekend. Screw it. He had no intention of falling all over himself just because Tom Baines had decided to spend a few hours with him.

Never mind that his stupid sister seemed to think

otherwise. Oh, she did a pretty good job of not letting on to their father that she missed him, but Pete hated that girly hope in her voice when she'd told him their dad had called about the weekend. Didn't she get it? Dad just showed up when it suited him.

Disgusted, Pete leaned over and scooped up the globe. There it was looking at him—the latest pin. Stuck smack-dab in the middle of Indiana. Riverbend. At least Kuala Lumpur sounded exotic. And before, he'd been able to brag about his dad, flash around some of his "Hot Spots" columns. Now what?

Libby had been all excited when she'd learned their dad would be living for a while so close to Chicago. Maybe she'd pictured one of those sloppy sentimental family reunions like you see in movies. Maybe even that their parents would get back together. Yeah, sure.

He stood up and stared at the open closet door, where dirty clothes and shoes littered the floor. Then, defiantly, he threw the globe into the back corner where it came to rest on top of a pair of muddy hiking boots.

Okay, so he'd get through the weekend somehow. But he wasn't going to make it easy for his dad. No way.

TOM PULLED into a parking place in front of his aunts' place, climbed out of the truck and ambled to the door. After yesterday's disturbing encounter with Aaron, he was looking forward to a quiet dinner with Ruth and Rachel.

As if dealing with Aaron wasn't enough, there was the unsettling matter of Lynn. When he'd gone into seclusion, he hadn't counted on meeting a woman who, by quiet example, challenged many of his assumptions. It had been several days since he'd seen her. He'd been caught off guard by how much he missed her. He'd call her after he left the aunts, see if he could visit her later. The little dinner get-together would break up early, so surely he wouldn't scandalize Lynn's neighbors if he stopped by for a while.

Aunt Ruth flung the door open before he raised his hand to knock. "Come in. You're late."

He planted a kiss on her cheek. "Don't tell me you've started the cocktail hour without me."

She linked her arm through his and sent him a sly glance. "No, but you've kept three beautiful women waiting."

"Three?"

"Think you can handle that many?"

"If they're beautiful? A piece of cake."

Ruth drew him into the formal parlor where, sitting on the sofa, was the Reverend Lynn Kendall, her eyes dancing. "Lynn, may I present my nephew Tom Baines." Lynn nodded her head and smiled demurely. "Tom, this is our pastor, Lynn Kendall."

He started to confess he already knew Lynn, but Ruth and Rachel's expectant looks stopped him. He and Lynn had clearly been set up. Because he didn't want to spoil his aunts' pleasure, he'd play along, at least for a while. He crossed the room, leaned over and picked up Lynn's hand, then winked by way of soliciting her complicity. "Pleased to meet you."

She signaled acquiescence by squeezing his hand. "Likewise I'm sure. I've been hearing a lot about you," she said coyly.

He straightened and faced the aunts. "From these two?"

Ruth bustled forward and ushered him to a large overstuffed chair. "I only told Lynn the good parts."

Perched on a hard-backed chair, Rachel added, "We wanted at least her initial impression to be positive."

"And it is." Lynn's low voice trembled with concealed amusement.

Ruth sat down beside Lynn, a smug expression on her face. "We'll save the truth for another day."

Tom feigned a put-upon look. "You malign me, Auntie dear."

"We love you, anyway," Rachel said, turning to Lynn. "You'll have to forgive us. We're rather partial to our nephew. We tend to spoil him."

"As well you should." Lynn assessed him. "He looks like he could use a little feminine attention."

Tom's pulse quickened. He knew exactly the kind of feminine attention he needed, but the aunts' formal parlor was hardly the appropriate venue. He spread his arms expansively. "Bring it on, ladies. You won't find me resisting."

"I'll start, then, by taking your drink order. I already have Lynn's." Ruth rose. "Rachel, could you bring in the hors d'oeuvres?"

While the two were out of the room, Tom whispered, "Did you know about this in advance?"

Lynn shook her head. "I was as surprised as you. Eventually, however, honesty is going to compel me to confess we've already met."

"Not yet. They're enjoying this too much." Then, hearing Rachel returning, he grinned and put a finger to his lips.

Rachel had just set down the tray of cheese and crackers when Ruth brought the drinks. "Lemonade for you, Lynn.'' She handed Lynn a tall crystal goblet, then turned to Tom. ''Your scotch and water, Tom.''

''Are the two of you still drinking sherry?'' He pointed to the wineglasses the aunts held.

Rachel held up her wine. ''It's good for the digestion.''

Ruth laughed. ''That's as good an excuse as any.'' Then, as if she was commenting on a prize rose in a horticultural show, Ruth proceeded to sing Lynn's praises, touting her many accomplishments during her time in Riverbend.

Finally Lynn held up her hand and laughingly protested. ''Oh, dear, Ruth. Enough. Heaven help me if I have to live up to that list of virtues. We don't want to mislead Tom. You both know I have many flaws, too.''

''I know no such thing,'' Rachel said indignantly. ''I can't name one.''

''I can,'' Lynn said. ''For instance, I seem to have totally misjudged Prentice Jewett and his reaction to Meacham House.''

''Oh, *that*.'' Ruth's chin quivered indignantly. ''Prentice is a first-class fool.''

''An influential one who's causing quite a stir.'' Lynn's voice sounded strained. ''I had a tense meeting with him yesterday.''

Rachel glanced quickly at her twin as if checking for permission, then smiled enigmatically. ''Don't you worry. Ruth and I have a plan.''

Tom noticed Ruth's eyes light up. ''Watch out, Lynn. The aunts are noted for their nefarious schemes.''

''Nefarious! The idea,'' Ruth snorted. ''You know

very well we have always been quite successful in influencing public opinion.''

''I'm not questioning your success. It's your methods.'' Tom grinned. ''You two could put the CIA to shame.''

Lynn looked from Ruth to Rachel. ''I have to admit I'm curious.''

Rachel took a sip of her sherry. ''You'll see, Lynn. You have right on your side, as well you should.''

''And if these two are involved,'' Tom offered, ''*might* as well.''

He listened while Lynn and his aunts explored the Meacham House subject more seriously. Some downtown business owners were objecting on several levels—the teens would make too much noise with their loud music, their coarse language and disreputable appearance would offend potential customers, and the house would degenerate into a gathering place for drug users, turning the downtown into a commercial wasteland. Tom grimaced. He hated the thought of bigoted busybodies interfering with what was clearly a project close to Lynn's heart.

At dinner Tom watched with interest the interplay between Lynn and his aunts. They clearly adored her, and she impressed him by holding her own admirably in a discussion of several bestselling books. Ruth had been right. He was in the company of three beautiful women.

Over dessert, the conversation took a turn when Ruth abruptly put down her fork and said to Tom, ''Perhaps now we can talk about your visit with Aaron.''

Tom frowned. Was this an appropriate topic for Lynn? Before he could find a tactful way to pose the question, Rachel anticipated it. "It's all right, Tom. As our pastor, Lynn knows about the situation. Ruth and I would like her to be a part of this discussion. Perhaps she can help us find a way to make peace with it all."

"I'll do what I can," Lynn said, folding her napkin and carefully setting it next to her empty plate. "But in the long run this is something you will have to work out among yourselves. And it will take time."

"Lynn, do you know Aaron?" Tom asked.

"Not well, but he's been helpful in talking with the Meacham House volunteers about the teenagers and their problems."

"He and Lily Bennett Holden make a striking couple," Ruth said.

"An odd pairing, though," Rachel added.

"At first glance they might appear mismatched," Lynn agreed, "but you only have to be in the same room with them a few moments to feel their connection. It's positively incandescent."

Ruth nodded. "Aaron has been looking for someone like Lily all his life."

"We're straying from the subject," Rachel reminded them. "How did Aaron react to you, Tom?"

"Given that he hasn't seen me in years and we were never friends, about what you might expect. Minimal civility with a healthy dose of hostility."

"Some bitterness would be understandable," Lynn suggested softly.

"After we found out about Abraham's role in Aaron's life, we called Aaron," Ruth said. "He was polite. Very controlled. But he did say he had no hard feelings where we were concerned."

Rachel leaned forward. "In fact, he said we'd been

among the few folks in Riverbend who'd always treated him with respect.''

"He was pretty hard on Uncle Abe yesterday.'' Tom winced, remembering the hot waves of Aaron's anger.

"I'm sure our brother did what he needed to do,'' Rachel said.

"We're biased, sister. From Aaron's viewpoint, it wouldn't necessarily appear that way.''

"No, it doesn't,'' Tom said. "In fact, I wouldn't blame him if he never gets over his resentment of us.''

Lynn looked from one to the other. "Abraham isn't here, so Aaron can't confront him. It's natural he might take his anger out on the family.''

"Oh, dear,'' Rachel murmured. "That puts you on the front line, Tom. How did you feel about him?''

Tom finished the last of his pie, then said, "Believe it or not, I liked him.''

Lynn sought his eyes across the table. "I can believe it,'' she said softly. She turned to Ruth and Rachel. "Find the small openings, look for the good and build a bridge.''

Ruth raised her brows hopefully, then responded, "I pray it will be so.''

Just as Tom knew that Aaron's angry words were justified, he also knew that healing the family breach wouldn't be easy. Not for the first time, he wished like hell Jacob was here. If and when he returned, there'd be another huge hurdle to leap with Aaron. He and Jacob were half brothers, after all. Tom leaned back in his chair, determined to change the subject. "Thank you, Aunties, for a delicious meal.''

Lynn stood and began clearing the dessert plates.

"Quit that,'' Rachel said. "Ruthie and I want our

guests to be exactly that—guests. We'll take care of this later."

"Meanwhile, why don't you two run along? We old ladies turn in early, you know." Tom could swear there was a conniving gleam in Ruth's eyes.

"Lynn lives only two blocks down on East Hickory. But it's dark out. Do you think you might drive her home?" The affected innocence of Aunt Rachel's question almost made Tom laugh out loud.

Lynn demurred. "I can walk by myself."

Tom gallantly presented his arm. "I wouldn't hear of it." Warmth spread in his chest as Lynn tucked her hand through his arm.

Ruth patted them both on the shoulders. "You make such a nice couple, don't they, Rachel?"

Beside him, Tom could feel the giggle welling up in Lynn. "Is that what my devious aunties are up to? Matchmaking?" he asked.

The aunts looked flustered. "I…we…" Ruth, rarely at a loss for words, was tongue-tied.

Lynn withdrew her hand and turned to embrace the women. "Remember when I told you I have flaws? Well, I've been guilty of one tonight. I—" she looked at Tom "—*we* haven't quite been truthful with you."

"You haven't?" Ruth sounded incredulous.

Tom moved to put at arm around each aunt's waist. "It's my fault. I led Lynn astray. I was having too much fun."

Rachel cocked her head to look up at him. "Whatever do you mean, Tom Baines?"

"We've already met," Lynn, looking abashed, volunteered.

"You have?" Rachel sounded both confused and pleased.

Tom pulled the aunts closer to him. "Yes, and while I appreciate all your elaborate machinations this evening, I have to tell you—no matchmaking is necessary." He found Lynn's eyes, warm with affection. "We've already taken care of it." He kissed each aunt, released them and grabbed Lynn's hand. "Thanks for a great time. I'll talk to you soon. Meanwhile I have a beautiful woman to escort home."

Lynn murmured thanks as he whisked her out the door, leaving the aunts speechless. But he took satisfaction from their expressions. No doubt about it— they were delighted by his revelation.

"I LIKE YOUR HOUSE," Tom said as he walked around the living room, studying the watercolors displayed on the garden-green walls. "It has a cozy feel."

"It should." Lynn laughed from the kitchen where she was making coffee. "It's tiny. These Victorian cottages aren't known for spacious rooms."

He sank onto a chintz-covered sofa with a rounded back. The lace curtains, potted ferns, wicker rocker, glass-enclosed bookcase and antique chest that served as a coffee table showed her knack for making a room welcoming. None of the pieces matched, but somehow it all worked.

Draped across the high back of a wing chair, the large black cat she'd introduced as Benedict stared at him unsettlingly. "Invading your territory, am I?" Tom challenged. The cat merely closed his eyes, yawned and resumed his scrutiny. "Could you at least give me a chance, fella? I kind of like the lady of the house."

"Talking to yourself?" Lynn entered the room with a tray, two mugs and a coffeepot.

"No, Ben and I were just having a man-to-man chat."

"About?" Lynn sat beside him and served him a cup.

"Staking my claim."

She raised an eyebrow. "To?"

He set his coffee aside and stilled her hand before she could pour her own cup. "You." He gathered her in his arms. "You," he repeated against her ear.

"And what did Ben say?" she asked softly.

"I believe his exact words were, 'Go for it, dude.'"

Lynn chuckled against his neck. "No way. Ben's far too possessive for that."

"What do you say we give him something to be possessive about?" He raised her chin and kissed her, first lightly, then with increasing pressure. He could feel her fingers clutching his head, sense the same urgency in her body that thrummed in his. Reluctantly he pulled back and cleared his throat. "Um—" he nodded at the windows "—the lights are on and those lace curtains aren't exactly opaque."

"Why, Mr. Baines, are you embarrassed?"

She constantly surprised him with her wonderfully earthy flirtatiousness. "The last thing I want to do is compromise you."

She laughed. "Why is it I don't believe you?" She picked up her coffee and moved to the rocker. "But I do see your point. You stay there—" she pointed to the sofa "—and I'll sit here."

Tom threw a baleful look at the cat. "Help me out here, Ben. Next thing you know, she'll want me to leave my calling card in a silver tray and politely withdraw." Ben regarded him with what was clearly disdain.

Lynn rocked back and forth. "I told you so."

"What?"

"That this wouldn't be easy." She paused. The delicate chime of the clock on the mantel rang nine. "I'd like nothing better than to sit on that sofa and neck with you."

"Neck?" The old-fashioned word amused him. Besides, he definitely had something more in mind.

"We have to be sure, Tom, both of us, before we take this much farther. And—" she blushed "—you need to know there's a point beyond which I can't go." Her eyes signaled a silent appeal.

Of course. Why hadn't he thought of that himself? She had a moral example to set. It wasn't as simple as two adults satisfying their mutual needs. She was drawing the line. And to step over the line meant commitment. "Hey, I understand." He laughed self-consciously. "You were right. It isn't easy." He swallowed, then cleared his throat and found himself saying, "I want you." The words ricocheted around the room, bald in their truth. "Before. Now. Tomorrow." His body was tense with desire.

She had stopped rocking and was clutching the arms of the chair. Finally she spoke. "I want you to know it is taking every bit of willpower I have to stay in this chair."

Her full breasts rose and fell with her breathing, and he felt the evidence of his own desire. He cast about for a way to defuse the moment, then again turned to the cat, who had crawled down the back of the wing chair and now sat curled in the seat. "I guess I should take some comfort from that, huh, fella? But it's not easy for us tomcats, is it?" He looked back at Lynn, whose luminous eyes and flushed cheeks betrayed her emotions. "Lynn, you told me the other night you wouldn't ask of me more than I can give. I want to make the same promise to you."

She raised her fingers to her lips and tenderly blew him a kiss. "Thank you," she whispered.

"I think maybe it's time I was going." He managed a grin before rising to his feet. "While I can still keep that promise."

She followed him into the small entry hall, where she put her arms on his shoulders, reached up and brushed his lips with hers. "When will I see you again? I want to, you know."

He held her by the waist, not tempting himself by moving any closer. "I'll be out of town this weekend."

"Weekends aren't good for me, anyway."

"That's right. You're on duty then."

She chuckled. "That's one way of putting it."

"What about Monday? I'll pick you up and take you to my place."

"It's a date." She kissed him again. "Have a good trip. Where are you going?"

There was no reason not to tell her. But if things didn't go well... "Chicago."

"Oh." She waited.

Hell, this was stupid. Surely it wouldn't jinx anything to confess the truth. "I'm going to see my kids."

He could swear she was looking through his eyes and into his soul. Her hands relaxed on his shoulders and the smile she gave him put light where before there'd been none. "Good."

That was all she said. But the way she said it was like a one-word benediction.

He turned to leave. She followed him out and stood on the porch watching him depart, her arms snugged protectively around herself. When he was halfway to his truck, she called his name softly. He stopped and turned to face her, relishing the way the interior lamp backlit her golden hair. "What?"

"Thank you for giving Ruth and Rachel such delight and especially for telling them we've done our own matchmaking." He almost bounded up the steps, heedless of his promise, but before he could move, she smiled and waggled her fingers at him and said one last thing that warmed him all the way home. "You're a good man, Tom Baines."

CHAPTER SIX

"A GOOD MAN"? Tom slammed shut the drawer of the motel-room dresser and stuffed his dirty clothes into his overnight bag. Thank God Lynn hadn't witnessed this weekend's debacle with the kids. The "good man" would've died on her lips.

He grimaced. Not that he'd expected a warm, fuzzy Brady Bunch-type reunion. No. For Pete and Libby, a piranha might have been a more welcome weekend companion. It wasn't merely that he didn't speak their language, know any of their friends or behave in a "cool" manner. Their hostility went beyond that, as if they were determined not to permit him a way back. Hell, why should they?

The truth was, he'd known even at the time that part of his eagerness to globetrot in the name of work derived from his fear that he had no notion how to be a father. Bottom line, parenthood scared the crap out of him. Certainly his own father had been too busy to be much of a dad; and for Tom, committing to staying in one place had felt frighteningly confining, even though for a time he'd tried. So what had he done? He'd run. There. He'd said it. No wonder Selena had finally, though reluctantly, given up and divorced him. Who could blame her? Maybe it would be easier on everybody if he simply faded out of the picture instead of trying to win his way back into his children's good graces.

He zipped up the bag, tossed the card key on the dresser, then doused the lights. Easier for them? Maybe. But not for him. Guilt and need clawed at his guts, reminding him that *easy* demanded a painful price.

THE AIR HELD a hint of fall Wednesday noon when Lynn joined Kate outside the church for their customary triweekly walk. "Sorry I couldn't come Monday," Lynn said as they turned the corner onto East Oak, "but I had a few things on the front burner."

"Like Meacham House?"

Lynn nodded.

"The aunts are in a tizzy over Prentice Jewett. They're spending hours plotting his downfall."

"Although it would be uncharitable of me to hope for their success, I do wish he'd give up his opposition."

"Lots of folks are behind you on this, Lynn. It's the right thing to do."

"I know." They stepped up their pace, passing showcase Victorian homes with sweeping lawns where ancient trees shaded wide front porches.

"That's not all the aunts are in a tizzy about lately."

Lynn could feel it coming. "Oh?" she asked innocently.

"No." The two paused at the corner of Adams Street to let a delivery truck pass. "I understand Tom made their day by playing one-upmanship in the matchmaking game." Kate shot Lynn an amused look, then grabbed her arm and started off across the street. "So what's going on in the romance department?"

"Hmm. A cautious courtship, maybe?"

"That doesn't sound very exciting."

"Prudent, though. I wouldn't tell anyone else this, but if I'm not careful, this could become a lot more exciting than either Riverbend or I am ready for."

Kate laughed. "Aha! He turns you on, then."

Lynn felt her face flush, maybe from the exertion. "More than that." Her brows knit. "There's a deeper part of him that intrigues me."

"Sure you're not simply trying to save him?"

Now it was Lynn's turn to laugh. "You know me too well. That, too, I suppose. But a lasting relationship has to be built on more than rescue."

"And so?"

Lynn waved to one of her parishioners who was out sweeping her front walk. "We've agreed to move slowly and see where it goes."

"When did this happen?"

Lynn decided to come clean. "I had dinner with Tom Monday evening at his farm. The seclusion there keeps us out of the public eye. Once I get him talking, he's a great conversationalist, and I love hearing him reminisce about Riverbend." She stopped short of admitting how troubled she was, however, by the topics he'd avoided discussing—his work and the details of this past weekend in Chicago with Pete and Libby.

Kate nudged her with an elbow. "Surely good conversation isn't all that went on."

"You're relentless, you know that?" Grinning, Lynn slackened the pace. "Okay, true confession. Being alone with him is pretty heady, and 'moving slowly' requires every last ounce of my willpower."

"Are you worried about the reaction of people at the church?"

"That's a consideration, but in the long run I have to follow my heart."

"Good girl," Kate said. "I have to admit I'm a bit envious. The twins are wonderful and keep me more than busy, but a love life would be a welcome novelty. Guess I'll just enjoy yours vicariously."

Lynn's sympathy welled up. She admired her friend for her upbeat attitude, but she knew her marriage had been a disaster and that, as a single parent, Kate struggled—although her five-year-old twin daughters, Hope and Hannah, were the light of her life. Lynn almost felt guilty for the way her heart expanded every time she said Tom's name. She wanted Kate to be able to feel that rush of love and desire for a man, too. Surely someday the right one would come along for her.

"Kate, I can't tell you what a relief it is to be able to talk about Tom." There it was again—that flood of well-being. "I don't know how this could happen so quickly, but I can't stop thinking about him."

Kate stopped dead in her tracks and framed Lynn's face with her hands. "It's called love, honey. And you're as entitled to it as the next woman." Then Lynn felt herself enclosed in a warm embrace. "I'm happy for you," Kate whispered.

Lynn's eyes misted with gratitude and with the knowledge that she, too, was happy.

FRIDAY NIGHT Tom rested the latest John Sandford thriller on his chest and closed his eyes. Even the intriguing plot twists weren't holding his attention. His mind kept returning to two subjects—Lynn and his kids. He'd planned to take Lynn out tonight—until she'd called from the hospital to say she needed to stay with a family whose father was having emergency surgery. When his plans had been thwarted, he'd experienced a twinge of resentment. Not good, he reminded himself. That was the part of her life she'd warned him about. The part he'd have to accept if he wanted her.

Earlier in the evening he'd worked on a letter to Pete and Libby. Twice he'd torn it up. Once because it sounded pathetically like begging, and the second time because the caustic tone spoke all too clearly of his irritation at their indifference. Over dinner Monday night Lynn, in her tactful manner, had suggested he keep trying with them. As she'd reminded him, the relationship hadn't fallen apart overnight and it wasn't going to be mended overnight, either. But for a man accustomed to action, patience was difficult.

He tossed the book aside, left the easy chair and stood for a moment listening to the moody Dave Brubeck number playing on the stereo. Smooth jazz and a good book—his usual antidotes to loneliness, and neither had worked worth a damn this evening. Might as well go to bed. See whether insomnia was lying in wait—or worse, bad dreams. He turned off the stereo and dimmed the lights.

Before locking the front door, he paused, staring out at the cloudy, moonless night. Beyond the line of trees at the edge of his property, where usually there was no sign of life, he thought he saw a flame flicker. He looked again. Nothing. He rubbed his eyes, chalked off the illusion to exhaustion and hauled himself off to bed.

Around one-thirty he became aware that the stac-

cato pops and high-pitched metallic bursts he was
hearing were not part of the Gulf War nightmare from
which, with difficulty, he finally emerged. He grabbed
a T-shirt, pulled it on over his briefs and stumbled to
the front porch. From there, it was clear someone was
shooting fireworks from the same general area where
he'd earlier seen the flame—an area all too near the
cemetery so dear to Lynn.

He returned to the bedroom, hurriedly donned jeans
and shoes, then set off in the truck to investigate.
Nearing the cemetery, he could hear the thrumming
bass of a car radio or boom box. *Brmm. Brmm.* The
steady rhythm jolted his psyche. As he rounded the
curve right at the cemetery, he encountered at least a
dozen pickups and souped-up cars. He jumped from
the truck and started up the hill. The heavy-metal music was deafening. Just then another set of firecrackers
exploded, punctuating the night with bursts of sound
followed by raucous shouts and laughter.

Son of a bitch! If anyone had desecrated that cemetery... And there they were, fifteen to twenty teens,
some dancing drunkenly around a campfire, several
huddled against the wall drinking beer and smoking
God knew what, and a couple sprawled in the shadows so engrossed with each other they were unaware
of his presence. Locating the boom box, Tom hit the
off switch and wheeled on the group. ''What the hell
do you think you're doing?''

A chorus of protests rained on him. One of the
smokers looked up blearily and said, ''Piss off, man.''
A long-haired, black-clad youth with a pencil-thin
brush of facial hair on his upper lip said to the others,
''Lemme handle this.'' A cocky sneer distorting his

mouth, he took his time sauntering over to Tom and stopped just short of crowding Tom's space.

"I want you off this property right now," Tom said.

"Think you can scare us? You don't own this bone dump." The teen postured for his friends as if to say, *Get a load of this guy.*

Tom stood his ground. "If you don't pack up and get out of here, you'd be well advised to be scared."

"We got as much right to be here as you do."

"You're trespassing on private property, drinking illegally, not to mention desecrating a graveyard."

"You musta aced your ACT test." A big-breasted redhead in tight jeans ambled over. "'Desecrating'— I'm impressed," she said, her blue eyes ice-hard.

"Lemme straighten you out, man." The ringleader poked a finger in the direction of Tom's chest. "We're not leavin' here, and there ain't nothin' you can do about it."

"If you're not out of here in ten minutes, I'll call the sheriff."

"Who made you boss?" the girl challenged.

Tom winced. The hell of it was, he could picture himself at their age doing exactly the same thing these kids were doing.

"Okay, okay." He held his hands up in a conciliatory gesture. Others who had been on the fringes of the conversation now massed behind their spokesman. "Look, I worked my butt off helping to get this cemetery looking nice again. You don't need to party here. Plus, the fireworks are disturbing the peace." He decided against mentioning the music.

The redhead rolled her eyes. "Like there are so many places to have fun in this hick county."

"Let me put it this way," Tom said. "You leave here now, I won't call the sheriff. But if I ever catch you out here again, I won't even hesitate."

Some of the girls started gathering up blankets and snacks, and Tom heard one of them say, "My folks would kill me if we got caught."

Tom pointed to the empty beer bottles and fireworks boxes. "You need to clean up this mess."

The young man with the mustache glared at Tom, seemingly oblivious to the grumbles and preparations going on behind him. "I got only one thing to say to you, man." Then, in explicit street language, he told Tom precisely what he could do with himself.

"You've got quite an attitude, son."

"And you ain't improving it. And just for future reference—" he pronounced it ree-fur-ence "—nobody tells Damon Hudson where to party."

"I don't care where you party, so long as it's nowhere near this cemetery." Tom started toward the truck, then turned around. "Ever consider using that mouth of yours to accomplish some good?"

"Oh, yeah. Right." The kid spread his arms in disbelief.

"You hear of Meacham House? You might give it a try when it opens."

Damon laughed derisively. "I got a news flash for you, pops. You'll never catch me in that place. I don't need no reformin'."

"Who said anything about reforming? You might find it's an okay place to hang out."

"Screw it." Damon started to walk off.

"You afraid?" At Tom's words, the youngster stopped in his tracks. "Afraid your buddies'll think you're a wimp? Afraid you might like it? Why don't you bring them and come see? The center opens the Monday after Labor Day.''

The kid whipped his head around, sending his dark hair flying. ''You really think those church—'' he almost spit the word ''—ladies want us hangin' around?''

''Yeah, I really do.'' Tom thrust his hands in his pockets. ''I dare you to give it a try.''

The redhead moved closer to Damon. ''It might be a kick to let them see what teenagers are really like.'' For all her attitude, Tom could swear he saw in her eyes a flicker of vulnerability.

The boy seemed to consider the idea. He looked from side to side at his cohorts. ''Whaddaya think, guys? Wanna give Meacham House an in-ter-est-ing send-off?'' Mean-spirited laughter and exchanges of high fives greeted the suggestion. Damon held up his hand and the group quieted. ''Tell ya what, big shot. We'll come under one condition.''

Tom waited. ''What's that?''

''You come, too.''

''Me?''

''Yeah,'' Damon drawled.

By no stretch of the imagination was he a youth worker, Tom thought, and he had zero desire to encounter any of these yahoos in the future. ''Deal. I'll see you there September eleventh. For now, though, pack up and get out of here.''

Tom strode quickly down the hill, and as he got into his pickup, to his chagrin, he heard the boom box blast the night again. His words had apparently made little impression. All he'd succeeded in doing was recruiting a bunch of kids who very well might sabotage the opening of Meacham House.

Beyond that, the smart-ass kid had succeeded in manipulating him. The very last thing he wanted was to get involved with a bunch of misguided teenagers. He already had his hands full with his own two.

He reached down to press in the cigarette lighter before he caught himself. Damn. Meacham House.

"I MAY AS WELL tell you," Tom said the following Monday evening as he sliced the tomatoes Lynn had set out on the small counter in her tiny kitchen. "I hope I haven't ruined the Meacham House opening."

She glanced up from the pot she was stirring. "Really? Single-handedly?" He looked so serious it was almost comical. "How?"

"You may have more teens opening night than you counted on. Not model citizens, either."

She crushed some basil between her fingers and threw it into the stew. "And this is a problem?"

"They're wise-ass troublemakers with big mouths and no desire to be rehabilitated."

"Good." Lynn thumped the ladle on the rim of the pan and set it in a spoon holder. "They're exactly who the program was designed for."

Tom set down the paring knife and frowned at her. "But—"

"Are you trying to protect me? These are the very kids we want to reach. We know they'll be defensive and resentful to begin with."

"That's putting it mildly." Then Tom filled her in on his confrontation with Damon and his gang at the cemetery. "So," he concluded, "they may set out to defy you."

Pushing up the sleeves of her sweater, she smiled

at him. "And defy you, too, from what you're telling me." She couldn't help it. The chuckle erupted.

"It's not funny, Lynn."

"You're right, it's not funny. I'm well aware their appearance en masse may fuel Prentice's objections and create some challenges for our staff. But it's still worth doing. If it's trial by fire from the very first, maybe we'll be all the more successful sooner."

He placed his forehead against hers. "Are you always such a Pollyanna?"

She circled his waist, hooking her hands behind his back. "Always."

"Isn't that a bit unrealistic? You know, there are some bad people in the world."

She raised her head and looked into his troubled eyes. "I know that. I can be optimistic without being blind or uninformed. In the long run, though, I believe people are inherently good. Our job with these kids is to give them a chance to prove it."

"Then we have our work cut out for us."

She smiled. "I like the sound of that 'we.'"

He nuzzled her neck. "Me, too."

"I think the aunts do, too," she whispered.

He paused in his ministrations long enough to say, "Oh?"

She could hardly concentrate for the insistent sensations warring with rational thought. She molded her body to his. "Rachel found me after church yesterday and very discreetly but obviously—" He shushed her with a toe-curling kiss. She struggled to continue. "Your aunt voiced her opinion that you had finally exercised some good sense."

"I was merely waiting for the right woman." He

kissed her again in a way that left her feeling she was that woman.

His hand was straying from her shoulder to the button at the neck of her sweater when she heard a popping noise from the stew pot. More than just their supper was coming to a boil. She pulled from his grasp and removed the pot from the burner. ''Saved.''

He moved away, then with the tip of the knife, pushed the tomato slices from the cutting board onto a plate. ''What? The stew or you?''

''The stew, of course.'' To herself, though, she admitted she was learning a great deal about temptation. Tom was a very male, very sexy kind of guy who easily made her forget she needed to exercise caution.

Later, over fruit, cheese and coffee, Tom again made passing reference to his disappointment concerning the weekend in Chicago with his kids. Lynn decided to press him. If she was serious about him, she needed to be serious, as well, about his son and daughter. ''Please tell me more about Pete and Libby. About what's happened between you and them.''

His lips thinned, and for what seemed a long time he didn't say anything. ''You're not going to like it,'' he said finally.

''How do *you* know?''

Picking up a section of apple, he traced circles on his plate. ''They couldn't care less if they ever saw me again.''

''I don't believe that!''

He held up his hand. ''Let me go on. I don't blame them. It's hard to relate to an absentee father, especially one who hasn't given them the time of day for years on end.''

''Why, Tom?''

He dropped the apple slice, then rocked back in his chair. "Several reasons, none of which qualifies as an excuse. First, I didn't know how to be a parent. Second, the lure of journalistic achievement, even glamour, was powerful. Third, I suppose Selena and I should have realized early on we were ill suited. She's a great person, but a homebody by nature. She never understood my wanderlust."

He linked his hands behind his head and stared at the ceiling before going on. "I cared nothing about diapers, potty training, nursery schools—all the stuff that consumed her. Even when the kids were older, I didn't seem to know how to talk to them, how to understand what was important in their lives. And I can't say I made much of an effort. It was easier to turn from the uncomfortable to the comfortable. I was a damned good reporter with an ego the size of a small country. I enjoyed thinking of myself as 'our man on the scene.' When you're halfway around the world and gain a good deal of attention from important people, it's hard to get excited about the first time a kid rides a bike without training wheels or learns to do a back flip in gymnastics class."

"And now?" Lynn could feel his pain as if it was her own.

He lowered his hands, then shook his head wearily. "I don't know. Pete just looks at me with this mocking sneer as if daring me to prove something to him. Damned if I know what or how. And Libby? She's taken eye-rolling to an art form and acquired an unlimited supply of words like 'gross' and 'embarrassing' to describe my every move. That makes it darned difficult to pull off the hey-kids-I'm-back number."

"Their actions are understandable, given their history. But not insurmountable."

"Easy for you to say." The words were laden with irony, but Lynn concentrated on the sadness in his eyes.

"You can never retrieve the past, but you have years in front of you to be a father." She smiled warmly. "Even a grandfather. It's important that you keep trying."

"I'm not sure I can."

She experienced a surge of irritation, which she quickly squelched. Anger on his children's behalf would not be a productive response. "I think you have to, Tom." The air crackled with tension and she remained silent, watching hot wax form ribbons down the stem of the candle burning in the middle of the table.

Finally he shrugged. "We'll see."

She worked to mold the wax to the taper before it dripped onto the table surface. "What about the other one?"

His brow furrowed. "Other one?"

"The boy in the photograph in your bedroom. Terence."

Tom raked his hand through his hair, and Lynn didn't know if the candlelight was playing tricks, but she could have sworn his eyes filled. "Ah, Terence." He sighed heavily. "That's another story."

When he didn't elaborate, she suggested they move to the living room where they'd be more comfortable. Apparently still lost in thought, he picked up his cup and drained it.

She blew out the candle, then stood and led him to the sofa. A small Tiffany table lamp spread a rosy light. He sat down, then pulled her across his knees, cuddling her against his shoulder. For a time the only sounds were their quiet breathing and the creaks of the old house, bending to the stiff wind outside. "Terence is all that's left of a time in my life I don't talk about." He stopped as if gathering his words. She didn't move, sensing that whatever was coming was critical for him.

"First, I have to tell you about Gordy Maxwell, the toughest, bravest man I ever met. He was my cameraman for eight years. He ventured into places the hounds of hell would've fled. And his photos? What can I say? He was a genius. He had a talent for capturing faces that gave war a hauntingly human dimension, in a way my most eloquent words never could." Tom rubbed a hand up and down Lynn's arm as if buying time. "He was also the best friend I ever had. We got our asses shot at, closed down more pubs than I care to think about and joked around like brothers."

Lynn raised her head slightly. "*Was,* Tom?"

His hand stilled on her arm and she watched his eyes narrow. "The bastards blew him up." His controlled anger was more jarring than if he had screamed the words. "It was a terrorist bomb in Ireland," he went on tonelessly. "We were in the wrong place at the wrong time."

"Go on," Lynn encouraged.

Tom told her the whole miserable tale, finishing with, "I found a boy, still breathing, underneath Gordy's body." Tom paused. "Gordy had saved him."

"Terence?"

Tom nodded. "Yes."

"So you saved him, too."

"Don't make me a hero, Lynn. I was still on the sidewalk when that bomb went off."

Lynn reared up. "What became of Terence?"

"His wounds were superficial. He was more traumatized than hurt. He and his parents wanted to do something for me. *Me?* I was so angry about Gordy, I could hardly be civil. But it wasn't the kid's fault he survived and Gordy didn't. So I told him to send me a picture, write occasionally if he wanted to."

"And?"

"Faithful as clockwork. I've been sending him my address changes, and every month I get a letter from him."

Lynn clasped his hands in her lap. "Do you think it should've been you, instead of Gordy, who got killed?"

He pulled his hands away. "What's this? Are you playing shrink now?"

"*Do* you?"

He stood and paced to the far side of the room, where he stopped, gripping the back of a desk chair. His voice filled the room. "Hell, yes. Gordy was worth a dozen of me. Nothing about it makes any sense."

"No, it doesn't."

He turned around and fixed his eyes on her. "I thought you'd have all the answers."

"Well, I don't."

"I'll bet you could come up with some platitudes if you tried." She bit her lip, trying not to take his attack personally, knowing he needed to vent. "How about 'Everything happens for the best' or 'Ours is not to wonder why'? Then there's my personal favorite. 'God has His reasons.'"

"You're asking a mighty big question," Lynn said.

"So why aren't you answering it?"

At times like these, Lynn felt her inadequacy especially keenly. And what she said now could be significant. She slowly rose and went to him. She touched him lightly on the shoulder. "Because my answers might not be your answers. At this moment I can be either your counselor or your woman. Which do you need from me?"

He crushed her to him. "Right now? Just hold me."

She reached up, feeling the rigidity of his shoulders, then ran her hands up and down the tense muscles of his back. "I can do that." Then softly but firmly she repeated the words. "I can do that."

CHAPTER SEVEN

OVER THE NEXT FEW DAYS, in addition to her regular duties, Lynn was swamped with details concerning the opening of Meacham House. Molly Linden, a nurse new to Riverbend who had agreed to direct the program, had already put in an unprecedented number of hours cleaning the property, scrounging furniture donations, laying in a supply of food and training the adult volunteers. Lynn didn't know which was her bigger fear—that few if any kids would show up, or that there would be so many they would feel overwhelmed and quit participating before giving the program a chance.

The volunteer staff had decided food, music and a nonjudgmental atmosphere were key to hooking the teens. After that, they'd promote activities, tutoring and a peer-counseling group. It would all take time, and Lynn prayed Prentice Jewett would cut them enough slack to prove to doubters that Meacham House could succeed.

At the end of a particularly grueling afternoon, Lynn wandered out into the church garden and sank gratefully onto a stone bench facing a large flowering crepe-myrtle bush, its lush magenta blooms brilliant against the lawn.

She closed her eyes, waiting for her interior monitor to stop hounding her with uncompleted tasks.

In a few days she'd learn if this grand experiment would fly. At times she'd questioned whether she should attempt such a large-scale outreach project so early in her Riverbend tenure, but she'd concluded Meacham House would be a boon for many and a genuine blessing for some. If she was wrong? She clutched the edge of the bench and leaned back, exposing her face to the sun. She'd cross that bridge when she came to it.

If Tom was correct about the group of rebellious teens he'd encountered at the cemetery, she'd have her answer sooner rather than later. She recalled his concern that he'd sabotaged the opening. Ah. That evening.

She straightened and stared past the crepe myrtle into space. She hadn't known how to help him. He wasn't ready for the usual pastoral responses. She hadn't found the right things to say to him. Not about his children, not about his friend Gordy and not about the cosmic ''Why?'' that had erupted from the depths of his anguish.

Then had not been a time for words, only for reaching out with the best-known antidote for fear and loneliness—connection to another human being. He had held her so fiercely she knew he'd been unaware of the strength of his grasp. His pain had been forged in the white-hot flame and fueled for a very long time under crisis. It would not be assuaged overnight.

She rose to her feet and approached the crepe myrtle. She cupped a blossom in her palms, awed once again by the beauty, variety and fragility of nature's gifts. If only she could wrap her hands around Tom's hurt and soothe it away. When he was ready, *if* ever he was ready, she could perhaps help him. But only in his time. Only if he asked.

Meanwhile, if she wasn't very, very careful, she would watch his spirit curl into itself and wither just as, with the first hint of cold, the flower she cradled in her palms would.

Somehow she had never expected that loving a man would be this difficult.

THE FIRST MONDAY evening after Labor Day, an eclectic group gathered on Washington Street in front of Meacham House. Its gabled two stories spoke of another era; however, signs over the large wraparound front porch announcing music and food were strictly contemporary. Lynn watched nervously as a few stray teenagers loitered on the lawn, looking distrustful. Molly, a smile wreathing her face, her bright red curls bobbing, hurried to greet the young people. If anybody could charm them up the walk and into the house, it was the effervescent director.

From the backyard, Lynn heard the music begin. One of her parishioners led a five-piece band, which was donating two hours tonight, and beyond that, the leader had agreed to offer weekly guitar lessons. Molly had been scrupulous in securing permission from town officials to forestall neighbors' objections to the music, and most of the property owners contacted had been cautiously receptive.

Lynn wasn't quite so optimistic about Prentice Jewett and others like him. She hoped he wouldn't show up. But she had a sinking feeling that nothing would keep him away.

Off in the distance she noticed Ruth and Rachel Steele making their way toward Meacham House.

Wally Drummer, the retired high-school coach, and Mary, his wife, were already on duty dishing out pizza and soft drinks to the five or six kids Molly had lured inside, and now several other kids, attracted by the music, were walking around to the back of the house.

Lynn felt someone touch her arm and turned to see Aaron Mazerik. He had been a tremendous help when the idea for Meacham House had first been broached and had taken a genuine interest in the project. "How's it going?" he asked.

"Slowly. But I guess that's par for the course with something like this."

"Don't be discouraged. It's early yet. I overheard some of the kids talking at school today. It's a peer-group thing. Nobody wants to be the first to arrive, to appear uncool. Then there are others who think the idea is dumb. Of course, those are the very ones who could profit most from what you're offering here."

Lynn sighed. "I know you're right. I'm trying hard to be optimistic."

"Atta girl."

"Where's Lily?" One of the town's recent hot topics of conversation had been the announcement that Lily Bennett Holden, a young widow who had recently come back home to Riverbend, and Aaron were soon to be married.

"She'll be over later. We thought it might not be so great to overwhelm the kids at first with too many adults."

Lynn inclined her head toward the group of onlookers, mainly adults, standing near the street. "Good thinking. I'll suggest to them that they make themselves less conspicuous."

"Okay. Meanwhile, I'll see if I can snare that

bunch.'' He pointed toward the corner where a group of teens dressed mostly in black milled around, smoking. ''I know those kids. Some of them are real pieces of work. But Meacham House is exactly what they need. Wish me luck.'' Shoving his hands into his pockets, he sauntered casually toward the group.

Meanwhile, Lynn made her way to the adults, mainly interested church members. ''Thanks for coming. We appreciate your support. However, it's been suggested the kids might feel freer to join in if there weren't so many of us hanging about.''

Grace Pennington looked around, then grinned. ''It does come across as running the gauntlet, doesn't it?''

''Why don't you visit with the kids inside?''

At her invitation, some of the adults made their way toward the house while others dispersed. Out of the corner of her eye, she saw Aaron talking with the group on the corner. One young man with shoulder-length black hair and a scraggly mustache kept gesturing. Finally Aaron left the teens and moved back to Lynn. ''Got any idea who promised to meet them here? Damon Hudson, the kid with the attitude, said he wasn't coming near Meacham House unless this dude showed up.''

''Tom.'' Lynn's heart sank. Where was he?

''*Tom?* Tom Baines?''

Lynn nodded.

''He's the last person I can imagine being involved with that bunch.''

''It's a long story.''

Aaron leaned over and studied Lynn's face. ''You look worried. Is he supposed to be here?''

''He said he'd come.'' Before she could say anything further, they were interrupted by a voice coming from a loudspeaker. In moments a flat-bed truck rounded the corner. Banners hanging from the bed read Save Our Square, Say NO to Meacham House, Protect Your Property. The voice emanating from the speaker was unquestionably Prentice Jewett's.

"Citizens of Riverbend, what do you want in this historic neighborhood? Deafening rock music, drug transactions, public indecency? Many of you have worked hard to build your businesses, rehabilitate these fine old homes, improve your properties. You enjoy a peaceful quality of life. Are you going to let a bunch of teenagers ruin all you've built up?"

Lynn felt a knot forming in her solar plexus. The band stopped playing, and out of the corner of her eye she saw the formless group of kids on the corner ambling closer. One of the boys, who sported spiked purple hair, shook his fist and shouted an obscenity in the direction of the truck. Wonderful. A confrontation in the making. Prentice would undoubtedly call it a "rumble" and enjoy every minute of being proved right.

Volunteers clustered on the porch, and Aaron and Molly hurried to join Lynn. By now the truck was slowing in front of Meacham House, and Prentice's rhetoric was becoming more impassioned. "It doesn't take much, folks, to turn a decent, God-fearing neighborhood into a slum. Take a look at these kids! Do you really want the likes of them lounging on the sidewalks presenting that kind of disreputable image to visitors? I urge you to talk to the town council and..."

Before he could finish, the boy Aaron had identified as Damon stepped in front of the truck and stood defiantly, arms outstretched, daring the driver to hit him.

Lynn watched Prentice, jowls quivering, lean out of the window of the cab. "Whatsa matter?" Damon challenged. "You afraid of us, pops? Afraid we're too 'disreputable' for this town? I got news for you. We belong here as much as you do."

About this time, to Lynn's everlasting relief, Tom, who must have been on the other side of the street obscured by the truck, stepped forward and put his arm around the shoulders of the belligerent teen, who shrugged him off. Then Tom said something to him. The boy frowned, seeming to consider the words, then turned back to Jewett. "You ain't seen the last of us, grandpa."

As if deliberating his next move, the youth stared at Meacham House. Then, shooting Tom a cryptic look, he gestured to the other teens, who followed him and Tom up the steps and onto the porch, where they all turned to witness Jewett's reaction.

About this time Ruth and Rachel arrived on the scene. Lynn saw the two of them look at each other, nod triumphantly and approach the truck. "Get out of there, Prentice," Ruth said in a peremptory voice, audible to the entire group.

"Now," added Rachel.

"Why should I?"

"Because if you don't, sister and I have a little surprise for you that won't be particularly pleasant," Ruth said.

Anticipating additional fireworks, the few bystanders remaining on the sidewalk edged closer to the truck.

"Remember old man Fenter's outhouse?" Rachel prodded.

His face flaming, Prentice stepped down from the truck. "What are you two up to?"

Ruth withdrew a handful of photographs from her handbag. "Would you like these to be made public?" She handed them to Prentice, who quickly shuffled through them.

"You wouldn't dare."

"Wouldn't we?" Rachel linked her arm through his. "You of all people ought to understand the mischievous ways of young people when left to their own devices. The trouble they can get into."

Ruth commandeered his other arm, and together they propelled the hapless Jewett up the walk toward the porch. "Just think," Lynn heard Ruth say sotto voce, "if there had been a Meacham House back in our day, certain obstreperous young men in Riverbend wouldn't have gotten into so much trouble."

"But then," Rachel went on, "those days are gone. And we certainly wouldn't want those former, er, indiscretions to affect anyone's judgment about all the good some of those youths have subsequently done, now would we?"

Between them, Jewett sputtered, but when Ruth tightened her grip on his arm, he must have reconsidered his position, because he didn't say a word.

Lynn was rooted to the spot. Unbelievable. The sisters were blackmailing Prentice. And the price? The answer came swiftly.

"Rachel and I ask only one thing. That you spend some time at Meacham House, see what these folks are trying to accomplish and then make your judgment. Give them some time to prove themselves. We have a store downtown, too. But we think Reverend

Lynn and the others deserve a chance to make this work. Now, what do you think?"

Trailing them up the sidewalk, Lynn stifled a grin when she heard Prentice mutter, "There never was any getting around the two of you. I suppose I could give it a look-see."

TOM HAD DEBATED about even coming this evening to the Meacham House kickoff. He hated being snookered by some punk of a kid. He studied the living room, set up with folding chairs, beanbag chairs and huge floor pillows, the walls festooned with colorful posters. The teens clustered in groups of two or three taking full advantage of the food still piled on the dining-room table. Others drifted in and out of the backyard or took up a spirited game of Foosball in the downstairs bedroom, now a game room. A few were upstairs using the computers. Most of the adult guests had gone home, including Prentice Jewett, who had stayed only long enough for the most cursory of tours. However, Ruth and Rachel were involved in an animated discussion with Damon's well-endowed female companion, Keri Mellon. Tom smiled indulgently. His aunts seemed totally oblivious to the girl's nose ring, tattoo and pseudo-sophisticated expression. Ruth caught his eye and gave him a triumphant wink.

Aaron materialized beside him. "I didn't expect to see you here."

"Believe me, neither did I." He shrugged. "Somebody has to protect the aunts."

"I think there's a little more to it than that." Aaron inclined his head toward Lynn, who was talking to a younger boy who watched her intently. "You can't take your eyes off Reverend Lynn."

Tom mentally groaned. So much for discretion. "She's quite a woman."

Aaron scrutinized his expression, then lifted an eyebrow. "That she is." They stood quietly in the doorway until Aaron spoke again. "What did you say to young Hudson out in the street to get him in here?"

"I told him if he wanted some fun, he could stay and watch a pair of old ladies put the screws to Prentice Jewett. Then I reminded him of his promise."

"Promise?"

"Yeah, a little deal between him and me. He's the main reason I came, though I wouldn't have bet he'd show up. Nor that if he did, he'd actually come in."

"Hudson could use someone to take an interest in him. His mother died when he was six, and his alcoholic father works the night shift at the foundry. Kid's basically been on his own for years."

An edge in Aaron's voice reminded Tom that Aaron hadn't had it so easy, either, and they both knew why. Was this Aaron's way of sticking it to him about Uncle Abe?

About that time Damon sauntered in from the kitchen, his dark eyes sweeping the room, a curl on his lips.

"Know anything about photography?" Aaron's question to Tom seemed completely out of the blue.

"By osmosis. Hard not to pick up some stuff as a journalist."

"You might mention that to Damon. He's a bright enough kid who doesn't care a thing about school, but the art teacher told me he's shown a real talent for photography. There's a darkroom in the basement. Could be the hook we need with him." Aaron walked away as abruptly as he'd come.

Tom gritted his teeth. He didn't know all that much about photography, and what he did know he'd learned mainly from Gordy. Those memories were still painful. And clearly he didn't know squat about kids. But what could it hurt to sound Damon out?

"Hey, kid." He jerked his chin at Damon. "Seen the darkroom?"

For just an instant the boy's features relaxed before his mask of indifference slipped back into place. "Didn't know there was one."

Tom didn't give him a chance to say no. "C'mon, I'll lead the way." Aaron had said the darkroom was in the basement. How hard could it be to locate it?

As they started toward the cellar steps, the younger kid, not more than ten or eleven, who'd been talking to Lynn, stood up. "Darkroom?"

Lynn rose and put her hand on the boy's shoulder. "Tom, I don't think you've met Mitch Sterling's son, Sam. Sam, this is Tom Baines and his friend Damon Hudson."

Son of a gun, Tom thought. Mitch's kid. Tom noticed that Lynn made a point of facing the boy as she spoke. Was he hearing-impaired?

"Pleased to meet you, Sam. Your father and I were good buddies when I used to visit Riverbend a long time ago."

"Really? Were you a River Rat?" The boy formed his words deliberately, enunciating with care.

Tom nodded. "Sure was."

"Cool." Sam looked at Tom, then at Damon. "I like cameras and stuff. Could I come with you?"

Damon shrugged. "It's a free country."

From behind Sam, Lynn smiled at Tom, then discreetly cupped her hand to her ear. The smile was almost sufficient reward for taking these two unlikely kids in tow.

Tom easily located the darkroom, and both boys found it a source of endless fascination. Damon became almost civil when Tom offered to lend his expensive camera to Meacham House for use by the participants. Sam seemed interested both in the camera and in Damon. In fact, if Tom wasn't mistaken, when Sam looked at Damon, incipient hero worship lit up his face. What would Mitch think of that? Well, it wasn't his worry.

When they went back upstairs, the volunteers were cleaning up. Only Keri, Damon, a few of his sidekicks and Sam remained. Lynn, her arm around Keri's waist, approached them, a satisfied expression on her face. "Damon, I hope you and your friends will come back. On Wednesdays we're serving supper at six-thirty. We'd love to have all of you."

Damon's eyes flickered to Keri. He shrugged indifferently. "Maybe." He paused as if waiting for something.

"You gonna bring the camera on Wednesday, Tom?" Sam's eyes were shining.

Damn. He'd made his one token appearance. He hadn't counted on getting roped into another. He'd intended to lend the camera to the center, not become involved himself. He looked away from the approval he saw in Lynn's eyes. Unjustified. "Are both of you going to be here?" Sam nodded enthusiastically and Damon gave another shrug. "Okay, guess I'll see you then."

"Unless something more important comes up," Damon said skeptically, as if recognizing Tom's reluctance. "Let's blow this joint, Keri." They started toward the door, then Damon turned and addressed Lynn. "Did that Jewett prick back off?"

Tom opened his mouth to suggest that "prick" wasn't a word used in conversation with a minister, but when he looked at Lynn, she was unperturbed. In fact, she was smiling at Damon. "Thanks to you and the Steele ladies for standing up to him, he seems willing to give us some leeway. I hope we can win him over."

"We gotta," Sam said, looking admiringly at Damon. "Him and me can help."

"Runt, I ain't makin' no promises. I do exactly what I want. It's just a question of *if* I want. Got it?"

Sam turned his gaze to the floor. "I guess."

Damon gave a grunt of approval, stared around the room as if memorizing it, then grabbed Keri's hand and stalked out the door.

Lynn looked at Sam. "We'd better call your dad to come get you." She started toward the phone.

The boy nodded. Tom waited while Lynn dialed, then mouthed to her, "Later?"

She shook her head. "Not tonight. I'm bushed." Then she spoke into the phone. "Mitch, Sam's ready for you to come get him.... How did it go? Generally speaking, it was a positive beginning."

Tom, his arms hanging at his sides, stood there feeling useless. He had mixed feelings about the whole evening—about his awkward conversation with Aaron, about this odd alliance with Damon, about Lynn's unwillingness to see him later. He supposed she *was* tired, but on the other hand, wouldn't she want to share tonight's success with someone she professed to care about?

Molly, her fair face flushed, came in from the

kitchen and put a hand on his arm. "Thanks for all your help, Tom. We could sure use you on a regular basis."

He hoped his answer didn't sound churlish. "I'm not really into kids."

She smiled as if his comment hadn't fazed her in the least. "They'll win you over. You'll see."

After he made his farewells, he walked down the darkened street toward his truck, troubled by his mixed emotions. Why was he getting involved with other people's children when his own would barely speak to him? It was nuts.

LYNN HAD BARELY time enough over her lunch hour the next day to dash into the bookstore. Kate greeted her with a hug. "Congratulations! From what I hear, the opening was a great success."

Smiling, Lynn returned the embrace. "I wouldn't go that far. We did have a fair turnout, although clearly some of the kids came primarily for the food. The proof will be how many come back regularly."

"They'll be there. You'll see."

"I hope so. Are Ruth and Rachel here?"

"They're in the office."

"I want to thank them for their help with Prentice Jewett."

"They've been pretty hard to live with this morning. They are *very* pleased with themselves." Kate chuckled. "They've had so much fun plotting his comeuppance."

"What in the world did they say to him?"

Kate took her by the arm. "Come on. You need to hear it from the horses' mouths."

When the two slipped into the office, Rachel looked

up from the computer, and Ruth, who'd been writing a letter, set down her pen. "Welcome, Lynn," Ruth said. Rachel smiled sheepishly.

"Is this Command Central?" Lynn joked.

Ruth eyed her smugly. "The brain trust assembled here."

Kate excused herself. "Somebody has to tend the store, after all."

Lynn pulled up a chair. "Okay, ladies. I'm dying of curiosity. Out with it."

"My, the Lord does work in mysterious ways," Rachel offered, her eyes twinkling behind her glasses.

"His wonders to perform," Ruth added.

"I'm not so sure about the Lord," Lynn said. "In fact, I think He might have some serious reservations about your methods." She grinned. "But I'm delighted with the results."

"It was an inspired plan," Rachel said. "Sometimes the end does justify the means."

"I'll bet you didn't know Prentice Jewett has a questionable past," Ruth explained. "One he hoped no one remembered."

Rachel pursed her lips. "One he has tried very hard to live down. But with the help of some of our contemporaries, we were able to reconstruct some of the notorious incidents Prentice was involved in as a youth."

"Turns out we weren't the only ones who had photographic evidence," Ruth crowed. "Axel Morrison and several other boyhood accomplices of Prentice's had recorded his escapades for posterity."

"Like?" Lynn couldn't wait to hear what they'd cooked up.

"Like the time Prentice stole a farmer's outhouse,

broke into the school and put it in the high-school principal's office. Like the time the old-maid geometry teacher walked out on her porch only to find it covered with cow patties. We could go on, but you get the drift.'' Ruth sat back in her chair and crossed her arms, the picture of satisfaction.

"Prentice was a wild one in those days," Rachel continued. "He had more scrapes with the law than you can shake a stick at. A real doozy, that boy!"

"So we rounded up a few of our classmates who still live here, put our minds to it and the rest is history." Ruth continued to wear her tickled-pink smile. "The photographs showed Prentice digging a new latrine for the outhouse. That was part of his punishment."

Rachel erupted in a laugh. "We figured the least we could do for the youth being served by Meacham House was to remind that jackass Prentice that he needn't come off holier-than-thou so long as we're around."

Lynn shook her head in a cross between disbelief and admiration. "Even though I'm risking moral compromise by approving of your scheme, I want you to know I think you two are something else! Thank you so much for defusing what could have been an ugly confrontation."

"If it saves one youngster," Rachel said, "it will be more than worth it."

"I only hope nobody remembers any of my youthful escapades," Ruth said with a mischievous grin.

"There's always one person who will," Lynn suggested.

Both she and Ruth turned to Rachel, who adopted

a superior smirk. "Rest assured, I've got the goods on her."

Lynn rose to leave. "I'll see you both in church on Sunday?"

"As always," Ruth said. "Besides, we need to get ourselves right with the Lord."

Lynn smiled, then gave each of them a hug. "A prudent course, always."

TOM SHOVED his chair back from the computer, re-reading what he'd written about last night's Meacham House opening. Not his usual stuff at all, yet not half-bad. Just the act of putting words on paper filled him with a sense of purpose he hadn't had since Ireland. Returning to international journalism wasn't in the cards, nor was that morbid book proposal of Harry Milstein's. For the moment he'd write whatever came into his mind. Later he could worry about trying to sell again.

He stood up, stretched, then wandered around the living room, thinking on his feet, frustrated about Lynn. She had a lot of people looking to her for support, advice and encouragement. The last thing she'd needed was for him to dump his past on her. At least she hadn't tried to "fix" him.

When the phone rang, he pulled himself together and answered it.

"Hi, Tom. This is Lily. Where have you been keeping yourself, anyway?"

"Even after I've seen Paree, I still like to come back to the farm."

"Consensus is you've holed up long enough. As you may have heard, Aaron and I are getting married a week from Saturday, and we'd like you to come.

We're having a small church wedding, followed by a reception at our house. Most of the old gang will be there. Please say yes.''

Tom hesitated. "You've cleared this with Aaron?''

"I'll admit you weren't at the top of his list, but he's trying, Tom, really trying to come to grips with the past. He knows Riverbend is a small place. It's going to take time for him to adjust to the news that your uncle was his father, with all the implications of that fact. But avoiding the issue or hiding from the Steeles isn't Aaron's style. Since you and he have already had a couple of encounters, I think your coming to the wedding will help others see that Aaron doesn't want to foster ill will.''

"What *does* he want?''

"I'm not sure he knows yet. But this is a step, Tom. Please say you'll come. It would mean a lot to me.'' She paused. "In the long run, I think it will be meaningful to Aaron, too. And perhaps to you.''

Lily Bennett had always been difficult to refuse. "All right.''

"And just in case you're interested, Lynn Kendall will be performing the ceremony and attending the reception afterward.''

"What are you suggesting?''

"Maybe you'd like to escort her to the reception.''

Jeez, the town was full of matchmakers. "I'll think about it.''

They concluded the conversation and Tom hung up. Before he could change his mind, he called Lynn and made the date. At the very least he'd get a reading on Riverbend's reaction to his interest in Lynn.

Maybe, too, he could get a reading on his own emotions, not only about Lynn but about being back in Riverbend. About whether he could ever fit in.

CHAPTER EIGHT

TOM WAS A FEW minutes late to the first Wednesday-night dinner at Meacham House, but the aroma of garlic and tomato sauce had him mounting the front steps two at a time. He was starving. Three teens sat at the porch table wolfing down platefuls of spaghetti. One of them deigned to look up and raise a forefinger. "Hey, man."

Tom stopped and laid a hand on the back of the youth's chair. "Looks good. Save any for me?"

"Better hurry," a listless-looking girl with stringy blond hair said, motioning with a fork toward the kitchen.

Not a smile in the bunch, and wariness blanketed their eyes. But they were here. That was the main thing. And the food was clearly a hit.

Inside, six or eight kids had found perches and were balancing plates on their knees. He looked around, searching for Lynn. Molly, who was dishing up the pasta, waved and smiled. "Soup's on," she mouthed.

He had to step over a long-legged kid who was sopping up tomato sauce with a crust of French bread. "'Scuse me." By way of response, the boy moved his leg a scant three inches. Tom set his camera down on top of a bookcase and headed for the dining room.

Molly extended a plate of steaming spaghetti. As he took it from her, he jerked his head toward the living room. "The dinner looks like a real draw. I don't think you'll have to worry about leftovers."

She smiled. "I just hope we have enough. Several who still need to eat are upstairs on the computers, and that doesn't count any others who walk in off the street."

He couldn't help himself. "Where's Lynn?"

"She'll be here later. She had a meeting at the community food bank. She's on the board, you know."

He didn't know, but he wasn't surprised. "Damon?" he asked, looking around.

Molly's smile faded. "Not yet. Several of his buddies are here, but he's still a no-show."

He felt someone tug on his sleeve. "Tom, come eat with me, okay?" Sam Sterling looked up hopefully.

Tom turned to pick up a piece of French bread. "Sure, kid, just a minute."

"Tom, please? Come eat with me. The big guys don't want me."

What was the matter with the youngster? Hadn't he heard him the first time? Molly set down her spoon and took hold of Tom's elbow and turned him to face the boy. "Now tell him."

He'd forgotten. Sam read lips, so of course he hadn't "heard" Tom's response. He felt like a heel. "Hey, Sam," he said. "Get your plate and we'll find us a place." He nodded at the soft drinks. "Root beer okay with you?"

"Sure."

Tom grabbed two soft drinks, then found seats on the stairs. Both of them dug into the food. After a few minutes Tom tapped Sam on the shoulder to get his attention. "What makes you think the big kids don't want you?"

"I'm not a teenager. But I heard they have art and photography and stuff here. I like to draw. Reverend Lynn said if I wanted to try it, I could come."

"But you're not quite sure?"

"Most of 'em don't pay any attention to me, but I liked that Damon kid. I saw him at the square yesterday after school. He said, 'Hi, runt. See ya tomorrow night.'" Sam twisted a fork through lank strands of spaghetti. "But I guess he forgot or something."

Poor Sam. He must be very lonely if a *hi* from the likes of Damon Hudson made his day. "Maybe he'll come later."

"Maybe."

"Meanwhile, when we finish, I'll introduce you to my camera."

Sam shifted and moved a few inches closer. "Cool."

After dinner a few of the teens left, but most stuck around, some heading for the computers, others taking seats in the art room where a local artist was offering instruction in watercolor painting. Molly steered a few of the boys to the basement rec room, now converted to a music room where the bandleader from Monday was setting up to teach guitar. Several hung out in the living room studying or talking.

Just before he and Sam got down to business, Lynn breezed in carrying a large box. "Look, guys. We have a present." Some of the teens quit talking and stared at her. "The owner of the office-supply store donated a printer. Now we'll be able to put out our own newsletter. Who likes to write?"

The listless-looking blonde held her hand up tentatively. "I prob'ly wouldn't be any good, but I'll help."

Several others shrugged as if to add their willingness to hers. Lynn winked at Tom by way of greeting, then rushed on, "Okay, then." She set the box on the coffee table and sat on the floor amid the kids. "Let's start brainstorming. Who needs to receive a newsletter and what do we want it to say?"

Tom and Sam found a quiet corner in an upstairs bedroom set up as a study hall. Tom removed the camera from the case and was starting to explain the various parts when they heard a loud racket from the stairs.

"Whaddaya mean, no smoking? What kind of stupid place is this, anyway?"

Tom recognized Molly's cool, objective tone as she explained.

Then another outburst. "Look, lady, you can't tell me what to do. Nobody tells Damon Hudson where to get off."

Tom walked quickly to the head of the stairs. "Need some help, Molly?"

"Ooh, here comes the big man with the muscle." Damon stood at the bottom glaring up at him.

Tom leaned against the wall, folding his arms across his chest. "No muscle, Damon. But if you're going to hang around here, you need to remember you're expected to behave courteously."

"Hey, man," Damon said in a whiny voice, "she told me I couldn't smoke here."

Tom nodded to Molly to indicate he'd handle Damon from here on. "You'll get no big lecture from me about the dangers of tobacco. I used to smoke, and we both know it's not good for us. But give Molly a break. I'm sure the fire marshal had something to say about the rule."

Damon's eyes narrowed, as if considering the logic of Tom's argument. "Where's the kid?" he said in an abrupt change of subject.

"Up here with me. We're looking at the camera. You're welcome to join us." Tom turned away and walked slowly toward the study hall, his ears cocked for the sound of feet on the stairs. Nothing. A tough nut, that kid.

"Okay, Sam." Tom leaned forward, making sure his lips were in Sam's line of vision. "This is the F-stop. Let me explain how it works." Several minutes passed before Tom became aware that Damon was leaning against the doorjamb, listening.

Tom beckoned to him. "Pull up a seat." Then he went on with his explanations. "You missed the spaghetti," he said offhandedly as he pulled off the lens cap.

"So? I thought the runt here would be home with mommy eating his supper."

In a voice louder than usual, Sam said, "I don't have a mommy."

"Everybody has a mom, stupid."

"Do you?" Sam challenged.

Damon's cocky attitude underwent a subtle shift. Tom waited. Something important was going on. "Used to."

Sam stared at the floor. "Me, too. Used to."

Where was Lynn now that he needed her? Tom thought. She was the one with the expertise. How was he supposed to make anything right here? Before he could intervene, Damon clamped Sam on the shoulder. "But look, kid, we're doin' okay, know what I mean? Who needs a mother, anyway?"

The answer to the question was apparent in the

weighted silence that ensued. "Maybe, well, maybe—" the hopefulness in Sam's voice was heart-breaking "—we could be like...buddies."

Damon withdrew his hand. "I dunno, runt."

"I don't see why that wouldn't be a good idea," Tom interjected.

Damon jerked to his feet. "Hey, man. This is between the kid and me. Ain't none of your business, got it?" His eyes were hostile. Clearly this conversation had struck a nerve.

Tom held up his hands in surrender. "No problem. Do it your way. Now do you or do you not want to learn anything about my camera?"

The youth stood silent, as if weighing the cost. Then he slumped into his chair. "Might as well. I'm here, ain't I?"

THE DAY OF AARON'S WEDDING, Tom shifted uneasily in the pew, watching dust motes dance in the shafts of late-afternoon light streaming through the tall stained-glass windows. He was barely aware of Rachel's organ prelude, the hum of anticipation as ushers seated the guests or Ruth's presence beside him. However, the tattoo of his heart and the shallowness of his breathing were all too apparent. It wasn't merely that he hadn't been in church for a long time—it was the anticipation of seeing Lynn in her clergy role. It had been easy enough to avoid the reality, as long as they kept her profession and their personal lives separate. He had no idea how he would react this afternoon or what such an innocuous event as a wedding might imply for their future.

The music stopped and a rustle of expectation spread through the nave. When the organ resumed,

Aaron, tall and erect in his dark suit, escorted his
mother down the aisle. Evie wore a pink dress in some
sort of satiny material, and her eyes were fixed with
pride on her son's handsome face, as if looking at the
guests, many of whom she'd served as a waitress,
would incite their disapproval of her and Aaron's
changed status in the community. After Mrs. Bennett
took her place in the first row of the bride's side,
Rachel began to play Clark's "Trumpet Voluntary."
Tom scarcely took in the bridesmaids who passed his
pew in a pearl-gray haze. Because he had eyes for
only one woman. While everyone else turned to watch
the bride start down the aisle escorted by her father,
he stared at Lynn, who had emerged from a side door
and stood at the altar steps, clothed in a lace-trimmed
white alb and stole, a welcoming smile radiating from
her face. He didn't know when he had ever seen a
more beautiful woman. He swallowed the lump in his
throat.

When Lily reached Aaron, Tom noticed Aaron's
usual guarded look vanish. In its place was a kind of
awed joy. Two of the unlikeliest people in the world
to find each other, and yet watching them, Tom sensed
the depth of their love and commitment. And on a
level that disturbed him, he found himself envying
them.

"Dearly beloved," Lynn began in a clear, pure
voice. And from that moment, Tom was lost. He
didn't believe in angels, but he'd swear one was performing this ceremony. It was as if the three—Lily,
Aaron and Lynn—were enveloped by an aura, setting
them apart. With a sinking sensation Tom realized he
was intensely uncomfortable. This couldn't be the
Lynn who teased him about being the big, bad wolf,

the Lynn whose laughter had a rich, earthy quality, the Lynn who responded so enthusiastically to his kisses. The woman before him was…untouchable.

Beside him, Ruth dabbed her handkerchief to her eyes and sighed with pleasure. Tom clasped his hands between his knees and bent forward, blotting out the scene. Yet the words Lynn spoke were inescapable. "We come together as a community of family and friends to witness the vows of Lily and Aaron, whose union is a beautiful example of 'amazing grace.' Each of them would admit that in their own ways, they were 'lost.' They rejoice today in the fact that they now are 'found,' and have found in one another a future filled with promise."

She went on speaking, but Tom had stopped listening. He, too, was lost. And finding himself was proving damned difficult. Would he ever be man enough to stand before a congregation and pledge his undying love for Lynn? He knew, beyond the shadow of a doubt, that he could do so only when he could offer her a whole man, one worthy of her love. His heart contracted. That was a tall order.

The rest of the ceremony passed in a blur. Only when he heard Lynn's delighted laughter did he look up. Her amusement was because Aaron was kissing his bride in a manner that left no doubt as to how he felt about her. In a curious way, the laugh gave Tom hope. Most angels didn't have such an uninhibited manner of expression. At least he didn't think so.

The triumphant chords of Handel's "Water Music" filled the church, and the beaming couple, with eyes only for each other, made their way down the aisle. Ruth nudged Tom with her elbow. "Did you ever see a more beautiful bride? That ice-blue sheath is perfect on her. And the flowers…simply exquisite." She continued prattling about the details of the service while Tom stared at the front of the church, where Lynn, head bent over the Bible clasped in her hands, walked from the sanctuary.

This new Lynn had given him serious pause for thought.

"REVEREND LYNN, it was a lovely ceremony. Thank you." Lynn stood at the punch table beside Eleanor Bennett, Lily's mother, both of them watching the bride and groom make the rounds of the guests. The usually serious Aaron was grinning from ear to ear.

"They're a wonderful couple, and they deserve happiness. I'm glad I could be a part of this special day in their lives."

Eleanor cocked her head, a smile teasing her lips. "Didn't I see you come in with Tom Baines?"

To Lynn's relief, the smile looked encouraging. "Yes, you did."

"Lily has always been so fond of him. We all hope he'll stay in Riverbend." When Lynn didn't respond, Eleanor went on, "Judging from the way he looks at you, dear, I think you might have a great deal to do with his decision." With a nod of her head, Eleanor indicated Tom, who was standing across the room.

Lynn felt a quickening of her pulse as his eyes found hers. "I take it you would approve?"

The bride's mother gave a knowing chuckle. "Approve? I'll dance at your wedding."

She and Tom were a long way from that eventuality, but it was gratifying to know that at least one denizen of Riverbend would entertain the notion. "Now if you'll excuse me, I need to circulate."

Lynn took a tentative sip of the refreshing punch and was about to go join Tom when Genevieve Potts, one of her more cantankerous elderly parishioners snatched at her sleeve. "Reverend Lynn. Lovely ceremony."

"Hello, Genevieve. Nice to see you."

"I was Lily's piano teacher," she said by way of justifying her inclusion on the limited guest list. "Such a talented, refined young woman."

"Yes, she is. I'm glad to see her so happy."

Genevieve's nose quivered. "It won't last, you know."

"I beg your pardon?" Lynn was dumbfounded.

"Not with that Mazerik fellow. He's way beneath her."

Lynn set her cup on the edge of the table. "I'm sorry, but I can't agree. Aaron is a fine man, and the two of them deserve all of our good wishes."

"Humph. We'll see." The woman smiled smugly. "And as for couples, didn't I see you come in with Ruth and Rachel Steele's nephew?"

Lynn bit her tongue. "Yes, you did."

"Well, you can't be too careful, my dear. You have to remember your position in the community." She leaned forward confidingly. "That man has sown his share of wild oats, you know."

Lynn straightened to her full five foot six. "I, for one, believe there is good in each of us. And I see a great deal of good in Tom Baines. I hope you will look for it, too."

Genevieve's mouth dropped open and she stammered a reply. "Well, er, I suppose that is what we're taught, but—"

"Forgive me for ending our conversation, but I

haven't congratulated the groom, and he's coming this way right now.'' Lynn greeted Aaron with a warm hug. ''Much happiness to you both,'' she said to him.

''Thanks.'' Aaron then nodded toward Tom, in conversation now with Beth Pennington and Charlie Callahan, whose recent unexpected reunion, much to everyone's delight, had rekindled their love. ''And may I say the same to you?''

Blushing, Lynn found Aaron's twinkling eyes. ''I think those sentiments are a bit premature.''

''Maybe. I'm only now getting to know my cousin.'' The word came out with forced familiarity. ''He and I have had our differences in the past, but he's not a bad fellow.''

''No,'' Lynn murmured, ''he's not.'' She patted Aaron gently on the cheek. ''You're neglecting your bride. Go.''

After linking her name with Tom's in her own mind for these past few weeks, Lynn found it odd to hear them linked on the lips of others. During today's ceremony, she'd focused solely on the bride and groom, but afterward, while she was unvesting, she had become aware of her ongoing and all-too-human desire. Like Lily, she wanted to be married to the one true love of her life. And despite the odds, it was Tom, only Tom, who fit that definition.

He had seemed unusually quiet on the drive from the church to Aaron and Lily's house. She hadn't asked him why. Perhaps they were both a bit on edge about making their entrance as a couple, knowing that they would be greeted by reactions as varied as Eleanor's and Genevieve's. Upon their arrival, Lynn had been swept up by guests wanting to discuss the wedding, Meacham House or other church matters, but she had noticed Tom seemed content to stand against the wall in the corner of the dining room, visiting with those who approached him, but making no effort to mingle.

Beth and Charlie had moved away, and he stood there now, his arms crossed over his chest, his eyes making a slow circuit of the room. She smiled to herself. Ever the observer. A journalistic attribute, she supposed. That was one difference between them—she plunged into things, while he studied them. She accepted people at face value; he appraised them before forming an opinion. Yet, she reminded herself, even in her own premarital counseling sessions, she talked with couples about valuing such complementary traits and understanding they had the potential to strengthen a relationship. She certainly hoped so.

Just then Tom's eyes stopped on her, and a lazy grin spread over his features. He walked slowly across the room toward her. The whirl of color, the hum of conversation and the high-pitched laughter of a woman ladling punch seemed to be coming from another place. Lynn waited, hands at her sides, until Tom, his eyes riveted on her, put an arm around her waist. "How are we doing? Am I behaving myself?"

"Let's see." She made a pretense of checking off numbers on her fingers. "By last count, only a half-dozen guests have bolted the reception to run through the streets to announce that we're an item."

"Seriously, you're sure our being together isn't putting you in an awkward position?"

"I'm proud to be with you, Tom. Please don't feel you have to walk on eggshells. The people who matter will understand. As for the rest—" she shrugged "—it'll take them longer, but they'll come around."

"That's my girl. Ever the optimist." He ran a finger under his shirt collar. "I could sure use some fresh air. How about you?"

She smiled up at him. "I thought you'd never ask."

As they strolled toward the porch, she couldn't help overhearing a murmured comment from a woman she'd never seen before. "Isn't that the pastor? Who is that man with her? I thought she wasn't married."

"She isn't," her companion responded. "And I doubt Baines is the man for her."

Lynn glanced up. Tom must've heard, too. His jaw was working. She poked him playfully in the ribs with her elbow. "What do they know, anyway?"

"Only what I've been thinking."

"Tom?" She stopped dead. "Give yourself a break. When the time comes, the only person who will decide who's right for me will be me. And the very last criterion I'll use is what other people think. So there."

He pulled her closer and through clenched teeth muttered, "That's easy enough to say, but other people *do* matter."

"Not as much as you do," and with that, she stood on tiptoe and planted a quick kiss on his cheek, an act accompanied by the indrawn breath of Genevieve Potts, who was lurking behind a flowering plant.

"ALONE AT LAST," Tom gloated, throwing his suit jacket over the back of a chair and extending his arms to offer Lynn a bear hug.

Lynn snuggled into his embrace, rubbing her cheek against his shoulder. "Not exactly," she said, jerking her head toward the window ledge where Benedict surveyed them with seeming utter disdain.

"I'll take my chances with him," Tom said just before capturing her lips with his. It had been too long since they'd been alone, too long since he'd felt his body come alive in response to the smell and feel of her. With every fiber of his being, he longed to scoop her up, transport her to the bedroom and learn every intimate detail of her body. But much as he might want to, he couldn't. That right would not be his unless...until...

She disengaged her lips and laid a gentle palm on his cheek. "Mmm, good," she murmured. "Can we try that again?"

He gladly obliged. But just as he was getting with the program, his blood near the boiling point, the incongruous image of Lynn officiating at the wedding came to him. He stiffened. Sensing the change in him, she pulled away, then gazed at him quizzically. She looked as if she wanted to say something, but instead, turned and headed toward the kitchen. "I'll put on some coffee. Make yourself at home."

He stripped off his tie and rolled up his shirtsleeves before sinking onto the sofa. From the kitchen he could hear the faucet running, the clatter of a canister lid. Because of the startup of Meacham House and a series of pastoral emergencies, they hadn't been alone together—really alone—for more than a week. He'd missed her. The kisses tonight were nice, but he could no longer pretend everything was hunky-dory. Before seeing her officiate at the wedding, he hadn't fully realized how improbable this whole thing was. They needed to talk. Now.

When Lynn returned, she set the mugs on the coffee table, kicked off her shoes, then perched beside him, tucking her legs up under her. "Okay, something's on your mind. Out with it."

It was disconcerting that she read him like a book, but the time for sidestepping the issue was long past. "I met the vacation you, I've gotten to know the Riverbend you, but today I saw another you."

Smiling wistfully, Lynn twisted a strand of hair around her finger. "The reverend me?"

"Yes."

"And?"

He rubbed his palms on his thighs. "I don't know what to think. You were...something else. It was as if I was seeing you for the first time." He threw his head back on the cushion and stared at the ceiling.

"It scared you?"

This was harder than he'd expected. "That's putting it mildly. You are so loving, so perfect, I—"

"Here we go again."

"What do you mean?"

Lynn clutched the hem of her skirt. "The mistaken notion men get of me as, I don't know, Lynn the Madonna. Tom, I am graced by having the ability to help others on occasion. That does not overwhelm who I am as a woman or diminish my need to love and be loved."

"But your example is pretty hard to live up to."

"How many times do I have to say it? I am far from perfect. In fact, at the reception I very nearly lost my temper with Genevieve Potts. I can be as petty, selfish and mean-spirited as the next person. And until you see me as that flawed human being, I don't know how to reassure you."

Tom reached for her hand, aware of the depth of her distress. "Help me understand, Lynn. What you do isn't anything I've had much experience with." He looked intently into her eyes, filled with longing and something else. Desperation?

"Maybe if I tell you about my upbringing, it will help." She looked away as if gathering her thoughts, then turned back to him. "My father died when I was five, and my mother took my older sister, Pam, and me to live with her widowed mother. Nana was a powerful influence on me. In fact, I'm named for her—Elizabeth Lynn. She was full of life, never called anyone a stranger and was generally loved by everyone she met. She believed we should live each day as if it were our last, and that it's our duty to leave the world a better place. My mother's brother, Uncle Will, was a minister and the closest thing in my life to a father. From the time I was tiny, I've always known that his ministry is simply part of who he is. Integral, natural, if that makes sense. Not something separate, or an acquired or cultivated behavior."

She looked pleadingly at Tom, but he simply nodded for her to continue.

"When you grow up without a father," she said, "there's a yearning that's never quite satisfied."

He averted his face. "Or when you grow up with an absentee father."

Benedict diverted them from the painful silence when he leaped from the ledge and padded down the hall. Lynn continued. "Couple that need with the wonderful ways in which Mother, Nana and Uncle Will cared for me, and it's little wonder I always wanted to help people. Especially help them to discover where they belong and to understand how much they are loved. When I was a girl, my favorite pastimes were playing church and doctor. And since blood isn't my favorite thing..." She smiled self-deprecatingly.

He decided he needed to lighten the tone. "And here, all along, I thought you had to be struck by a thunderbolt."

"Heck, no. That's the easy way. And I never do anything the easy way." Her eyes mellowed. "Like falling in love with my doubting Thomas."

His throat constricted, and he choked out his disbelief. "Say again?"

She pulled his hand from her lap, grazed his palm with her lips, then glanced up at him, her beautiful gray eyes swimming with affection. "I love you."

He was sure she could hear the rattling of his heart in his chest. How could he possibly respond? He had the capacity to make her life more complicated than she could imagine. Rather than risk saying the wrong thing, he simply pulled her to him and held her, running his fingers gently through her hair. He knew she was waiting for him to speak. His mind rioted with exhilaration and fear. And with the realization she might get hurt because of him.

The shrill of the telephone startled them both. Lynn sent him a searching look before crossing the room to pick up the phone. He couldn't help overhearing her end of the conversation. "Calm down, Mae.... You say he's left...? What about the children...? Don't say that, honey. Stay where you are, and I'll be right over.... No, it's no trouble. I wouldn't think of having you be by yourself tonight." She concluded the conversation, then turned to Tom. "I'm sorry, but I have to leave. Now."

He stood and took a step toward her. The timing couldn't have been worse. There was so much left unspoken. "Lynn, please. Do you have to go?" He was aware his tone sounded accusatory. The room was charged with tension.

She walked past him, slipped her feet into her shoes and picked up her purse. Before she turned around, he saw her swipe a finger across her eyes. Then she faced him, a reproachful look on her face. "Yes, I do. Don't you understand, Tom? It's who I am."

They left the house together, neither saying another word. What was there left to say except, "I love you, too"? And *that* he couldn't bring himself to utter.

IT WAS AFTER FIVE the next morning when Lynn wearily let herself into her house. Benedict, waiting in the entry hall, rubbed against her legs and purred madly. She scooped him up, draped him over her shoulder and nuzzled his neck. "Oh, kitty, it was not a pretty sight." Mae's tearstained face, hollow eyes and defeated sag of the shoulders weighed heavily on her heart. When Lynn had arrived at the run-down old ranch house, the tiny porch light had done little to illuminate the way. She'd nearly tripped over the bikes, plastic toys and gardening tools littering the lawn. She wasn't surprised. She'd only seen Merlin Farrell a couple of times and never in church. He had struck her as the kind of man who feels entitled to a good time and views his family responsibilities as unwelcome burdens.

Unfortunately, tonight, that impression had proved correct. He had stormed out of the house, telling Mae he was leaving her for good. Mae, a dependent sort, was beside herself. How could she provide for the children—three under the age of ten? Where could she go? What could she do? Beyond that, she was further devastated by the news that her husband had found another woman, one who, in his words, "knows how to make a man happy in bed and out." The poor woman had been frantic.

Lynn carried Benedict into the living room and sank gratefully into the rocker. She'd done what she could to calm Mae. They'd talked, prayed and finally, after a cup of warm milk, Mae had said she was exhausted and should go to bed. Lynn had promised to put her in touch with a social worker and Legal Aid. The destruction of a marriage was always a sad event and, regrettably, all too common.

Lynn leaned her head back and closed her eyes, too tired even to attempt to crawl into bed. Besides, today was Sunday and she was due at the church for the early service at eight. She'd curl up here in the living room for an hour or so, then take a bracing shower to prepare for her day.

Setting Benedict aside, she moved to the sofa, unfolded an afghan and stretched out gratefully. She turned on her side, scrunching a decorative pillow under her head. Then her heart sank. From the street lamp casting light through the lace window curtains, she could just make out the two mugs sitting on the coffee table. Untouched.

Helpless, she stared at them through tears that seemed to come from nowhere. She could rationalize that they arose from her exhausted state. But she knew better. She'd bared her soul to Tom. For once, she'd risked putting her feelings out there. And had been rejected.

She raised herself on one elbow, retrieved a tissue from the end table, blew her nose, then fell back, unable to stem the sobs. She'd told him. Said the words she'd never uttered to any other man. And they were as true right this moment as they'd been then. She loved Tom Baines. Deeply, everlastingly. Hopelessly?

Yet at some almost subconscious level, she understood he'd been fighting the connection between them, holding back in ways that had more to do with him than with her. It was as if they were involved in some complicated dance figure—approach, connect, withdraw. Painful and difficult as it would be, if she loved him, she would have to wait. After all, she'd stated her feelings. It was his turn now. If he chose to take it.

Benedict jumped on her chest and made himself a nest. Even though she was exhausted, Lynn lay for a long time, staring into space. "Oh, Sir," she finally whispered, "have I fallen for the wrong man?"

SUNDAY AFTERNOON Tom planted the tee in the grass, then stood gazing down the fairway, lining up his shot.

"Since you last played here, they've put a trap on the left about sixty yards from the green," Mitch Sterling said.

Tom nodded appreciatively, gave one last glance down the fairway, then whacked the ball, which took a good bounce and landed just right of center.

"Nice shot." Mitch stepped forward, took a couple of practice swings, then hit his drive.

As they rode down the fairway in the golf cart, Tom experienced a tug of satisfaction. He'd learned to play on this course, and although he'd golfed on some of the finest courses in the world, there was something in the smell of the grass, the familiar tree markers and undulations of the terrain that spelled home. He'd been pleased yesterday at the reception when Mitch had suggested today's outing.

Beside him, Mitch chuckled. "Remember our famous River Rats tournament?"

A memory came to Tom, one he hadn't had in years. "You mean the time we wouldn't let the girls play? Told them it was a guys-only event?"

"That's the time." Mitch slowed the cart a few yards from his ball. "Lily and Beth somehow convinced the pro to let them in the bag room."

"That's right. And they took all our clubs except for a driver and a putter."

Mitch laughed again. "Made for an interesting round, didn't it?"

"I can still see Lily's triumphant look when they met us afterward in the grill room for hamburgers. And how Jacob stuck her with the bill. Those were special times."

"Yeah." Mitch left the cart, hit his second shot, then returned and steered toward Tom's ball. "You know, I hope my kid can have some of those good times."

Tom sensed a sadness in his partner's voice. "Sam? I've met him at Meacham House. He seems like a fine youngster."

"He is, but he has a lot to deal with."

Tom had heard the story about Mitch's wife leaving him and her hearing-impaired son. "He has some challenges, all right, but from what I've seen, he's handling them well."

"He's a good kid, but I wish…" Mitch shook his head. "Never mind." He didn't have to say anything further.

"How's Caleb doing?" Tom remembered Mitch's grandfather with great fondness.

"Thank heaven for him. He's been a godsend with Sam, an ideal sitter and companion. Until lately. He's recovering from hip surgery now. Slowly."

In his friend's face, Tom saw the worry lines deepen. Knowing Mitch, Tom figured he'd handle whatever came his way. But he was facing a lot. Alone.

Mitch parked the cart on a path near the green, but made no move to get out. "I'm grateful, too, to Lynn Kendall for taking Sam under her wing and letting him participate at Meacham House even though he's only ten. With Caleb being out of commission and my store manager quitting, I'd have been in a real bind without her." He smiled ruefully. "Small-town neighborliness. You can't beat it."

When they reached the twelfth hole, they were held up by a foursome playing in front of them. Mitch tipped back his hat and spread his arm across the back of the seat. "Have any plans to stay around here?"

Plans? There was that ugly word again. "I don't know, Mitch. I'll have to make some decisions soon. The only thing I know for sure is that I'm not going to be a foreign correspondent anymore."

"There are quite a few of us who hope you'll find a reason to stick around." Mitch turned and looked at him challengingly. "But maybe you already have."

"What are you talking about?"

"Another characteristic of small towns—gossip. Tongues are already wagging. Maybe Lynn will provide you reason enough to stay. She's a quite a woman."

"Tell me about it," Tom muttered as he jumped

from the cart, grabbed his driver and strode to the now-empty tee box. No way was he going to tell Mitch he'd lain awake half the night cursing himself for being such an insensitive, indecisive ass. What was so damn difficult about telling Lynn he was crazy about her? About telling her how, more than anything, he wanted to make a life with her?

He teed up, and in a burst of anger swung hard and let the ball fly. "Fore!" he shouted, as helplessly he watched the ball land a mere yard or two behind one of the men in the foursome, who turned and shook a fist at Tom.

Mitch strolled up beside him and laid a friendly arm around his shoulders. "You don't have to take it out on the ball, buddy. It was me who asked the wrong question."

Tom drubbed the head of his driver into the grass. "No. You asked the right question. But the hell of it is, I don't seem able to answer it."

Mitch slid his own driver through his fingers, then set up his ball. Before he hit, however, he said something else. "Love's a lot like golf, Tom. A game of patience." And then Mitch hit a perfect drive right down the middle of the fairway.

Some guys are just in the groove, Tom thought with envy.

SUNDAY EVENING after the golf game, Tom stared at the draft of his column about Meacham House. He needed to do more with the unlikely cooperation between Sam and Damon and the developing chemistry between the adult volunteers and the kids. Volunteers like himself. He groaned. Not only had those two kids gotten under his skin, demonstrating real talent in photography, but they'd convinced him to show up every Monday, Wednesday and Friday. And he'd done it all last week, when things were going well with Lynn.

But last night had been a disaster.

He shuffled the papers on his desk. Lying there to further complicate his life was the contract Harry Milstein had sent him. Harry was many things, but a liar he wasn't. The six-figure advance was very attractive. Tom knew he could write the book. Even do a creditable job of it. And make a mess of himself in the process. The day might come when this was a subject he could revisit. But not now. Maybe not ever. In his mind, the cries of children echoed too loudly, too hauntingly.

Abruptly he turned to the computer and typed his rejection of Harry's offer. He knew the editor wouldn't understand, but that was tough. Some things were beyond the reach of money. This was one of them.

The printer was clacking out the letter when the phone rang. He picked it up. "Hello?"

"Tom?" He'd know that voice anywhere. "It's Selena."

She rarely called him unless it was an emergency. "Is something wrong with the kids?"

"No." She paused. "It's my mother."

"Lila?"

"She's had a major stroke. Right now my sister's in Trenton taking care of her, but we need to make other arrangements as soon as it's practical."

"I was always fond of your mother. I'm sorry to hear about this."

"I've located a nursing home. A patient is moving

out at the end of the month.'' She hesitated. ''I was wondering if…well, if I could send Pete and Libby to stay with you while I get Mom settled.''

An immediate objection occurred to him. ''What about school?''

''They're good students. They could miss a few days. Besides, three of those days they'll be out of school, anyway, for the teachers' conference break.'' She sounded anxious. ''It would only be for a week or ten days.''

A week or ten days! What would he do with two teenagers for that long? Particularly when they had so little use for him? ''I don't know how Pete and Lib will feel about that arrangement.''

''More important, how will you feel about it?'' There it was, the subtly put, but familiar challenge to his parenting skills.

''I'm okay with it,'' he lied smoothly. ''In fact, it might give us a chance to establish some common ground. My weekend with them wasn't a rousing success. Maybe it was too short a visit.''

''Maybe.'' She hesitated, then went on, ''Actually, Tom, they could stay with friends. But I don't think that's best. They need time away from the social whirl here. Frankly, some of their friends are a bit too sophisticated for my tastes. And they need time with you. For what it's worth, your weekend in Chicago wasn't the disaster you seem to think it was.''

''It wasn't?''

''No. Of course, they wouldn't give you the satisfaction of telling you they enjoyed it, but the trip to the Navy Pier was a big success. Libby wears the T-shirt you bought her so often I can scarcely get it off her back to wash it. Give them a chance, Tom.

They're teenagers, after all, and their behavior reflects it. If you say yes, I'm not planning to give them a choice.''

Tom recognized that his ex-wife was handing him a golden opportunity. One that might never come again. One that scared the hell out of him. He raked a hand through his hair. What the heck? "Sure, Selena, send them on. I'll handle it somehow. Let me know the details. Oh, and when you see your mother, give her my love.''

"I will. And, Tom...thanks. I don't think you'll regret having the kids. I appreciate your willingness to help out.''

"Sure thing. Call me when you know something more.'' He hung up and sat staring at the phone, feeling more inadequate than he had in years. His first instinct was to call Lynn and solicit her help.

But after last night, that was out of the question.

PETE SLAMMED his bedroom door, cranked up the volume on his CD player and tried to lose himself in the vibrating rhythm of Mötley Crüe. Sweeping the magazines, books and dirty clothes off his bed, he flopped down, then threw an arm over his eyes, determined not to cry. He wouldn't give either of his parents the satisfaction. Besides, he was too old and too angry to cry.

His mother had broken the news right after dinner. She was actually going to send him and Libby to stay with his father for a week in that hick town in Indiana. He'd only been there once. The place had these spooky-looking houses with steep roofs and gaping windows, kind of like that Addams-family house he'd seen on TV reruns. Some of the kids there even wore boots and overalls. It was a wonder they didn't have straw and manure sticking to their feet.

Most of the time, he could manipulate his mother. This time nothing he said got through. She just kept talking about how he and Libby needed to be cooperative, that this was the best way they could help Grandma. Bull. They could help a lot better if they stayed right here with friends, but no. Mom just kept saying, "The best place for you is with your father." Right. Like the famous Tom Baines had ever given them the time of day. Like letters from places with names he couldn't pronounce would make a difference. Other guys had dads who helped with that stupid Pinewood Derby in Cub Scouts, actually took them to watch the White Sox, and not only showed up at soccer practice, but put in a good word with the coaches. Hell, he might as well be an orphan. At least then he wouldn't have to talk about his dad to all those gaga adults who seemed to think being in the middle of a war in Bosnia was some big deal.

Libby had pulled her you're-ruining-my-life-and-it's-not-fair routine, complete with big tears and the grand finale, "Mo-ther, how could you do this to me?" Zilch. His mother was like someone he'd never seen before—what was that new vocabulary word they'd just learned for the PSAT? Yeah, "obdurate." That got it.

So now he had to pack up and leave just when he'd gotten Polly Bridges all warmed up and on the verge of letting him cop a feel and who knew what else? Crap. Riverbend. What kind of a dumb name was that, anyway? About as original as Treestanding or Browndirt.

No way was he going to tell his friends where he

was actually going. Let 'em think he was on some cool trip with his famous journalist father. And contrary to what Dad might have in mind, no way was he going to be caught dead with any of those rubes in that butt-ugly town. He'd hole up in that stupid farmhouse and play Nintendo till his eyes bugged out first.

That settled, he sat up on the edge of his bed, grabbed the phone off the desk and dialed Polly's number. Might as well start laying it on about his "exciting trip" and how much he'd miss her and all that other mushy stuff girls grooved on so that maybe when he returned home, she'd let him get beyond first base with her.

CHAPTER NINE

Tom LEANED his elbow on the desk, cupped his chin and stared at the words on the computer screen. It was no use. His mind wasn't on the work. Monday was Lynn's day off, although she'd probably show up tonight at Meacham House. All he had to do was call her. Pick up the phone, dial the number and talk. And say what?

"I know I hurt your feelings"? "I'm sorry I can't commit"? Hearing her say she loved him had knocked the pins out from under him. There'd been no game playing, no coy flirtatiousness, no expectations. And because of that, he'd believed her.

Rubbing his tired eyes, he rocked back in the chair. An "I love you" deserved some kind of response. She'd told him she wouldn't ask more than he could give, yet, at this moment, he wasn't sure she hadn't. Even without the complication of Pete and Libby's pending visit, he and Lynn had issues to work out, not the least of which was how he really felt about her being a minister.

Still. He couldn't simply pretend nothing had happened. He stood up and paced to the window, staring out at the sunny September day. His need to see her warred with his confusion about what he'd say when he did. Hell, he'd faced SCUD missiles, mud slides

and firebombs more easily than he could brave Lynn.
But he had to.

That decided, he switched off the computer, picked
up his keys and left the house before he could change
his mind. She was either home or she wasn't.

It turned out she wasn't. He rang the doorbell several times, all under the scrutiny of Benedict, who
glared at him from his perch in the living-room window. Disappointed, Tom decided to stop at the cemetery on his way home. He hadn't been back since
Damon and his pals had partied there. Maybe he
should check to see if they'd cleaned up their mess.
He'd hate for Lynn to find the site trashed.

After parking the truck, he strolled up the knoll now
covered with crimson sumac and mustard-tufted prai-
rie grass. Then he saw it, half-buried in the tall vegetation. A bicycle he'd know anywhere. He hurried
the last few yards, then stopped, holding his breath.
Lynn sat with her back to him, her arms wrapped
around her drawn-up knees, gazing out over the scene
before her, now a riot of brilliant yellow-gold and
wine-red foliage bordering fields of browning corn-
stalks. Wisps of her strawberry-blond hair lifted in the
breeze. So still. So lost in thought. He felt like an
intruder.

As if sensing his presence, she slowly turned her
head. "Hi," she said softly, as if she'd been expecting
him.

He started toward her. "Hi, yourself." He stood
over her. "Mind?" he asked, indicating a spot by her
side.

"Not at all." She hugged her knees even closer to
her chest.

He settled beside her and joined her in studying the

distant river. Finally he spoke. "Am I disturbing your day off?"

Without looking at him she said, "You're never a disturbance."

"I'm glad." He couldn't judge her mood. She wasn't rejecting him, nor did she seem angry as most women would and as she had every right to be. She just seemed...pensive, sad maybe.

Moments passed during which he tried to formulate words to tell her why he'd sought her out today. To tell her of the love he felt for her, to say how much he longed to gather her in his arms and stay isolated in this place always. But his reluctance to commit, which he knew he couldn't justify, stopped him.

Finally she turned her head, smiled wistfully and said, "I've made things difficult for you, haven't I?"

Her clear gray eyes arrested any glib response he might have made. "Not you, exactly."

"I did come on pretty strong."

"Lynn, I—"

"I meant every word."

"I know." Just when he thought he could no longer bear the hope he read in her face, she lowered her gaze.

His eyes narrowed as he stared at a man fishing from a small boat in the middle of the river. "I want to be able to give you the sun, the moon and the stars." Beside him, he heard her sigh. "But I can't right now."

"It's okay. I'll wait."

His heart expanded, nearly breaking out of his chest. He disengaged one of her hands, cool to the touch, and enfolded it in his. "Until I get my life straightened out, it would be unfair to make any promises.''

"I understand,'' she murmured before laying her head on his shoulder.

He was afraid to move, afraid to break the spell that her acceptance of him had woven. It was as if they were suspended in a time and place the real world couldn't touch, although he knew it would intrude soon enough. God willing, one day he would be worthy of her.

"What brought you here today?'' she asked.

"Thought I'd better see if the kids cleaned up the cemetery. I didn't want you finding a mess after all the work you've done.'' He glanced around. "Looks like they did a pretty good job.''

"Except for that beer can.'' She nodded toward the wall.

"What about you?''

"Me?''

"What made you come?''

She withdrew her hand and shifted position so that she faced him, her legs crossed. "I'm still training for a charity bike ride in West Lafayette. But why here? Why today? It's the anniversary of my grandmother's death, and this seemed a comforting place to be.''

"Your nana?''

"Yes.'' She rested her hands on her knees. "She taught me so much about living. But ironically, perhaps her most important lesson was about dying.''

"In what sense?''

Lynn turned and gazed at a nearby headstone. "See that? When I was a child, I thought cemeteries were spooky and death was scary.''

"It is.''

"It can be. But it can also be beautiful."

He shot her a skeptical look. There had been nothing beautiful about Gordy's death.

Without reacting to his expression, she continued, "When Nana was diagnosed with cancer, I had just graduated from college. I made up my mind to go home and help care for her for as long as it took. She faced the chemo, the hair loss, the pain, everything, as she had faced the rest of her life. With optimism and faith. Caring for her, I got to know her in a way I never would have otherwise. Time was short, and she still had stories to tell, wisdom to pass on, love to give. She made the most of every moment. Toward the end she kept telling me I shouldn't be afraid for her. She pictured death as a journey, much like birth, into a bright, promising new world."

"What happened?"

"Her actual passing was apt. Beautiful. My mother, Uncle Will, my sister and I were all gathered at her bedside. Her labored breathing eased. Then she held out her hand and, one by one, we held it. It felt warm and her grip was stronger than it had been for many weeks. She looked at us with recognition, a tiny smile hovering around her lips. Then we all became aware of a presence in the room...or a quality of light or something. It's hard to explain. She simply smiled and said, 'Verne,' my grandfather's name, then her eyes closed and she was gone. Oddly I've never felt a greater sense of peace. All of us in the room knew we had shared in a mysterious and lovely rite of passage."

Though tears stood in her eyes, she seemed to glow with inner joy. "That's how I know there's more,

Tom, much more than we have any glimmer of. For Nana and for Gordy and all the others.''

''I'd like to think you're right.''

''But you don't?''

''I just don't know, Lynn. I really don't.''

A cold breeze ruffled his hair, and he stood up, unsure how to conclude such an intense conversation. He studied the sky. ''Not much daylight left. You'd better be getting back to town. Would you like a lift?''

She got to her feet, brushing dirt off her fanny. ''Thanks, but I need the workout.'' She checked her watch. ''If I leave right now, I can make it fine.''

They started down the hill together. When they reached her bike, she straddled it. He stood holding the handlebars, reluctant to let her go. ''Thanks for giving me space.''

A tiny smile lit up her features. ''Patience is a virtue, we're told.'' She sobered. ''Besides, I know you have a lot on your mind with your kids and all.''

''Speaking of the kids, they're coming to visit.''

''For the weekend?''

''No.'' He explained Selena's situation. ''I'm not sure what I'll do with them.''

''They'd be welcome at Meacham House.''

''Somehow I can't visualize Pete having much in common with kids like Damon.''

She brushed back a wayward lock of hair. ''You might be surprised. Will I see you there tonight?''

He let go of the handlebars. ''Sure. Be careful.''

When she started pedaling down the road, he stood watching until she was a speck in the distance. Pete and Damon? *Surprised* wouldn't begin to describe it. *Flabbergasted* would be more accurate.

Not for the first time since Selena's call, he felt his

gut clench. He had no idea what to do with a pair of teenagers, especially when his whole future with them might hinge on these next few days.

ALTHOUGH THE CONVERSATION at the cemetery this afternoon had changed nothing, Lynn was relieved she hadn't had to come to Meacham House tonight amid a crowd of teenagers and face Tom for the first time since her declaration of love. And a crowd was what they had. Three kids huddled around a coffee table, their math homework spread in front of them. Two girls sprawled in the armchairs barely looked up from their books to acknowledge her. Hoots of laughter erupted from the dining room where Molly was supervising the construction of posters advertising a community open house in October. The beat of rock music reverberated from the basement. Lynn sighed contentedly. So far, so good.

Upstairs she found Keri and the skinny blonde, Angie, working on the layout for their first Meacham House newsletter.

"Hi, Reverend Lynn," Keri said. "How's it going?" She might be a pretty girl if she smiled, but her expression conveyed perpetual boredom.

"Great. Need any help?"

Angie's lusterless hair fell over her face obscuring her eyes as she answered, "Not really."

"When you finish, why don't you print out a copy to show me? I'm eager to see it."

"It'd be better if we had a scanner," Keri complained.

"Then we could print photos," Angie added.

Lynn leaned against the doorjamb, considering. "That's a great idea. Some of the kids are getting into photography. We could use their pictures. Maybe we can get someone to donate a scanner.''

Keri squinted at the monitor. ''Don't hold your breath on the photos.''

''Why not?''

''Damon's not coming back.'' In her tone Lynn sensed both triumph and regret.

''Why not?''

''He says he don't care about the stupid darkroom. Says it's no big deal and he's got better things to do.''

''Like what?''

Angie looked up with a cynical smirk. ''Don't ask, Rev. You don't wanna know.''

Lynn stepped forward. ''But I do. Is he in trouble?''

''When hasn't he been?'' Keri said.

Lynn struggled to remain calm. ''Do you know where he is?''

Both girls shrugged. ''Beats me,'' Angie said.

''Would you tell me if you knew?''

''No,'' Keri said, as if Lynn's question was incredibly naive.

Lynn had known all along there would be rough spots. Apparently they'd hit their first one. And there was only one person who might have a chance with Damon. ''I'll be downstairs if you need me,'' she said. Nodding toward the monitor, she added, ''I'm really excited about what you're doing.''

Back on the main floor, she looked in vain for Tom. Had he stayed home, after all? She stepped out onto the front porch, gathering her sweater around her. On the swing sat Sam, one toe dragging along the cement as he pushed himself to and fro. She stood in front of him. ''Mind if I sit down?''

He shrugged. It was the evening of shrugs, it seemed. She hitched one leg up and sat so she could see his face. He was not happy. She tapped his knee. He turned to look at her. "What's wrong?"

"My friend didn't come."

"Who?"

"Damon."

"What about some of the others?" She nodded her head toward the living room.

He swung back and forth a couple of times. "They don't want me."

"Oh?"

"They think I'm a baby." His face flushed with the epithet. "Only Tom and Damon want me here."

"I want you here."

He didn't say anything, just shrugged again. Her heart ached for the little guy. She knew from Mitch that he was desperate to belong. He was convinced his hearing impairment made him unacceptable. The fact that he hung around here, instead of with his peer group, revealed the degree of his isolation.

"Sam? That you?" The familiar voice sent shivers through her. Dressed in a maroon jogging suit, Tom strode up the walk.

Lynn moved closer to Sam and cupped his head to turn it toward the steps. Sam's shoulders straightened. "Tom? I thought you weren't coming."

"Well, here I am." He smiled down at the boy. "Better late than never."

"Sam, why don't you go on down to the darkroom? Tom will be there in a minute." She laid a restraining hand on Tom's arm and waited to speak until Sam was inside. "I need your help."

"How's that?"

"Damon."

Tom let out an exasperated sigh. "Trouble?"

"I'm afraid so. Keri and Angie said he isn't coming back. I'm worried for two reasons. First, the girls indicated he's up to no good. Second, Sam seems to have developed quite an attachment to him. One thing that young man doesn't need is further rejection."

"And what exactly do you propose I do about it?"

"Find Damon. Talk to him."

Tom hooted. "Me? I'm the guy who can't even communicate with his own kids."

"Will it hurt to try?"

He stood there frowning for a minute, seemingly at war with himself. Then he shook his head helplessly. "Jeez, lady. The things I'm willing to do for you. I'll go work a while with Sam, then I'll set out. Damned if I know where to look."

No way could she stifle a chuckle. "Given what I hear of your checkered past in Riverbend, I'll bet you know *exactly* where to look."

He put an arm around her. "Well, since you put it that way, perhaps I do have a few leads."

She smiled up at him. "Thanks, Tom. I—"

The front door opened and Keri Mellon stood observing them. "Rev, what're you doin' out here with the party Gestapo?"

Lynn nearly choked. "The party Gestapo?"

"If you'll excuse me, I have something developing in the darkroom," Tom said, beating a hasty exit.

"Yeah, he busted us." Keri studied Tom as he brushed past on his way into the house, then turned back to Lynn. "You know what? He was putting the moves on you just now." Before Lynn could pick her chin off her chest, the girl went on. "He's not my type, of course, but for somebody older like you, he could be okay, I guess.''

Lynn composed herself, hoping her blush wasn't visible in the dark. ''Are you ready to show me the newsletter?''

''Anytime.'' Keri stood aside to let Lynn pass through the door. Then, for the first time, the girl smiled, adding quietly, ''Maybe he's even more than okay.''

AFTER HELPING SAM develop his picture of two boys playing hoops at a playground, Tom sent him upstairs. He lingered in the darkroom fingering the edges of a photograph of Damon's he'd just printed. The remarkable picture depicted one of his long-haired buddies playing a guitar. The use of light and shadow forced the eye to the guitar. The grace and power in the long fingers poised on the strings drew the viewer's attention from the hard, cynical features of the performer. The photo made a statement: Even a streetwise, alienated youth can find solace and meaning in music. Damn. How could Damon drop out of this program? He had such talent.

Tom flipped off the darkroom light and, as an afterthought, tucked the photo under his arm. Where the hell was he supposed to find the kid, and if and when he did, what was he supposed to say to him?

Although he knew it was fruitless, he started by driving to Damon's home, if you could call it that. A garage apartment with rickety wooden stairs in a neighborhood whose best times had occurred long before the Great Depression. The place was dark, and his vigorous knocking on the scarred door produced no response. From there he tried the neighborhood pool hall, a used-car lot where gangs of kids often hung out and finally the park alongside the river. Nothing. He turned the truck around and started back through the now-deserted downtown. Out of the corner of his eye, a flicker of light caught his attention. The flare of a cigarette from the alley behind the Sunnyside Café.

It was worth a try. He parked a little farther down the street and started back up the sidewalk. As he approached the alley, he could hear two voices, one louder than the other. "'Scuse me? You think *that*'ll buy you a score? Not tonight, dude. This is high-grade stuff."

"I'm not made of money, you know," Tom heard Damon say.

"I've got a news flash for you, sonny. I don't take no charity cases."

Tom stepped into the entrance of the alley, wondering belatedly if the pusher was armed. "Damon," he called forcefully. "What's going on here?"

At the sound of his voice, the guy who was obviously a dealer turned and ran out the other end of the alley. Propelled by the adrenaline pulsing through his system, Tom raced toward Damon, who had hesitated a beat before trying to run away himself. What in hell was the kid into? He outran Damon and, grabbing him by the arm, whipped him around so that they were eye to eye. "You got mush for brains or what?"

"Get your friggin' hands off me!"

The boy twisted away, but was no match for Tom's iron grip. "You're not going anywhere until we have a little talk."

Damon's cold, implacable eyes fixed on Tom. "I'll yell for the cops. Tell 'em you're molesting me."

"Go ahead." Tom stared back. "That'll save me the trouble of notifying them myself about your failed transaction. They'll watch you like a hawk from now on."

There was a brief flicker of fear in Damon's eyes. "So what's new?" Tom had to hand it to the kid. He wasn't backing down. "I don't know what's with you, man, but you're a pain in the ass. Leave me alone. My life's none of your damn business."

"You're the one who's the pain in the ass. And, believe me, I'm sorely tempted to leave you alone, but I'm not going to. You know why?"

Damon didn't blink, nor did he answer.

"Because, besides the fact that you're determined to ruin your life before you even hit eighteen, you're one damned talented guy, and I have a peculiar aversion to seeing talent go to waste. So that makes your life my business." Still holding Damon by the arm, he turned him around and propelled him toward the street. "I want you to see something. And if, after you do, you still want to smoke and snort your brains out, that's your decision."

Although the teen kept trying to jerk away, Tom marched him resolutely toward the pickup. For Lynn as much as for the kid, he'd give this his best shot. After that, he was through. Let someone else do the saving. When they reached the vehicle, Tom swung open the door and jerked his head at Damon. "Get in."

"You gonna make me?"

"If I have to." Apparently something in Tom's tone of voice or stance proved persuasive because, with an insolent smirk, Damon climbed into the passenger seat. Tom kept his eyes on the youngster as he rounded the pickup, then opened the door and took his place behind the wheel. He picked the photograph off the dash and handed it to Damon. "Hold that while we go for a short ride. What I want you to see is at my house. When we're finished, I'll take you home."

Hostility emanated from the boy, and neither of them said a word until Tom pulled to a screeching halt at the farmhouse. "This'll only take a few minutes. If you're as smart as I think you are, it may change your life. C'mon." He didn't give the boy a chance to argue, but started toward the house.

Behind him, he heard the passenger door open and close. When Tom reached the front door, he turned and studied Damon, who had stopped on the bottom porch step, the photo clutched in his hand. The boy scowled at him. "What are you up to anyway?"

"Judge for yourself," Tom said, opening the door and holding it wide for Damon. "Ever hear of Gordy Maxwell?"

The boy didn't move. "No."

"How about Gordon Parks? Ansel Adams?"

"They were photographers."

"Bingo." Tom turned on an interior light. "If you like photography, I've got a real treat for you."

With a sideways glance, Tom took in the boy's indecision, the genuine temptation he'd placed before him. Maybe there was a glimmer of hope, after all. He moved briskly toward the bookshelves in the living room, laying his hands immediately on the volume he wanted. Once again he heard footsteps behind him. Damon had made it as far as the entry hall.

Tom laid *Collected Photos of Gordon Maxwell* on the library table and switched on the table lamp. Damon edged closer. "Take your time. Look all you want while I get us a couple of sodas." Tom left the room, mentally crossing his fingers.

Tom breathed a sigh of relief when he returned with the drinks. Damon had pulled a chair over to the table, set aside the print and was slowly turning the pages, examining each photograph intently, seemingly oblivious to Tom's presence. He waited, drinks in hand, until Damon reached the final page, then started across the room. "What do you think?" He set Damon's soda on a coaster.

Damon looked up, his usual sneer gone. "Awesome," he said.

The word, not just the throwaway teenage comment, but a heartfelt reaction, required no response. Tom dragged a straight chair to the table, straddled it and draped his arms over the back. Damon had turned to the beginning of the book and was starting back through the pages. "I agree. Awesome."

"This guy signed your book. Do you know him?"

"Yeah, I knew him." Tom struggled to keep his tone neutral. "We worked together for eight years."

Damon flipped back his dark mane of hair, leaving his face exposed. "What happened to him?"

Tom took a swig of his soda and swallowed slowly. "He was killed in a bomb blast."

"Oh."

"At thirty-two. Too young."

"Yeah," Damon muttered, then continued turning pages. At last he reached the photo Tom was waiting for. "Hold it." Tom laid his hand in the middle of the page. When he withdrew it, there was Gordy's picture of the tank commander standing in the turret of the metal monster. A human being encased by heavy armor, a modern warrior invincible in his steel skin. Until you looked into the soldier's face. Again Gordy had managed just the right angle. In the officer's expression was courage, but also a vulnerability, a fear, that rendered the portrait haunting.

"Now," Tom said softly, "give me your photograph." Damon looked up, puzzled. When he carefully handed over the print of the guitar player, Tom placed it beside Gordy's photo of the tank commander. He paused to allow Damon time to see what he saw. "Gordy was killed before he had a chance to live up to his full potential. Why are you trying to kill yourself before you even begin to live up to yours?"

The only sound was the hum of the refrigerator. Tom waited. Damon swallowed. "What do you mean?" he finally asked.

Tom scooted his chair closer and dared to put an arm around the boy's shoulders. "Don't you see it?"

"What?"

"You could be every bit as good a photographer as Gordy was."

The boy shrugged, as if loath to admit the possibility.

Tom pointed to the pictures. "See the similarities? You have the same concern for light and shadow, the same commitment to bringing out the soul of a subject."

"You think?" Tom heard the suppressed longing in Damon's voice.

"With training and experience, you could be as good a photographer as he was. But there's an even more important question."

"What?" Damon was moving his finger over Gordy's photo, tracing the lines of the tank.

"Can you be half the man he was?" Tom stood up and moved the chair back to its normal position. Damon remained motionless. Tom hoped he'd gotten his attention. "I'm going to answer that question for you. Not unless you decide to make something of yourself. Gordy didn't have a bed of roses as a kid, either, so you can't use that as an excuse. But that's a story for another day. Bottom line, you've got talent. Loads of it. Now you can either piss it down the drain or you can do something with it. Booze and drugs aren't part of that picture, understand? So you've got a decision to make." He leaned over and flipped off the table lamp. "C'mon. I'm taking you home."

Damon stood up, his face obscured by his hair, one finger still trailing over the cover of Gordy's book.

It was probably an impulsive thing to do, but Tom couldn't stop himself. "Would you like to borrow the book for a few days?"

Damon looked up, the rigid set of his face momentarily betrayed by hunger. "You wouldn't mind?"

"Not if you bring it back when you come to Meacham House next time." Tom watched the boy struggle with his thoughts. "And you will come, right?"

Damon picked up the book, inserted his own picture between the covers and finally looked evenly into Tom's eyes. "Yeah. I'll come."

LYNN HAD JUST CRAWLED into bed when the telephone rang. She glanced at the clock. After eleven. In her business, it was rarely good news at this time of night. As always, her heart thudded as she picked up the phone. She took a deep breath to relax before she said hello.

"Hi, it's me." Hearing Tom's calm voice, she exhaled and settled back against the pillows. "I thought you might want the Damon report."

"I do. Please tell me it's good news."

"Okay, then. It's good news. But it still won't hurt to cross our fingers or, in your case, send up a prayer or two."

"I'm already doing that," she murmured.

"Figured you might be." Then he launched into the story of his evening with Damon and concluded by saying, "So photography is the motivating force."

"I think there's more to it."

"Like what?" Tom sounded puzzled.

"Like attention from a man who won't let him off the hook and who believes in him."

"Wait a minute." She could hear the oh-no-not-me in his voice. "This was a one-time deal."

"Not if you really want to rehabilitate the young man." She scooted to a sitting position. "You're the key, Tom. He desperately needs you to monitor him, to help him restore his self-esteem."

"All this because I lent Meacham House a camera?"

"Just another example of God's mysterious ways," she said innocently.

"Easy for you to say." She could almost see the frustrated frown on his face.

She smiled. "Yes, it is."

"I've got my own responsibilities. The kids arrive Friday night."

"You said Damon would come back Monday evening."

"Yes."

"Without you there?"

His silence signaled big-time hedging. Finally he answered. "Probably not."

"In that case, we'll all look forward to meeting Pete and Libby then."

"What if they won't come?"

"There's only one reason they won't."

"What's that?"

"If you give them an out." She wondered if she should go on and finally decided to risk it. "They're looking for direction from you, Tom. Remember, you're the parent. They're the kids."

"I haven't had much practice with that."

"Then it's time to start."

"You don't give a man much wiggle room."

"Not about this, I don't. But on some other things…"

His voice dropped. "Yeah, I know. You might wait a long time. I wish—"

"Shh. I'll take my chances."

"You're something else, you know that?"

"Thank you. But be on your guard. I'm holding out for 'happily ever after.'"

"You drive a hard bargain." The need in his voice, so clearly echoing her own, sent a shimmer of warmth through her.

"We're worth it," she whispered before saying good-night and gently replacing the receiver.

She lay back down, pulling the blanket around her bare shoulders and plumping her pillow just so. Her body told her she needed him now, her head reasoned it wasn't time, and her heart promised that somehow, someday, they would be together.

Benedict, as if sensing her aloneness, padded into

the room, leaped onto the bed and curled up by her head. ''Ben, I wish you could help me. I said I'd be patient. But it's not easy.'' The cat purred as if in sympathy. ''Not when I want him so much.''

CHAPTER TEN

PETE KICKED a puke-green hedge apple ahead of him down the dirt lane. He had to get out of that stuffy old farmhouse, away from his jerk of a father whose idea of entertainment was to shoot clay pigeons and fish in that yucky river. His friends at Weymouth Prep would bust a gut laughing if they could've seen him out there in that stupid cornfield target-shooting. His dad had acted like it was some big-deal father-son thing to handle guns. The whole time they were out there, he was missing the World Tennis Association match on TV.

And dumb Libby had acted as if she'd been given special status or something. A girl asked to shoot. She'd looked like a klutz trying to shoulder the heavy gun. Worse, now she was complaining about a bruised shoulder. Well, duh. If she'd have done what their father told them to, she wouldn't have a problem. That was just like her, thinking she knew stuff she didn't.

Spotting a pair of large blackbirds ahead of him, he sent the hedge apple flying toward them, dispersing them amid a grating series of cackles. Corn, cows and crows. Man, this was the middle of nowhere.

Only two good things so far. The warm oatmeal cookies Dorrie had brought them and the visit to his father's aunts, Rachel and Ruth. At first he hadn't wanted to visit the two old ladies. He'd met them before the one other time he'd been in Riverbend. But he was a little kid then and couldn't remember much about them, except that one of them smelled like gingerbread. He forgot which.

So he'd been surprised when the plump one made him laugh and took him into the bookstore, even though it was closed for Sunday, and let him pick out any two books he wanted. He'd gotten one with all these pictures of tennis stars and then a sci-fi adventure by his favorite author.

Damn. Those retarded crows had landed again right in his path. Again he kicked the hedge apple at them, and again their outraged squawking erupted.

Oh, one other good thing. Today was Monday and he wasn't in school. He could picture his classmates bent over their smelly biology-lab stations, hear them in French class repeating parrotlike those artsy-fartsy phrases like "*Je m'appelle Pierre,*" and falling asleep after lunch while old man Hazelhorst droned on about supply-and-demand.

He reached the end of the lane and looked up and down the country road. One tractor going about negative-five miles an hour. That was it.

Reluctantly he turned around and headed for the house. Tonight would be the worst. His father had made a big deal out of telling them about the Mitchum House, whatever it was. He was supposed to be excited about meeting some other kids. Retards, prob'ly, if they lived in this place. Besides, he couldn't picture it. His father with a bunch of teenagers?

He felt a tightening in his stomach. Why would his dad be interested in going there? He hardly had time to come visit him and Libby in Chicago. It made him mad just thinking about it.

He stopped, staring down the road with disgust. This time he picked up the hedge apple and flung it with everything he had at those creepy birds.

IF SHE HADN'T SEEN IT with her own eyes, Lynn wouldn't have believed it. Ruth and Rachel Steele huddled at the dining-room table at Meacham House surrounded by several teenagers who defined the word *grunge*. Neither of the women seemed remotely perturbed by the purple fingernails, pierced lips and noses and weird hair. Keri scooted her chair closer and watched over Ruth's shoulder as she flipped the black pages of a photo album.

"This is the old high school." Ruth pointed to a black-and-white photograph.

"Whaddaya mean 'old high school'? You're telling me our rattrap of a school is new?" A skinny boy with a pimply face and head shaved but for the ponytail popping out of his crown, looked at his peers for approval. One snickered, but several of the girls had the grace to look embarrassed.

"It's all relative, I suppose," Ruth said. "It seems like yesterday we graduated from Old Main—" she gestured at the photo "—but to you it must seem like ancient history."

"What happened to the old school?" one of the girls asked.

Ruth shook her head sadly. "Burned to the ground right after we graduated."

"Good riddance," a surly-looking, heavily made-up girl with orange hair muttered.

"Now, you don't mean that." Ruth adopted a serious tone. "Education is very important."

The girl rolled her eyes. "It's boring."

"Let's see what we can do about that," Rachel suggested. "Why don't you bring some of your assignments and let Ruthie and me help you? Maybe it's boring because you don't feel very successful."

"Yeah, Kala," one of the boys taunted. "Those D's ain't gonna get you on no honor roll."

"Tell you what," Ruth intervened. "Sister and I will spend forty-five minutes helping you each Monday and Wednesday night, and then for fifteen minutes we'll tell you some of the secrets of Riverbend."

"Oh, right," the orange-haired girl said, tossing her head dramatically. "Like there're so many."

Unperturbed by her skepticism, Ruth went on, "So you don't want to know how the school burned down?"

There was silence. The fellow with the ponytail seemed to be considering. "Forty-five minutes? That's all?"

"That's all," Rachel echoed.

He looked around at the others. "What else have we got to do? Hey, it'd be worth it to see Fleerbaum's face if we all passed one of her tests."

Lynn chuckled when Rachel threw her twin a triumphant look over the rims of her glasses. One of Lynn's hopes when she had suggested the program was that it would become intergenerational. Thanks to the Steeles, she hadn't had long to wait.

Speaking of waiting, Lynn glanced nervously at the door. Damon had already been upstairs twice ostensibly to get something to drink. The first time he'd sauntered to the front window and had stood for several minutes sipping a root beer and gazing at the sidewalk. The next time he'd sidled up next to her, his hands hidden in his baggy trousers' pockets. "Tom coming?" She'd told him as far as she knew he was, but from Damon's increasingly nervous mannerisms, she had the uneasy sense he was ready to cut and run. And even if—*when*—Tom came, he'd have Pete and Libby with him. It was anybody's guess how Damon would react.

Even though she usually left the chore to the kids, Lynn walked around picking up empty plates and soda cans. She shared Damon's edginess. She had no idea what to expect from Tom's children. He'd called late Sunday night fit to be tied. With the possible exception of a visit to Ruth and Rachel's, nothing he'd done to make them feel at home had succeeded. He said it was as if they were determined not to like anything. Knowing it would be cold comfort to tell him these things take time, Lynn kept silent.

Besides, the more she'd pondered the situation, the clearer it became that a large part of what was going on with Tom was tied to belated desire to connect with his kids. Even though she recognized that step as a significant one in his healing, there was a personally important aspect. She'd finally been able to admit it would be difficult, if not impossible, to commit to a relationship until and unless he could resolve his family issues. Because she desperately wanted a family. Including children of her own. She suspected, however, he wouldn't be ready to consider having another child until he'd made peace with Pete and Libby. If then.

She put a stack of plates into the sink and ran water over them, aware of a heaviness in her heart. What had started as a heaven-sent attraction now involved burdensome baggage. She closed her eyes briefly, inhaling the steam from the hot water. "Please, God, help us find our way," she intoned under her breath, before wiping her hands, arranging her facial features into a pleasant expression and returning to the living room where, just inside the front door, stood a harried-looking Tom, a teenage boy with a shock of dark hair, ruddy cheeks and a sullen look, and a slightly built, auburn-haired girl who seemed to have gathered herself into a taut, expressionless stick figure.

Lynn crossed the room saying, "Welcome to Meacham House. You must be Pete and Libby." Even to herself her greeting sounded falsely cheery.

Tom stepped forward, pressing a palm into his son's back. "Pete, this is Lynn Kendall, the minister I told you about."

The boy gave her a swift appraisal, but mumbled only, "Hi."

"And this is Libby." He sent his daughter a smile of encouragement.

"Nice to meet you," she dutifully replied, her braces causing an unnatural thickness in her words.

Lynn swept her arm expansively toward the others. "Please come join us."

Pete glowered at his father. "I can hardly wait," he muttered.

Rachel saved the day, shoving away from the dining-room table and coming to greet her great-niece and -nephew. She put an arm around each of the children. "Nice to see you both again." She ushered them toward the group of teens. "You might enjoy meeting my friends."

"Friends?" Libby, peering at the group around the table, sounded incredulous. "Those freaks?" she whispered.

Lynn detected Tom's fleeting wince.

Pete said nothing, but over his shoulder sent his father a look of total incredulity.

"Oh, God," Lynn heard Tom groan beside her. "I knew this was a mistake."

Lynn had to admit that the two squeaky-clean Baineses, with their clear skin, designer-label clothes and salon haircuts stuck out here like hothouse orchids in a dandelion patch. She reassured herself that kids are kids and that once they got past appearances, miracles could happen. And looking at Tom's face, they could do with one right now.

But once again she was forcefully reminded that God's timing was not hers, because just then, Sam and Damon emerged from the basement. Damon walked straight to Tom and balanced menacingly on the balls of his feet directly in front of his mentor. "Hey, where ya been? Or was all that talk the other night just so much bull?"

"I don't deal in bull." Tom stared intently at the boy. "What have you been working on tonight?"

"Sam and me was waiting for you."

"It's time to begin counting on yourself."

Damon emitted a lifeless chuckle. "Like whaddaya think I been doin' all my life?"

"With the photography. Trust your instincts. I'll help along the way, but you know enough to go ahead without me."

"Yeah?" There was a catch in Damon's voice.

"Yeah." Understanding seemed to pass between the two. From the dining room Lynn observed Pete scowling at his father.

Sam tugged at Tom's sleeve. "What about me?"

"You follow Damon's instructions. He's in charge."

Something about the words *in charge* caused Damon to straighten imperceptibly. "Okay, kid, c'mon."

"I'll check on you later," Tom said as the pair headed for the basement door.

"It's all your fault," Tom said under his breath to Lynn as he linked his fingers with hers and hid their clasped hands in the folds of her skirt.

"Genus teenageri?"

"Getting me into this mess."

"But judging from your intervention with Damon, you're pretty effective."

"Hah!" He nodded over her head to the dining room where Pete had refused to sit, and just stood, his arms crossed, looking down his nose at the group, and where Libby was noticeably cringing from proximity to the ring-nosed Keri.

Lynn attempted to inject a note of levity. "You know what they say. 'A prophet is without honor in his own country.'"

Tom shook his head wearily. "This is a disaster."

Lynn squeezed his fingers. "I'll grant you it looks that way now." She disengaged from his grasp, glancing toward the dining room where Ruth and Rachel were putting on their coats. "Let me see what I can do. Meanwhile, your aunts are about ready to leave. Why don't you walk them home? I can guarantee Pete and Libby aren't going to give you the satisfaction of letting you see them enjoying this place. Your best bet is to keep a low profile."

He looked so hopeless it was all she could do not to give him a hug right there in front of everyone, including his own kids. She nudged him toward the dining room and, taking a deep breath, watched as he offered himself as an escort.

Distaste written all over him, Pete avoided his father, returning to the living room where he flopped into a beanbag chair and picked up the TV remote. He looked up at Lynn. "This thing work?"

"Yes. But we only turn on the television if everyone in the room agrees."

"Yeah, so? It's just you and me."

"The others are saying goodbye to the Steele sisters. They'll be coming in here. Then you can check with them."

His lip curled. "What do we do? Vote?"

"If necessary."

Pete flipped on a baseball game. "If they want to change the channel, they'll have to make me."

"Who is it you're trying to punish here?"

He looked up, his pupils hard as buckeyes. "What's that supposed to mean?"

"What did these kids ever do to you?"

He shrugged. "Nothing. Yet."

"Isn't it your dad you're upset with?"

"Him?" He nodded at his father who was taking the aunts by the arm and assisting them onto the front porch. "He's no big deal."

"That's where you may be wrong, Pete. I think he's a very big deal to you." She crossed her fingers and went on gamely. "And I know you're a big deal to him."

Pete, fiddling with the remote, avoided looking at her. "Right. I'm such a big deal he forced me to come to this stupid place against my will."

Lynn sensed he'd had enough. "Well, since you're here, would you like something to eat?"

"Got any chips?"

"Sure, I'll get them." She knew he wouldn't relinquish his control of the remote to secure the food himself. When the others joined him, maybe he'd relax a bit. Give the Meacham House kids a chance. She was down to small miracles.

On her way to the kitchen, she noticed that Keri Mellon had somehow broken through Libby's reserve, and the two were chatting about the boys at Libby's school. It was a start.

TOM PUT AN AUNT on each side of him and started slowly up the street. Lynn's suggestion had given him a welcome reprieve. Inside, he hadn't known what the hell to do with himself, with his kids, with Damon, with anybody! He had the sick sensation that bringing Pete and Libby there had muddied the waters even more.

"There is no need to escort us," Ruth said. "Nobody's foolhardy enough to attack the Steele sisters at this late date in our lives."

"Or desperate enough." Rachel chuckled.

"I know there's no need, but I'm enjoying your company."

Ruth winked knowingly at Rachel. "Oho, I do believe our nephew wants something."

Tom spread his hands innocently. "Are you accusing me of ulterior motives?"

Rachel nodded emphatically. "Definitely. After all, deviousness runs in the family, doesn't it, Ruthie?"

After a long silence in which he sensed his aunts waiting, Tom explained his dilemma. "I'm glad the kids are here, but—"

"You're scared to death." Ruth matter-of-factly completed his thought.

"Why wouldn't I be? I've never been a candidate for Father of the Year, and they've as much as told me they'd rather be anyplace else."

"Poor babies," Ruth said with an unsympathetic look on her face. "They may have to do something they don't want to do."

"That's the trouble with teenagers today," Rachel added. "They think they control their parents."

"How can I control them if they'll hardly speak to me?"

Ruth laced her hand through his arm. "Why do you think that is?"

"They don't like me."

"Nonsense," Ruth said.

On his other side Rachel linked her arm through his, too. "For starters, show them you care. Don't let them get away with murder."

"Set boundaries," Ruth said.

"Unplug the television," Rachel added.

Tom could hear the strain in his voice when he said, "And then what?"

"Spend time with them," the twins said in unison.

"Doing what?"

Ruth squeezed his arm. "For a grown man, you are incredibly dense."

"What have you done so far?" Rachel asked.

"We went fishing in the river, did some shooting. Believe it or not, Libby liked it better than Pete."

Ruth harrumphed. "That's not so surprising. Libby liked doing something special with you, but Pete is determined not to let you win him over."

"That's encouraging." Tom was more bewildered

than ever. "I compounded my mistakes by bringing them tonight."

"That wasn't a mistake," Rachel said.

"You saw them. They hated it. They have nothing in common with those kids."

"You're judging by appearances," Ruth said.

Tom felt himself getting hot under the collar. He should've known better than to seek their advice. The aunts were too old to have a bead on today's teens. "Hell, yes, I am."

"Then you're a fool." Ruth stopped in front of the bookstore. "Those young people all have more in common than you could guess from the surface. They want to feel good about themselves, to be approved..." She paused, then looked up at him. "To be loved."

Beside him, he heard Rachel sigh. Very quietly she added, "Not so different from you, Tom dear."

Simultaneously, as if they'd communicated their intention by telepathy, they each stood on tiptoe, kissed him on the cheek, then turned toward the house. He watched as they unlocked the door and disappeared inside.

Maybe it was easier to see the big picture when you didn't have any children of your own. Or maybe they didn't have the answers, any more than he did.

But they were right about one thing—he needed to be loved. Why did he find it so damned difficult to admit? And Lynn was standing in the wings, waiting for him to accept her love. He plunged his hands into his pockets, kicked at a pebble and headed back toward Meacham House.

But he was waiting for something more. He was waiting to feel worthy of her.

WHEN HE RETURNED, Tom nearly tripped over Keri, Angie and a boy who looked somehow familiar—all sprawled on the living-room floor, drawing on a huge square of orange cloth. As he studied the kid, a light-bulb went on. "Say," he addressed the teenager, "didn't I see you and Charlie Callahan the other day in Sterling Hardware?"

The boy shrugged. "Prob'ly. I'm Nathan Turner. Charlie's kinda my adopted dad."

Tom had heard how Charlie had taken the young-ster under his wing. "Lucky you. I've known Charlie ever since we were kids. He's one of the best."

The boy smiled shyly. "Yeah, he is."

Tom noticed Libby sitting cross-legged nearby stuff-ing batting into a narrow green cloth sack that looked somewhat like a stem. Pete was nowhere to be seen. Nor Lynn. Apparently she'd already left. Maybe she'd had a call to make. Tom surveyed their work. "What's going on here?"

Keri looked up long enough to say, "We're making Halloween decorations for the retirement center."

"So what's that?" he asked pointing at the cloth.

Libby threw him a long-suffering look. "Dad, it's obvious. It's a pumpkin."

Maybe, but they had a long way to go. Retirement center, huh? That was a picture he could hardly imag-ine—these kids and octogenarians!

Molly, carrying a large piece of white poster board, sailed into the room. "Anybody game to draw a ghost?"

Nathan stood up and relieved her of the poster board. "Casper, here I come."

Tom gestured toward the slowly emerging pump-kin. "Is it that time of year already?"

Molly's eyes twinkled. "Once October comes, it's soon enough for me. Halloween is one of my favorite holidays. How about you?"

Tom's chest felt hollow. "I never had much experience with it. We were almost always overseas."

"We'll fix that, right, kids?" She continued talking as she hunkered down between Keri and Angie and studied their progress. "Meacham House is throwing a party at Golden Fields. Halloween is always such a big deal in Riverbend that this coming Friday was the only weekend night the social director could work us in. I know it's early in the month, but we're having no trouble getting into the spirit. You and your children will be coming, won't you? In fact," she rattled on, "I could use another driver. Can I count on you?"

The three of them—Pete, Libby and him—at a Halloween party for senior citizens? But it was something to do, and at this point he was clutching at straws. "Sure."

"Don't forget to wear a costume."

He stuck his little finger in his ear and jiggled it. "Say what?"

Molly's grin was downright mischievous. "We're all wearing costumes, chaperons included."

Libby looked up with an innocent smile. "Yeah, Dad. You could be the Grinch."

"Gee, thanks." He hopscotched across the room to avoid stepping on the materials. "Seen Pete?"

"I think he went downstairs," Libby said, turning back to her task.

Under the supervision of one of the sponsors, several youngsters with guitars were practicing riffs in the rec room. Pete slouched against the wall, watching them intently. Tom stood quietly in the door observing his son. His dark, short-cropped hair, lean, well-toned build and air of indifference were a far cry from the curly-haired, eager youngster who used to greet him enthusiastically when he returned from overseas assignments. Tom's eyes narrowed. The hell of it was that, sadly, he recognized in his son that same defensive attitude of worldly ennui that had characterized himself as a teen. An unexpected surge of love caught Tom by surprise. Along with an overwhelming feeling of helplessness.

Finally, before Pete spotted him, he turned and knocked on the darkroom door. Damon let him in. Hanging on the wall were several prints of the guitar player, all the same exposure, but each revealing minute variations in the developing or cropping process.

Damon slumped against the wall, his hair obscuring his face. Sam bounced excitedly beside him. "Which one, Tom? Which one's best?"

Tom slowly examined each print. Each had its particular subtleties, and all of them were good. Very good. At the conclusion of his inspection, he stood back and took in the entire display. "It's hard to say."

Sam tugged at his sleeve. "I can't hear you."

Tom turned the boy so he could face both youngsters when he spoke. Sam moved closer to Damon, almost protectively, as if he feared Tom's judgment. "They're all fine in their own way, but I prefer the one where the contrast between the fingers and strings is clearest. It has a lot to say about the way music is made."

Sam hung his head. "I wish—"

Damon punched him lightly and mouthed, "Speak up, kid. Can't hear you."

The next words, high-pitched and uncontrolled,

filled the tiny room. "I wish I knew how music is made. But I can't hear it!"

Damon raked a hand through his long hair, as if he'd never contemplated such a deprivation. "Man—" he exhaled audibly "—I never thought about that. That's tough."

Tom knelt in front of Sam. "Damon's right. That *is* tough. But there are lots of things you can do. Didn't you play basketball this summer?"

"Yes." Sam's eyes filled with tears. "But I couldn't hear the whistle. Coach had to stay right with me."

"Forget it, runt," Damon said. "Sports are for dumb jocks."

"Whoa, fellas." Tom struggled to find the right words. "Sports aren't for everyone any more than music or photography are. The important thing is to find something that you do well and that gives you satisfaction. Your passion." *Like writing.* Out of nowhere the thought burst into his consciousness. A truth he hadn't stopped to examine. Not recently.

"Like what?" Sam challenged.

Tom remembered a comment Mitch had made during their golf round. "Don't you like to draw?"

"Yes."

"And you like photography, right?"

"Yes."

"Have you ever thought about being an artist?"

Sam bit his lip. "Do you think I could?"

"Sure, if you want it badly enough."

As Tom stood up, Damon caught his eye with a look that seemed to say, "I hear you, too."

THIS WAS THE BEST PLACE in this whole crappy teen center, Pete thought as he listened to the CD the guitar dude was playing to demonstrate some musical stuff. He liked the mellow sounds of the music and the way the guy didn't talk down to them the way so many adults did. Some of what the man had said he'd never considered before. He'd just taken the music for granted, never really thought about what went into it. Man, he'd sure been wrong. Maybe he could get his dad to buy him a guitar. He owed him something for making him spend ten days in Riverbend. Yeah, a guitar.

Where was his dad, anyway? He'd just dumped him and Libby the minute they'd come in the door. It couldn't take those old ladies *that* long to walk home. While he'd been waiting, he'd heard some of the kids call his dad Tom, like he was a regular guy, not a pain-in-the-ass parent. Go figure.

Several of the girls had wandered into the rec room and now sat on the floor grooving to the CD. He eyed the one in the tight black T-shirt appreciatively. She had hooters that almost made him forget Polly. Quite a sight as long as you didn't look at her ears—they had enough metal poked through them to activate an airport detector.

He felt weird. He was the one with the stylish threads, the one with the money, the cool one, for cripe's sake, so why did they all look at him like he was the alien? Well, screw 'em. He didn't care. He'd be back home soon where he could forget all about this bizarre—yeah, there was another of those PSAT words—chapter in his life.

The music stopped and the kids stood up, some of them milling around the instructor asking questions and crap like that. Where the hell was his father?

Surely it was time to leave. Maybe he'd gotten too tied up with some loser who called him "Tom."

Finally, at the other end of the basement a door opened and he saw his dad emerging, one arm around the shoulders of a kid of maybe ten or eleven and another arm around a guy who looked kinda like that rocker dude Tommy Lee. A sour taste rose in Pete's throat, a taste like after you heave up your guts.

"Hey," Pete called. The group was heading toward the stairs. Maybe with all the conversation swirling around, his dad hadn't heard him. He shoved some girls aside and got closer. "Where've you been?"

The long-haired dude must've heard him, because he shot him one of those looks that don't need a genius to interpret. *Who the hell are you?* it said.

"Dad?" Finally his father must've heard because all three stopped and turned around. "Where you been?" he repeated.

"In the darkroom."

"With *them?*" Pete couldn't seem to help himself. His famous father, who had never given him the time of day, had holed up with these misfits?

"What's wrong with us?" the long-haired dude said, stepping forward.

"Look at you." Pete pointed to the boy, then back to the long-haired creep. "You're a coupla weirdo retards."

Before he had time to process the shocked expression on his father's face or hear the howl rising from the onlookers, he felt first a blinding pain near his eye, then his nose exploded in blood and snot and he found himself on the floor, looking dizzily at the blurred distorted image of Tommy Lee.

CHAPTER ELEVEN

LILY MAZERIK'S FATHER, Julian Bennett, had been the doctor on call at the hospital when they'd arrived and had recommended keeping Pete in the hospital overnight where the staff could check on him and monitor his pain medication. A concussion and blowout fracture of the orbit, Dr. Bennett had said. After the CT scan and X rays, Tom had been weak-kneed with relief to learn there appeared to be no bleeding into the brain. Pete wouldn't be playing any tennis matches in the next few days, but he was lucky. It could've been much worse.

Looking at his son from the foot of the bed in the light of day, Tom was hard-pressed to recall the handsome face he'd studied in the rec room only hours before. The bruised cheeks, puffy eyes, bandaged nose and pale skin bore testimony to the force of Damon's outrage.

Where did they go from here? All of Pete's pent-up hostility had found a target—Sam and Damon. Hell, who could blame Damon for retaliating? Particularly considering the conversation they'd just had in the darkroom about Sam's impairment. Thank God for Molly. She'd gotten the other kids to go, then driven Sam and Damon home.

Libby had sat in the car, scrunched against the door, not saying a word, while he drove to the hospital.

There had been no way to tell what she was thinking. Nor had she been any more communicative this morning when he'd dropped her off at Ruth and Rachel's. How many more ways could he botch this visit?

A nurse bustled into the room, affixed the blood-pressure cuff and took Pete's vital signs. At her touch, he groaned.

Tom cleared his throat. "How's he doing?"

"Resting comfortably. But he isn't going to feel very well when he wakes up." She smiled reassuringly. "What did the other guy look like?" she asked teasingly.

It hadn't been that sort of fight, Tom thought. Damon had been justified—there'd been no excuse for Pete's insult—and Pete had been in no condition to hit back. Lately he'd been moody as hell and had made no secret of his unwillingness even to try to fit in here. But Tom had never thought his son was bigoted. Pete stirred in his sleep, flinging one arm across his chest. While Tom had had his back turned traipsing all over the globe, had his son turned into a bad kid? Was his hostility that deep-seated?

The nurse paused in the doorway, her ministrations completed. "Can I bring you anything?"

"Thanks, no. I'll get some coffee in the cafeteria later."

Morning sun streamed through the vertical blinds, and Tom stepped to the window to adjust for the glare falling on Pete's face. Leaning against the window ledge, he folded his arms across his chest and continued studying his son. What should he say to him when he woke up? On the one hand he was furious with him, but on a deeper level his heart was in splinters.

He had only himself to blame. He had not been there to help shape his son into a man. Was it too late?

A shadow fell across the entrance to the room. He looked up to see Lynn standing tentatively in the doorway. "May I come in?"

He didn't know when he'd heard more welcome words. When she shut the door behind her, he crossed the room and pulled her into his arms. "I'm glad you're here," he breathed into her hair.

For several seconds neither of them moved, and almost as a physical sensation, he felt himself drawing strength and calm from her embrace. Finally she whispered, "I'm sorry I wasn't there last night."

"You couldn't have prevented what happened." That was the sorry truth. There wasn't anything anybody could have done. Except him. A long time ago.

Gradually she extricated herself from his arms, then walked to Pete's bedside. "How is he?" she asked, laying a hand over the boy's and looking at him with such love and concern that Tom felt his insides turn upside down.

He swallowed the stone in his throat. "His body will heal."

She smoothed Pete's hair off his forehead with her other hand. It struck him that he himself hadn't touched his son even once. "And the rest of him?"

He shrugged. "I don't know."

She paused, one hand on Pete's forehead, one still clasping his fingers, and closed her eyes. The only sound in the room was the gentle exhalation of his son's breathing. In the hall Tom could hear the clatter and conversation that signaled morning hospital rounds. Lynn, however, seemed totally oblivious, deep into whatever she was doing. Praying, he supposed. Well, it couldn't hurt.

When she opened her eyes, it was like the sun rising after a stormy night. She gave Pete's hand a pat, then turned, smiling, to Tom. "Feel like buying a girl a cup of coffee?"

"Don't you have other hospital calls to make?"

She poked him playfully on the arm. "Trying to weasel out?"

"Not at all, but—"

She took hold of his arms. "Yes, I have other calls to make. I'll do them later. Right now, you look like you could use a break. And a friend."

"Both," he agreed. He took one last look at Pete, whose lips twitched in a half smile. A good dream? He certainly hoped so.

Most of the breakfast traffic had cleared out of the cafeteria, so they were able to settle at a table by a window overlooking the cancer survivors' rose garden. Tom cupped his hands around the mug and found himself staring at the cross suspended from a thin silver chain Lynn wore around her neck. The sun had caught it just so, highlighting it against the dark blue of her sweater, making it difficult when he looked up, to forget she was a minister. Even though, to him, she was so much more.

"How did you find out?" he asked.

"About the fight?" She stirred a container of cream into her coffee. "This is Riverbend, remember? Molly called me first thing this morning."

"Did she tell you everything?"

"You mean about Pete's insulting remark?"

He stared into the black depths of his mug. "Yeah."

"Yes. No one thinks Pete's actions were admirable, but they're understandable."

"I wish I thought so." All he could think of was the one time he had mouthed off to Uncle Abe and the very clear lesson he'd learned as a result. Pete came by his mouthiness naturally, but that didn't excuse it.

Lynn sipped her coffee and gave a small sigh of satisfaction before continuing, "He's jealous."

Tom sputtered a mouthful of coffee. *"Jealous?"* He picked up his napkin and wiped his lips. "Of what?"

"Of your work, of your glamorous career, of all the other people in your life. Of anything that takes you away from him. In this instance, Damon and Sam. Can't you see? They're a threat to him."

Tom set down his cup, then leaned forward and rested his elbows on the table. "Let me get this straight. You're suggesting this kid who ignores me, turns away from me any time he can, is jealous?"

"His belligerence has root causes. Can you suggest anything else?"

When she put it that way... "Okay, for the sake of argument, let's suppose you're right. If he's jealous, it must follow he doesn't hate me."

"Far from it. Forgive me for smiling, but is it so hard to believe he loves you very much?"

"Then why does he act like he hates me?"

"Because it's safe."

"Safe?"

"It's a natural protective response. He rejects you before you reject him."

Tom shook his head, confused and frustrated. "But that's just it. I'm *not* rejecting him." He didn't know how much longer he could bear to look into the crystal depths of those understanding gray eyes and find himself mirrored there.

"Not *now*. But how's he supposed to know that?"

"Hell, I've come home, haven't I?"

"Have you?"

He turned and stared out the window at the cold stone statue of St. Francis standing ankle-deep in a carpet of autumn leaves. He heard someone scrape a chair across the tile floor and set down a tray on a nearby table. The sound grated.

Had he? Come home? Or was this just another way station on his life's journey? Was his kid supposed to be a mind reader?

Over the tinny intercom, he heard a female voice page a doctor, but the words didn't seem connected to his brain. At last he turned back to Lynn, patiently awaiting his answer. "Are you always this perceptive?"

Her mouth curved gently. "Not always."

"So you're saying I have something to prove to my kids."

"No, I'm not saying that. *You* are." She pulled both his hands into her warm grasp. "They've said goodbye to you so many times in their young lives. They don't want to have to say it again."

"But their experience suggests this isn't any different from any other time. Is that it?"

"They're very bright children, Tom."

"I know." He paused, his chest tightening. "I love them."

She squeezed his hands. "That's obvious, at least to me. Now you need to make it clear to them."

"How?"

"Think about it. Are they so different from you when you were their age? What did you want? What would have made you feel loved and secure?"

Unbidden, that remembrance of not belonging rose like gorge in his throat. He hadn't wanted to be on his own. Hadn't wanted to grow up before it was time. Hadn't wanted his father's handshake. What he'd wanted was...a hug. A place to call home, where he had people he could count on.

He withdrew his hands and picked up the tab. "I have no idea why you bother with me, but I'm grateful as hell. Thanks, Lynn, for being you." He shoved back his chair and stood up. "Now if you'll excuse me, I want to be there when Pete wakes up."

"Good. You know something? I think the rest of Pete is going to heal, too." She placed her forefinger and middle finger against her lips, then withdrew them and turned them to him in a silent kiss.

As he walked briskly toward the cash register, he wondered what in heaven's name she saw in him. Whatever it was, he never wanted to lose it.

AFTER VISITING two hospitalized parishioners, Lynn decided to stop by Ruth and Rachel's to check on Libby, who had to be wondering what was going on. Rachel greeted her with a worried frown. "I'm glad you've come. Our young guest hasn't said much, and she's tight as a tick. Ruth's taken her over to the bookstore, hoping to interest her in some reading. But I'm not optimistic that'll help. She's an unhappy little girl."

Rachel took Lynn by the arm. "Come through here." She ushered Lynn to the passage connecting the house and bookstore. "Good luck, my dear."

Lynn figured she could use it. Tom, of course, needed to be with Pete, but Libby had to be feeling very alone in a strange place, not to mention worried about her brother. She seemed to be a quiet, introspective girl. It might be difficult to get her to share her feelings, but it was worth a try.

When Lynn entered the bookstore, Kate waved, then advanced toward her, arms extended. Lynn gratefully stepped into her embrace. "You've had an interesting last few hours, I imagine," Kate said as she stood back and studied her friend's face. "How's Tom's son?"

"Not a pretty sight at the moment. But he'll be fine, at least physically. Emotionally, I'm not so sure."

Kate cocked an eyebrow. "Oh?"

"Beyond the damage to his pride, there's the underlying issue of his feelings about his father."

"Heavy stuff."

"Heavy for Tom, too. And Libby, of course, in a different way. I've come to see her."

Kate nodded toward the young adult section of the bookstore. "Ruth's trying to keep her occupied, but I know she'd welcome reinforcements."

Lynn fingered her cross. "That's why I'm here."

Laying a hand on her arm, Kate momentarily delayed her. "I care how *you* are, too. This whole thing must raise some interesting issues for you and Tom. If you need to talk, just give a jingle."

"Thanks, I know I can count on you," Lynn said. She approached the table where Ruth and Libby were bent over a stack of books, examining them one by one. "Mind if I join you?"

"Not at all," Ruth said, sounding relieved. Libby merely shrugged.

Lynn slipped into a vacant chair. "What have we got here?" She picked up *Cold Sassy Tree* and thumbed through it. "This is one of my all-time favorites."

"It is?" Libby appeared mildly curious.

Lynn slid it across the table. "I think you'd like it."

"The main character is a boy. I like female narrators."

"I do, too, usually." Lynn tapped a finger on the cover. "But this one's different. Tell you what, why don't I buy it for you, and if you don't like it, we'll donate it to Meacham House?"

"Better yet, why don't I give it to you?" Ruth interjected. "I'd really like you to have it."

Libby pulled the book closer to her. "Thank you," she mumbled.

"Have you had breakfast, kiddo?" Lynn asked.

"Dad gave me a bowl of cereal."

"But you're still hungry, I'll bet." Lynn waited for the nod of the head. "I'm dying for one of the Sunnyside Café's gooey caramel rolls. Will you let me treat you?"

"I am kinda hungry," Libby admitted.

"You're in for a treat," Ruth said as she stood up, then aligned her chair under the table. "Lucky neither of you has to worry about calories."

Libby threw Ruth a skeptical look. Lynn sighed. Adolescent girls always worried about calories. Too much.

As Lynn and Libby crossed the street to the Sunnyside, Lynn reassured her about Pete. "He isn't going to win any beauty contests, but he'll be fine. In fact, he'll be coming home this afternoon."

"None of this would've happened if Dad hadn't made us go to Meacham House." She studied the courthouse cupola while they waited for the green light. "Or if Mom hadn't made us come to Riverbend."

"But it *has* happened." Before Lynn could go on, the light changed and Libby jumped ahead of her, as if eager to put distance between them. Lynn gave up pursuing the subject until they were in the café and had ordered their rolls. "I don't mean to intrude, Libby, but I'm a good listener. Aside from last night's unfortunate events, what is it about Riverbend you don't like?"

"All my friends are in Chicago. There are things to do there. Dad thinks this is such a wonderful place. For him, maybe. But not for me."

"Have you given it a real chance?"

"I went to Meacham House, didn't I?"

"Yes. And it looked to me as if you were getting along all right."

"Not really." Libby set her menu aside when the waitress delivered the rolls. "Those kids are such freaks."

Lynn, affecting a nonchalance she didn't feel, picked up her fork. "All of them?"

"Well, certainly that Damon guy. What a creep!"

Lynn let that pass. "What about the others? Keri, for instance?"

Libby carefully tore off a corner of the roll and put it into her mouth. "She dresses funny, but she's okay."

"So you might give her a chance?"

"I guess I'll have to if we're going to that dumb Halloween party."

"Is bringing cheer to some senior citizens 'dumb'?" Lynn chewed contemplatively on a morsel of roll, waiting while Libby mulled over the question.

"Not the old people. That part's okay. But if I was at home, I'd be going to the football game."

"You're not home."

Libby looked straight at her, her neck stiff. "You keep saying that. I know I'm not home. So what's your point?"

"My point is that, whether you like it or not, you're here. I want to help you make the best of it."

"Fat chance."

Lynn carefully kept any anger out of her voice. "How do you feel about spending time with your father?"

With daintily crooked fingers, Libby pulled off another piece of the roll. "I dunno," she said tonelessly.

"I think you do know." Lynn prayed she wasn't pushing too hard.

"It's kinda weird being at his house." Lynn said nothing, hoping Libby would go on. "It's like he doesn't know what to do with us. Oh, we've done some stuff—fishing, shooting, hiking. But it's like, I dunno…" She screwed up her face in concentration. "He can't relax around us."

"Maybe he's scared."

"Scared? *Dad?*" Libby gave a brittle little laugh. "He's bailed out of a plane, had people shoot at him and all kinds of scary stuff."

"I'm not talking about that kind of scared. His physical courage is a given. But maybe there are other things he doesn't feel so confident about."

"Like what?"

"Being a father." Lynn deliberately took her time

chewing another bite. Watching Libby, it was as if she could actually see the wheels turning in her brain. "As I understand it, he hasn't had much experience. But I can tell you one thing." Libby looked up hopefully. "He's finally figured out he wants to be a good father."

"You think so?" The girl's voice wavered.

"I *know* so. Maybe you could help him out."

"How?"

"By not fighting him every step of the way."

"I haven't been."

"Haven't you?"

Libby licked her finger and lowered her eyes. Her thin shoulders protruded from the tank top she wore underneath her designer overalls, and Lynn's heart melted. The girl was trying so hard to maintain her stony defenses. "Maybe."

"Love is hard, isn't it?"

When Libby raised her eyes, Lynn was moved to see tears gathering. The girl, in an effort for control, merely nodded.

Giving Libby time to compose herself, Lynn went on, "It's hard for adults, too. The most difficult part is the risk. I mean, what if we show or tell someone we love them and they reject us? It hurts. Worse yet, it makes us afraid to risk exposing our feelings again. Nobody likes to be hurt." Just as she'd told Tom she loved him and... But she couldn't go there, not now. Getting through to Libby was too important. She spoke softly. "Did it hurt, Libby, every time your dad left to go on assignment overseas?"

With her finger Libby made circles in the gooey caramel frosting on her plate. "Yes."

"And when your parents got divorced?"

A nod.

"So you don't like saying goodbye. I don't blame you, especially when it's someone you love."

A noisy group of city street workers sat down in the adjacent booth, masking the awkward silence with guffaws and loud voices.

Lynn had to lean forward to hear Libby say, "What if Dad leaves again?" The vulnerability in her eyes was heartbreaking.

"He won't."

"How do you know?"

"You'll have to take my word for it. He has put his work and his other relationships all aside for one reason. You and Pete." Lynn picked up her paper napkin and dabbed her lips. "So do you think you could cut him some slack? Give him a chance?"

Another pitiful shrug.

"I know it's scary. But your dad is a brave man, and once he makes up his mind to do something, he's very good at it. Can you risk letting him love you?"

Libby picked up *Cold Sassy Tree* and clutched it to her small chest. "I'll try."

Lynn nodded and smiled. "Great. That's all anyone could ask."

The waitress put the check under the saltshaker and inquired if they wanted anything more. Lynn dug out change for a tip, then looked at Libby. "Ready to go back to the bookstore?"

"Yeah." The girl slid across the seat and stood up, the top of her head reaching only to Lynn's shoulder. "You must be a pretty good preacher," Libby said softly.

"Why do you say that?"

Libby's answer brought a huge grin to Lynn's face. "Because you ask such good questions."

Thank you, God. This conversation could have been a disaster. But Libby was quite the young woman. Lynn hoped she'd get an opportunity to know her better.

But that all depended on the results of her one very big risk. The risk of loving Tom Baines.

TOM SAT IN THE CAR outside Mitch and Sam Sterling's house late Wednesday afternoon waiting for his son to come out. When Pete had awoken yesterday morning in the hospital, he had complained groggily. He hurt. He hated Riverbend. And he particularly hated Tommy Lee. At first Tom had been puzzled, but finally Pete had made it clear that he'd identified Damon with the rock star. Despite his inclination to light into Pete, Tom had restrained himself, concluding he needed to let the pain medication wear off before they had a serious discussion of the incident. Besides, he needed more time to think about what Lynn had said.

Finally, on the way home from the hospital, when Pete had seemed more himself, Tom had spoken up. "It's time we talked about the situation. Help me to understand why you lashed out like that."

Pete had given him the usual rationalizations—the Meacham House teens were weird, the little kid had no business being there, it was Tom's fault for making him go. Then he'd said, "Besides, you couldn't care less. You took us there and then disappeared."

Tom admitted that by taking the aunts home and then going into the darkroom, he had seemed to disappear, but he argued the point about his concern for

Pete. "I'm sorry if you think I don't care. Nothing could be further from the truth."

Pete had merely grunted. Just before they'd reached the farmhouse, Pete spoke again. "What's wrong with that little kid?"

"Sam? He's hearing-impaired. But he reads lips. Can you imagine what he must've felt when you called him a weirdo retard?"

Nothing more had been said, but when Tom had gone upstairs last night to check on Pete before turning in himself, he'd found him lying on his back, his hands behind his head, staring through puffy eyes at the ceiling.

"You okay, son?"

"I'm thinkin' I should apologize to that Sam kid."

Tom sat on the edge of the bed and laid a hand on his son's shoulder. For once, Pete didn't wince when he touched him. "That would be the right thing to do."

"I'm not a bad person, you know."

"I know that." Tom listened to distant thunder, wondering how to phrase his next question. He decided the less said the better. "Damon?"

"*Him?*" Pete snorted. "What about him?"

"Don't you owe him an apology, too?"

"For what? He almost knocked my head off. No way."

Tom's shoulders sagged. From Pete's point of view, it was asking a lot. Then again, he needed to take responsibility for his part in the altercation. "I won't say any more tonight, Pete, but I want you to think about why things got out of hand. Then we'll talk about it tomorrow."

"If you think I'm gonna go crawling to that dude—"

Tom stood. "Tomorrow," he said with finality.

And now tomorrow had come. The day had passed, yet neither of them had raised the issue of Damon. Tom hoped fervently that Pete would spare him having to insist. Compelling him to apologize would simply widen the already serious breach between him and his son.

When Tom looked up, he saw both Mitch and Sam accompanying Pete to the car. Mitch held open the door for him and waited until Pete climbed in. Then, with a broad smile at Tom, he clamped the boy firmly on the shoulder. "This is a good kid you have here, Tom." He turned to Sam. "Right?"

"We're friends now," Sam said proudly.

"I'm glad," Tom said. "Thanks, Mitch, for giving Pete the opportunity to tell you how sorry we are."

"It's over," Mitch replied. "Forgotten."

Tom had driven several blocks before Pete said anything. "Sam doesn't have many friends."

"Is that what he told you?"

"Yeah." Pete seemed surprised by the concept. "I guess some of the kids his age make fun of him. He told me about how he'd like to be an athlete or a musician, but how that'll never happen." Pete looked out the window for a while. "I said we could be buddies. At least while I'm here."

"How about *whenever* you're here? I hope you'll be back often."

Tom drove along River Road back to the farm, encouraged that Pete hadn't said, "No way."

After last night's rain the fall foliage was particularly vivid, and the setting sun burnished the copper-orange of the oak leaves to a high luster. Even without Pete's next words, the sight was cause for optimism.

"Dad, I've been thinking."

"Yeah?" Tom held his breath.

"Do you know where Damon lives?"

"Uh-huh."

"Could you take me there?"

Tom executed one of the speediest U-turns in driving history. "You got it, son."

NOW WHERE HAD THAT DUMB IDEA come from? Pete wanted to talk to that Damon guy like he wanted to throw himself over Niagara Falls. Then there was this weird look in his dad's eyes. All soft and glowy. A friggin' Hallmark moment!

Damon was a creep, no denying that, and Pete hadn't the foggiest idea what he'd say to him when they got to his house. And getting there seemed to be taking forever. They went clear through town and into this ratty neighborhood where people had rusty old boats and dented cars parked in their front yards. Some of the houses had paint peeling off them, and this one dump had aluminum foil covering the windows. If he'd known Damon lived someplace like this, he might've changed his mind. But Dad was counting on him. Like this was a big deal.

When his father parked in front of some crummy garage, Pete asked, "Why are we stopping?"

"This is where Damon lives."

Pete looked around. "Where?"

His dad pointed at these ramshackle wooden stairs. "Up there. In the apartment over the garage."

"You're kidding, right?"

Tom stretched an arm across the back of the seat.

"No, Pete. I'm not." It was nearly dark, and only one dim-wattage bulb illuminated the steps. "Do you want me to come with you?"

Oh, sure, that'd be really cool. "No. I'm fine." He climbed out of the car and slammed the door.

An odor of motor oil and stale garbage greeted him at the foot of the stairs. As he climbed, he could hear faint canned laughter from a TV getting louder and louder. Was Damon hard of hearing, too? Pete drew in a thick breath and knocked on the door. Nothing. Just another outburst of audience hysteria. He knocked again. Louder. He figured that was plenty. If nobody was home, he could at least say he'd tried.

The door opened so suddenly Pete nearly fell inside. "What do *you* want?" Damon slouched in the entrance, holding a fork and a can of pork-and-beans and barring Pete from seeing much of anything except the tube and a sagging, mud-brown sofa.

"I was outta line Monday night," Pete mumbled.

"No kidding," Damon responded with a sneer. With the handle of his fork, he nudged Pete's face into the light of the entry lamp. "Gotcha good, didn't I? Serves you right, dork."

Pete pulled himself to his full five foot nine. "I *said* I was sorry."

"Let me give you a clue. Damon Hudson don't need no candy-ass preppie tellin' him which way is up. Got it?" Without losing eye contact, Damon spooned a forkful of beans into his mouth. "Did Daddy make you come?"

Pete was aware his hands were clenched at his sides. But no way was he going to give this jerk the satisfaction of getting his goat. "No. It was my idea."

"Gee, maybe you're not as dumb as I thought."

"Besides, my father and I don't get along. I make my own decisions."

Damon continued chewing. "Your old man seems like an okay guy to me."

"Well, lucky you." Pete had just about had enough. "Maybe you've had better experiences with fathers than I have."

"Ha! Mine?" Damon swallowed just before the beans were in danger of spewing out of his mouth. "The mysterious disappearing man? The one who calls a bar stool his office? That's rich."

For a brief moment Pete felt a weird kinship with this guy. "Look, I've said my piece. I'm going now."

"Don't do me no favors. See ya around."

And the door shut firmly in his face.

Okay, he'd done it, but he sure as hell didn't feel any better. Screw it!

RACHEL STOOD in the doorway of the guest bedroom, her mind going in several directions. "Papa's tuxedo isn't in here. Where could it be, Ruthie?"

Ruth emerged from her bedroom and stared at her twin as if she'd taken leave of her senses. "Good Lord, we haven't had it out in years. Why do you need it?"

"Tom just called. He's in a panic."

"Somehow I can't visualize our intrepid nephew in a panic."

Planting her fists on her hips, Rachel peered over her glasses. "Well, you didn't talk to him. I did. He needs Halloween costumes for Pete and Libby for Friday night's party at Golden Fields. I suggested Pete could be the Phantom of the Opera. That way his poor face won't be such a problem."

"Why didn't you say so in the first place?"

Rachel shook her head in frustration. "Because you didn't let me."

"Be that as it may, I've got another idea. Mama's opera cape."

Rachel relented and clapped her hands. "Great idea, and Papa's white gloves. But…"

"Where are they?" they both chirped at once.

"Let's try the trunk in the attic," Ruth suggested. "Maybe we can unearth one of Mama's old evening gowns for Libby."

They hurried up the attic stairs. "What about us?" Rachel paused at the top, panting.

"Us?"

"We're Meacham House volunteers, right? When was the last time we were at a costume party, Ruthie?"

Ruth hugged her sister impulsively. "Years and years. And you know what I think?"

"Yes, I do," Rachel responded smugly. "We'd better go while we can before we're the ones in the wheelchairs."

"Exactly," Ruth said, crossing to the old steamer trunk under the eaves.

Rachel hugged herself. This was going to be such fun!

LYNN LEANED BACK in the claw-foot tub in her tiny bathroom and laid her head against the rim, closing her eyes and relishing the delicious drowsy feeling induced by the hot water, fragrant with almond-scented bath oil. Had it been only this morning that Molly had called with the news about Damon and Pete? It seemed days since she'd been to the hospital.

And she would need days to process her conversations with Tom and Libby. It was next to impossible to maintain her objectivity where that family was concerned. Had her personal stake been too high? Had she overstepped her boundaries? Said too much?

Was she being foolish to wait for Tom? Once he finally got his situation with his kids straightened out and decided what kind of work he was going to pursue, what was to keep him in Riverbend? She opened her eyes with a start, realizing she'd never contemplated that obstacle. She reached back and fanned her hair over the edge of the tub. So many unknowns. Would he stay here? Could he give her emotional support in her work? Would he want more children?

And, of course, the big one. Did he love her?

Surely kisses don't lie. Or do they? His kisses. Just thinking about them was dangerous. Even though the water was still warm, she trembled. She wanted him as she had wanted no other. *Oh, please—*

The phone rang in the bedroom. She was tempted to stay where she was, but it could be Mae, who was extremely vulnerable now and who found lonely nights the worst. The phone rang a second time. She shoved herself up, grabbed a towel and stepped onto the bath mat, quickly drying herself before dashing to the phone, where she stood clutching the towel sarong-style. "Hello?"

"Reverend Kendall, this is Prentice Jewett." His solemn tone held no hint of amiability. She should've stayed in the sanctuary of the tub. But of course that had been out of the question. Now the other shoe would drop. "I just heard about the brawl Monday evening at Meacham House. What do you have to say for yourself?"

Thud.

CHAPTER TWELVE

LYNN HAD AGREED to take a carload of the Meacham House girls to Golden Fields an hour early Friday so they could decorate the activity center before the residents assembled. They stashed their costumes and several jack-o'-lanterns in her trunk and held the rest of the decorations on their laps, all except for the huge stuffed pumpkin. Tom was bringing it in the pickup.

"Do we have everything?" Lynn asked before they set out. "Masking tape? Staple gun? Candles?"

"I don't know where we'd put anything else," Angie said.

"You've got a point." Lynn turned on the ignition. "Okay, here we go."

Keri, sitting in the front seat, tuned in a radio station, and for several minutes the girls sang along with Shania Twain. In the rearview mirror Lynn observed Libby, who was smiling as she sang, her fingers snapping rhythmically, seemingly at ease with the group.

Angie punched Libby on the shoulder. "You go, girl. That's some voice you got."

"Yeah," Rosita Diaz, perched in the middle of the backseat, seconded. "You oughtta sing with a band."

Lynn risked another glance in the mirror. Libby was blushing. "I'm not that good."

Keri squirmed around to look at Libby. "Don't

gimme that crap. I'd give anything to sing like you do.''

''And I'd give anything to have your boobs.''

Lynn managed not to laugh and simultaneously keep the car on the road.

''These?'' Keri placed her hands under her breasts and hefted them. ''They're nothing but a pain. How would you like to look like me and be cursed with the last name of Mellon? It's not funny, I can tell you, but guys seem to think it's hysterical.''

''They're still better than nothing,'' Libby said. ''Which is what I've got. Boys never even look at me.''

Keri folded her arms, as if attempting to hide her breasts. ''Count your blessings, kiddo. They wanna do a lot more than look with me. It's disgusting.''

''Damon, too?'' Angie asked knowingly.

''He's different,'' Keri mumbled. ''At least when we're alone.''

Rosita leaned her elbows on the back of the front seat. ''Like how?''

Keri shrugged. ''I dunno how to explain exactly. He's not so tough.'' As if reluctant to say more on the topic, she cranked up the radio, effectively ending the discussion.

Amazing what you can learn when you keep your mouth shut, Lynn mused. Who would have thought that brazen, assertive Keri, who at times seemed to flaunt her sexuality, was so sensitive? And it wasn't too surprising that Libby at her age was concerned about her developing body and about boys. The fact that she had felt comfortable confiding her insecurity to the others gave Lynn a warm feeling. Libby had let her guard down, an encouraging sign.

Lynn ventured a remark. "I looked like a piece of string until the end of my sophomore year in high school."

Keri's jaw dropped. She adjusted the radio volume. "Well, the boob fairy certainly came through for you."

In the backseat, the other girls giggled. The Golden Fields sign was just ahead. Lynn flicked on her turn signal. "I used to wear these huge baggy sweaters, hoping no one would notice I was flat as a pancake. I didn't have a real date until I was a junior."

"I'll bet you don't have that trouble now," Rosita said.

"As a matter of fact, I don't date much."

"Why not? You're a hot-looking woman," Keri said.

Little was to be gained from telling them that a minister has more trouble attracting a man than the average woman. "Thank you for the vote of confidence. I guess I just haven't met the right guy."

"We'll fix that." Angie looked at the others as if soliciting their agreement. "Any of you guys know somebody for Reverend Lynn?"

Keri, Angie and Rosita began suggesting names, then arguing over suitability. Amid the babble, Lynn thought she heard Libby say softly, "I might." But the others didn't hear her, and then they arrived at the parking lot.

The girls piled out of the car, and after loading themselves with costumes, strings of cardboard ghosts and one or two skeletons, made their way to the main entrance of the retirement center. Libby fell into step beside Lynn. "They're not so bad," she said, nodding at the trio ahead of them.

"I know."

After several seconds Libby moved closer to Lynn. "Were you really flat-chested, or were you trying to make me feel better?"

Lynn chuckled. "I really was."

Libby looked up, a tentative smile bringing a sweetness and vulnerability to her expression. "Maybe there's hope for me, then. Thanks."

If her arms hadn't been full, Lynn would have given Libby a hug. Sometimes it was easy to forget that kids had a whole lot on their minds, not all of which was obvious to adults.

PETE STOOD IN A CORNER of the activity room observing, glad as hell that his half-mask covered the worst of his bruised face. Nathan's life-size ghost, propped in the doorway looked good, and the girls had done a pretty decent job of decorating this place. But, jeez, the old people. Some of them never changed expression except that their eyes would shift from side to side like tortoises checking to see if they could cross the road. Lots of the old ladies, though, seemed real excited and were making a big deal of the kids' costumes.

So far he'd been able to avoid Damon. Just as well. Damon wasn't wearing a costume and would probably laugh his ass off when he caught sight of Pete's old-fashioned cape and tux. Guy'd probably never heard of *Phantom of the Opera*. Anyway, old Damon was so busy acting like a hotshot photographer he maybe wouldn't notice.

Libby, who didn't look half-bad, for a sister, in the long dress Aunt Ruth had given her, and several of the other girls were distributing plastic jack-o'-

lanterns full of cough drops and tissues and junk like that to the residents. If that was the "treat," he'd hate to see the "trick."

Just then, those standing near the door began pointing and laughing. Pete stepped forward to see what the ruckus was about. And almost lost it. There, framed in the doorway, stood Aunt Rachel and Aunt Ruth wearing knee-length red-and-white-striped stockings, balloonlike bright blue knee-length pants, red suspenders and matching white shirts with huge red bows around their necks. On their frizzy gray heads they wore funny little hats with propellers on the top. Their cheeks were bright with spots of rouge. Aunt Ruth wore a sign that read Tweedledum, while Aunt Rachel's read Tweedledee. Pete had a vague recollection of his mother reading something like that to him when he was a little kid.

The aunts held their pose so that Damon, the "boy wonder" photographer, could snap away with his camera, then they laughed and started around the room greeting some of the old people. Prob'ly a bunch of their friends lived here. It was a nice enough place, he guessed, but he sure hoped the aunts didn't end up here. He felt a sudden twinge of guilt remembering he was in Riverbend because his mother was putting his grandmother in just such a place.

He noticed that his dad seemed to know a few of the folks here, too. Pete was glad his father hadn't made an idiot of himself dressing up. All he'd done was wear a cowboy hat, western shirt, jeans and boots. Not too embarrassing.

"Hey, Pete. Come join the party." Ms. Linden, looking kinda foxy in her Peter Pan suit, took hold of his arm. "I want you to meet Axel Morrison. He knew your grandmother."

And before he could say anything, she steered him over to a wheelchair-bound man with a carefully trimmed silver beard and piercing black eyes. Pete tried to avoid looking at the empty pant leg neatly pinned above the man's left knee.

"So you're Celia Steele's grandson, eh?" He extended his hand and they shook. "She was quite a gal. If your grandfather hadn't grabbed her, I'd have had a go myself."

Weird to think of this old geezer having the hots for his grandmother. "What was she like?"

After ten minutes Pete had learned more than he'd ever wanted to know. It was a relief, then, when Damon came up to him and said, "Hey, dork, lemme take your picture." He started walking toward the lobby. "Over here. I like the light."

He flipped off the overhead and moved a floor lamp so that it illuminated only one side of Pete's face. "I'm goin' for the sinister look. Stand still."

Damon fiddled with the camera settings, then had Pete tilt his chin. "This is stupid," Pete groused. "Hurry up."

"Hey, you look cool, man. Classy. This could be a great shot." When he clicked the shutter, Pete started back to the party.

"Not so fast." Damon looked up and down the hall. "Want a cigarette?"

His dad would kill him if he saw him smoking. Besides, Pete had tried it. The stuff tasted like crap. "Not particularly."

"Keep me company, then."

Pete hesitated. It was either go with Damon or go back to the golden oldies. "Okay."

Out in front of the retirement center was a row of metal lawn chairs. Pete remembered seeing a bunch of seniors sitting out here one time when he and his dad had driven past. Damon wasted no time lighting up. Then he threw back his head and exhaled three smoke rings. "Have a seat."

They sat side by side, their feet on the porch railing. Damon drew on his cigarette again. Out here in the cool night air, the tobacco didn't smell half-bad compared to that antiseptic smell inside. Pete didn't have a clue what to say. He'd said all he needed to the other day.

"You got guts, man."

Damon's words took him by surprise. His tone was almost admiring. "Me?"

"Yeah, you. See anybody else out here?" He took one last drag and flipped his cigarette expertly, end over end, into the flower bed bordering the porch. "Most guys wouldn't have apologized."

Pete fingered his sore cheek. "And most guys don't connect with such a kick-ass punch."

"Hurts, huh?"

"Not especially."

Strains of "Monster Mash" filtering from inside kept the silence from being awkward.

"You see much of your father?" Damon asked.

"No."

"Me, neither. Mine, I mean. He's either at work, sleeping or drunk."

Pete had a sudden flash of the dump where Damon lived. Of the can of pork-and-beans. He glanced sidewise at Damon, sitting with his shoulders hunched, his hair falling across his face. Pete felt a peculiar sense of allegiance to his dad. "Mine's not so bad, I guess."

Damon raked his fingers through his hair. "Hell, yours is great. Don't you like him?"

Pete considered the question. He didn't know whether he liked him or not. But an ache slowly grew inside him. Even if he didn't like him, he guessed he loved him. That was why it hurt so bad that he couldn't seem to get through to him. Maybe that was what made him so angry. Even old Damon could get his father's attention, spending time in the darkroom and stuff. But it was like the guitar. He'd told his dad yesterday he wanted one. And what had he said? "You've never shown any interest before. It's a big investment." Like his dad was poor or something.

Damon leaned over and cupped his ear in an exaggerated way. "Hey, I didn't hear you."

"That's because I didn't say anything."

"That heavy, huh?"

Pete looked into Damon's eyes, again registering with surprise the growing bond between them. He sighed. "Yeah, that heavy."

Damon was reaching for another cigarette, his hand poised at his pocket, when he cocked his head. The front door opened. "Boys, I've been looking for you." Ms. Linden looked faintly disapproving. "We need some more partners for 'Monster Mash.' We don't want any of our guests to be wallflowers."

Damon shot Pete a commiserating glance and muttered, "Jeez, Louise." Dutifully they followed her inside, where to Pete's amazement, the costumed teens had the old people, even the ones in wheelchairs, out in the middle of the floor gyrating to the thumping beat of the Halloween perennial.

"Yoo-hoo, Phantom!" A little raisin of a woman waggled her fingers at Pete. "May I have this dance?" she said, and then, honest to God, she—wait the word was coming—simpered. He gave himself a mental high five. *Simpered.* His finest pullout yet.

LYNN HAD BEEN so busy at the refreshment table, helping the youngsters fill cups and load plates for the residents, that she only now had time to survey the scene before her. In short, it was wonderful. Something about being in costume had helped the Meacham House kids overcome their initial shyness with the residents. Nathan was holding a woman by the elbows, her walker between them, swaying to one of the classic big-band numbers the kids had selected in deference to the elderly folks; Rosita sat at a table, helping a gentleman with palsied hands direct his cup of punch to his lips; and Pete, bless his heart, had in his arms a tiny little lady who daintily held up a corner of her long skirt as they swayed to the music.

Lily and Aaron Mazerik, their arms entwined, left the dance floor and approached the punch table. "You two still have that honeymoon glow," Lynn teased.

Lily looked adoringly at her husband. "I hope we always will."

Aaron gave his wife a killer smile and pulled her closer. "This is a great party, Lynn. The generation gap has all but disappeared."

"It was nice of you to come. Thank you."

"Wouldn't have missed it," Aaron said. "Besides, a couple of my students would've blacklisted me if I hadn't come to see their costumes."

Lily glanced at the refreshment table. "Do you need any help here?"

"No, I think we've served just about everyone. The kids can handle the rest."

"In that case," Aaron said, "I'm going to get my wife back out on the dance floor."

"You don't fool me. You just want to get your hands on her again."

Aaron pointed a finger at Lynn. "Bingo." With that, he gathered Lily and twirled across the floor.

Until that moment Lynn had done her best to avoid looking at Tom. No tall-drink-of-water Texan could've looked leaner, meaner or sexier than he did. He was lounging against the wall, his hat pulled dangerously low over his eyes, one foot cocked over the other, and it was all she could do not to rush over and drag him out onto the dance floor just to feel his arms around her. Until this moment it hadn't hit her how much she'd missed being alone with him since his children arrived. But then, being alone with him might not be all she hoped. Unfinished business stood between them.

As if reading her mind, he lifted a finger to his hat brim and nodded at her before shoving off from the wall and making his way through the crowd toward her. She hoped no one could overhear the timpani of her heart. Finally he stood before her, his eyes hungry, his voice husky. "I should have known. I like it."

"Like what?"

"Your costume." He touched the tip of her hood. "Little Red Riding Hood never looked *this* good."

She lowered her eyes in studied demureness. "Thank you, sir."

"Red's very becoming on you."

She wondered if that included the flush coloring her cheeks. Out of the corner of her eye she spotted Keri, dressed like a Gypsy fortune-teller, bearing down on them. On her way she motioned to someone. "Hey, Libby, come over here. Get Angie and Rosita."

Tom turned just in time to avoid having Keri run him down. He reached out and took hold of her shoulders. "Whoa, there. What's your rush?"

Keri looked somewhat embarrassed, but recovered when Libby joined her, trailed by Angie the witch and Rosita the ballerina. "I wanted to ask your opinion about an idea I—" she checked with the others, who all nodded "—er, we have."

Lynn stifled a grin. No telling what this group of connivers was up to.

In an affected Texas drawl, Tom said, "Well, ma'am, if ah can, ah'll be happy to oblige."

"Good." Keri looked smugly at the others.

"Go for it," Libby said softly.

Keri nodded, then, like an approving duenna, placed one hand at the small of Tom's back and one at Lynn's. "We think you should ask Reverend Lynn to dance."

"Why, ladies, if y'all will excuse me, ah'd be more than happy to step around the floor with this little lady." Then, sweeping his hat from his head, with a flourish, he said, "Miz Kendall, may ah have the honor of this dance?"

Lynn was flabbergasted, first that the girls would try such an obvious maneuver and second that Tom had gone along with the fun so obligingly. She hadn't seen much of his playful side before. She had no time though for further reflections, because Tom grabbed her elbow and escorted her to the center of the floor.

There, amid the witches, monsters and ghouls, he took her in his arms, just as she had imagined, and holding her closely, fit his body to hers and began moving to the music.

Her hood fell back, freeing her hair, and when he spun around, he pressed his chin to her temple. He was a breathtakingly good dancer, and she, who seldom had the chance to dance, felt detached and featherlike in his arms. Slowly she became aware that others had stopped dancing and had formed a circle around them. She caught sight of the aunts beaming, of Keri and the matchmakers giggling delightedly, and then, more disturbingly, of an unsmiling Pete standing with Damon.

Yet she was helpless to break the spell. The beautifully nostalgic strains of "Let the Rest of the World Go By" moved her even more profoundly than when she'd first heard it in the film *Out of Africa*. It so fit Tom. Like the singer, he, too, needed someone, good and true, with whom to find a place where he could forget, where he could indeed let the rest of the world go by. The haunting violin carried them, as lost in each other's arms, they danced until she barely had the wit left to pray she could be that someone.

Just as the last chord quivered in the air and before the onlookers started to applaud, she overheard Damon say, "Hey, dork, it looks like your dad's got the hots for Reverend Lynn."

"Will you friggin' shut up?" she heard Pete hiss. Then out of the corner of her eye, she watched as the boy made a hurried exit, stage left.

Tom dropped her hand. "Now what?" he muttered.

"Go to him, Tom. If he was jealous before, how do you think he feels now?"

Tom nodded his head, then threaded his way through the crowd toward the door where, to Lynn's horror, stood the last person she'd expected to see here tonight. Prentice Jewett.

"SON, WAIT A MINUTE." Pete was halfway down the walk to the parking lot before Tom finally caught up with him.

When he grabbed his son's elbow, Pete shook him off. "Leave me alone, will you?" The boy continued walking.

Tom maneuvered in front of him, blocking his path. "Not until we get a few things straight."

Pete ripped off his mask, revealing stony eyes. "Great. Now I have to listen to the fatherly lecture."

"I'm not here to lecture. I'm here to find out what's going on with you. With us."

"And what would that be? I'm here visiting because that's what Mom wanted us to do. I'm going home Sunday and you'll be rid of me. So what's to discuss?"

Tom felt exasperation threatening to choke off reason. "Maybe the fact that I love you. You're not a nuisance to me, you know."

"Gee, you coulda fooled me."

"Pete, I know I haven't been the world's best father." The withering look on Pete's face said it all. "I want our relationship to be different. Better."

"How?" Pete regarded him coldly.

"First I need to change some things about my life." Tom took a deep breath. "I need to stay in one place so I can spend more time with you and Libby. Be a part of your lives."

"Why start now?"

"Because now is all I have." He corrected himself. "All *we* have."

"What about Reverend Lynn? What was *that* all about?"

Tom plunged his hands into his pockets, wondering how the hell to explain when he didn't know the answer himself. "First of all, there will always be room in my life for you and Libby, and I intend to do a better job of proving that. Believe it or not, Pete, I'm not too old to learn a thing or two. I used to think I could take on the world single-handed. That I didn't need anyone else." He paused, searching for an explanation. "I was wrong."

At those words, his son turned and looked at him strangely, as if seeing a father he didn't know.

Tom struggled to continue. "I need my family and my friends. And I need that someone special."

Pete looked up. "Reverend Lynn?"

"Maybe." Tom cleared his throat. "I hope so. But she and I have quite a few things to work out first."

"It figures." Pete was giving no quarter. "So Damon was right, huh?"

"About?"

"You having the hots for her."

Tom pulled his hands out of his pockets and dared to drape an arm around his son. "That's one way to put it, I suppose." Tom started strolling back toward the retirement center, Pete at his side. It was good to be able to touch his son with affection. "What do you think about that?"

He felt Pete's shrug. "She's a nice lady, I guess." They walked a few more paces. "Does that mean you might stay in Riverbend?"

Taut muscles somewhere in the vicinity of Tom's

gut suddenly relaxed. A slow grin spread over his features. "Yeah, son, I think it does."

When they reached the porch, Tom spotted a furtive movement to their right. Damon putting out a cigarette. Tom chuckled to himself. Some things never change. How many clandestine smokes had he sneaked in his day?

"Hey, butthead, where ya been?"

Pete looked up to see if Tom was going to object to Damon's language. After a beat, Pete responded, "Talking with my dad."

"Lucky you," Damon replied. Tom looked at the boy. There was nothing in either his tone of voice or his expression that indicated sarcasm.

"I'll leave you here, son. I have a little unfinished business inside."

In Pete's eyes was the faintest glimmer of a smile. "Good luck."

TWEEDLEDUM ELBOWED Tweedledee. "Uh-oh. Here comes trouble." Ruth nodded toward the door.

"Saints preserve us," Rachel said, shaking her head. "What's Prentice doing here?"

"Who knows? But I don't like that look on his face. C'mon." Ruth grabbed her sister's hand and they made a beeline for their nemesis, who was charging directly toward Reverend Lynn, his face reddening with each step.

Rachel had no idea what her sister had in mind. All she knew was that somehow Prentice needed to be headed off.

"Prentice, why, what brings you here this evening?" Ruth trilled in a delighted falsetto. She clutched his arm with her free hand and maneuvered herself and Rachel between him and Lynn. "Isn't this a grand party?"

Prentice gaped. "What in tarnation are you two thinking? You look ridiculous in those outfits." He harrumphed. "Grown women," he muttered.

Rachel pasted on her most welcoming smile. "We're Tweedledum and Tweedledee."

"And I'm the Mad Hatter, emphasis on the *mad*." He craned his neck to look beyond the twins. "Where's Reverend Kendall? She's making a mockery of these senior citizens. Whose idea was this, anyway?"

Out of the corner of her eye, Rachel saw Lynn making her way toward them. "I think the staff of Meacham House is to be commended. We're all having a grand time. Why, even old Mrs. Hankins did the Monster Mash and—"

"The *what?*" Rachel had only thought Prentice was red-faced before. Now he was positively beetlike. "She could've had a heart attack right on the spot."

"Prentice," Ruth said acerbically, "the staff approved the party and they've been on duty. Somehow I think they're more qualified than you to judge the suitability of this affair."

"Besides," Rachel added, "better to have a heart attack having fun than to expire of boredom."

Prentice threw the sisters a scathing look just as Lynn reached them.

"Prentice, how kind of you to drop by." Lynn's smile didn't conceal the worry in her gray eyes. Rachel held her breath.

"Kind, is it? I see that nothing I said to you in our little meeting yesterday made a bit of difference."

Lynn's voice was steady. "I told you then and I'll

tell you now—this program deserves a fair trial. We can already point to positive results.''

"Like what?'' He gestured helplessly around the room. "Upsetting a bunch of old people?''

"Upset? Who's upset?'' Axel Morrison rolled his wheelchair between Prentice and Lynn. "About what?'' He looked around. "This? Why, Jewett, it's the best thing that's happened here since they got rid of that sorry excuse for a cook.''

Rachel pursed her lips, not daring to smile. The twinkle in Ruth's eyes was unmistakable. *Sometimes God just steps in and takes a hand.* She censored the thought. She didn't mean to be blasphemous. Although with that elegant beard, Axel did look a bit like Moses.

Axel clamped a hand on Prentice's arm. "You've met Reverend Lynn, of course. Great things she's doing with our young people, if you ask me. Why, I've half a mind to help 'em out at Meacham House. The reverend here—'' he nodded in Lynn's direction "—was telling me about some needs you have over there.''

At the *you,* Rachel noticed Prentice cringe. But he couldn't afford to cross Axel, who was the major investor in Jewett's real-estate holdings.

"I'm thinkin' about donating a van for the kids so they can go on field trips. And your preacher here, she told me they could use a—whaddaya call it?'' He looked inquiringly at Lynn.

"A scanner for our computer.''

"Right, and you could probably use another computer or two maybe?''

"That would be very welcome.'' Wonder was written all over Lynn's face.

Axel smiled broadly at Prentice. "So ante up, Jewett. Help the kids out. Tell Reverend Lynn you're good for the computer stuff."

Rachel had to hold a hand over her mouth. This was too delicious. Prentice's eyes bulged and his cheeks went in and out, but finally he choked out his answer. "I'll send a check first thing Monday morning."

Axel winked conspiratorially. "It's only fair, Jewett. After all, think of the trouble you and I used to get into."

At that point, Ruth piped up, a mischievous grin on her face. "Yes." She eyed Prentice pointedly. "Just think."

BY THE TIME Tom returned to the activity room, the party was breaking up. Earlier he had noticed Prentice Jewett and was surprised to see he was still there. Tom hoped the man had been visiting a friend, not causing trouble.

He sidestepped aides who were wheeling some residents back to their rooms while some of the kids assisted those who were ambulatory. Molly, Lily, Aaron and Lynn were packing the decorations into sacks and boxes as the teens handed them over. Libby, Angie and Keri were huddled around Axel Morrison, and at one point, he heard Keri say, "Cool. Now we can have photos in our newsletter."

Ruth and Rachel sat at one of the tables, their heads together, absorbed in conversation. Tom wondered if they ever ran out of topics. When they spotted him, they motioned for him to join them. "Have we got news for you!" Ruth crowed. Then Rachel filled him on Jewett's latest comeuppance.

When she finished, Ruth surveyed the room. "Where's Pete?"

"Outside. With Damon."

"Damon?" they chorused.

Tom chuckled. "An unlikely pair. It's funny, though. I think they'll be good for each other."

"I think so, too." Rachel patted Tom's hand. "Rather like you and your cousin," she added wistfully.

Ruth suddenly straightened and looked over their heads toward the hall. "Hmm, I wonder what that's all about?"

"What?" Tom followed his aunt's line of vision.

"Lynn. She just went racing out, looking very worried. I hope it's not trouble."

Tom jumped to his feet and went after Lynn, who began running once she cleared the front door. "Lynn," he called. But she was already too far away to hear him. He hesitated, heard an engine sputter to life and then watched her car pull out of the parking lot onto the main road.

"Tom?" Aaron laid a hand on his shoulder. "Lynn had an emergency call from the hospital. She seemed unusually rattled. Stayed only long enough to ask me to tell you, so you could take Libby home since she came with Lynn. Lily and I will drive Damon and the other girls."

Tom registered one word. "Rattled?"

"Yeah. Lynn's usually pretty calm, especially in emergencies. But she looked about ready to cry."

Without making a conscious decision, Tom started toward the parking lot, backpedaling to speak to his cousin. "Aaron. Change of plan. Please ask our aunts to keep Libby and Pete until I get back." Something powerful was propelling him toward his car. Something he had no right to question.

"Go," Aaron said. "I think Lynn needs you."

Tom was halfway to the hospital before he realized he'd referred to Ruth and Rachel as *our* aunts. Naturally. Without thinking about it.

CHAPTER THIRTEEN

TOM SPOTTED Lynn's car under a halogen lamp in the hospital parking lot beneath a sign reading Reserved for Clergy. He circled until he found a place near the street. How many times had she been called for this kind of duty? Not knowing whether she would be dealing with the living or the dead? Yes, she, too, was well acquainted with death. How arrogant he'd been to suppose he had a corner on it. Violent or peaceful, it was still death. Still a wrench for loved ones left behind. What had she found tonight?

He hurried through the double automatic doors and found himself in the brightly lit emergency-room waiting area. A burly man with bloodshot eyes and a day's growth of whiskers sat in a corner staring into space. A worried young couple holding an obviously sick youngster across their laps didn't even look up. The irritating hum of vending machines was the only sound, besides the child's whimpering. He stepped up to the reception window and waited impatiently, thrumming his fingers on the laminated surface. Finally a woman dressed in maroon surgical scrubs entered the cubicle. She had a harried air about her, but paused long enough to say, "May I help you?"

"I hope so." His chest felt tight. "I'm looking for Reverend Lynn Kendall."

"She's with a patient right now." She eyed him

quizzically. "Do you want to wait? She may be a while."

Again that weird stomach lurch. He didn't even know what was wrong, but intuitively he knew whatever it was, it was bad. And that somebody needed Lynn far more than he did. He glanced around for a pay phone. Spotting one, he said, "Yes. I'll wait."

He made a quick call to Ruth and Rachel's, explained the situation, told them he might be very late and asked them to keep the kids overnight. That done, he helped himself to a cup of stale coffee, picked up a dog-eared copy of *Golf Digest* and tried, unsuccessfully, to read.

His conversation with Pete pecked away at him. He'd more or less committed to staying in Riverbend. Close to Chicago and close to Lynn. Close to home? All kinds of people—Uncle Abe, his aunts, Mitch Sterling, hell, even Aaron—had made it home. Almost all his childhood associates. Except for Jacob. He looked at the ceiling. A longing, born of memories and nourished by hope, welled up. Could he make Riverbend his home? Even…his and Lynn's?

Across from him, the parents shifted their son, who cried out in his fitful sleep. Just then a nurse appeared in the door. "Mr. and Mrs. Hayes, we'll see Parker now." The mother sagged in relief, while the father lovingly cradled his son in his arms.

"Good luck," Tom said softly.

The father paused. "Have kids of your own?"

With an ache in his heart, Tom nodded. "Two."

"Then you know how it feels. Thanks." The three of them disappeared beyond the partition.

Setting the magazine aside, Tom steepled his fingers and placed them against his lips. Did he? Really?

Know how the worried parents felt? Selena would for sure. What had she handled on her own that he never even knew about?

Pete had every reason to be skeptical of him. Tom knew he'd still make a few mistakes, but maybe that was what parenting was all about. Making mistakes and going on, anyway, because you love your kids.

After fifteen more minutes, the same nurse reappeared. ''Mr. Jankowski?''

''Yeah?'' The man in the corner stood up.

''We've moved your mother to a room. You can see her now. Please follow me.''

The silence closed around Tom. He couldn't imagine what could be taking Lynn so long. Then the image came to him of her leaning over Pete's bed, of the calm and compassion she exuded, of his gratitude to her for touching his son when he had not thought to do so. Someone else needed her now. Just as he had. Just as others would. Who was he to question or begrudge her gift? Especially when, he realized with sudden clarity, that was one of the main reasons he loved her.

The hands of the overhead clock crawled to eleven. A few minutes later the woman in the maroon scrubs poked her head through the window. ''Sir, the chapel is open. Perhaps you'd be more comfortable there. It's down the hall on your right.''

More comfortable? He doubted it, but the cafeteria was closed and he'd welcome a change of scene. ''Thanks. I'll give it a try.''

His cowboy boots echoed in the empty corridor. Near the end was a sign reading All Faith Chapel. He pulled open the door and stood in the back of the small sanctuary, just big enough for an altar and six rows of pews on either side of the center aisle. The dim interior lights contributed to the comforting aura of the place. He slipped into the far side of the back pew and sat quietly. Muted spotlights were focused on a Star of David and a cross on the wall behind the altar, above which an illuminated stained-glass window, rich in rainbow crimsons, golds and sapphires, carried the message "Peace to all who enter here."

Tom sighed, then rubbed his hands up and down his denim-clad thighs. Admittedly there was a different kind of silence here. Not the humming quiet of the waiting room, but a hush, both expectant and calming. He fingered the worn velvet of the pew cushion, wondering how many had sat here beseeching their God to heal pain, end suffering.

He stretched out his legs, leaned into the corner and closed his eyes. Lynn. Almost subconsciously he found himself saying over and over again in his mind, *Please be with her, please be with her.*

THE FORMLESS MASS crowded her lungs, pressed against her throat. Somehow Lynn managed brief polite farewells to the night-shift personnel before turning the corner and hurrying toward the chapel. If she could just get there before…before… She grabbed the cool metal handle, opened the door and sank gratefully into her customary place in the second row. It was coming. She wasn't going to be able to control herself any longer. She pulled down the kneeler and sat forward, gripping the pew in front of her and resting her forehead on the smooth wood. "Oh, God. Oh, God."

The mass gave way in a cataclysmic sob, and Lynn yielded at last, releasing the bottled-up anguish of this horrible night, succumbing to the temptation, so long and necessarily held at bay, to cry out her guilt and loss.

Her shoulders shook and the tears came, flowing in runnels down her cheeks. She sucked in breath after gasping breath, helpless to stop. She fumbled in her skirt pocket for a tissue, then wiped at her eyes, which continued to rain tears. Another paroxysm seized her and she bent nearly double with the painful emotions.

Why hadn't she seen it coming? It should never have happened. What could she have said? Done?

Slowly she eased back and contemplated the window and its proclamation. *Peace to all who enter.* She prayed it would be so.

When she calmed her breathing, she had a strong sense she was not alone. Looking around, her eyes widened, and then, when she recognized Tom, began streaming once more. He slid into the pew beside her and gathered her into his arms, cradling her head against his shoulder, smoothing her hair away from her face, murmuring soothing syllables in her ear. She couldn't stop shaking, couldn't stop crying. ''There, there,'' he whispered. ''It'll be all right.'' She nestled closer, seeking his warmth, pulling strength from the storehouse of his arms.

She didn't know how long she stayed protected by his embrace. It could've been seconds or minutes. She only knew that gradually her tears abated and her breathing slowed and became even and calm.

At last she raised her head and found his eyes, molten with concern. ''Oh, Tom. Thank you for coming. I've never needed anybody so much in my whole life.''

''Anybody?'' His voice sounded thick.

"You." She buried her head in his neck, inhaling the special scent that was Tom. Only Tom.

He ran his hand up and down her arm. Finally he tilted up her chin. "Can you talk about it?"

She lowered her lashes, bit her lip, then locked her gaze on his. "Remember the night I had to leave you and respond to an emergency?"

He nodded.

"Mae Farrell's husband had just left her. I've done everything I knew to help her. Referred her to counselors, social workers." Her breath hitched. "But it wasn't enough." She felt his hand on her face, his thumb wiping away fresh tears. "She committed suicide tonight." She clutched his arms. "Tom, I couldn't do anything to save her."

FINALLY HE PERSUADED LYNN to let him take her home. They left his truck and took her car. He figured she shouldn't be alone. Besides, he didn't want to leave her. In the morning he could walk from her house to the aunts' and get one of them to take him back to the hospital.

Lynn permitted him to lead her outside like a child. During the silent ride to her house, she huddled close to him, winding a tissue around and around her fingers.

When they reached her front porch, she was still so shaky she couldn't insert the key in the lock. "Here, let me do it." Tom took the key and opened the door, then stood aside to let her in.

She paused, then said, "Thank you, Tom. I don't know what I'd have done without you."

"I'm coming in." He put his hand at the small of

her back and nudged her over the threshold. "You shouldn't be by yourself tonight. I'm staying."

"But Pete and Libby—"

"They're at Ruth and Rachel's. End of discussion." He removed her red cape, no longer a symbol of playfulness, and led her to the living-room sofa. He sat her down, gathered the afghan around her, then picked up Benedict, who had been meowing fiercely at his feet, and placed him in Lynn's arms. "Tea or coffee?" he asked.

She managed a wan smile. "Tea, I think."

He left her and went to the kitchen, filled the kettle and located the tea bags. While he waited for the water to boil, he leaned on the counter trying desperately to sort out his emotions. She needed *him?* Throughout their relationship, he'd assumed she didn't need anyone. That she had it all together. She always seemed so capable, so...hell, perfect. Tonight had shaken him to the core. He'd felt helpless in the face of her massive need. Yet she'd clung to him, holding on to him in a way that made him, at the same time, feel almost indispensable to her.

The kettle whistled just as the lightbulb went on in his head. He needed her, too. Life without her was unimaginable. He grabbed the kettle from the burner. In the sudden silence he realized he was as scared as he'd ever been. Scared of being that needful of another human being. *Human being.* Yes, that was what she was. All she was. A human being, not a saint. The thought was reassuring. A beautiful, loving, giving human being. And she needed him.

He dropped tea bags into two mugs, then poured the water over them, watching intently as the liquid in the cups grew deeper and richer in color. The comforting aroma calmed him. Finally it was ready. He carried the mugs into the living room and set them on the coffee table. He studied her closed eyes, her ivory complexion dusted with faint freckles. Her lids fluttered, then she smiled gratefully.

"Here," he said. She scooted upright, her back against the arm, snugged the afghan around her and nodded at the space at the other end of the sofa. He settled in the indicated spot, an arm stretched across the back of the couch.

She reached for her mug, then took a sip. "Mmm." She pulled up her knees and balanced the mug on them. "I feel better now, thanks to you."

He studied her thoughtfully before speaking. "Lynn, you can't save everybody."

"I know," she said sadly. "But I try, and it hurts when I can't."

"Yeah. I, of all people, ought to know."

Her eyes found his. "Gordy?"

He nodded. "Maybe that's one reason I've been so disillusioned. Up till then, I'd managed to steel myself, hell-bent on getting a story. Maybe even looked on the wounded and dead as nothing but statistics. That might have made me a more objective journalist, but it didn't make me a better man. Then, like a big wake-up call, came the explosion. Once I permitted myself to relate to events on a personal level, I lost myself."

"And now?"

He considered her question. "I'm feeling my way along. But...I think I'm going to be okay."

She blew on the hot tea. Several moments elapsed. "Maybe we all have our private hells. You, me, Mae, Pete, Libby."

"So how do we face them?"

She looked up, a tiny grin playing on her lips. "Don't do that, Tom. Don't look to the minister for all the answers."

"I'll bet the woman has an opinion, though, right?"

"Okay." She sobered. "How do we face them? Never alone. Always together."

He set down his cup, then slowly and deliberately relieved her of hers and set it aside. His eyes never leaving her face, he took hold of the afghan, pulled her close and reclined into the cushions. She settled against his chest with a contented sigh. He kissed her forehead. "I like the sound of that. Together."

Within a few minutes she was asleep, but he continued holding her, thinking about what he needed to do to assure that never again would she be alone when she had need of him. Or when he had need of her. He moved his hand gently over her back, grateful for the gift she had given him tonight. Her vulnerability.

He, too, had nearly drifted off when he became aware of something soft rubbing against his head. He blinked. To his amazement, Benedict lay curled up beside his head purring with what sounded like feline approval. Tom chuckled softly. Maybe there was indeed hope if he'd succeeded in winning over her cat.

SELENA CALLED TOM at home late the next morning. She said she'd gotten her mother settled and would be returning to Chicago the following afternoon in time for Pete and Libby to come home to attend school on Monday. He realized he'd be disappointed to see them go. After the disastrous start, Tom figured the week hadn't gone too badly. He hadn't made giant steps with them, but he hadn't expected to. He'd happily settle for the tiny cracks developing in their armor.

"Hey, guys," he said, walking out onto the porch where they were carving jack-o'-lanterns for Mitch Sterling's annual Halloween pumpkin-carving event, "your mother called, and I'll be taking you home tomorrow."

"Good," Pete mumbled as he wedged the paring knife into the thick top of the pumpkin.

"How's Grandma?" Libby asked, a worried frown creasing her brow.

"She's comfortably settled, your mom says."

Libby set down the pen she was using to draw a face on her pumpkin. "Do you think her place is as nice as Golden Fields?"

"Nice?" Pete scoffed as he worked at hacking out a lid. "Don't be stupid. Nobody wants to go to one of those homes."

Tom eased down onto the top porch step. "For some people, it's the best alternative. Aging is no fun, but you're given good care, and you get to meet a lot of interesting people—like those you met last night." Pete looked skeptical.

"I liked Mr. Morrison," Libby said.

Tom nodded. "Yeah, he's quite a guy. But to answer your question, yes, I'm sure your grandmother's place is nice, too, and that she's getting good care."

He watched Pete dislodge the top of the pumpkin, then dig into the pithy center, coming up with a handful of seeds and stringy pulp. "Look, Libby. Guts!" He threw several strands at his sister.

She shrank back. "Gross. You're disgusting."

"Before you start a pulp fight, there's something I'd like us to talk about." Tom's dry throat closed. It was pretty serious when you couldn't even talk to your own kids without suffering an attack of nerves.

"Yeah, what?" Picking up a large spoon, Pete continued his disembowelment.

"I was wondering how you'd feel about coming here to visit on a regular basis." They both looked up at him. He rattled on. "Of course, I'd come to Chicago, too. Often. I want to see you play tennis, Pete, and come to your swim meets, Libby. And anything else you invite me to."

Libby pulled her pumpkin into her lap and wrapped her arms around it. Her eyes were big and she was biting her lower lip.

Pete simply continued scraping the inside of his pumpkin. Dead leaves, disturbed by the wind, rattled against the base of the porch, and the odor of wet pumpkin filled Tom's nostrils. The sound and smell of disappointment. He'd been foolish to think one week could turn around years of neglect.

Libby spoke first. "How do we know that..." She hesitated.

"I'll follow through?" Tom finished her thought.

She hung her head. "Yeah."

"First of all, because I'm not going anywhere."

She looked up wonderingly. "You're not?"

"No." He glanced sideways at Pete, whose lower lip jutted out in concentration as he continued scraping an already hollowed-out pumpkin. "Second, because I want to be here for you in whatever way I can. I told Pete last night that I'd made a lot of mistakes in my life. Not putting family first was one of them. But I hope I'm not too old to learn, to change." He swallowed. "And finally, because I love you guys even more than I realized."

Pete's head jerked up and Libby's eyes filled with tears. "You do?" Her voice quavered.

"I'm sorry I ever gave you occasion to doubt it. So what do you think? Can we start fresh from today?"

Libby played with the stem of her pumpkin, as if considering the matter. Finally she said quietly, "Yes. I think we can."

"Pete?" His heart pounded as he waited for his son's answer.

"How do I know you'll come?"

Tom laid a hand on Pete's shoulder. "Because I am making you a solemn promise."

"And we'd have to come visit you in Riverbend?"

"It's not so bad," Libby piped up. "And Meacham House is cool."

"It'd be better if I had a guitar." Pete, the opportunistic little scoundrel, looked right at Tom.

"I'd like you to be enthusiastic about visiting with or without a guitar."

He pouted. "What about Reverend Lynn? Will she be here, too?"

Libby stared at her brother. "Reverend Lynn? What are you talking about?"

"Didn't you seem 'em last night, dorkess? All mushy-gushy?"

"*See* them? Keri and us girls got them together."

Pete flipped his spoon at his sister. "I don't think so. The way they were lookin' at each other, I'd say they already had something going. Am I right?"

Tom laughed and held up his hands in surrender. "I can see I'm going to have to get up pretty early in the morning to put anything past you."

Libby edged closer to him and rested her head on his shoulder. "It's fine with me, Dad. I like her a lot."

"I do, too," he whispered. "I do, too."

Pete gathered up the newspaper with the pumpkin mess and stood up. "Then do something about it, for crying out loud." Then he walked down the steps past Tom, headed for the garbage can in the garage.

Tom sheltered his daughter in his arms, pondering Pete's challenge. He had a few loose ends to tie up before he could "do something about it," but if he hadn't already had a powerful incentive, his kids had given him one. Their approval.

LYNN BOWED HER HEAD in silent prayer as she always did before entering the church for a service. She gave thanks for the colorful Sabbath morning—the brilliant blue of the October sky, the panoply of fall foliage, the crisp bite of the cool air—for the opportunity to love and serve and for all those who had touched her life in special ways. She opened her eyes and picked up her hymnal and service leaflet. This had been a particularly rich week for having her life touched—Axel Morrison, the girls at Meacham House, the aunts, even Prentice Jewett. But especially Tom. She clutched the hymnal to her chest as the first chords of the opening hymn sounded.

She had never realized before quite how *much* she loved him, not only because of their powerful physical attraction, but because he helped her laugh and play in joyous times, and gave her comfort and support in sad ones. Love, Tom's love and hers for him, was something rare and beautiful. Something to cherish.

At this early service, there was no processional. When the congregation began singing "Morning Has

Broken,'' she entered from the side and took her place at the top of the chancel steps. At the conclusion of the hymn, she looked out over her flock—and found herself momentarily speechless, unable to utter the words of the opening prayer. There, in the third row, sat Pete, Libby and Tom, gazing expectantly at her. Her eyes filled, and she sent them a smile she hoped conveyed the love in her heart.

With difficulty she drew her concentration back to the worship service, but once engaged, the familiar words took over and she managed to conduct the service with a heaven-sent grace, especially welcome when she led a prayer for the repose of Mae Farrell's soul. When she faced the congregation to give the benediction, she was humbled again, as she was every time, by this role to which God had called her. A moment of silence followed, then Rachel Steele pulled out all the stops for ''All Things Bright and Beautiful,'' the recessional.

As was her custom, Lynn waited outside the front entrance to greet those who'd attended the service. She understood that the ''nice sermon'' comments were usually perfunctory, but every so often someone would address a specific way her words had lifted their spirits or spoken to a need. She treasured these few moments when she could reach out and touch each person individually.

She noticed Tom and his children loitering in the foyer, letting the stragglers go ahead of them. Finally the threesome approached. Pete was first. ''Good morning,'' she said. ''It's a treat to have you here.''

''We had to get up awful early,'' he mumbled as she took his hand.

Libby threw her brother a disgusted look, then elbowed him out of the way. "Don't pay any attention to him. We had to get up early, anyway." Laughing, Lynn put her arm around Libby and gave a gentle squeeze.

Tom stood just beyond his daughter. The way he was staring at Lynn, intently and lovingly, turned her legs to limp noodles. "Their mother is home. I'm taking them back to Chicago today." He hesitated. "They, er, wanted to say goodbye."

She couldn't resist. She smiled mischievously and asked, "Is that the reason you came this morning?"

He locked his eyes on hers and smiled back, as if he was playing along with her, but also as if he had something very important to convey. All he said was, "That, too."

Neither the ringing of the church bells, nor the conversational hubbub on the church lawn distracted them from holding each other's gaze.

Libby broke the spell by throwing her arms around Lynn's neck. "I'm coming back soon."

Over Libby's shoulder, Lynn saw Pete raise a hand. "See ya."

"I'll call you later," Tom said as he turned to leave.

Libby remained beside Lynn, watching her father and brother. "Guys are such dorks," she commented.

Lynn chuckled. "Not all of them."

Libby glanced up at her. "Not Dad?"

"Definitely not your dad."

A huge metallic smile broke across Libby's face. "Good. That means you'll risk letting him love you, right?"

"Oh, honey, that's exactly what it means."

"Good," Libby said before joining Tom and Pete on the sidewalk.

Lynn stood in the doorway of the church, the breeze ruffling her hair and lifting the hem of her robe. Then she looked skyward. "Indeed, Lord, You do make all things wise and wonderful. Thank you."

CHAPTER FOURTEEN

BEFORE IT WAS TIME to begin the organ prelude prior to the later service, Rachel located Ruth in the church fellowship hall where she and Molly Linden were holding the ends of a banner while Lily Mazerik stood back, assessing how high to hang it. "Over that way a little." Lily cocked her head. "Perfect!" She beamed, and Ruth and Molly affixed it to the wall with thumbtacks.

Meacham House
Open House
Sunday, October 22

Rachel hoped Molly and Lynn would have a good turnout for the event, their first attempt to showcase the programs and, more particularly, the talents of the teens. The Halloween party at Golden Fields had been a good start toward helping folks think positively about Meacham House, and if the open house went well, perhaps even the doubters would change their tunes.

As soon as Ruth finished her task, Rachel pulled her off to the side. Ruth, ever the gregarious twin, hissed, "What's so all-fired important? I need to visit with Lily about helping with the open house art exhibit."

"This won't take a minute." Rachel rubbed her palms together in anticipation.

"Well, don't stand there grinning at me like you just gave birth or something. Out with it."

Rachel permitted herself a smug smile. "Guess who was in church this morning?"

Ruth raised an eyebrow. "No. I'm not playing guessing games. I'll be here all morning."

"Hmm, you could be right. Because you'll never guess."

"Then tell me."

Rachel could see that her sister was losing patience. "Aren't you going to beg even a teeny bit?"

"This better be good." Ruth crossed her arms and tapped her foot impatiently. "Okay, I'm begging. Who was in church this morning?"

"The Baines family."

Rachel took gleeful satisfaction from watching her twin's eyes pop and her mouth drop open. *"Tom?"*

"Know any other Baineses?" Rachel took one last look at her sister's stupefied face before heading toward the choir robing room. She'd let Ruth stew for a while before she added the best part. *The way Lynn and Tom had looked at each other.* It was enough to make tone-deaf angels sing.

THE FOLLOWING SATURDAY MORNING Tom sat hunched over his computer desperately trying to get words to flow. Earlier in the week he'd attempted to write a travel piece about Vancouver, one of the places he'd visited before coming home to Riverbend, and had ended up scrapping it. He'd focused, instead, on a profile of a politician he admired. But that wasn't coming together, either. Besides, he wasn't interested in traveling to Washington, D.C., to interview the subject. He had too many things going on here. He leaned back and let his gaze wander to the window and the idyllic Indian-summer day.

He had a sudden, fierce longing for Lynn. It was a day to play in the leaves, eat candied apples and take a long walk in the woods. It would be a night to build a fire, drink hot chocolate and kiss the whipped cream off her nose, before nipping lower and lower... He cursed under his breath. These thoughts were serving little good except to increase the ache in his groin.

Restless, he stood and walked out to the porch, where he inhaled deeply in an attempt to clear his mind of distracting and arousing thoughts. Lynn had left yesterday with a group from the church to participate in the charity bike ride she'd been training for. He supposed this was only one of many times she'd have to go off and leave him. He grinned, then, just thinking about the kinds of little reunions they could have, about the ways he would show her just how glad he was to see her. Ways he hoped would light up her eyes, cause her breathing to quicken, elicit tiny whimpers of pleasure.

He groaned. This was not a helpful train of thought, either. Sexual satisfaction was the least of his worries, but that, too, might soon improve. Just as soon as he figured out what he was going to do. He was a writer, for heaven's sake. Surely he could think of something.

His eyes narrowed. In the distance he saw Shep's ramshackle truck approaching. He walked down the steps and was waiting at the edge of the drive when Shep slowed to a stop.

"Thought I'd bring your mail," Shep said, and proffered the bundle through the open window.

"Thanks," Tom said, taking it. "How's Dorrie?"

"Missing those kids. And I'm suffering for it. I've already gained five pounds eating the leftover cookies."

Tom watched while Shep unwrapped a piece of gum and carefully folded the foil before popping the stick in his mouth. Tom knew the signs. Something was on Shep's mind. He waited.

"So how are you and the reverend gettin' along?" Shep asked. "I been noticin' she's a regular visitor here."

Whether it was his own question or one Dorrie had put him up to didn't matter. They were his friends. "Cross your fingers for me, Shep. I may not be good enough for her, but I'm going to do my damnedest to make her happy."

Shep's cracked lips spread in a grin that exposed a number of stained teeth. "Can't think of anybody better to do it, son."

The vote of confidence meant a lot, because more than anything, Tom wanted to be worthy of Lynn, to be the kind of man who put his wife and family first. "Thanks, Shep."

The older man's lined face wrinkled further with a frown. "She know how you feel?"

"I'm working on it."

Shep nodded his head several times in approval. "Okay, then. See you in church tomorrow." And before putting the truck in gear, he gave Tom a broad man-to-man wink.

Walking back to the house, Tom sifted through the mail, pausing when he came to the envelope bearing Irish postage. *Terence.* The memory blindsided him, as it no doubt always would. He slit the envelope with a knife, then sat back down at his desk and began reading.

Dear Tom,
Thank you for your letter. I liked hearing about Riverbend and about the boys and girls at Meacham House. I wish we had a Meacham House. Then I would have more friends. I live far from school. I can't play much as the bus ride is so long. Also, since the explosion, I don't always hear very well. Some of my classmates make fun of me. Terry Whadjasay, they call me. Ma says to ask if you are well. I hope someday you will come visit me again.

Your friend,
Terence

Tom stared at the letter, saddened by the boy's pain and isolation, and maddened by the insensitivity of his peers. If only he could do something to help. Terence did, indeed, need a Meacham House. Just like Damon, Keri, Sam...

Sam. *There* was an idea. He thumbed through the phone directory till he found *M. Sterling*. He dialed and waited anxiously. Mitch picked up on the fourth ring. "Hey, Mitch. It's Tom. Got a question for you. How would Sam like a pen pal?"

When he concluded the conversation, Tom sat back in satisfaction. It was a natural. Communicating by mail made anybody's hearing impairment irrelevant. And friendships, he knew, could span time and distance.

Friendships. His friendship with Gordy. Tom's fingers hovered over the keyboard, then slowly began tapping out his thoughts as memory after memory flooded his brain. The serious, the profane, the comic and the heartbreaking. More and more rapidly the words appeared on the monitor, but Tom didn't look up. He wanted to capture it all—the jokes, the back slaps, the boredom, the adrenaline rushes, the mind-numbing fear.

Finally, around five o'clock, he stopped and began rereading the text. Halfway through, he slumped forward, burying his face in his hands. "Oh, my God," he whispered. "It's the book."

Not the book he'd been asked to write, but the book he was *going* to write. A book dedicated to Gordy and devoted to exploring, not the cold-blooded atrocities of the end of the twentieth century, but the human beings caught up in events beyond their control, and the heroism and friendships forged in such a caldron.

He couldn't wait to tell Lynn. But first he needed to talk to Harry Milstein.

IT WAS THE FOURTH SUNDAY in October. Although the temperature had dropped into the midforties, the sky was blue and cloudless. Lynn squared her robe over her shoulders and peeked out her office window, gratified to see the parking lot filling up. She turned back to Molly, Nathan and Rosita. "Looks like we'll have a good crowd."

"That's a positive sign," Molly said, smiling at the two youths.

"If I don't screw up," Nathan said, nervously cracking his knuckles.

"Not possible," Lynn assured him. "Whatever you say will come from the heart. That's what counts."

"We have lots of good things we can tell them about, don't we?" Rosita, dark eyes shining, looked to the adults for approval.

"You certainly do," Molly agreed.

Lynn moved to the door. "Ready?" Nathan gulped and Rosita nodded. "Remember, you'll be sitting on either side of me, and I'll introduce you when it's time."

"Break a leg, kids," Molly said.

Lynn escorted them to the foyer and the processional began. She could hardly keep her mind on the hymn, so full was her heart. The church was packed. Dr. and Mrs. Bennett, the Drummers, the Mazeriks, Shep and Dorrie, the Penningtons, Charlie Callahan, Mitch and Sam Sterling, dear Kate and her dynamic duo, Hope and Hannah, and others too numerous to count. Ahead of her, petite Rosita, her bright red skirt flaring around her knees, and Nathan, tall and handsome in his blue suit, did Meacham House proud. As she passed Tom's row—he was on the aisle—he winked and gave her a thumbs-up.

When the time came for the sermon and she stepped to the pulpit, she couldn't avoid noticing Prentice Jewett, sitting expressionless in the front pew, his arms folded defensively across his chest. She paused, taking a moment to center herself before beginning. "Dear friends, this is a day of celebration for Riverbend Community Church and for Meacham House. As God's people, we must always remember that we are part of a larger community and that He has blessed us with resources beyond our imagining. Sharing those resources, easing others' burdens and enabling each of God's children to build upon his or her unique talents and gifts is what we are called to do.

"At this church, part of our response to that call has been the establishment of a community program for young people, Meacham House. Many of you are already involved. Others may be curious about the nature of the program and its benefits. So, in lieu of my sermon—" she held up her hands and smiled "—I have asked Molly Linden, director of Meacham House, and two of the participants, Nathan Turner and Rosita Diaz, to share their thoughts with you. Molly?" She stood aside as her friend mounted the pulpit.

After thanking the church for its financial and volunteer support, Molly outlined the activities taking place and those planned for the future. "But for the real story, no one is better equipped than our young people to share it. Nathan Turner, who moved to Riverbend this summer, will begin."

"Go get 'em, Tiger," Lynn whispered as Nathan got awkwardly to his feet.

Reaching the pulpit, he gripped it like a drowning man clutching a ring buoy. "Molly asked me to tell you what Meacham House has done for me." He cleared his throat twice. "I didn't want to come live here with Charlie, at first. Not because he's such a bad guy, I mean, well, you know." Several in the congregation tittered.

"But I didn't know anybody here. There was nothin' to do. Nobody to hang out with. The only reason I went to Meacham House, besides Charlie making me go, is that I heard they were offering art classes. So I went, and it's made a big difference. Now I have friends. And I'm not the only one. Da-

mon, Sam and the other guys—we all have friends.
Some of them are even grown-ups like Molly and
Tom.'' Appreciative laughter from the congregation.

''I'd like to invite all of you over after church to
see some things we've done. I hope you'll like my
paintings, too.'' He turned and looked at Molly as if
checking to see if he'd said enough.

She nodded and moved to the pulpit. ''Thank you,
Nathan. Now, we'll hear from Rosita Diaz.''

Lynn couldn't wait. Rosita was a born actress and
loved nothing better than an audience. Even though
she could barely see over the lectern, she was not
intimidated. ''On behalf of myself and the Meacham
House kids, I want to thank all of you for giving the
teens in this town a safe place to go. More impor-
tantly, for giving us a place to belong. A place where
we can laugh and study and just talk about life. And
where there are adults who don't think we're so bad.
Who listen. Who think we're worth their time and
attention and love.''

Lynn held her breath. You could have heard a pin
drop in the sanctuary. Molly threw Lynn a teary look
that clearly said, ''Aren't these kids something?''

Rosita went on, her confident voice filling the
building. ''There's lots of bad stuff going on. You
know that. You watch TV. You read the newspapers.
But there's good stuff, too. And we want you to come
see some of it today. Please, after church, come home
with us to Meacham House.''

When Rosita returned to her seat, Lynn was nearly
too overcome with emotion to go on. But, she realized, there was really nothing further to be said. So
instead of more words, Lynn caught Rachel's eye,
confident of her organist's musical flexibility. Rachel

peered over her glasses, then nodded. Lynn stood, and after she announced a hymn number, the congregation rose and began a heartfelt rendition of ''Now Thank We All Our God.''

By the time Lynn reached Meacham House after the service, the crowd was spilling out into the backyard, where the teenage musicians were holding forth. Inside, little kids ran up and down the stairs shrieking delightedly, grandmas perched on folding chairs brought in for the occasion, and men stood in groups, balancing cookies and coffee.

A young couple engaged Nathan in an intense discussion of his art, while next to him one of the girls explained to an elderly gentleman the media she'd used for an abstract collage.

After being stopped numerous times by people greeting her or asking questions, Lynn finally made her way to the rec room where Damon and Sam had mounted a collection of photos. The display was entitled ''Our Town.'' In the center was a striking photo of the courthouse at dawn, surrounded by studies of Victorian homes, Riverside Park, the First World War memorial statue and other points of interest. Lynn clapped her hands delightedly. Damon, his hair hiding his face, skulked in a corner, as if daring the world to like anything about him.

Lynn felt an arm snake around her waist and looked up to see Tom smiling with satisfaction. ''They're good, aren't they?''

''Very good.'' She turned and, with Tom at her side, walked over to Damon. ''You do us great credit,'' she said softly. ''Those are incredible photographs.''

He tossed his head. ''You think?''

"Yes, I do."

A tall man with a craggy face and a crooked smile approached them. "Baines, is this the fellow you were telling me about?"

"Yes. Damon, this is Court Reeves, editor-in-chief at the *Riverbend Courier*. He has something to say to you."

Damon eyed the stranger warily. "You have a great future ahead of you," Reeves said to him. "I'd like to do a full-page spread in the Sunday paper of your photos. I can't pay you what they're worth, but something is better than nothing."

Damon stood stock-still. "You're kidding, right?"

Reeves laughed. "No. Not only am I not kidding, I hope you'll come around and see me at the newspaper office. I'd like to put you on the payroll."

Damon looked from Reeves to Tom. "Does he mean a job? Taking pictures?"

Tom put an arm around Damon's shoulders. "That's exactly what he means."

Lynn linked her fingers through Tom's and squeezed just as Damon blew out a breath and uttered a single word. "Awesome."

Leaving Damon and Reeves to work out details, Tom and Lynn wandered hand in hand upstairs. Either everyone knew they were an item, or no one noticed their joined hands. Regardless, it felt so right to have Tom there with her, touching her, claiming her.

"Psst." Putting a finger to her lips, Ruth motioned them to join her. "Over here," she said in a low voice.

Lynn normally disapproved of eavesdropping, but it was too late. Ruth pointed to a group of men standing just inside the downstairs game room. Prentice

Jewett faced away from them, holding court. "Listen," Ruth whispered.

Prentice clasped his hands behind his back and rocked on his heels. "…so I said to them, never mind. I'll take care of it. These Meacham House people are doing fine things, and if I can provide them with state-of-the-art computer equipment, it's the least I can do for such deserving young people."

Ruth signaled a "Watch me" look and sailed into the middle of the group. "I couldn't help overhearing, Prentice. We all know you as a very generous man. I understand Meacham House can use a new oven. May we count on you for that, as well?"

Lynn almost felt sorry for Prentice. Like a fish mouthing the side of an aquarium, his lips moved, but nothing came out. The other men looked at him expectantly. Finally he sputtered, "Why, Ruth, dear, it'd be my pleasure."

Tom led Lynn into the living room. "I don't want to be anywhere near the scene of that crime." He leaned over and whispered in her ear. "Where I want to be is alone. With you. You busy later?"

"What a lovely idea. Will four o'clock suit you?"

"Perfectly."

Lynn smiled up at him. Days didn't get much better than this.

WHEN HE PICKED HER UP, Tom noticed that Lynn had changed into jeans and an avocado turtleneck that brought out greenish highlights in her eyes. He helped her into her gold fleece anorak and whisked her out to the truck. She looked puzzled. "I thought we were planning to be alone."

"We are."

"Then where are we going?"

"It's a surprise," he said.

"I like surprises."

He certainly hoped so. He couldn't believe how nervous he was. He'd been in tight situations before, but never one where the result depended so heavily on saying just the right thing.

A bulky object knocked against the front seat. "What's that?" she said, cranking around to look.

"A guitar."

She giggled. "Are you planning a serenade?"

It was a good idea. Too bad he hadn't thought of it. "No. It's for Pete. I'm going to Chicago tomorrow. Libby asked me to come. She has a swim meet. I'm taking it to him."

"He'll love it."

"I hope so. He's been bugging me about one. I figured it might be a good way to involve him with the kids at Meacham House."

"Like I've said before, you're a good man, Tom Baines."

Good *enough?* That was the question.

"Ah." With one hand she braced herself against the dashboard. "You're taking me to the cemetery."

"Yes, I am." He squinted at the road, studiously avoiding looking at her. "I kind of think of it as our place."

He slowed, then pulled off the road and parked. After helping her out, he took her by the hand and began the ascent.

"It's funny," Lynn mused. "Most people wouldn't pick a place of death as a sentimental landmark."

"I don't think of it as a place of death," he said seriously. "I figured I could make a choice. To let death control my life or to make peace with it. It was here I began to find that peace.'' He squeezed her fingers. ''With you.''

When they crested the rise, Lynn sucked in her breath. ''Oh, Tom.'' She turned tear-filled eyes to him. ''It's…it's lovely.''

He'd loaded the pots of vermilion and yellow chrysanthemums into the pickup after church and had had just enough time to decorate the cemetery with them before picking her up.

She slowly turned her head, taking it all in. ''They're everywhere. By each and every marker. On the wall. It must've taken hours.''

He shrugged, then grinned. ''You're worth it.'' He sobered and tilted his head toward the graves. ''And they're worth it.'' With a thudding heart, he pulled her toward the wall. ''I want to show you something and ask you something.''

He put his arms around her waist and lifted her onto the low wall, as nervous as if he were still that scared little kid at a new boarding school. Slowly, standing before her, he extracted a thick envelope from his inside jacket pocket. ''Here,'' he said, handing it to her.

Her eyebrows knit in inquiry. ''What is it?''

''Open it.''

She pulled out the papers and began to read. He could tell when she came to the important words, because her mouth fell open. Then she looked up, her eyes shining in wonder. ''Is this what I think it is? A book contract?''

He took the sheaf of papers from her and refolded them. ''Yes. I didn't want to bring you here and ask you what I'm going to ask you until I figured out who I am.''

"And now? Have you figured it out?"

He picked up both her hands and drew in a deep breath. "I am a writer. But beyond that, I am a man who has learned a lot and has a lot still to learn. The main thing is, I'm willing to try." He cleared his throat and concentrated on the encouragement he saw in her eyes. "The most important thing I've learned, and what I couldn't say until now, until I felt worthy, is that I love you, Lynn Kendall, and want you to be my wife."

The love he read in her face nearly undid him. "Tom, you've always been worthy."

He was gripping her fingers so hard it was a wonder she didn't cry out. "Is that a yes?"

Her merry laughter warmed his soul from the inside out. "Of course it is." She flung her arms around his neck. "I've been waiting for you all my life."

Before she could kiss him, he held up his fingers and stayed her. "There's one more thing." He thought he knew what her answer would be, but he needed to hear it from her. "Up until recently, I've not been the best father. If you're willing," he stammered, "I...I'd like to try parenthood again—from the beginning. With you."

She pushed herself off the wall into his hug and fastened her lips to his. Her mouth was sweet and warm. He hadn't known such joy, such oneness, was possible. And he had a lifetime of this to look forward to. How long they stood locked together was anybody's guess. The sound of geese calling to one another finally brought him back to his senses. He pulled his mouth away and pointed to the sky. The flock flew closer and closer, almost directly overhead, winging their way south.

"They're leaving home," he said. "But they'll return in the spring."

She leaned against his shoulder. "And what about you? Have you returned? Are you home?"

He thought about her question and realized he'd known the truth for several weeks. He turned her in his arms so they faced the distant river and the setting sun. "Riverbend is a wonderful place, full of fine people and good memories. But it isn't home."

She lifted her head, bewilderment darkening her pupils. "It isn't?"

"No, love." He cupped her face and drank in her serene beauty, knowing he would never forget this moment. "My home is wherever you are."

HARLEQUIN®
SUPERROMANCE®

You are now entering

WELCOME TO **RIVERBEND**

POPULATION
8793

Riverbend...the kind of place where everyone knows your name—and your business. Riverbend...home of the River Rats—a group of small-town sons and daughters who've been friends since high school.

The Rats are all grown up now. Living their lives and learning that some days are good and some days aren't—and that you can get through anything as long as you have your friends.

Starting in July 2000, Harlequin Superromance brings you Riverbend—six books about the River Rats and the Midwest town they live in.

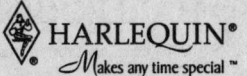

HARLEQUIN®
Makes any time special ™

HARLEQUIN *Super* ROMANCE®

They spent a snowy night in each others'
arms. Now there's a baby
on the way....

SNOW BABY by *Brenda Novak*

(Superromance #939)

Chantel Miller has fallen for Dillon Broderick, the man
who held and comforted her during the blizzard. Then
she learns that her estranged sister is in love with him.
The sister whose affection Chantel's trying to regain. The
painful coincidence becomes even more devastating
when Chantel discovers she's pregnant.

On sale September 2000

Available wherever Harlequin books are sold.

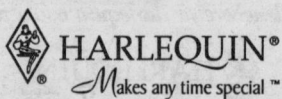

HARLEQUIN®
Makes any time special ™

"Do you realize something is happening between us?"

"No." Natalie tore her gaze from Jake and shook her head helplessly. "No, Jake, I can't accept that."

That was what she said aloud, but silently, inside, she was dazed by the sudden realization of the truth. Inside, somewhere deep and hidden, her feelings for him had been growing, intensifying, without her knowing it.

He must have read some of her turbulent thoughts. "You see?" He raked his fingers through his thick hair, his face twisted, a sign of his torment. "God, why do I feel like I'm cheating? I wish..."

At that moment the baby kicked Natalie, hard, as though to remind her of its presence. She winced and put her hand on the spot.

Jake's gaze dropped to her stomach. His expression closed instantly, like the slamming of a door between them....

Dear Reader,

There's so much to talk about this month that I hardly know where to begin, so I guess I'll start off with this month's American Hero, Race Latimer, in Kathleen Eagle's *Black Tree Moon*. Race is a smoke jumper, an elite fire fighter who attacks the flames from above. He's also a cocky, hell-raising kind of guy who meets his match in social worker Hannah Quinn. You won't want to miss their story.

We're also highlighting new author Kate Carlton this month, as part of Silhouette's PREMIERE program. In *Kidnapped!*, Kate has created characters you won't soon forget. Talk about on-the-run romance . . . ! Be sure to come along for the ride.

Emilie Richards's *From a Distance* is memorable not just for the way this talented author reunites Stefan and Lindsey Daniels, whose marriage had foundered on the rocky shores of discontent, but for the secondary character she introduces. Alden Fitzpatrick is more than he seems, but in ways most people are not yet ready to deal with. Are you? Read this book—and then look for Alden's story, coming in 1993.

The month continues with Marion Smith Collins's *Baby Magic,* a deeply emotional story of loving, of giving, of the miracles of science and the unpredictability of fate. Two people who'd never expected to share the ups and downs of parenting find themselves in just that position. Join Frances Williams in *Shadows on Satin,* as heroine Lori Castleton returns to the brooding mansion that was once almost her undoing. There she has to confront the specters of her past as well as hero Keith McKinnon, a man who can't bring himself to trust her—even though he loves her. Finally, join Desire author Beverly Barton as she makes her Intimate Moments debut with *This Side of Heaven,* a potent mix of the here and now with the shadowy forces of the past.

In coming months, look for books by such favorite authors as Kathleen Korbel, Dallas Schulze, Rachel Lee and Marilyn Pappano. Here at Silhouette Intimate Moments, we try to make all your reading experiences happy ones.

Yours,

Leslie J. Wainger
Senior Editor and Editorial Coordinator

BABY
MAGIC

Marion
Smith
Collins

Silhouette®
INTIMATE MOMENTS®

Published by Silhouette Books New York
America's Publisher of Contemporary Romance

SILHOUETTE BOOKS
300 East 42nd St., New York, N.Y. 10017

BABY MAGIC

ISBN: 0-373-07452-2

First Silhouette Books printing October 1992

Printed in the U.S.A.

MARION SMITH COLLINS

has written nonfiction for years and is the author of several contemporary romances, as well as one book of general fiction.

She's a devoted traveler and has been to places as far-flung as Rome and Tahiti. Her favorite country for exploring, however, is the United States because, she says, it has everything.

In addition, she is a wife and the mother of two children. She has been a public-relations director, and her love of art inspired her to run a combination gallery and restaurant for several years.

She lives in Georgia with her husband of thirty years.

To Ben and Sam, who brought magic into our lives.

Chapter 1

It rained the afternoon of Lisa Reed Armstrong's funeral.

One hundred percent humidity augmented two weeks of an energy-sapping, record-breaking August heat wave, and all along the southern coast, from Virginia to Florida, the air was almost unbreathable. That morning the newscaster on Savannah's radio station, WAEV, warned the elderly and people with breathing problems to stay inside air-conditioned buildings.

A sober-faced attendant from the funeral home held a large black umbrella over Natalie Robinson Armstrong as she got out of her car at the cemetery. "This rain sure hasn't cooled things off any," said the young man, trying to make conversation.

Natalie didn't want to talk. "No," she answered. Her normally quiet, evenly modulated voice sounded hoarse.

They joined the parade of other mourners, men and women dressed in dark colors, hidden under umbrellas, who made their way through a gray driving rain toward the grave site. A funeral tent had been set up to shelter them from the inclement weather. The only element of color in the scene, visible even from this distance, was the blanket of pink roses that lay atop the casket.

Natalie was in shock; her heart felt numb, her eyes were puffy from unshed tears and nausea sat like a knot beneath her collarbone. She and Lisa had grown up together in Charleston, South Carolina, forty-five minutes north of Savannah. It still seemed unbelievable to her that her sister-in-law, and best friend for most of their twenty-nine years, was dead.

Raindrops beat a noisy tattoo on the heavy nylon fabric over Natalie's head. She and the attendant skirted a low stone marker. Walking on the turf was like treading on a sponge; with each step Natalie's high heels sank into the ground, threatening to throw her off balance.

Finally the man noticed. He offered his arm, which she took gratefully. "Thank you," she said.

Her life had been intertwined with Lisa's since the day in first grade when the Jefferson boy, whom everyone knew was a bully, had squirted Mary Lou Delaney with his water pistol, making her cry. She and Lisa had responded quickly in their characteristic and complementary ways. Lisa had pushed Tommy Jefferson down and stomped his water pistol into plastic pieces, and Natalie had comforted Mary Lou, mopping her tears.

From that day on Lisa and Natalie were a team, as close as sisters. They had gone to Girl Scout camp together, giggled over boyfriends, experimented with makeup and hairstyles. They'd been cheerleaders together in high school, sorority sisters at the university and they'd married brothers.

Three years ago Natalie had lost her husband. Now her friend was gone.

Lisa, like a lovely butterfly, should not have to be buried in the rain, thought Natalie, sudden tears springing to her eyes. At the very least, yellow sunlight, a warm, bright reflection of her spirited personality, would have made this parting more endurable. This steamy, dismal day seemed to drain the vitality from Lisa's memory.

And Lisa shouldn't be buried before her life was complete. She should have been buried far into the next century, with grandchildren—even great-grandchildren—in attendance.

"Mind this step," said Natalie's escort, recalling her to the present. She straightened her shoulders, telling herself that she had survived the other crises in her life. She would get through this one. But she would never be the same.

The grave site was near an ancient oak tree, its branches dripping with water-soaked moss. Up close the green tent looked inadequate.

Natalie thanked the man with the umbrella again and ducked under a scalloped edge of canvas. Folding chairs had been arranged on a carpet of artificial grass, facing the bier. There were empty places in front, but she ignored them, making her way to a chair in the far back corner. Absently she picked up a wood-handled paperboard fan that lay on the seat.

She was feeling clammy and light-headed. She made use of the fan, dabbed at the perspiration on her forehead with her handkerchief and prayed that she wouldn't be nauseated again. The only dark dress she owned was long sleeved and high necked, appropriate for the circumstances but totally unsuitable for this weather. Though she had pulled her long, thick hair into a tight chignon to lift it off her neck, the heat and humidity had become enemies allied to sap her strength.

Natalie had none of that to spare. She would need every bit of endurance, fortitude and determination she could muster to get through the coming months.

She blinked to clear her eyes and glanced down at the cardboard fan. One side was decorated with a misty Eden-like photograph of a garden, and the other quoted scripture heralding the glory of God. At the bottom, of course, was a list of the advantages of using Lehey Funeral Home when your time came.

At last, when all the other mourners were settled into place under the tent, the doors of the long black family limousine opened. Two men emerged first, then they turned back to assist a woman. She was stooped with the weight of her grief, her face shielded by a mourning veil. Accompanied by the minister and the somber black-clad men from the funeral home, Lisa's parents and her husband walked slowly to the front row of chairs.

Natalie swallowed hard. She dropped the crumpled handkerchief into her small shoulder bag and took out a fresh one.

The minister took his place beside the casket and a hush sank over the group. He opened a worn prayer book and began to speak.

Mr. and Mrs. Reed, Lisa's parents, sat motionless as the minister intonated Lisa's wonderful qualities and her contributions to the community. Though their heads were erect, though they stared straight ahead at the roses that covered the coffin of their daughter, though they seemed attentive, Natalie doubted that they heard a word the man said.

She know how deeply their eyes reflected their agony; she'd seen it yesterday when they arrived from their home in Charleston. She'd seen their resentment, too, as she had greeted them. And she'd felt it even as they each hugged her and accepted her condolences. They resented her, alive and well, when their only child lay dead as the result of a grotesque automobile accident.

Lisa's husband, Jake, had also been unable to hide his antagonism toward his brother's widow. She had been the only one in the town house when the policeman had come to inform them about the accident. She'd been the one to break the news to Jake. She'd gone with him to the morgue. And she had made the call to Charleston.

She closed her eyes. Only two days ago Lisa had been alive and full of enthusiasm, racing off in one direction or another, always active with a project of some kind....

Natalie had been at the computer. The insistent knock at the front door had interrupted her train of thought. She muttered something unkind under her breath and went to answer it. She was surprised to see a young, fresh-faced policeman standing on the sidewalk. "Yes, Officer? Can I help you?"

He was backlit by the bright sunlight, and she couldn't see his expression clearly. "Is this the home of Lisa Armstrong?"

Lisa, Lisa, I told you your cavalier attitude toward parking tickets would catch up to you someday. Natalie grinned. "Technically, yes. But this is a separate apartment. Mr. and Mrs. Armstrong live upstairs," she said, stepping out the door to indicate the twin arms of the curved, split stairway that led to the main entrance of the house.

She could see his expression now and he looked very serious. "No one answers the door," he told her.

The grin slipped from her face. "I'm Natalie Armstrong. May I take a message?"

He held her gaze for a moment. "Ma'am, there's been an accident. I need to locate—" he glanced at the notebook in his hand "—Jake Armstrong."

Natalie stared, disbelieving, at the man. Suddenly an awful premonition seized her. "Lisa?" Her voice sounded shrill.

He hesitated. "You're a member of the family?"

"Lisa Armstrong is my sister-in-law—" she waved her hand in the air, a gesture to suggest the tangle that was her relationship with Lisa "—my late husband's brother's wife."

"I'm afraid I have bad news. She lost control of her car, ran it into a telephone pole."

"When? Where?"

"About an hour ago, ma'am. Out on the Isle of Hope."

"What hospital is she in?" She whirled to go back in for her car keys but his quiet words halted her abruptly.

"I'm sorry."

Dealing with her own grief, while having to tell Jake that his beloved wife was dead . . . it had been unbearable. That was why, though Natalie had been invited to accompany the family, she'd chosen to drive her own car to the funeral.

Jake sat as immobile as a statue on the other side of Mrs. Reed. Only his profile was visible, but it was enough to reveal his grief. The inherent strength and sureness that were so much a part of him had clearly been exhausted. His normally healthy, tanned face was worn gray; his full, dark mustache contrasted with the pallor of his skin. He'd not used an umbrella and his hair was wet, making it appear even darker. As she watched, a muscle tripped convulsively in his square jaw.

When the minister asked them all to bow their heads for a last prayer, Jake seemed to fold up into himself, his broad shoulders and dark head dropping forward. He took a deep shuddering breath and covered his eyes.

Natalie looked away quickly, unable to bear the sight of his sorrow. She hurt for all of them and for herself, as well. Funerals were barbaric, she thought, not for the first time.

The last prayer of the service was blessedly short. Mr. and Mrs. Reed and Jake returned to the limousine for the drive back to town.

The mourners came from the cemetery to the restored three-story town house where the Armstrongs lived. They had paid their respects to the deceased; now they would pay their respects to the family. They would bring casseroles and cakes, potato salad and deviled eggs, country ham and fried chicken. And they would make gallons of sweetened iced tea, laced with lemon. They would offer assistance, comfort, encouragement.

Fruitlessly.

Or, looking at this situation from a different perspective, the family was expected to play host to this lot of well-meaning people. Natalie knew from her memories of her husband's death that all any of them wanted to do was curl up alone somewhere and let the grief have its way with them, let the sharp knife of sorrow cut them to ribbons.

The narrow street in front of the house was congested as people searched for parking spots. Lisa and Jake had moved to Savannah as newlyweds eight years ago. They had both become successful in business here, and they had made many friends.

Natalie parked her own car in the rear alley behind the house. She entered through an elaborately wrought gate into a formal garden that had been Lisa's pride. She paused for a moment and drank in the beauty around her. The rain had stopped, and the garden was washed clean.

Planned as a disciplined riot of prolific color and myriad scents, the garden offered daylilies and hollyhocks lining the neat paths, backed by shaped boxwoods and Savannah holly trees. Old-fashioned roses perfumed the air. Bougainvillea climbed one corner of the brick wall that surrounded the area, and brilliant fuchsia spilled over another.

A tree, dripping with water and long wet tails of Spanish moss, shaded the garden bench that skirted its trunk. The high-gloss varnish of its slatted seat was beaded with raindrops.

A stray beam of sunlight reflected off a polished window. The beautiful house had been built with coral-colored brick, trimmed with black-green shutters and sparkling white trim. Originally constructed in the late-eighteenth century, the building had been purchased and lovingly restored by Lisa and Jake shortly after they moved to the city.

Natalie resisted the temptation to withdraw into the ground-floor apartment where she was living temporarily and close the door on the tragedy. Instead she climbed gracefully curved wrought-iron steps to enter the main floor of the house through the kitchen.

As expected, neighbors had prepared enough food for a small army. The dishes were now arranged in a variety of containers on the dining room table. Delicious aromas wafted through the rooms. The gracious old house was crowded, straining the capacity of the air-conditioning; the living room was nearly as sultry as the outdoors.

Natalie roamed through the crowd, greeting the few people she knew. She'd moved here less than a month ago and had not had time to meet many of the couple's friends. She felt like an interloper and wondered how long she would have to stay before she could safely slip away without offending Jake and the Reeds.

One group of people broke and reformed as she passed through them, some eyeing her curiously, others ignoring her.

How many of them knew about the circumstances that had brought her here?

It wasn't a secret. Lisa and Jake had never planned to hide the reasons for Natalie's leaving Charleston and moving into the street-level apartment of their town house, but neither had any of the three of them ever made a point of explaining.

She looked around for Mr. and Mrs. Reed, but they had disappeared. She assumed they had gone upstairs to the guest room to be alone.

Jake was in the hall, talking in low tones to three other men. She hadn't spoken to him since yesterday and at that time he'd been intensely formal and stilted, as though he were holding on to his reason by the merest thread.

Natalie's late husband had been this man's brother. Her best friend had been married to him. And they shared another, deeply personal connection. That very thought made her wary of approaching him.

One of the men in the group was Andrew Roberts, Jake's right-hand man and the vice president of Jake's successful shipping business. As she watched, the men shook hands all around, and Jake left the group.

He turned and caught sight of her. He hesitated and she inhaled sharply when she saw the expression that crossed his face—an expression of hostility, even more severe than his earlier antagonism, much more severe than the resentment of Lisa's parents.

It hurt. But despite her distress, she understood and she tried to stay calm.

Though the circumstances were different, though Joseph had died following a long illness, she'd felt something akin to the same emotion three years ago when her husband, Jake's brother, had died. She had probably looked at Jake in much the same way then.

It was natural, she told herself. But though she and Jake were in a rather unique situation, his reaction was still something of a blow. She waited quietly while he made his way toward her.

When he reached her side, he unbuttoned his suit coat and slid his hands into the pockets of his trousers, displaying a broad expanse of white shirt bisected by a dark blue tie. His gray eyes, bloodshot and sunken in their sockets, burned with emotion. He was larger than Joseph had been. His posture, as he stood looking down at her, underscored his size. Natalie, who was not a small woman, felt diminutive in contrast. And intimidated.

"Natalie," he greeted her evenly. "Are you all right?"

She pushed her sleeves as far up her forearms as they would go. Immediately she realized that for the nervous gesture it was and forced herself to stand still, fingers linked loosely in front of her. "Okay, I guess. How are you, Jake?"

How am I? Dead inside. Empty and hollow. Jake shook his head, not answering for a minute, and looked down at the floor. He could not bear to look at her. His lovely Lisa was dead, her car wrapped around a telephone pole. Suddenly he loathed Natalie with an intensity that overwhelmed him.

He struggled to regain control of himself. "I'll get by," he said finally, wondering if that were true.

"Is there anything I can do for you? Or for the Reeds?" She glanced toward the staircase. "Are they all right?"

"They don't need you to do anything for them," he said tersely. "They're upstairs packing to return to Charleston this afternoon. They most likely won't leave without saying goodbye."

Natalie was clearly puzzled by his wording and his sharp tone, but she nodded in her typically calm, composed way. "I see," she said.

Just then he thought he heard someone call his name. He glanced around, over the heads of the people in the room, but didn't see anyone paying particular attention.

"I'll talk to you later," Natalie murmured. She started to turn away, but he halted her with a touch on her arm. The contact disturbed him. He quickly dropped his hand.

"The Reeds aren't young anymore. As you might imagine, the funeral was a shattering experience for them," he said without any change of expression at all. "I'd appreciate it if you'd leave them alone, wait for them to come to you."

This time he knew his caustic remark couldn't be misinterpreted. She stiffened, staring at him, her blue eyes wide with hurt. "How could you say such a thing to me?" she demanded in a low, shaky voice.

He felt the sharp sting of guilt as he watched the color drain from her face. But he immediately mustered himself against any feelings for her. He couldn't afford them. Important decisions would have to be made very soon, and he was not going to let weakness or emotion dictate those decisions.

She went on with barely a pause. "I wouldn't dream of hurting the Reeds, or intruding on them if they don't wish to see me. And as for you, Jake." She shook her head, clearly bewildered. "If you don't want me here, please say so. I'll be happy to leave."

"Don't be childish," he snapped. "I simply—" The call was repeated; he looked around again, then raised his hand to acknowledge the minister's summons. "I'll be back in a minute. We need to talk." He moved away.

Natalie watched him go with a sense of helplessness; pain gripped her heart. She was fully aware of the movement of people around her; she heard their subdued voices. But she felt as alienated, as isolated, as she had ever felt in her life.

She looked down at her hands; they were trembling uncontrollably. She scanned the room, suddenly frantic, anxious to escape from this crowd of people. And from Jake Armstrong.

Nancy Hightower, a neighbor from the next block, appeared at Natalie's side and patted her arm. Her touch was warm and caring; Jake's, when he'd touched her arm a moment ago, had been cold.

"Hello, Nancy," she said, gratified that her voice didn't reveal her panic.

"Jake didn't mean to hurt you," Nancy answered, and Natalie realized that she had been a witness to the hostile exchange. If anyone had to overhear the conversation, Natalie was glad it had been Nancy. As the panic eased off a bit, she sighed.

She smiled, but there was no humor in her expression. "Rationally I know he didn't mean to be cruel. We say and do things at a time like this that we often regret, if we even remember them."

"But that doesn't make it any less painful for the one on the receiving end," said Nancy.

Natalie nodded. A tear tracked down the side of her nose. She quickly wiped the moisture away with her fingertips. "Lisa's death has been unbearably hard on him. And I know from experience the grieving will get much worse before it begins to get better."

Nancy looked at her, then toward the dining room table. "Let's get something to eat," she said gently.

Natalie shook her head. "No, thank you," she said. She tried another smile and flattened her hand against her midriff. "I'll eat later, but I couldn't swallow a thing right now."

"Lisa wouldn't want you to get sick," Nancy told her in a matter-of-fact tone. She broke off abruptly when she realized what she had said and took a handkerchief from her pocket. She mopped her red-rimmed eyes. "Sorry."

"I understand."

Nancy replaced her handkerchief and sniffed. "Your husband was younger than Jake, wasn't he? Were they alike?" she asked.

Natalie was thankful for the other woman's attempt to steer the conversation to another topic. "Jake was five years older. He wouldn't agree with me, but I thought they were alike in many ways." She paused. Jacob and Joseph Armstrong had been orphaned when they were very young, and they had been brought up in foster homes. Jake had gone to work when he was eighteen so that Joseph could have a college education. "Joseph idolized Jake."

She was surprised that she could speak calmly of Joseph during this emotional time. Even after three years she still missed him terribly.

She had met Joseph Armstrong at the grand opening of a seaside resort off the coast of Charleston during Thanksgiving holidays. She was finishing her senior year of college; he had been out of school for a year and was working as a tax specialist. They had married the week she'd graduated.

Though she and Joseph had been seeing each other for months, she had first met Jake at their wedding rehearsal. A big man, with a walk like a lazy cat and a face that was rugged rather than refined, he had electrified every woman there into silence. Including Lisa. It had been love at first sight for the maid of honor and the best man. In less than three months Lisa and Jake had married....

Voices cut into her memories. Someone behind her attempted to muffle laughter. Someone else commented about the recently completed portrait of Lisa, which hung above the mantel in the living room. It had been delivered yesterday, the day after she died.

Without warning Natalie's panic returned. The pain around her heart intensified; she couldn't seem to get her breath. Suddenly she craved solitude, escape. She turned her back on the room and spoke under her breath. "Nancy, I have to get out of here. I'm going downstairs. If Jake asks where—"

Nancy nodded. "I'll make sure he understands. Besides, I'm sure that deep down he realizes this is hard on you, too," she said, looking around at the crowd. "The kitchen is a zoo. Try the front door." She hesitated, touched Natalie's shoulder. "Natalie...if you need someone to talk to..."

Natalie covered the other woman's hand with her own and squeezed lightly. "You're kind," she managed to say. "I'll call you." She left by the front door and descended one side of the split stairway.

A group of five people were gathered at the foot of the steps, talking about the tragedy that had brought them together. "Excuse me," she said to a man—a stranger—who blocked her way.

He moved aside but his inquisitive eyes followed her. She could feel their weight on her back as she headed for the apartment a few feet away. She stopped between two urns filled with crimson geraniums that flanked the door, fished in her purse for her keys and promptly dropped them.

The man was there immediately. As he handed her the keys he smiled, the confident smile of a handsome man.

Natalie murmured her appreciation but ignored the smile.

She closed the apartment door behind her and leaned against it thankfully, shutting out everything, everyone. At last.

The old brick walls were solid. Not even sounds of traffic seeped in. The quiet was a relief. She shut her eyes and eased out of her shoes. She felt her muscles begin to loosen, her nerves unwind. She took a deep breath and let it out.

Natalie stood there for a long time. Finally, when her body informed her that her energy level had improved, and she was capable of moving, she pushed herself away from the door, scooped up her shoes from the floor and made her way back to the bedroom.

She hadn't slept for two days, not since the policeman had appeared. The two days had been a nightmare of telephone calls, arrangements to be made, people to be notified. Natalie had moved through them in a state of shock, yet she was better prepared to deal with certain details than either Jake or the Reeds.

She put away her purse and her shoes, stripped off her panty hose and set them to soak in the bathroom sink, then hung her dress in the closet.

Since she was clad only in her bra and panties, the cool air-conditioning on her sweat-dampened body was a shock. She unfolded a white comforter from the foot of the bed, lay down on her side and pulled it over her shoulders.

But before she could rest, she knew she had to cleanse herself of bitterness toward Jake and wipe out from her heart the things he'd said to her.

When Joseph had died, Jake and Lisa, but mostly Jake, had been there for her when she needed them desperately. So now she would not take his remarks too literally. Even when he said hurtful things, even when he lashed out at her, she would understand.

She vowed that she would be there for him as he'd been for her. She pulled one of the pillows out from under the spread and hugged it.

Somehow they had all made it through these past two days. Now, according to the minister, Lisa was at rest, at peace.

Natalie wondered about that. With so many things left unresolved in Lisa's life, how could her friend possibly find peace?

Night had fallen; the last of the mourners had left. Jake walked through the empty house. His friends and neighbors had cleaned the kitchen, stored the food, even straightened the living and dining rooms.

He pulled at the knot of his tie and opened the top button of his shirt. He locked all the doors, turned the lights off downstairs and, with slow, heavy steps, climbed to the top floor of the house.

He thanked God for the protective numbness that had carried him through the past two days, but he could already feel it begin to erode, leaving him with widening patches of raw grief. When the protection was stripped completely away, he feared what would come.

A few moments later, he stood alone in the center of the bedroom he had shared with Lisa. The four-poster bed was neatly made, scattered with her needlework pillows. Her dressing table was cluttered with all her small feminine accoutrements, her perfumes, her lotions. He picked up a silver-backed brush he'd given her last Christmas. He realized that his hands were shaking, and he dropped the brush. It bounced against the edge of the dresser and fell to the floor. He left it there.

The house was so damned quiet. He stumbled to the bed, sat on its edge and ran both palms down his face. They came away wet.

Lisa, damn you, you always did drive like a bat out of hell. Now look what you've gone and done.

Suddenly, with a muffled cry, he surged to his feet. He crossed the room to yank open the closet door. He hadn't the slightest notion where he was going, but he had to get out of this room, out of this house.

Swiftly he shed the dark suit and tie and white shirt. He took off his leather shoes and grabbed a warm-up suit from the closet shelf. He stuffed some sweats, underwear and socks and a couple of knit shirts into his gym bag. He grabbed his shaving kit from the bathroom and headed for the stairs. He was halfway through the garden, headed for the garage, when he heard Natalie call his name.

Hell, he'd forgotten all about her. Natalie and the complications she represented, the talk he'd resolved to have with her, meant less than nothing to him at the moment. He had to get away, and he fiercely resented her for delaying him. She should realize that he could not deal with this now.

The night was black; the garden was filled with shadows. He turned toward the light that spilled from the back door of the apartment, but he didn't retrace his steps.

She came outside and stood with her back to the doorjamb, her arms crossed protectively at her waist. "Are you okay?" she asked quietly.

She didn't try to approach him and for that he was grateful. He didn't want anyone anywhere near him, especially not her. "Yeah. I guess." He choked on the lie and scraped a hand through his hair. "Look, I'm going away for a few days. I don't know how long I'll be gone. If anything comes up...if...ah, hell! If the house burns down, call Andrew." He spun away, digging into his pocket for his keys as he disappeared into the garage.

Natalie watched him go, making no protest. She stood where she was until she heard the sounds of the car engine fade away. She knew what it was to try to flee from the anguish, the heartache of death. She also knew that it didn't work. But she couldn't tell Jake that; no one could. He would have to find out for himself.

She tightened the belt of her robe and wandered into the garden, taking solace in the darkness, the unseen beauty that surrounded her, in the scents, in the peace. Moving slowly she traversed the paths, coming at last to her starting point, to the open door. She went inside, closed and locked it behind her.

When Joseph had died, she had run as Jake was running now. For her, running away had been totally out of character. In fact, her flight had been one of the first completely spontaneous things she could ever remember doing.

But the memory helped her now, helped her to understand his need, his urgency; she wouldn't have dreamed of trying to stop him.

* * *

Jake was gone for more than a month.

The days were endless. Television didn't interest Natalie and music had no appeal. She bought a book and it lay on the bedside table unopened. Worst of all she couldn't work.

When night fell, she roamed the rooms of the apartment.

The place was a perfect size for her, and Lisa's professional decorating acumen had made it into a cozy, restful retreat, which, if she could relax, was probably what she needed right now.

The ceilings were lower than the ten-foot ones in the house above. The floors were well-worn brick, extravagantly softened by vintage oriental rugs.

The front door opened directly into the large living room. To the left was a brick fireplace, flanked by rich dark mahogany built-ins, bookshelves and cabinets that held the stereo and television. The furniture had been chosen for comfort, but nothing had been lost in charm. A sofa was covered in floral chintz; two deep-cushioned leather wing chairs flanked the fireplace. Straight ahead through a door at the back of the room was the sun-bright yellow kitchen.

To the right, through an archway, was a hall with steps leading upstairs. Also off the hall were the bedrooms, two of them, each with its own bath. The front bedroom had a floor-length window that looked out onto the sidewalk. Natalie had set up a temporary office there, and she had a view of LaFayette Square across the street. Open carriages carrying tourists often passed. The back bedroom, the one in which she slept, had French doors opening directly into the garden.

A week went by, then two, before she finally received a call from Andrew, Jake's assistant.

"I'm afraid Jake isn't coming home anytime soon, Natalie. He said that he would stay in touch, but he needed time to come to terms with Lisa's death. He said you'd understand."

She released her breath, relieved that Jake was safe. She hadn't known until that moment just how worried she had actually been. Jake had been distraught and visibly exhausted when he'd left. She rubbed at her temple with two fingers. "I do understand, Andrew. God, it's so hard, but time away may help him. Is there anything I can do?"

Five minutes later she was beginning to regret that she'd asked. Too clearly, she recalled the many essential details that followed death.

Lisa's car had been sold. Lisa's business had been put on the market. Natalie squeezed her eyes shut at that.

Andrew asked her to pack Lisa's clothes and personal things. "Jake was adamant," Andrew explained. "He said to call Goodwill. He wants it all gone before he comes back."

"Everything? What about Lisa's parents? Won't they want anything?"

"Mr. and Mrs. Reed have left all decisions to Jake." He hesitated. "He also wants the portrait destroyed, Natalie. The one over the mantel. He was most insistent about that."

She put her fingers to her trembling lips. "Oh, Andrew, I'm not sure I can do this."

"I understand. If you feel you can't take care of it, let me know. I'll... hell, I'll do something."

She was silent for a minute. "I'll try," she said at last.

When Jake finally did return to Savannah one evening in late September, he looked as though he'd spent the entire six weeks in a prison camp.

Dusk was gathering, slowly leeching the color from the garden. Natalie hadn't heard the car, so it was a shock to glance out the kitchen window and see him step through the gate. He'd lost weight, a lot of weight. His square jaw was unshaven; his clothes were a wrinkled mess, as if he'd been sleeping in them the whole time he'd been gone. She froze at the sight, a vegetable peeler in one hand, a carrot in the other.

He didn't spare a glance toward her door, but went straight upstairs.

An hour later she was standing at the sink once more, rinsing the last of her supper dishes under running water, when he came downstairs again. She held her breath until he bypassed the path that led to the garage and headed toward the apartment.

She let out the breath in a rush, turned off the water and put the dish in the dish rack. She caught a towel from the counter to dry her hands and went to the door.

The outside light was not kind to him; up close he looked even worse than he had from a distance. But at least he'd made an effort. He'd showered and shaved and changed from the clothes he'd arrived in to a clean pair of khakis and a black cotton turtleneck. He'd pushed up the sleeves of his shirt to his elbows and she could see that his distinctive tan had faded a bit. He needed a haircut and his mustache needed trimming.

But there was one encouraging note—the dazed look in his eyes when he'd left Savannah six weeks ago had been replaced by a harsh glint of acceptance. He'd begun the long process of recovering.

She smiled. "Come in, Jake. I'm glad to see you." Her voice was as warm and caring as she could make it, though she wrung her hands beneath the cover of the towel. "How are you?"

He shrugged and moved past her into the kitchen. "I'm better than I was when I left here. I can deal with . . . things . . . that I need to deal with. By the way, thanks for taking care of the packing upstairs. Andrew told me that you—"

"Nancy Hightower helped me. We were both glad to do what we could." She closed the door behind him. It had actually been a distressing experience. She couldn't have done it alone. Nancy and she had packed and sent Lisa's clothes off to Goodwill as directed.

But she didn't tell him, as she hadn't told Andrew, that they had stored Lisa's personal things in boxes and secreted them in a dark corner of the attic. And the portrait was stored right here in the apartment, in the closet of the room she used as an office. She and Nancy had decided that someday Jake might be grateful that they'd ignored his decree.

Carefully she folded the towel and hung it on a bar beside the sink. When she turned to him again, she made her voice light. "I just finished supper. I have two crab cakes from the take-out seafood place down the street and plenty of salad left over. Can I fix some for you?" She had also picked up fresh yeast rolls from the bakery and their luscious aroma lingered in the room.

"No," he said quickly. "I'm not hungry. I'll only stay a minute."

She almost told him that he was much too thin, that he should eat something, but she bit back the words just in time, remembering all the well-meaning advice she had received, and often resented, during the months after Joseph's death.

Each person reacted to the loss of someone they loved deeply in a different way. She could only imagine the ordeal Jake had been through, what fears and regrets had tormented him over these past weeks. But she could see that the first stage of grief—the disbelief—had passed. Now he simply looked grim...and determined.

She wondered about the determination as she sat at one side of the kitchen table. What was coming? She felt a moment of inexplicable dread.

"How are you feeling, Natalie?" he asked, pulling out a chair at right angles to hers. He didn't relax but sat forward with his elbows on his knees.

Actually she felt really good. She'd read that the middle three months of pregnancy were the easiest, and she believed it. Despite the trauma and upheaval in the first trimester, her physical well-being had established itself firmly. She studied his profile for a minute, then attempted a small laugh. "I'm feeling very fat," she answered. "I can't get my slacks buttoned."

He looked over, his gaze drawn to her middle.

She knew that her stomach wasn't clearly defined; she had on a big man-tailored shirt. But the agony—worse than before—was back in his eyes. It was clearly a struggle, but he gained control again.

"The baby is due in February?" he asked. His voice was toneless, not the vibrant baritone she was accustomed to hearing.

Jake knew exactly when this baby was due. His question was clearly a denial of the baby's existence. It brought a burning sensation to her eyes and tears clogged her throat. But Natalie repeated the vow she'd made to herself the day Lisa was buried. She would be strong for him, as he'd been for her when Joseph died.

"The end of February," she said gently. "Jake, I know you have to deal with this in your own way. But is there something, anything, I can do to help?"

He sat motionless for a long minute, as though he were reluctant to voice his thoughts. Jake was a vigorous, intelligent man. Tall—six foot plus—and solidly built, he was not conventionally handsome, but his square jaw projected a impression of strength.

Now he seemed to call on all his concentration, all his strength, all his command, when he raised his head and straightened in his chair. He looked at her again. His eyes were passionless, his expression determined. "There *is* something you can do, Natalie. And it will help a great deal."

Her breath had caught somewhere in her chest. The sense of dread she'd felt earlier grew to frightening proportions. She waited for him to explain.

"You can consent to have an abortion."

Chapter 2

Natalie's hand flattened the big shirt to her stomach in an unconscious gesture of protection as she stared at him, unable to believe what he'd just said.

The big electric clock on the kitchen wall swept away the seconds. Slowly the chilling effect that accompanied shock worked its way into her bones. For a moment, she did not, could not, speak.

An abortion.

She wondered if she should have seen this coming. Because this baby she carried, that Jake had just asked her to dispose of, was not hers. Not related to her in any genetic way. The baby was Lisa's and his child.

Silently he watched her, his gray eyes noncommittal, and waited for a reaction.

At last she said, "I'm eighteen weeks pregnant, Jake. Approaching the legal limit for termination. But I can't have an abortion." She was grateful that her voice hadn't stumbled over the word. "That you would even suggest such a thing is—is—'' Then her voice did break under the emotional impact. ''How *could* you, Jake?'' she whispered.

He looked away. ''How could I not?'' he asked quietly. He seemed to be speaking more to himself than to her, having drawn inside himself somehow.

She might as well not have been in the room. After a moment she got to her feet and went to look blindly out through the six-paned window of the kitchen door, out over Lisa's garden.

Lisa's garden, Lisa's house, Lisa's husband. Good God, what was *she* doing here? She leaned her forehead against a cool glass pane.

Lisa's baby...

It was another bond—a tragic one—that she and Lisa had shared. The inability to bear children.

Lisa *could* not carry a child because of an accident she'd suffered many years ago. Her womb had been destroyed.

Natalie *would* not carry a child because she might pass along the terrible gene she carried in her body.

She squeezed her eyes shut and bit her lips together hard, feeling the edge of her teeth grind against the tender flesh, deliberately arousing physical pain to distract her from the pain in her heart.

She'd carried the pain with her ever since she was old enough to understand that though she was healthy and free of the disease, she could pass this gene to any baby she might have.

She'd never been willing to take that chance, and she'd grown accustomed to the idea that she would never be pregnant. She didn't even think about it much until she'd met and fallen in love with Joseph. She had told him, of course, long before they had become engaged. They'd discussed adoption, but Joseph had gotten sick....

Then a little over a year ago, everything had changed when Lisa had come to Charleston for a visit with her parents. The first night, Lisa had called Natalie to invite herself to dinner. Over the meal, she'd introduced the concept of using in vitro fertilization—and her body—to make a baby.

Natalie had dismissed the idea out of hand. "Lisa, my friend, you are nuts." She'd grinned to take the sting out of the words, but her meaning was straightforward.

Lisa's dark eyes had sparkled like the Fourth of July. "No, I'm not, sweetie. My body is still capable of producing an egg, and Jake has no problems. It's all done in a clinic. I've brought you some materials to read that explain the process.

"You wouldn't lose anything either, Nat," Lisa had persisted. "The timing is perfect. Jake and I would insist on an allowance, so you wouldn't have to worry about working. You can move to Savannah, into our downstairs apartment, sit around and get fat while you finish your book."

Natalie scowled at her friend for using that as an argument. Though she was happy with her job as a feature writer for Charleston's evening newspaper, it was her dream to write fiction. Her editor at the paper was from New York and knew someone who knew someone.

She had sent off a proposal for a novel based on colonial history of the coastal area. After several weeks of self-doubt, she'd recently received a positive response from a well-known New York agent, saying he would be delighted to read a completed manuscript. How long did she think it would take? She'd estimated that she could have a completed manuscript within a year.

Naturally she'd called Lisa in Savannah immediately, to share the exciting news first with her best friend. It was an opportunity she didn't want to ignore. And Lisa knew it.

Surely Lisa didn't imagine she would do something like carry a child for money. Before she could voice her objection to such an outrageous idea, Lisa read her mind.

"Of course, it wouldn't be like taking money for having a baby for some stranger." She grasped Natalie's hand in both of hers. "We're family, and we would naturally want to help you fulfill your dream as you would be helping us fulfill ours."

Her grip tightened; she shook Natalie's hand a bit. "Just think of it, Nat. All these years, neither of us ever thought we could produce a child. But one of the best in vitro clinics in the state is right there in Savannah. The three of us—we could *have* this baby. Jake and I will be the genetic parents, and you will give the baby life. But it wouldn't stop there, you would always be involved. Like another mother. What a lucky kid! And Joseph would have loved it, too, wouldn't he?"

Natalie's eyes had swum with tears during the impassioned appeal. The mention of Joseph caused them to spill over. Even nearly three years after his death, the memories still hurt terribly. She wiped the tears away with the back of her hand. "I can't do this, Lisa. You know I love you, and if I could help you get a baby, I would. But—" she shook her head decisively

"—no." She turned her hands palm up and shrugged her shoulders. "I'm not a risk taker."

"But you're so strong, Nat."

"Me?" she said, surprised.

"You're the strongest woman I know," Lisa had answered seriously.

Was she? wondered Natalie. Was she strong enough?

Lisa never had been one to take no for an answer. It was what made her so successful. "Just think about it, Nat. That's all I ask. What was it my mama used to say about someone who was pregnant? 'She has a bun in the oven.' Well, I'll furnish the bun, and you'll be the oven." She laughed then, and Lisa's laugh was irresistible.

Almost.

"No," Natalie repeated. "Besides, what would you do with a baby? You're so busy." Lisa had opened her home-decorating service the year she married, and it had become an extravagantly successful venture. She was often away from home several days a month, shopping for antiques in Europe, fabrics in the Far East.

"Jake and I will work it out," Lisa said breezily, then she sobered. "I know it's a rather startling suggestion. But please think about it."

"You could get another—"

Lisa interrupted her immediately with a determined shake of her head. "I would never consider letting anyone else carry my baby. You're my sister."

She'd meant it, of course. And Natalie understood completely. Had their situations been reversed, she would have felt exactly the same way. "Jake agrees with this crazy idea?"

Lisa pretended to be offended. "Of course, I'd never make a decision like this without consulting him."

"Consulting?" Natalie laughed dryly. Lisa joined in. They both knew of Lisa's talent for persuasion. Her husband seldom objected to her plans.

Lisa's grin faded, to be replaced by a wistful smile. "You know Jake. He doesn't reveal his feelings as openly as I do, but you should have seen the look in his eyes when I first mentioned it. He would love a child, Nat."

"I'm really sorry if you've had your heart set on this, Lisa, but I can't. *Won't.*" She added the latter, more forceful word so that her friend would know she meant what she said.

"You won't even think about it? Nat, I've never known you to be closed minded before."

Natalie had continued to refuse, but in the end she'd promised to read the material that Lisa had brought and think about the request.

And think, she did. Once the idea had been suggested, she found that she could hardly think of anything else. Eventually, after weighing the pros and cons carefully, she had decided that she would do it.

She'd finally gone to Savannah to spend a weekend and had told Lisa and Jake that she had pondered their proposal. She still had reservations—mainly because of Lisa's high-pressure job—but one look at Jake, at the bright gleam in his eye, convinced her that he would hold up his end of the bargain.

So she had agreed to carry a child for Lisa and Jake. And then, for the rest of the weekend, they'd used every argument they could think of to dissuade her.

Finally, in exasperation, she'd demanded to know if they'd changed their minds.

Lisa, her pretty dark eyes shining with amusement, had grinned at her husband, then jumped up from the sofa where she'd been sitting beside him. She hugged Natalie. "Of course we haven't changed our minds, sweetie."

"We simply wanted to make sure you didn't have any lingering reservations, Natalie," Jake added as he joined them. He draped his arm over Lisa's shoulder. "What you're doing for us—" He shook his head, obviously touched. "We wouldn't want you to be unhappy."

Lisa stood back then, gripping Natalie's shoulders, and looked into her eyes. "But you haven't. You really do want to do this, don't you?" she asked, her voice husky with emotion.

Natalie smiled at her friend. And at Jake. "Yes, I really *do* want this," she answered softly. "I really do." She took a deep breath. "And I think Joseph would want it, too." *It's the one last thing I can do for him,* she added to herself.

The complicated process took a long while. Even so, they were luckier than most. And sooner than any of them had expected, Natalie was pregnant. In July, when the doctors had confirmed her condition, she'd resigned her job, giving half-a-month's notice, and moved from Charleston to Savannah.

Now, as she stood staring into the garden, she was almost to the halfway point of the pregnancy. And the father had decided that this child should not be born.

This baby might not be related to her in a genetic way. But, dammit, it was related to Joseph. And she had been his wife. And this baby was inside her body. Didn't that give her the right to have some say-so?

She rolled her forehead against the glass and fought off the tears. What rationalization could she use with Jake? How could she convince him that what he'd asked was impossible? At last she lifted her forehead from the window and licked her dry lips. Another memory flashed suddenly in her mind. Bright morning sunlight, Jake leaving for work, she at the open kitchen window.

It had been her first morning in Savannah; she was still trying to get used to this upheaval in her well-ordered life. He'd seen her there and detoured from his course.

"Good morning." He'd smiled. "How is the pregnant lady?"

"Fine." She had smiled, but something of her nervousness must have shown in her face.

He'd come in, fresh like the morning in a spotless starched shirt and dark casual slacks, carrying a charcoal-gray sports coat. He had spoken to her gently, reassuringly. "Lisa tends to see most things from her own perspective. But this has been very difficult for you, uprooting your life, hasn't it?"

She nodded.

"I hope you know we're here for you, Natalie." He never had shortened her name like Lisa did. "Anything, *anything* you need—including company when you're lonely or jokes when you're blue—you have only to ask."

His understanding had eased her fears. She smiled. "I know, Jake. Thank you."

The pleasant memory faded. She looked over her shoulder. The gentle, considerate man was gone, probably forever replaced by this angry, bitter one.

He seemed to have regained his balance and determination. A muscle jumped in his jaw once and then again while he held her eyes with his steady gaze.

Her eyes skittered away first. She came across to sit in the chair opposite him, the table between them this time. She placed her elbows on the hard oak surface, her arms outstretched, palms up in a beseeching gesture. "Jake, I think I can understand your feelings..."

The commonplace opening didn't have the desired effect. Her heart sank as she watched his hard expression change to pure granite.

Jake narrowed his eyes as a caution to the woman seated across from him not to argue. Not now. He'd watched the emotions, the memories, chase across her face. He knew what she was thinking, but it was impossible for Natalie to understand what he was feeling. Impossible.

And he recognized from her expression what her reply was going to be. She was going to fight him on this. He maintained his unflinching demeanor. "No, you can't understand." He could tell that hurt.

"I grieved when I lost Joseph," she reminded him evenly.

Impatience and anger crept into his voice. "Joseph was sick. Sick and in terrible pain. There was no hope of his recovering. His death was a relief, for him and for all of us."

His words were like lashes, flaying her heart. She shook her head. "No," she whispered. "Never a relief, never that."

"Lisa was alive," he went on harshly, ignoring her protest. "We had dreams. The baby was a part of them. She's gone, the dream is gone." He broke off for a moment, trying to gain the upper hand over his emotions, the sting in his eyes, the hard mass in his throat. "You here…seeing you every day…pregnant. I can't live with it."

"Jake, you're not being fair," she protested. "I should have the right—"

"Fair?" The anger roiled through him like hot lava. "Life sure as hell isn't fair. You are carrying a—a fetus that is not yours, Natalie," he said brutally.

He saw the effect of his words. Her face paled, her features became wooden, her hands clenched together on the tabletop until her knuckles were white. For the briefest second he deplored his callous handling of the situation. Then he shook his head, hardened his heart against all regret. A clean break with the past was the only way he could survive.

During the time he was away he had forgotten about the child. No, that wasn't right; he hadn't forgotten. The knowledge was there, but he had confined it to a brittle glass sphere and rolled it into the back of his mind for later reflection.

The day Lisa was buried, he'd fled. He'd headed up the coast, driving until total exhaustion had overtaken him. He'd found himself in North Carolina, where he'd pulled into the first motel he came to, checked in and slept for twenty-eight hours. It was the only peace he would know for more than a month and a half.

After the one call to Andrew, he didn't talk to anyone. He walked the beaches; he ate only when weakness reminded him. Lisa's birthday in early September passed in an alcoholic blue haze.

Finally, after weeks of existing in a vacuum, he had begun to pull himself together, to come back to life. It was only yesterday as he was slowly making his way back to Savannah that he remembered the child.

Without warning the glass sphere had shattered; the memory had hit with the force of a tornado. He'd had to pull the car off the highway until he could breathe again. His thoughts were scattered, chaotic. He gripped the steering wheel and rested his forehead on his clenched hands, squeezing his eyes shut against the pain.

Images. Of Lisa. Of himself. Of Natalie and Joseph. He couldn't seem to focus.

At last, thankfully, he'd realized that unlike Joseph's debilitating disease, unlike Lisa's sudden and tragic end, this was a dilemma that he could do something about. It was the right thing to do. The only thing. Lisa was gone.

Abortion was not a crime, and he would not be swayed by an emotional appeal from Natalie. She would have to accept his decision.

At his harsh outburst, she had looked down at her clasped hands. She sat stone still; except for the slight rise and fall of her breasts she might have been carved of marble. He was fully aware that she was confused and hurt by his bringing up the idea of abortion. Hell, he was confused, too. And hurt. God, did he hurt.

Now she murmured something in a low voice. He didn't catch the words. "What?" he said, glaring at her classic profile.

Slowly, with an obvious effort, she raised her head, as though the weight were too substantial for her delicate neck to support. Her hair was tumbled. She'd run her fingers through the mass a number of times. The whole picture was of a disarming fragility. Her facial expression was determinedly composed, serene.

Jake knew that her grief did indeed run deep, but the only hard evidence of her distress was the defenseless expression she couldn't quite hide completely in her wet, wide blue eyes. He hardened his heart against the vulnerable sight. He would not be swayed. She would have to—

"I said, 'I think I felt the baby move.' Last week, for the first time. It was a tiny quiver, like a butterfly, inside me. It felt very... real." Her voice broke; she moved her hand absently. "And I remembered what we went through to make this baby, what a miracle it seemed. I can't understand, Jake, how you could even..." Her chin rose. "You see why I have to fight you on this?" she finished.

Jake stared at her, paralyzed by her words. If she had slammed him in the gut with a railroad tie, he couldn't have been more stunned.

At last he shook his head, managing with effort to break off the eye contact. She could feel the baby.

Moving inside her. His baby. Lisa's. Dear God.

Numbly he rose to his feet and, without a word, headed for the door. He felt as if he were a hundred years old. He finally made it outside, pausing to breathe deeply of the clear, cool air.

Slowly he climbed the steps, pulling himself up by gripping the cold rail, and went into his dark house. He didn't turn on any lights, but made his way, stumbling once, through the darkened kitchen and dining room.

In the living room, there was a faint reflection from the street lamps. He found the sofa and sat down. He felt that if he moved too abruptly he would break into a thousand pieces.

Over the past month and a half, he had achieved a certain fragile calm, and, he thought, acceptance of his wife's death. Only now did he realize how wrong he'd been.

His head fell back on the cushions and he stared at the ceiling. A car's headlights illuminated the moving shadow of a tree branch outside the window, making an eerie pattern across the ceiling.

He looked to the bare spot over the mantel where the portrait had hung. "Lisa, Lisa," he whispered harshly, when what he wanted to do was scream. "Damn you, Lisa. Why the hell did you leave me?"

Downstairs, Natalie fought off nausea by taking deep breaths. When she was able to stand she circled the apartment, turning off lights, until she reached the bedroom. She lay down on top of the bedspread, staring at the ceiling, her emotions swirling in a black fog, her heart knocking painfully against the wall of her chest. Finally she drifted into an uneasy sleep.

Natalie stayed away from the kitchen window until she heard the car and knew Jake had left for work. What was she going to do? Jake didn't want this child, didn't want any reminders of Lisa. It followed, logically, that he wouldn't want her here, either.

For Natalie, the most difficult part of this arrangement was having to forgo her independence and her established life-style for the duration of the pregnancy. She had known it wouldn't be easy.

She had been on her own for many years, since the death of her parents when she was eighteen. Even before that, really. Her parents were older than those of her friends. They'd never quite reconciled themselves to this young person who had surprised them with her appearance about the same time her father was ready to retire. Somehow she'd sensed their ambivalent feelings toward having her so late in life.

Even as a very young child she'd always been quiet and careful not to disturb. Some of her contemporaries took her reserve for snobbery. As she grew older, others, including her teachers, thought she was quiet because she was brainy. Even though she was now an adult, only those who knew her best realized that the quiet dignity she had established around herself stemmed from that childhood feeling of vulnerability.

Joseph had known. Being married to him had been wonderful. He had stripped some of the reserve from her; he made her laugh and feel deeply.

After he died she'd been more alone than ever before. She'd had to start all over to shape her autonomous life-style. And when she came to Savannah, Lisa had understood, without discussion, her need to maintain a certain independence during this interval.

So Lisa had arranged the apartment, which served mainly as guest quarters, to be separate from the rest of the house. She had installed a door at the head of the stairs, and she had locked it, giving Natalie the key. "We'll come and go through the outside doors just like neighbors." Lisa had smiled. "It would be too easy for me to pop in anytime I felt the urge. And I don't intend to distract you from your writing."

The financial arrangements had been made through the lawyers. A living allowance was deposited into her account on the first of every month.

At first, Natalie had been uncomfortable about taking money from her friends for something she'd decided she wanted to do. But when practical considerations were taken into account, she'd acquiesced. If she were to quit her job, give up her apartment and move to Savannah, she would have to take the money. Her savings wouldn't be sufficient for her to live on for seven or eight months. So she had agreed to move as soon as her pregnancy was confirmed, to be near the doctors.

Now that conditions had been so drastically altered, she would have to make some more difficult decisions—about where to go from here. And she would have to make them quickly. She hated that. She liked to think things through very carefully, very completely.

Jake parked his sedan in the garage next to Natalie's coupe. Seeing her car there, in Lisa's spot, always gave him a jolt.

It had been a hell of a day, he thought as he turned off the engine and reached in the back seat for his coat. Every day he'd been back had been a hell of a day.

The men around him acted as if they were scared to walk or talk too loudly. But at the same time he could feel their probing stares. They watched him carefully, waiting.

His company had been on the verge of a very large expansion when Lisa had died. When he left after the funeral, all plans had come to an abrupt halt. Now he had to make some decisions.

Andrew had advised him to go ahead with the expansion. "It will be good for you to have work to focus on," he'd said. And Andrew had reminded him that, in anticipation of receiving a bank loan, he'd already hired a number of men. If he abandoned the expansion plans they would have to be laid off; their families would suffer. As if he needed Andrew to remind him. His damn sense of responsibility did a bang-up job of that.

But what about him? Dammit! What about what *he* wanted? He left the garage, pushed through the gate and crossed the garden.

Suddenly Natalie's voice came out of the darkness. "Jake."

Startled, Jake spun around to see her wraithlike figure sitting on the circular garden bench around the oak tree. If she hadn't been wearing a light color, he wouldn't have been able to make her out on this moonless night. "Natalie."

She didn't move. Damn, a confrontation with her was all he needed. He cast his coat over his shoulder, hooked on two fingers. The night was warm and clear. He stood very still for a moment, looking up into the starlit heavens. *Lisa, help me.*

"Were you waiting for me?" he asked at last, resigned to the necessity of this meeting. He came over to sit beside her, laying his coat across his knee.

"Yes. You've been avoiding me," she accused, not unkindly. She wore light slacks and a loose, gauzy top. Her legs were drawn up to her chest and her arms were wrapped around them. She was barefoot.

"Yeah," he admitted, frowning. "Aren't your feet cold?"

She ignored his question; folding her arms across her knees, she rested her chin there. "And now I've caught you unprepared," she said, staring straight ahead.

He sighed, wearily. "Natalie, I'm not sure I will ever be prepared."

"I realize we need time to get used to—" Her voice broke. Abandoning her position she set her feet on the ground and gripped the edge of the bench. She struggled with the rest of the sentence. "Not having Lisa with us." Then she took an audible breath and let it out, and her voice was stronger when she continued. "But we can't put this discussion off much longer."

He leaned back against the tree trunk behind them. The leaves rustled in an unfelt breeze. "You're right. I apologize for avoiding you." The words had to be dragged out of him.

She shrugged dismissively. "I understand. And I'll give you time to think about what you're going to say. Tomorrow is Sunday. I'll cook Sunday dinner and afterward we can talk."

"I can't...oh, the hell with it." He broke off the automatic response.

Natalie surged to her feet and planted her hands on her hips as she glared down at him. "Look, Jake. I don't mean to nag you, but I think you're being pretty damned selfish. There are decisions to be made and other people involved here. Me, for one, and this baby." Natalie held her breath. It was a calculated gamble.

His head snapped up; his eyes narrowed.

"This may sound cruel, but life doesn't stop, Jake. And the problems that go along with it don't just disappear."

"I know. God, I wish—" He paused. "Okay," he said, finally resigned. "What time do you want me to be there?"

"How about one o'clock?"

"Fine. I'll see you at one." He got to his feet and brushed past her. When he reached the steps he took them two at a time.

Natalie remained in the garden for a while longer. The traffic sounds were muted, the night was pleasant. She spoke silently to the stars. *Lisa, I need you to help me out tomorrow. Help me find the right words to comfort Jake, as well as convince him.*

Chapter 3

Natalie put on large silver earrings and took a last look in the mirror. Her sapphire-blue silk dress had a soft easy waist—thank heavens—and a full skirt. She had put her hair up into a no-nonsense chignon. She was probably overdressed for a casual lunch, but she decided that she looked very capable, very efficient, ready to justify her case. That was important to her today.

There was no dining room in the apartment, just a lovely old maple drop-leaf table against one wall in the kitchen. Natalie set out place mats, napkins and silverware there. They would serve themselves from the counter, where she had arranged a platter of smoked ham slices and asparagus salad. A warming tray kept both a casserole of candied sweet potatoes and a loaf of crusty French bread at the right temperature. She wanted everything to be ready when Jake arrived. She didn't want to be bustling around the kitchen and trying to talk at the same time.

When she heard his footsteps on the back stairs she poured iced tea into the glasses at each place. She had raided the garden for sprigs of mint. She left the pitcher on the table for refills and smoothed the skirt of her dress. She made herself wait until he knocked to let him in.

She realized her mistake as soon as he walked in the door. All her careful preparations left her with nothing to do to fill the uncomfortable gap of silence that followed their initial greetings. "Would you like a glass of wine before we eat?" she asked.

Jake noted Natalie's nervousness with a certain wry amusement. It was so unlike her that he smiled. The movement of his lips felt stiff, strange. He realized that it was probably the first time he'd smiled since... since... "No, thanks."

He looked at the food on the counter, arranged attractively and emitting delicious aromas. He was distracted for a minute, wondering when he'd last eaten a well-balanced, well-prepared meal. "I hope you didn't go to a lot of trouble," he mumbled absently.

Natalie snapped her jaws shut on a comeback. There was no sense in antagonizing him again, not when she was about to ask for a considerable concession. "No, no trouble at all," she lied. The truth was she didn't particularly like to cook and, before this pregnancy, was content to grab a bite of whatever was handy without thought of the nourishment within. But now, for the baby's sake, she made an effort to eat the right things.

"It looks good," said Jake.

"Please, help yourself," she answered, handing him a plate.

They served themselves. The only sound in the room was the clink made by serving spoons and forks, which sounded unnaturally loud in the heavy silence. Jake waited politely while she filled her own plate, then held the chair for her.

The silence continued for a few minutes longer as they applied themselves to the food, but at last he laid down his fork, took a swallow of tea and spoke. "I haven't been hungry lately, but this is really good, Natalie."

"I'm glad." She hesitated, but they couldn't skirt subjects related to Lisa's death forever. "I noticed you've lost weight." She caught her breath, waiting for the shutters to fall back over his eyes.

"As I said, I haven't been hungry."

Natalie breathed again, in relief. Maybe it would be all right. "I wish I could say that. Nowadays I always seem to be hungry."

They continued to eat, but the atmosphere had eased a bit. The tension was less charged; the silence, if not companionable, was tolerable.

When they had finished eating, Natalie picked up both plates and went to the sink to rinse them. Jake followed with their glasses. "Thank you. Everything was delicious, Natalie."

"I'm glad you enjoyed it. Why don't you go sit in the living room? Just let me put some things in the refrigerator, and I'll be right there."

He frowned and looked around the kitchen. "I forgot there wasn't a dishwasher down here. Can I help you with the dishes?"

"I'm going to leave them for now. I'd rather we talk." Again she held her breath, waiting for a reaction, but again he surprised her.

She entered the living room a few minutes later to find him browsing through her books. At the sound of her footsteps on the brick floor, he glanced back over his shoulder.

"Your tastes in reading are certainly eclectic," he observed, replacing the book he held and joining her near the fireplace.

She smiled to herself. "I probably didn't have to bring all my books, but somehow I couldn't stand to leave them in storage. They smell so musty when they've been packed up."

She chose a straight-backed chair; Jake settled on one end of the sofa. He stretched his arm along the back of the cushions and crossed one ankle on the opposite knee. It was a position designed to project a casual attitude. But it didn't quite work.

He seemed to be waiting for her to speak first. She decided to plunge right in, using the truth and assuming that the issue of abortion was now moot, though he hadn't exactly said so. "I've always believed that when there was something unpleasant to be gotten through, it was best to get it behind you." She laid her hands in her lap and studied them for a minute. "I feel that I owe it to you to try to explain my feelings. Some of the things I have to say, you've heard before, but maybe not from my point of view. So I have to define my thoughts in sequence. If you'll indulge me...?" She raised her gaze to meet his gray-eyed stare.

"Go ahead," he answered curtly.

"I loved Lisa, Jake. You know that. She was the sister I never had. When she first approached me with the idea of having this child I didn't want to do it. I'm sure she told you."

His eyes met hers. He nodded.

Suddenly Natalie couldn't sit still. She got to her feet and began to roam around the room, absently touching the back of her chair, a book, the edge of the mantel. On one of the shelves was a picture of Joseph. She picked it up. "At the time she brought the idea up, I'd recovered from—from the awful apathy I'd felt after Joseph's death." She replaced the picture and began to roam again. "I'd finally begun to care about life again, about my career at the paper and the free-lance work I'm doing. I didn't want to leave Charleston." She came to a stop before the cold fireplace, her back to him.

"But after I'd thought about it for a while, the idea began to seem more and more . . . right.

"So I changed my mind. I sincerely wanted to bring this life into the world. Partly as a tribute to Joseph's memory, I admit. Partly for me. Partly for you and Lisa." She laughed under her breath and shook her head. "If that isn't a mixed bag of motives, I don't know what is," she muttered.

At last she did turn to look at Jake. He was watching her, his expression noncommittal. She could not read a reaction in his eyes or in the set of his mouth; his posture had not changed by so much as an inch.

"Now, with the situation changed, I've discovered that I want this wholly for myself, Jake." She resumed her position on the chair facing him and leaned forward trying to communicate her sincerity. She laced her fingers and rested her elbows on her knees. "If you'll agree, I'd like to adopt this child."

It was Jake's turn to move. He got to his feet. He slid his hands into the pockets of his trousers and walked a few steps. Then he halted. The silence was thick, absolute.

Natalie could hear the echo of her heartbeat in her ears as she stared at his back. His broad shoulders were bowed under the weight of the decision he had to make. She waited, motionless, afraid to speak. She'd presented her proposition. Now it was up to him.

"Can I let you know tomorrow?" His voice was a husky whisper.

He was crying.

Instantly Natalie's hand flew up, covering her mouth to keep a whimper from escaping. Oh, God. Her eyes filled with tears that threatened to spill over. She wished she dared let them.

She nodded, then realized that he couldn't see her. She breathed deeply through her nose and let her hand fall away from her mouth. "Of course," she said evenly. "I assumed you would need time to think."

Jake lay stretched out on the sofa in the living room, staring at the small portable television set, heedless of the golf game that was being broadcast.

Why had he hesitated? Wasn't Natalie's proposal the best answer? Lisa's parents were too old to take on the responsibility of a child, and he was unwilling to.

He'd thought he'd come to terms with Lisa's death. And, in a sense, he had accepted the reality of it, though the years stretched out before him bleak and empty when he thought of living the rest of his life without her. Yet when faced with a practical matter like this, a decision that needed to be made immediately, he was uncharacteristically indecisive. He couldn't seem to focus beyond tomorrow, and he didn't seem to know what was right anymore.

He linked his fingers together behind his head and wondered if he would have been able to follow through on the idea of an abortion. That night when he'd returned to Savannah to be greeted by Natalie, he had felt a profound and primitive rage—he'd wanted to lash out at her. He'd wanted to wound her. As he was wounded.

It wasn't fair to her, he knew that. But somewhere on the side of the highway between the North Carolina beach and Savannah, he'd lost his sense of perspective.

Could he have gone through with it? He would never know. He'd realized that the presence of a baby in the house would do nothing except generate painful memories of Lisa, memories that would be a further threat to his tenuous hold on rationality.

But since that night, he'd had time to think. They'd all gone through so much in order to have this baby, the weeks of lab work and blood tests, of interviews and counseling and lawyers. The months of waiting.

How excited the three of them had been when, in July, they'd found out she was pregnant. He smiled sadly at the memory.

Like most other newlyweds, he and Lisa had dreamed big dreams eight years ago. Some of the unimportant dreams fell by the wayside; some were fulfilled. And finally their biggest dream—of having a child of their own—was coming true.

Most of the dreams had died with Lisa. A few days ago, he would have said all of them had.

This was the reason for his hesitation, he realized. With the possibility of this child, a piece of the dream remained. And that tortured him.

Natalie decided to change into comfortable clothes before she did the dishes. She donned a faded pink exercise suit, comfortably stretched, and an old pair of sneakers. As she pulled the pins from her hair and let it fall, she told herself again that she was going to have to do something about clothes. Nothing fit comfortably. A barrette secured the thick mane at her nape. She also needed a haircut.

One aspect of pregnancy that she'd found difficult was adjusting to the changes in her body, which no longer belonged only to herself. Though her waist was thick, she hadn't developed much of a bulge in front. But each morning, it seemed, there was something new and mysterious to discover about her own body.

She cleaned the kitchen, lingering over the task, polishing copper-lined pans that already shone. She straightened the living room. Then she stood looking around for something else to do.

The silence was oppressive and amplified her loneliness. She went to her office and sat in her swivel chair, staring at the black computer screen. But she couldn't bring herself to turn it on. Nothing she'd written since the funeral seemed right. She'd used the delete button more often than the one to print.

At last she returned to the living room and flipped on the television, more for the comforting sound of another human voice than because of any interest in a particular program.

She curled up on the sofa and pulled a warm rose-pink afghan over her legs, finally acknowledging the private war that was going on inside her. This indefinite situation piled on top of the pregnancy, her move and Lisa's death had set her emotions into conflict with her normal, rational thought.

What on earth was she going to do if Jake said she could not adopt this child?

For that matter, what on earth would she do if he said yes? Along with the responsibility for a child, she was inviting monumental disorder into her ordered life.

Frustrated, Natalie wrapped her arms around a soft sofa pillow and rubbed her cheek against the smooth nap. With determination she called forth the practical side of her nature. She wouldn't be able to decide what to do until he gave her an answer. So there was no point in dwelling on it.

She put the subject out of her mind. The soft, hypnotic tones of a golf announcer was making her sleepy. Her eyes slowly closed.

She had no idea how long she slept, but the daylight had dimmed when she was awakened by a knock at the front door, the one that opened directly onto the sidewalk. She tossed the afghan aside and got to her feet, still groggy from the aftereffects of a dream she couldn't even remember.

"Jake?" Her surprise was disturbing, as was her accelerated heartbeat.

He'd also changed from the clothes he'd worn at dinner. Despite the weight he'd lost, he was a big man and very strong. His black running shorts and red tank top revealed his broad chest, his flat-as-a-board belly, the long powerful muscles in his legs and arms. And when he gripped the ends of the towel that was slung around his neck, his biceps flexed.

The unexpected sight of so much hard muscle and tanned skin unsettled her. "Sorry. I fell asleep." She shook her head in an attempt to clear the lethargy from her brain. "Come in." She stepped aside to let him pass.

Jake took in her heavy-lidded gaze, slightly out of focus, her tousled hair. He felt a smile relax his lips, ease the tension around his eyes. In the old warm-up suit she looked very languid, very approachable, very...sexy.

Instantly he stiffened, blasting himself. Where the hell had such an inappropriate thought come from, anyway?

He could see past her into the room. The bright afghan on the sofa had been tossed aside. "I'm sorry I woke you."

She waved aside his apology and swallowed a yawn. "Don't be. I shouldn't sleep now, anyway. I'll have a hard time falling asleep at bedtime. Won't you sit down?"

He closed the door but remained standing beside it. "No, thanks. I just want to say this and get it over with." The next few minutes were going to be bitter ones, but he really had no choice.

He took a deep breath and faced Natalie, letting his hands fall loosely at his sides. When he spoke, his voice sounded forced even to his own ears. "I've come to tell you that I think your offer to adopt the baby is probably the best thing for everyone."

His statement wiped the languor from her soft blue eyes. She straightened. "You do?" she asked, a slow smile spreading across her features.

He clutched the ends of the towel again and looked at her steadily. He could see the relief rising within her, and begrudged it, when all he felt was desolation, wondering if he was doing the right thing. "I have every confidence in you, Natalie. I know you'll be a good mother to this child." That, at least, was the truth.

"I will try my very best, I swear it, Jake. Thank you." He watched her blue eyes grow dark with emotion, until they were almost purple. He looked away, unable to bear her exhilaration.

"I'm not sure what sort of legal arrangements will be necessary, but I can find out. I know this is best. And I would never shut you out of the child's life. In a few years you may decide you want to be involved—"

"No," he said harshly. "This child will always be mine in some ways, I can't escape that. But I want you to know that I'll consider it your child from now on. I don't want to have anything to do with it."

Or you, he might have added aloud. Natalie's loneliness suddenly seemed even more vast than before. The silence stretched between them while she searched for comfort in his consent to let her adopt the baby. "I'll make plans to move back to Charleston immediately."

He held up his hand. "I've thought about that, too." He paused as though choosing his words carefully. "It would be senseless to lie, Natalie. I'm very tempted to let you go, to try to get on with my life without any painful reminders. But your leaving isn't the answer. Even if you left, I'd still feel responsible for you as long as you're pregnant. You'll have to stay here until the child is born."

Her eyes flashed her annoyance. Then he remembered her independent streak.

"That sounded very much like a rehearsed speech," she said, irony strong in her tone. She also wondered why, if he was anxious to sever all ties with the baby, he was insisting so strongly that she stay. Responsibility aside, it didn't quite make sense.

She dismissed his puzzling logic and returned the focus to her own objections. "I don't want you to feel responsible for me, Jake." She folded her arms against her chest. "I don't want *anyone* to feel responsible."

"Nonetheless, I do. You've given up your apartment and your job. You are over four months pregnant, and you've uprooted your life for this child. Your doctors are here in Savannah. I think we should stick to the original agreement."

"No matter how averse you are to the idea?" she persisted. She shook her head decisively. "It won't work, Jake. The pregnancy is already becoming evident. In a short time I'll have to wear maternity clothes. You were right. You'll think about Lisa and the baby every time you see me."

Inadvertently his gaze went to her belly, then away. He raked his hand through his hair. She was so different from his Lisa. He hardened his expression. "Our personal feelings aren't the issue. The point is you have no choice."

He knew as soon as the words were out that he shouldn't have made it sound like a challenge. Hell! He wasn't handling this well.

Clearly provoked, she planted her hands on her hips. "I certainly do have a choice."

The militant reaction was so unlike her natural ladylike demeanor that he almost smiled. But he caught himself in time. *That* would have added the proverbial fuel to her fire.

"I always have a choice," she repeated.

He crossed his arms and looked down at her. "Oh, and what is that?" he asked mildly.

"I can move back to Charleston, find another apartment, another job, another doctor."

"It took a long time to find a doctor who would even take our case originally. It wouldn't be that easy to find another doctor now. Yours is not exactly a normal pregnancy."

He could see that he was only adding to her irritation by tearing down her arguments as soon as she put them forth. But he couldn't seem to stop himself. How the hell had this discussion deteriorated so quickly into a two-way power struggle?

"As I said, you have no choice," he told her flatly, hoping to bring the argument to a close.

To his horror, he saw the tears well in her eyes. But then his gaze narrowed. These were not tears of grief. They were tears of frustration and resentment. "Look, Natalie," he continued calmly, trying to calm her. "We're adults. We can work through any problems that might come up. The only practical answer is for you to stay here. You have a home, an allowance, a good doctor who cares about you. You'd be a fool to chuck all the arrangements we've made just because of false pride."

"A fool?" Another mistake. She glared at him. She started to go on, then stopped. Taking a long, deep breath, she made a clear effort to regain her composure. Finally she said, "Maybe you're right about some things." She pronounced the words as though they left a bad taste in her mouth, and he almost smiled again.

Natalie raked him with her angry gaze and struggled to control herself. He didn't move a muscle. She tried to think. He *had* made some important points. She liked Dr. MacGregor very much. She would hate to change. Also, she had to admit that to move again in her condition would be a problem.

Perhaps she could live here without seeing much of Jake. If she were really alert she might be able to avoid him completely. He had many friends; they would keep him occupied and out of her way.

She tilted her head back to meet his eyes. "All right. Maybe I should stay here where the doctors are, and where I have a comfortable home. But you can call off the allowance, Jake. Under the circumstances I wouldn't feel right taking money from you."

He gave her a disgusted look. "That's no argument. The money is in a trust. You know that. I couldn't stop the allowance if I wanted to—which I don't. How do you think you're going to live without money?"

I'll manage. Somehow I'll manage. "I'm pregnant, not an invalid. I'll get a job."

"I can't argue with you, can I?" When she didn't answer, Jake sighed heavily and reached for the doorknob. After this he was ready for a good hard run. He opened the door and stepped outside.

She followed and stood in the doorway. "I'll try to stay out of your way."

He threw up his hands in mock disgust and chuckled. "You drive a hard bargain, Natalie Armstrong. Get a job if you have to. I'll see you later." He headed out the door into the twilight and moved off at a slow jog. Despite his show of impatience, he felt fairly good about the outcome of this confrontation. He'd won

most of the disputed points. She was going to stay here
where he could keep an eye on her.

Natalie felt a grin spread across her face as she
watched him go. She felt okay about their shaky truce.
She'd won on the most important item.

Even if she couldn't stop the money in the trust
from accumulating, Natalie was determined not to use
it. She wanted to support herself. But finding a job
was not as easy as she had thought it would be. The
newspaper, while impressed with her credentials, was
not hiring. The major advertising firms in town had all
the copywriters they needed at the moment. She
searched the want ads for a week before she found one
that looked promising.

A gift shop on River Street was looking for a sales-
clerk. She had wanted to visit the quaint area as soon
as she'd arrived. But Lisa, self-appointed tour guide,
insisted that Natalie first had to see the fabulous
homes. So—they'd toured homes, and cottages, and
a plantation. They'd had such fun. She smiled at the
memory.

River Street was a narrow cobblestone road that ran
parallel to the Savannah River and was a favorite spot
for tourists and natives alike. The shops and restau-
rants there had an unobstructed view of the ships that
traveled upriver from the Atlantic.

Across the narrow road, beside the water, was a
broad esplanade with trees and benches and colorful
plantings. Outdoor concerts were often performed
there. And the Riverwalk was not far from Jake's
town house. If she could get the job, she could walk to
work when the weather was nice. That would fulfill

Dr. MacGregor's orders that she exercise every day. She had to get started on that, she reminded herself.

The store's owner, John Barnard, was young and male. And very, very French. His accent was easily understandable. He was dressed in velvet trousers, white silk shirt with pirate sleeves and sported a gold earring. Though slightly built, he seemed to have enough energy for two men. As she discovered during the short interview, he was an entrepreneur who owned a number of small ventures around the city.

He explained that he had come to the United States to study at Harvard and had simply decided to stay. That was ten years ago. He was often needed at the other locations, he told her with wide flamboyant gestures. She would mainly be left on her own.

He wasn't completely satisfied when he found out she was pregnant. "But you're the best of the bunch who've applied for the job, m'dear," he told her. "At least you have enough sense to figure state sales tax. Can you start today?"

Natalie hesitated a moment, then shrugged. Why not? She stored her purse beneath the counter and went to greet her first customer.

She found she liked the work. John was candid and pleasant and, she soon discovered, a shrewd businessman. People were in and out of the shop all afternoon—tourists, mostly, but a few local people, too. She enjoyed watching the ships pass. The large window that faced the cobblestone street gave the shop an unrestricted view.

"Why do the ships all blow their horns after they pass?" she asked during a break in the customer traffic.

"Oh, m'dear, it's a wonderful story," John explained. "It's called the legend of Savannah's Waving Girl."

Many years ago, a young girl had waited at the lighthouse downriver for her lover to return from the sea. When she received the news that he'd been lost, she was devastated. She began her custom of waving to every vessel that entered Savannah Harbor. The tugs and the bar pilots responded by blowing their ships' horns in reply as they passed the Elba Light. "Even today most of the captains honor the statue of her with a blast," John finished the tale. "You should visit there one day. You might get an idea for a story. Even if you don't, the statue is something to see. It was done by the sculptor who did the Iwo Jima Memorial in Washington."

She had told John that she was a writer, but she hadn't mentioned her novel. Still, it was a romantic, interesting legend and very possibly something she might use. She promised herself she would walk down to see the statue at her first opportunity.

When she dragged in that night at nine-thirty, Jake was waiting. He jogged lightly down the back steps to hold the gate open for her. "Where the hell have you been? Do you know what time it is?" he demanded testily.

She proceeded through the gate and toward the back door of the apartment. "I found a job and—"

Jake followed on her heels. "A job?" he asked, trying with a visible effort to maintain control of his temper. "Already?"

"Jake, I told you I would be looking for a job," she explained patiently.

"Where is this job? In Charleston?" he demanded gruffly.

"What?" she asked blankly. Then she realized that he thought she would be leaving town. That he would even care surprised her. "I'll be working in a gift shop on River Street near the hotel. The owner, John Barnard..." She glanced up at him. "He said he knew you."

"Yes, I know John."

"I put you down as a reference."

"You want to work in a gift shop? I thought you were a writer."

She ignored that. "John was in a kind of a bind today and needed me to begin right away, but I won't always be this late getting home." She took out her key, opened the back door and reached inside to flip the light switch. Then she turned back to him. "Did you want something else?"

He looked as though the question astonished him. "No. It's just that..." He made an impatient gesture. "You don't know a lot of people here. I was... no, I didn't want anything."

"I'll say good-night, then. I'm really beat." She smiled, her hand on the door.

"Good night." He left.

In the days that followed, Natalie's pattern was quickly established. "You're very trusting," she told John when he gave her a key to the shop. It was Wednesday; she'd started work on Monday.

"I checked your references," he assured her. "I want you to open the shop at ten every morning. This will leave my days free to check in with my other businesses. I'll relieve you at six each night and do the book work before I close the shop."

The schedule was ideal for Natalie. A clerk didn't make much over minimum wage, so she planned to supplement her income by writing short articles. She'd already been on the phone to the editors of several regional magazines for whom she'd written before. Putting her novel on hold for the time being worried her, but it couldn't be helped. She reminded herself to write a note to the agent who had been so kind and explain the delay. She hoped he hadn't forgotten her.

She enjoyed working in the shop; she liked the routine and the merchandise, and she loved meeting the people who came in. Her spirits were boosted by the contacts. John had a playful side that was reflected in his buying, and the shop was filled with unique items.

She rarely saw Jake that first week. She had no idea what time he left for work, but it was before she got up in the mornings. And she often heard him come in late. She knew he was working on an expansion plan for his business. The construction of new warehouse space and the purchase of new equipment had been started before Lisa died.

On Friday morning she dressed for work but kept her nine o'clock appointment with Dr. MacGregor. It was the first time she'd seen him since Jake had returned and they'd agreed on the baby's future.

The doctor told her she needed to gain some weight and asked if she'd kept to her daily walk. He frowned a bit when she told him she was walking to work.

"You have a job away from the house? I thought Lisa and Jake told me you were a free-lance writer. Weren't you writing a book?"

"Yes, but... well, things have changed." She hesitated. "Jake's back."

He nodded, gave her a keen look and asked a few pointed questions about the job. When she answered honestly, he shrugged. "Working won't hurt you. Just be careful about standing for too many hours at a stretch. And add a few calories to your diet."

"I have something I'd like to discuss with you," she told him after he had concluded his examination and she was dressed again.

He nodded. "Come into my office. We won't be disturbed there."

She sat in one of two chairs for patients that faced his ancient metal desk and crossed her hands on her lap. "This is difficult for me, Dr. MacGregor, but I feel I need to discuss it with someone." She paused. "Jake doesn't want the baby," she said.

Instead of retiring behind his desk Dr. MacGregor took the other chair, beside her. He didn't comment.

"He says...he has agreed that I may adopt..." Her voice caught in her throat.

"Oh, Natalie," he said with a sorrowful, bittersweet smile. "We never dreamed it would turn out like this, did we? The three of you had such high hopes."

His concern, his empathy, the first genuinely kind response she'd heard since Lisa's death, was nearly her undoing. "After all we'd been through to ma-make this baby, he wanted me to have an abortion." Her voice rose a bit on the last word, but she fought against letting the tears fall. She was afraid that if she ever started, she wouldn't be able to stop.

"I know," he said quietly. He plucked a handful of tissues from a box on the desk and handed them to her. "He came to see me before he talked to you."

Her eyes met his kind gaze as she crushed the tissues in her grasp. For a long, silent moment she was unable to talk. "He came to see you? Why?" she finally asked huskily.

"I'm not altogether certain." He shook his head slowly. "We talked a bit about Lisa, where he'd been, unimportant things, until finally he got around to the baby." He waved his hand dismissively. "I told him that the baby's future was a decision for the two of you to make."

"I guess we've made it."

He settled back in the chair and linked his fingers over his paunch. "Natalie, you mustn't blame Jake too harshly. He was deeply distraught, to a degree that he wasn't thinking clearly."

She had to remember that Dr. MacGregor was Jake's friend. He would make excuses for him. "I understand that. And I loved Lisa, too."

She concentrated hard on a picture of a sailboat hanging on the office wall, trying desperately not to lose the slender hold on her equilibrium. All her doubts, all the problems she'd put off facing, all the obstacles she'd put out of her mind with such determination, seemed to be rising up to taunt her.

He leaned forward to take her hand, holding it tightly. "It would help if you could cry, Natalie," he said, his voice low with compassion. "Cry it out here, where it won't matter. Let the tears wash away your frustration and unhappiness. You'll feel better for it."

With his kindness to brace her, she was almost persuaded to let go. Almost. To ease the pressure that at times was unbearable. The hand he held remained lax, but she clenched her other hand into a fist, digging her nails into her palms. The small hurt reminded her of bigger hurts. "No. I can't." *I might not be able to stop.* She tried for a laugh. "I have to go to work, and I don't want to show up with a blotchy face and red eyes. I'd frighten the tourists away."

She pulled her hand from his. He watched her reflectively. "Natalie, have you cried at all since Lisa's death?"

"No. I'm afraid to," she admitted.

He dismissed her excuse and smiled his patient smile. "Don't be afraid of tears. They often have a healing effect. You have good reason to cry. You've suffered an appalling trauma, and you've held your feelings in check far too long. Now you're faced with another major change in your life that you weren't prepared for. I realize that these are personal problems, but I have a stake in you and this child, too. If you need to talk—"

Natalie pulled her shattered composure together. "I appreciate that, Doctor. But Jake and I are reasonably intelligent individuals. It may take some time—it would be useless to try and rush it—but I'm sure that between us we'll work this out."

He seemed relieved. "I'm sure you will. Have either of you considered outside adoption? I could put you in touch with an agency."

Natalie caught her breath and stared at him. The question rocked her foundations. It upset her almost as much as Jake had when he'd suggested an abortion.

Give up this child to a stranger? The only child she would ever carry within her womb? Never.

Her backbone seemed suddenly to be made of steel. She shook her head, grateful to have recovered her balance and determination. Now she could give him a confident smile. "No, we haven't discussed it, but I don't think that would be an option for either of us. Thanks, Doctor." She checked her watch. "I've kept you too long."

"I can be here as long as you need me, Natalie."

She remembered Jake saying those very words to her on her first day in Savannah. And look what happened to *his* support. The memory served to remind her that the best person to depend on was herself.

"Nevertheless, I'd better get to work and let you do the same." She dropped the unused tissues into a wastebasket and reached for her purse as she stood.

"Very well." Dr. MacGregor sighed and got heavily to his feet. Before he released her, however, he gave her a few additional instructions and changed her vitamins. "Don't forget to make an appointment as you leave. I'd like to see you in three weeks." He jotted something down on a prescription pad. "Here's my home number. Will you call if you need me?"

She opened her mouth to tell him that she wouldn't need anyone, but then she closed it again. He was simply trying to be kind. And he didn't press her further on the personal issues. For that she was relieved. She gripped the slip of paper, anxious now to get out of the office. "Yes, I will. Thank you."

When she was back in her car she rested her head against the seat back for a minute. Outside adoption? Let someone else have the baby? She faced the prospect with a real feeling of repugnance. Not a chance. But it was odd that the thought had never even occurred to her.

And odd that the idea hadn't occurred to Jake, either. She wondered if she should discuss it with him, then dismissed the idea as unnecessary.

Chapter 4

The first difficulty with Natalie's job came at the end of her first week. She was supposed to have weekends off—John had a college student who worked with him on Saturdays and Sundays—but he called early Saturday morning to tell her to open the shop and plan to work all day.

She was tired, but of course she agreed. It was a good job in pleasant surroundings, and she didn't want to lose it. She dressed in a pleated navy knit skirt and a white sailor-style top trimmed in bright shades of crimson that covered her hips. Her navy shoes had heels higher than she liked to wear now, but they were the only ones she had that went with the outfit. She had planned to go shopping for clothes today.

When she dragged herself home at six-thirty that evening, she found Jake waiting. He took one look at her and demanded, "Did you have lunch?"

"I didn't have time," she admitted.

"We're going to Tibernio's," he said, mentioning an Italian restaurant a couple of blocks away that served delicious food. She'd been there with Jake and Lisa one night shortly after she'd moved in.

She didn't argue too strenuously. Maybe this would be a good time to see if there was a chance of their being together with any degree of comfort. But when he would have hauled her off immediately, she protested. "I have to go inside first," she said.

"Why? You look fine."

She knew that was a lie. She started to tell him bluntly that she had to go to the bathroom, that pregnant women did that a lot. Instead she said, "If we're going to walk, I'd like to change my shoes. These are beginning to pinch."

When she got inside, she took one look at herself in the bathroom mirror and groaned. No wonder he thought she needed food. The blush she'd applied to her cheeks that morning had long since disappeared, and she had rubbed off all traces of her lipstick. She was naturally pale; she didn't tan well so she avoided the sun. Combined with her pale hair and fatigue, her fair complexion made her look washed out even when she felt fine.

Hastily she made the repairs and changed into a pair of traditional loafers. They didn't complement her outfit but they felt good. She hesitated over her hair. It was fine and tended to be flyaway, so she rarely wore it down. But the pins that had held it up all day were beginning to aggravate her. If she was going for comfort, she might as well go all the way, she decided.

Jake waited in the living room. He turned when she entered and stood very still. He hadn't realized her hair had grown so long.

Or that it was so beautiful. The shining mass reached midway down her back. At the crown, it gleamed like highly polished gold and when she moved he could see silver lights in the curling ends. Honey and moonlight, he thought.

When he didn't speak, Natalie stopped. She'd used a twisted red scarf as a head wrap to hold the thick mass off her face. "Alice in Wonderland in a sailor suit, right?" she said with a disparaging gesture at herself. "The pins were hurting, but...should I put it back up?"

"No, no. I just didn't realize your hair was so long."

"I need a haircut. I'd planned to do that today, but then John called me in."

"It would be a shame to cut it," he said, then wished he hadn't. The comment was too personal. What did he care if she cut her hair?

Conversation was sporadic between them as they walked to the restaurant. But Jake was very much aware of the woman beside him. Too aware.

The maître d' greeted them at the door. "Good evening, Mr. Armstrong." After a discernable pause, he went on. "I was very sorry to hear about the accident, sir. We'll all miss Mrs. Armstrong. You know she decorated—"

"Thank you, Morris," said Jake crisply, cutting him off. Damn, he wished all the well-meaning people in town would just keep their mouths shut. "Do you remember my sister-in-law?"

The man looked chagrined, but he nodded politely to Natalie, who smiled.

Jake looked around the crowded restaurant. "It looks like business is good, Morris. I should have called for a reservation."

"Reservations are never necessary for you, Mr. Armstrong." He bowed toward Natalie. "Nor for your family."

When they were settled in a booth, Morris signaled for the waiter. Jake took her menu away from her. "I'll order for you," he said.

"I'm..." Natalie started to protest, then thought better of it. "All right." She listened in amazement as he ordered—clam chowder, house salad, grilled swordfish with a baked potato, vegetables, a glass of milk.

"And for dessert—"

"No," she finally broke in. "No dessert," she told the waiter herself. "Jake, I'll never be able to eat that much food," she complained amiably.

He nodded at the waiter. "Cheesecake," he told the man firmly. "We'll take it with us if she doesn't eat it."

"Why did he say that reservations were never necessary for *you?*" she asked, emphasizing the last word as the maître d' had. "At the door?" she explained when he looked blank.

"Oh. Lisa talked me into putting some money up. She thought a neighborhood restaurant would be a good investment."

Though she'd been here once before, she looked around with a fresh eye, noticing her friend's distinctive stamp on the decor. "Obviously Lisa was right. She always did have good instincts."

"I didn't think you worked on Saturdays," he said in a transparent attempt to change the subject.

She sighed and relaxed against the plump cushions of the booth. "I'm not supposed to, but the other clerk didn't show up today."

"Natalie, if you don't take care of yourself, who will?"

"I'm fine, Jake. I had an appointment with Dr. MacGregor yesterday."

He hesitated, then said, "I know. I called Mac last night. He said you'd told him what we'd decided. He also said it wasn't good for you to stand on your feet all day long."

She leaned forward to plant her elbows on the table. "Jake, we've been through all this. I'm going to work. I was lucky to find a job I enjoy, and if John has an emergency I'll do what I can."

"Even if it isn't good for you?"

She let the question slide, determined not to argue. "I've noticed you're putting in long hours, too. How are the plans for your expansion going?"

He raked a hand through his hair. The gesture said as much as words that he was under intense pressure. "I'm still negotiating for a piece of property that I'd like to have. It isn't vital, but it would give me a second rail spur. I don't want to begin construction until I have an answer."

She recalled a conversation they'd had months ago. "Is that the property that's tied up in the estate of the illiterate plumbing magnate?"

"You remembered that?" He seemed surprised.

"Sure. You talked about it when I first moved here."

He smiled deprecatingly. "God, I must have been boring."

"Not boring at all. Seven kids fighting over forty-three million dollars. That's the stuff of great American novels."

Jake looked across the table at her. He realized that since she'd moved here she'd shown more interest in his expansion than his beautiful wife had ever shown. Lisa had been bored by business, even the business end of her own decorating shop.

"When will you know about the property?"

He was still caught up in his thoughts. With an effort he recalled himself to the present, mentally setting aside his memories. "The first of next week, I hope. I signed a note at the bank yesterday for a hell of a lot of money." He'd finally deferred to Andrew's urgings to throw himself into his work, and he'd found that his assistant was right—initially, anyway. He wasn't sure how much it would help down the road, but it gave him a lot to think about today. "I don't want that money to sit in an account doing nothing for longer than a few days."

She shuddered lightly and smiled. "I can't imagine how it feels to borrow a lot of money." She looked down at the table and traced a design on the white cloth with an unpolished fingernail. "I've never even liked to make payments on a car."

He studied her bent head for a minute, wondering if she realized how revealing her statement was. He knew that Joseph had died leaving debts. Not more than his insurance would cover, but she had been left with very little after those debts were settled. She had never complained, wouldn't even discuss letting him help, but she'd sold their house and moved into an apartment.

The candle on the table between them illuminated her face. Her thick lashes cast shadows on her cheeks. "Would you like to drive out to the site tomorrow?" he asked suddenly. "See what all this talk is about?"

"Yes, I'd like to," she said with a smile. "I've always wanted to know what goes on around the docks."

"Nothing very exciting. I hope you're not disappointed."

"I won't be," she assured him.

Strangely, Jake believed her. The waiter arrived just then to place steaming bowls of chowder before them. "This smells good," he said, picking up his spoon.

Natalie made a sound of agreement and began to eat.

"Thank you, Jake. That was delicious," Natalie said as they left the restaurant. "Although I can't believe I ate the piece of cheesecake," she added.

When the evening had begun, she had wondered if they could spend time together comfortably. If her appetite was any indication of comfort, she'd been very much at ease. She slid a glance at Jake, who had eaten well, too.

"I'm glad you enjoyed it," he said absently. He walked along for a few minutes, his head bent. There was very little traffic on the narrow streets. "Would you like to see a movie or something?" he asked abruptly.

The invitation surprised her. First he'd taken her to dinner, then he'd suggested the trip to the construction site tomorrow, and now this. Did his sense of responsibility include thinking he had to entertain her?

"Thank you, no." She checked her watch in the light from a street lamp. "It's early yet. I want to write for a while tonight."

"Maybe another time."

Their footsteps echoed hollowly on the sidewalk. "Yes," she agreed. "Another time."

The next morning, as she dressed in yet another expandable warm-up suit, this one royal blue, Natalie reflected on the preceding evening. Heartened by Jake's concern for her health, she concluded that it had been a beginning of sorts. She just wondered how long it would last.

She slid her feet into her sneakers and bent to tie them. On the day of the funeral, and again after he had returned to Savannah with his ominous request, she had despaired of his ever being able to face her pregnancy with any equanimity whatsoever. But after last night, no matter what he said, she was beginning to hope that someday, when he could deal with it, Jake would want to know his child. And that would be good for all of them.

She entered the sun-washed kitchen, opened the refrigerator and stood there staring in, wishing she'd saved the cheesecake for breakfast.

The telephone rang in the living room. She let the refrigerator door swing shut and went to answer. It was Jake.

"Are you ready?" he asked.

"Jake, it's only eight o'clock," she said with a laugh. "I haven't even had breakfast yet."

"We can stop on our way. There's a pancake restaurant not far from the site."

Suddenly Natalie had a suspicious thought. "Jake, you said you'd called the doctor. Did the two of you happen to discuss my nutritional habits?"

"He may have mentioned that you could stand to gain a few pounds," Jake said after a short pause, then he laughed under his breath. "But the last time I saw him, he said the same about me."

That would have been the day Jake returned to Savannah. She remembered how thin he looked, but . . . "You're not— Oh, never mind."

All sorts of arguments about the right to privacy flew through her mind, but she discarded them. She was afraid they wouldn't apply in this situation. "All right. I'll be ready."

Natalie sat in the passenger seat of Jake's car and watched his profile. The sunlight streaming in through the windshield poured over them. She didn't know exactly when it had happened, but sometime during the course of the morning he had withdrawn into a place where she couldn't follow.

They'd stuffed themselves on buttermilk pancakes and maple syrup. At the pier he'd made her don a hard hat and had given her the "complete hands-on tour," as he'd called it, of his vast waterfront domain. She'd been curiously exhilarated by the sight of the operation, the huge containers that could hold hundreds of tons and the huge cranes to lift them.

Goods from all over the world arrived through the port of Savannah, and American goods departed from here to ports in Europe, the Far East, South America. Docked this morning, but idle except for the presence of security guards, was a large ship bearing automobiles from Germany and Great Britain.

In his conservatively decorated offices, which were a sharp contrast to the rough dockside, Jake had shown her the plans for expanded warehouse space. It all seemed unbelievably complicated.

"How on earth do you know which containers go where?" she'd asked. "Do you ever send anything to the wrong place?"

He'd laughed—his deep, husky laugh that she'd not heard since Lisa died. "Come with me," he'd said leading her to a large room. There he had explained the computer-driven program of accounts, inventory lists, bills of lading, time schedules, locations of ships and trucks and trains—until she begged him to stop, for her head was spinning. Later they'd walked over the property he wanted to purchase.

But sometime during those hours he had retreated, and she tried to recall exactly when it had happened. Surprisingly his retreat had not made conversation uncomfortable. He seemed able to function on two levels. Clearly he had become distracted by something he wouldn't discuss with her, but it hadn't affected his good manners. Not this time, at any rate.

"Thanks for the tour. I enjoyed it." Suddenly she realized what had caused the withdrawal. "Hands-on," he'd said; hands-on it was. He'd taken her hand as they stepped over waist-thick coils of rope. He'd laid his arm across her shoulders to turn her toward a scene he wanted her to see. He'd had to touch her, and it bothered him.

She felt the heat rise to her face and reached forward to direct the air-conditioning vent toward her.

"Are you still warm?" he asked, unaware of where her thoughts had taken her. After the tour they'd returned to the car to be hit by an oven-hot blast when they'd opened the doors. Now he'd adjusted it to a comfortable low breeze.

"A little bit," she answered.

* * *

Occasionally over the next couple of weeks, Natalie arrived home from work to find Jake waiting for her. She smiled to herself when she remembered thinking that if she stayed in Savannah she wouldn't have to see much of him. She suspected that he often timed his homecoming to coincide with hers.

Sometimes he took her out to eat; sometimes they had food delivered and once or twice she cooked. One evening he came for her at the shop and they walked down the cobblestone street to look at the statue of the Waving Girl. Jake added a few comments to what John had told her about the statue. Natalie was captivated by the expression on the girl's face, part sorrow, part hope.

It was all very platonic. As soon as they had eaten, Jake always left and she headed for the computer. There was no repeat of the physical contact that had occurred the day of the tour.

She was managing nicely. She'd finished two short articles for *Southern Life* and expected a check for them soon. She'd even gotten in some work on her novel, though not as much as she would have liked.

When she and Jake were together, they were both careful to avoid sensitive subjects, like her pregnancy—with one exception.

She happened to mention that Dr. MacGregor insisted that she walk every day for exercise. From then on, Jake seemed to think it was his responsibility to see that she complied.

However unnecessarily, he had taken her on as an assignment, and she couldn't fathom his motives. He didn't want to become involved, he'd made that clear.

She couldn't come up with an answer that satisfied her.

She had to admit to herself, however, that she hadn't probed her own motives too deeply, either. She told herself that she still didn't know many people in town, and she would be lonesome if it weren't for him. In fact, she enjoyed being with him.

One rainy evening she drove into the garage, parked and hurried to her back door. Something, some movement above, caught her attention. She looked up to find him standing silhouetted in his doorway, the light from the kitchen beyond illuminating his large form. Obviously he had been waiting for her.

"Hi," she called, shaking the moisture from her umbrella as she unlocked the apartment door.

"Hi, yourself. You drove to work today."

It was an accusation, but an amused one. She laughed. "Jake it was raining this morning. It still is, if you haven't noticed. Even though I drove the car, I still got soaked getting *to* the car." She indicated her wet shirt with a sweeping hand.

"Change your clothes, then, and we'll go over to the mall for your walk. We can get something to eat while we're there."

"Okay."

The mall, she thought, as she pulled on a pair of slacks. If she could get rid of Jake maybe she could do some shopping at the maternity store. No, she shut off that thought. To flaunt this pregnancy in front of him would be to deliberately inflict hurt.

But she was going to *have* to do something about clothes.

* * *

When they got home from the mall, Jake said good-night and waited while Natalie closed and locked her door. Back upstairs, he paused on the landing. The quarter moon cast a weak light on the garden below.

Fall had arrived. The blooms were fading on the roses, he noticed. Today's steady rain had drummed off some of the other flowers. The garden was a mess.

Lisa will have a fit. The garden is her pride and joy.

Then he remembered. The familiar pain hit and he gripped the rail with both hands, closing his eyes tightly against its power. God, he hated these flashes of memory that caught him unawares like this. He had an idea that tonight his conscience was reminding him—with a forceful nudge—that his wife had only recently died.

His conscience probably thought he needed the reminder. He thought about the day he had taken Natalie out to the docks. He was working diligently on his expansion and, spurred on by her interest, he found that he liked to talk to her about it. He also found that she was quicker than Lisa to grasp both the substance and the excitement of his plans for the business.

He chided himself for that disloyal thought. His enthusiasm had bored Lisa, and his wife seldom feigned interest in things that bored her. She hadn't been a hypocrite.

He had simply thought Natalie might enjoy a tour. The sensations had crept up on him slowly, when he'd taken her hand to help her over a rough spot. A few minutes later he realized that he still held a woman's hand in his. The dissimilarity between his large rough palm and her soft, slender one left him shaken.

And then he'd noticed her perfume, something light and floral, clean smelling and delicate in contrast to the heavy, masculine odors of the riverfront. Her laughter was musical; her wide eyes, as blue as the sky on that warm October day, were expressive; her gestures were expansive but very, very feminine.

Since then, the realization had grown stronger each time they were together. Tonight at the mall he'd again taken her hand without thinking. And as they'd waited for a table in the restaurant, they'd been squeezed together for a heart-stopping moment. He'd felt her breasts brush against him, his nostrils had been drowned in her scent.

She had felt it, too. Her eyes had darted to his, then she had hurriedly looked away.

Not that his response was to Natalie, per se, he persuaded himself. He'd responded because she was a woman, a very beautiful, very feminine woman. He and Lisa had shared an active sex life. It was only natural for him to begin to notice soft, womanly things.

The pain and his conscience began to ease. He went inside the house, locking up behind himself.

As he lay on his back an hour later, his fingers linked under his head, he recalled another occasion, years ago, when he'd told himself that something was "only natural." But there had been no danger then.

He felt a jab of conscience again. That incident at the hospital, when Joseph was so ill... Damn. Muttering obscenities, he switched on the light beside his bed. He reached for a manual he'd been planning to read.

Tomorrow he would call the man who had sometimes helped Lisa with the garden.

* * *

Halloween arrived and Natalie had found a terra-cotta jack-o'-lantern stored in one of the kitchen cabinets. She bought a warming candle to set inside and placed the grinning pumpkin face in one of the front windows. Sure enough, it attracted dozens of trick-or-treaters to her door.

Goblins and witches, princesses and green turtles screamed, "Trick or treat," and giggled as they held out decorated bags. She contributed wrapped fruit candies and packages of sugarless gum.

The main house above remained dark and quiet. She found out the next morning that Jake had been to dinner with friends, Billie and Matt Turner. And that he was not happy about it.

Evidently Billie had invited a number of people for dinner and she'd seated Jake next to a divorcée. "Can you believe the nerve of that woman? Trying to fix me up with a *date?* She was supposed to be Lisa's *friend.*"

"I don't know Billie, but I'm sure she didn't mean it in an inappropriate way," Natalie soothed, but she couldn't completely suppress a smile at his outrage. Lisa would have loved it; she was a notorious matchmaker herself.

When he saw her lips twitch, he scowled and stalked off to work.

One Saturday evening in early November Natalie arrived at the house, her arms loaded with packages. She had spent the entire day at the mall, but she'd bought only enough to get by. Pregnancy wasn't an experience she would ever repeat. But at last she had some clothes that would fit comfortably.

Jake had just parked his car in the garage. He saw her and came to help. "I'd say you cleaned out the store," he accused with a good-natured grin as he took two of the shopping bags she carried.

She hesitated briefly, but it was long enough to draw his gaze. "I was forced to buy some maternity clothes," she said. She'd also had her hair trimmed. Not cut short, as she had planned, but trimmed the slightest bit.

His grin disappeared like a puff of smoke. He nodded, his gray eyes clouded, his expression unreadable. "I see."

Jake deposited Natalie's packages on the kitchen table and left immediately. He knew he was going to have to get over this dislike of any mention of her pregnancy. It was a fact of both of their lives.

When she had wanted to move, he had been the one to convince her to remain, to point out all the reasons why she should stay in the apartment. And he was the one who initiated their contacts now.

It was almost as though he couldn't keep away from her.

He told himself it was because she was pregnant. And while he didn't want to spend all his free hours with her, he felt a responsibility to show his concern, to keep her from feeling abandoned and lonely. He couldn't forget that she was in Savannah because of him and Lisa.

The next night Jake was back. Natalie had just unlocked the door to the apartment when he drove in.

"Natalie?" he called out.

She dropped her purse on the kitchen counter. "Hi," she said, turning at the door to face him. He looked tired, she noticed as he reached her side. His tie was pulled free of his collar, his top shirt button open and the bulging briefcase he carried seemed to weigh him down.

In his free hand he tossed his keys and caught them in a fist. "I'm sorry about last night."

She nodded. "Please don't be concerned. I understand," she said.

"It's just that sometimes things like that hit without any warning."

And they always left him reeling. She didn't need to hear him say the words to know how he felt. She took a step forward to join him on the stoop. "I remember the feeling very well. It still happens periodically."

Her comment drew his sharp gaze. "You mean . . . after three years?"

She looked up at him, wishing for his sake that she could deny the truth, that she could give him a specific date in the future when he would be free of pain. But she couldn't. "Joseph was a vital part of my life. I'll never forget him. The sadness becomes a kind of nostalgia . . . like a deep regret for unfulfilled promises, but it still exists." She laughed lightly. "Listen to me. Joseph would say I was being wildly poetic."

He touched her shoulder in a gesture of support. "Have you made plans for dinner?"

She was surprised into answering honestly. "Not really."

"I thought we could walk over to Tibernio's," he said casually.

They'd eaten there several times; the food was always delicious. "Thank you, Jake, but not tonight. I'm really bushed. And—"

"And you want to write," he finished for her. He hefted his briefcase. "I have some work to do tonight, too. But we both have to eat," he urged.

He was sincere. And he was right; they had to eat. Mentally she reviewed the contents of her refrigerator. "Okay. I'd like that."

"Ten minutes?"

"I'll be ready."

Natalie had to redo her chignon. The slight trim had been just enough to make it difficult to keep all the ends tucked in. She had worn one of her new dresses to work. It was holiday red, a lightweight wool challis. And it was huge on her, falling straight from her shoulders to her knees. According to the saleswoman, though, during the last few weeks of her pregnancy she would be lucky if she could get into it. A broad white collar framed her face. She wore a new pair of comfortable black flats with it.

November had brought a change in the weather. Tonight it was cool, chilly almost, as it had been for the past week. The dress had long sleeves, but she put a sweater over her shoulder.

Jake was waiting when she joined him on the front sidewalk a few minutes later. He'd exchanged his sport coat for a leather jacket. "Are you going to be warm enough?"

"I'm fine."

The street lamps came on as they walked along the sidewalks toward the restaurant. They seemed to be directing their steps from one pool of light to the next, as though seeking warmth.

Unexpectedly Natalie flinched and put her hand to her stomach.

"Are you all right?" he asked quickly, reaching for her arm.

"I'm fine. It's nothing."

But it happened again and she couldn't control her start of response or miss his urgent look. She decided to explain before he could ask. "I think it's hiccups," she said.

"Hold your breath and count to ten," he advised.

"Not me. The baby."

"Oh," he said. "I didn't know that happened."

"I didn't, either, but that's what it feels like."

They didn't speak again until they were at the restaurant.

The weeks crept by. Nothing happened to mar the fragile harmony, and gradually Natalie and Jake began to relax around each other. Natalie's natural sense of humor began to reassert itself.

Early one morning, however, when that attribute would have served her well, it deserted her completely.

She had only been awake a few minutes when the doorbell rang. She hastily pulled on her robe, drew it across her ever-expanding middle and tied the sash. She opened the door a crack to find a deliveryman there.

"Clyde" was embroidered in white on the breast pocket of his lavender coverall, and beneath that the name of a pricey furniture store in the suburbs. The stub end of a cigar protruded from a corner of Clyde's mouth. It smelled like burning rubber.

"Mrs. Armstrong?"

"Yes."

He waved to another man who was unloading a large flat box from a truck, made a note on his clipboard and held it out to her along with a chewed-on pencil. "Sign here, please." The other man trundled his dolly up onto the sidewalk, unloaded the box and returned to the truck for another.

She opened the door, took the clipboard and scanned it quickly, but the items were listed by number, not name. "I haven't ordered anything," she protested, trying to give the clipboard back to him.

"You said you were Mrs. Armstrong."

"Well, yes, but—"

"This is baby furniture, a special order, placed..." He finally took the clipboard from her and ran a grimy finger across the top. "Last July."

Natalie closed her eyes. Oh, God. Now she remembered. As soon as Natalie's pregnancy had been confirmed, Lisa had placed the special order for the nursery she'd planned to decorate.

Natalie opened her eyes and stared at the man. "I'm not that Mrs. Armstrong."

He checked his clipboard again and rolled the cigar to the other side of his mouth. "Let's see...14057 East Harris." He checked the brass number embedded into the brick on the side of the house. "Nobody answered the door up there," he said, indicating the main entrance. "This is that address, too, ain't it?"

"Yes, but you can't bring it in here," she informed the man.

Jake must be in the shower. Or he might have gone to work. She hadn't heard him leave, but that didn't mean anything. Maybe this was a lucky break; she could get rid of these people and call the store to explain. She could just imagine the scene if he came out to find these men unloading a van full of baby furniture.

"Look, the stuff's already paid for, lady," the man said impatiently. "And I'm in a hurry. I've got a whole tractor trailer load to deliver today."

"But I didn't pay for it. It isn't mine. You'll just have to take it back to the store. Someone will be in touch."

He took a step toward her. "Look, lady, I ain't movin' this damn stuff again," he growled. A puff of noxious smoke hit her in the face. "This is the address on the order, and this is where I'm leavin' it."

She fought against gagging at the smell of the cheap cigar. "Get that thing out of my face," she ordered, her anger rising to meet his as she waved away the smoke. She planted her fists on her hips; her voice grew louder. "I told you, you *aren't* leaving it here. It isn't mine, and I don't know what to do with it."

His gaze dropped to her rounded stomach, barely enclosed in her robe and much more obvious than when she was properly dressed. "It looks to me like you might think of something," he said sarcastically, releasing another puff of smoke. "So where do you want it?"

"What's going on here?" said a deep voice as Jake stepped out of the door above them. His hair was wet from the shower. He wore trousers and a white shirt, but the shirt wasn't buttoned to the top and he hadn't put on his tie.

He hesitated for only the briefest second while he took in the sight of the men, the truck, the growing pile of merchandise on the sidewalk. Then he came down the steps to stand beside her, putting his broad palm reassuringly against her back. "Are you okay?" he asked tersely.

Her heart sank. She appreciated his concern, but wished he would disappear. She could deal with this. She nodded. "I'm fine. Jake—"

But he had turned the threat of his gaze on the deliveryman, who rolled the cigar to the other corner of his mouth. Jake topped him by almost a foot.

"Can I do something for you?" asked Jake pleasantly, but the threat remained in his eyes. The man at the truck had ceased his unloading and now stood watching interestedly.

"Yeah. I got a load of baby furniture for Mrs. Armstrong here."

Jake's hand fell away. She saw him breathe in and pale slightly as he glanced down at her stomach. He couldn't seem to look away. Finally he met her eyes and she recoiled from the accusation there. His gaze shifted to the items piled on the walk—a chest, a shelf, the long box.

His expression was noncommittal, though, as he turned back to the man. "Then unload it and get the hell out of here," he said in a low, dangerous voice.

The man started to say something, but he took a look at Jake and evidently thought better of it. He motioned to his partner. "Let's get movin'."

"Jake—"

Ignoring her, Jake crossed the sidewalk and headed back up the steps. Annoyed, Natalie watched him go; she knew exactly what he was thinking.

Before he went inside, he paused and spoke across the railing. "Hey, you."

The man looked up, surprised.

"Get rid of the cigar before you set a foot inside that apartment."

"Yes, sir!" The man stomped toward the truck. He balanced the stub of his stogie on its fender and climbed into the back, muttering to himself.

"Where would you like me to put this, ma'am?" said his partner politely. He had hefted the long, flat box in his widespread arms.

Natalie frowned at him. "What *is* that?" she demanded.

He craned his neck to see a series of numbers written on the bottom end of the box. "I think it's the pieces for a crib. It'll have to be assembled."

"Great," muttered Natalie. She stepped back from the door so he could pass. "In here."

The apartment had limited space—most of which was quickly filled with what appeared to be enough furniture for two babies. She had him put the long box, which indeed did contain parts of the crib, in the room she was using as an office. There was also a mattress for the crib, a chest of drawers, a bath and changing table, a high chair, two sets of shelves and boxes filled with exquisite imported linens.

It was a tight fit, but they managed to squeeze most of the furniture into the small room. They wedged the bassinet into an empty corner of her own bedroom. There was no space left for the last item, a lovely antique rocking chair. "Just leave it in the living room," she said at last.

After she had signed the invoice and the men had left, she went to the telephone. Jake answered on the third ring.

"I wanted you to know that I didn't order the furniture," she told him evenly.

He was silent for a moment. Then he sighed. "Yes," he said. "I figured that out."

"Jake, I regret that this happened, but I don't appreciate having the blame automatically placed on me for anything that upsets you. I wasn't the only one involved, you know."

"Sorry," he said.

Just the one word, nothing else. If he'd been in the room with her she would have shaken him. She gripped the telephone until her knuckles were white. "I am determined to be pleasant around you, even if we disagree. If something bothers me, I'm going to talk to you about it. Do you think you could manage the same courtesy?"

She paused, but when he didn't reply she went on. "If you can't, I would prefer we stop spending time together. It isn't good for my nerves."

"Nerves?" he shot back. "I didn't know you had any."

She caught her breath. "That was a rotten thing to say. Just because I don't—"

"Natalie," he interrupted, saying her name very softly. She could imagine his expression, hard, unyielding. His jaw would be clenched and he would be speaking through his teeth.

"Natalie," he repeated. "I will do what I can to make you comfortable for the duration of the pregnancy. After that, I will gladly bow out of your life."

"Fine," she said sharply. "That's exactly how I want it." She hung up.

Chapter 5

After Thanksgiving, the weather in Savannah turned bitterly cold. Though the winter months were not severe, autumn often delivered a damp, chilling wind off the river that was far from comfortable. Natalie began using her car to get to the shop. As a result she had to do her walking in the evenings.

Jake had worked straight through the holiday weekend. He was still pleasant, still checked on her, still walked with her when the weather allowed it, still took her to eat occasionally.

He was polite, but the warmth had melted away from his expression when he looked at her. Indeed, ever since the day he'd shown her the docks, he had avoided doing that as much as possible. And since the scene with the furniture men, things were different, more difficult between them.

Or was that when it started? Natalie thought back. She knew her appearance was at least partly to blame.

With her stomach growing larger every day, the pregnancy was too obvious to ignore. But she had begun to anticipate their times together, the congenial, benevolent atmosphere between them, and she was sad for the loss.

Christmas weekend was as bleak as any holiday she'd ever known. Jake knocked at her door on Christmas Eve to say goodbye. He was spending two days with Lisa's parents in Charleston. They had included Natalie—via Jake—in the invitation, but she had declined.

The first Christmas after Lisa's death would be a sad, tense time for all of them, but if she were there, in her condition, the tension would be unbearable. Besides, she wasn't sure she could endure it, either.

"I know you'll be lonely, Natalie," Jake told her. "And I hate to leave you." To his surprise the statement was true. He did hate to leave her alone. "But the Reeds need me to be there."

"I understand, Jake. Don't worry about me."

As she watched him walk away, she patted her stomach. "Just you and me, Mischief," she said, using the nickname she'd conferred on the baby. "I guess we'd better get used to it."

Wasn't talking to yourself an indication of some kind of mental disorder? She smiled. Talking to your unborn child was surely acceptable.

Christmas Day seemed to last at least a week. Natalie tried to make it festive. She rose early to put a recording of Christmas carols on the stereo, and she dressed in a long red caftan that Joseph had given her their first Christmas together. At eleven o'clock she put a ready-to-cook turkey breast in the oven. She even prepared a packaged dressing and opened a can of cranberry sauce. But when she sat down at the table alone, her appetite vanished.

She tried to remind herself that next year would be different; she and the baby would be a family. "Next year, Mischief, we'll have a tree to decorate and presents and everything," she promised the bulge, rubbing her hand comfortingly over her stomach.

The baby kicked, hard, as though in understanding. The communication, primitive as it was, heartened her. She felt better, less lonely, as she put the food away and sang along with the stereo as she washed the dishes.

Finally she stretched out on the bed and slept the afternoon away.

Unconsciously she listened throughout the evening for Jake's return. He came in sometime after eleven. When she heard his car, she went through the dark kitchen to the back door.

She wanted to say something to him, even if it was just to ask if he'd had a pleasant trip. She needed human contact, words spoken aloud, a smile; after all, it was Christmas Day.

But when she looked out the window, she decided against it. He walked slowly, head bent, a picture of desolation.

By the twenty-sixth, she was relieved to be back at work. Until she heard John's plans.

"A convention is scheduled in the riverfront hotel for the first week of the new year," he explained. "Ordinarily we close during that week to list the stock for tax purposes. But there are megabucks to be made, m'dear. This year we'll have to do the inventory after-hours."

Natalie smiled at his flamboyant gestures, but nonetheless she felt her spirits slump. She was seven months pregnant now and didn't move as easily as she had. Dr. MacGregor had suggested that she participate in the Lamaze classes given by the hospital. The first class was scheduled to begin next Sunday afternoon. She also had to finish an article about Savannah's city parks for *The Georgian*. She'd promised to have it ready by January 10.

Her reaction must have shown on her face. "Of course, I'll pay you time and a half for the overtime work," John added hastily.

She nodded. "All right," she told him.

On the evening of January 7, Natalie and John finally completed the inventory. It was the first night in a week she had gotten home before ten o'clock.

Just inside the door, she stepped out of her shoes. She flipped on the light and padded into the living room. She pulled off her coat, dropped it on the floor and dug her fingers into the small of her back. She caught a glimpse of herself in the mirror over the fireplace. Shocked by her appearance, she headed for the bathroom, where she turned on the overhead light and looked more closely.

There was no color in her cheeks at all, not even reflected color from the red maternity dress, which had become her favorite. She picked up a strand of her hair that had worked free from her chignon and brought it forward to examine it. Dull and lifeless—just like the shampoo ads warned. She let the strand fall over her forehead into her eyes. Extending her lower lip out from her upper, she blew the hair off her face.

She returned to the living room, noting that her coat still lay where it fell, and she collapsed on the sofa. She ached all over—her head, her feet and every bone and muscle in between. She maneuvered a pillow under her swollen ankles and lay back. As soon as she was prone the baby started kicking.

"I know, Mischief, I know," she soothed, rubbing her stomach. "We're hungry, aren't we?" She closed her eyes. In a minute she would get up and fix something to eat, she thought. Then she would have a long soak in the bathtub and go to bed.

The article for *Southern Life* was almost done; all week she'd worked late into the night, hauling out the reference books on Savannah history. Tomorrow was her day off, and if John Barnard knew what was good for him, he'd better not call her in. She would finish the article and get it in the mail.

Tonight she and Mischief needed rest. She had put the saltshaker away in November, so she knew that her swollen feet and ankles were a bad sign. If the swelling wasn't gone tomorrow, she would have to call Dr. MacGregor and make an appointment to have it checked. She refused to think about what she would do if the condition turned out to be something serious. Not tonight.

Instead her mind wandered to happier times.

When her stomach was flat.

On that thought, she fell asleep.

Jake's knock went unanswered. She was home. He'd seen her car come into the alley half an hour ago.

He was aware that she and John had been working late every night, taking inventory at the shop on the riverfront. He had worried about it earlier, but when he mentioned it to her she'd said it was only for a few days.

The lights were blazing from behind the kitchen curtains; she had to be up. She was careful about things like lights. He knocked again. Still no answer.

Puzzled, he backed off the step and circled around to the front of the house, let himself through the iron gate that shielded the narrow strip of side yard from the street. This door opened directly into the living room of the apartment.

The shutters over the front window were open, allowing light to spill onto the sidewalk. Not very smart, Natalie, he thought. Though this section of historic Savannah wasn't a high-crime area, break-ins weren't unheard of. He looked in.

She was sound asleep on the sofa. The rise of her belly looked as though it were too much weight for her. At least, he presumed she was asleep. She was facing away from the door. But he could see that her bare feet, propped high on a pillow, were severely swollen. One arm was crooked above her head, the other dangled off the sofa, fingers almost touching the floor.

His heart rose into his throat. The vulnerable position seemed to expose a defenselessness she was careful to hide when she was awake.

He knocked again, then returned to the window. She hadn't moved. Did the effects of pregnancy generate such heavy sleep naturally? Concerned now, he fished out his keys.

He entered the room and closed the door behind him, not attempting to mute the noise. The first thing he noticed was that the room was cold. She must have forgotten to turn up the furnace when she came in. He had on corduroy pants and a sweater and the chill was creeping in on him. She wore a light wool dress and no shoes.

He saw that logs were stacked in the fireplace, the same ones he'd stacked there a week ago. He thought about lighting the kindling beneath them to get this room warmed up. But first—

Hands planted on his hips, he stood looking down at her. Her beautiful face was pale and taut with weariness. Her eyelashes fluttered lightly, casting moving shadows on her cheeks.

Then he saw her coat on the floor. Negligence was so unlike her that his heart began to race, and he felt a moment of real panic. He hunkered down beside the sofa and brushed away a strand of hair that had fallen across her forehead. "Natalie," he said gently. "Natalie, wake up."

She stirred slightly, then settled back into a deep sleep.

He laid his hand against her pale cheek. Was she feverish? He couldn't tell. "Natalie," he repeated, louder this time.

She opened her eyes halfway, then closed them again. And her lips curved into a lovely, tender smile. "Hi," she said softly.

"Hi," he responded, relieved that he'd gotten a reaction. He relaxed and smiled. "I was worried when you didn't answer the door."

She moved her head, her lips brushed his palm and stayed to nestle there in an unquestionably affectionate gesture. Her skin was warm, smooth, silky. She was sweet and strong and—

Jake pulled his hand away, as though he'd been burned by her touch. What the hell was happening to him? Was he losing his mind? He stood, stumbling a bit as he regained his balance.

The abrupt movement brought Natalie fully awake. Her eyes grew wide as his stunned gaze met hers—met and held for a long breathless minute. Suddenly she raised herself on her elbows and looked around as though she didn't quite know where she was. "Oh, Jake. Sorry. I must have dozed off."

His eyes narrowed as he looked down at her. He wouldn't have thought she could have gotten any whiter, but she was. "You weren't dozing, Natalie, you were out like a light." His voice sounded strange—harsh and tough and angry. He moderated it before he spoke again. "Are you feeling all right?"

"I'm fine," Natalie answered automatically. But she wasn't, and she knew it. For just a moment as she was waking, she experienced a sense of happiness and contentment unlike anything she'd felt in years. Now she was simply cold. "I could use a hand getting up, though."

He bent beside her again to scoop his broad palm beneath her back. She sat up and swung her feet to the floor. Suddenly her head swam and her mouth was filled with a sharp metallic taste. She tried, unsuccessfully, to cover the moan that escaped from her throat as her head fell sideways to rest on his shoulder.

"You are not fine," said Jake accusingly, tightening his arm around her. His fear returned in a rush. "Don't move. I'm calling Mac."

"Jake, please wait." She put her hand on his corduroy-clad thigh to stop him.

Jake froze at the warm contact. He glanced down at Natalie. He must have looked shocked.

"I am a little dizzy," she admitted in response to his expression.

He breathed a sigh of relief and got himself under control. Thankfully she hadn't noticed his reaction. This woman was pregnant—sick—and here he was aroused because her hand felt so good on his leg. *Armstrong, you're a jerk.*

"I'm sure I'm just tired," she went on. "It's late. Let me get up, wash my face and see if I feel better before you call the doctor."

He searched her features for a moment, concerned. "Have you eaten?" he asked.

Natalie snatched at the excuse, for once grateful that Jake seemed to have a fixation about food. "No, I haven't had time. That's probably what's wrong with me."

He offered his hand to give her a boost.

The moment she stood the nausea hit. She clamped her palm over her mouth, forgetting her swollen feet, forgetting her headache and dizziness and every other symptom, in her rush for the bathroom.

Jake was right behind her as she attempted to shove the door closed. "No!" she wailed. Her stomach heaved then, and she forgot him, as well.

Jake took charge without asking her permission. Poor kid, he thought as he held her.

He supported her convulsing body with one strong arm around her shoulders, while he reached for a washcloth and wet it in the sink. He squeezed the water from it and was ready when she finally raised her head, gasping for breath. He continued to hold her as he bathed her pale face, gently soothing her brows. Her breath shuddered on a last sigh and she opened her eyes.

"Better?" he asked.

She nodded. "Thank you," she whispered. She started to pull away. But instead of letting her go, Jake lifted her in his arms and carried her into the bedroom. He deposited her on the bed and leaned down to brush her sweat-dampened hair away from her face. He hadn't realized until he'd lifted her how slender she was. For a pregnant lady, she weighed almost nothing.

She rolled to her side and curled into a fetal ball, her arms crossed protectively on her stomach. He pulled the comforter over her and patted her on the back. "Stay there," he ordered in a gentle tone. "I'll be back in a minute."

Natalie nodded. She felt too miserable to argue right now. But a few minutes later she was ready to. He returned to the room carrying her coat. "I don't want to go to the hospital, Jake," she protested when she realized his intentions.

"Sorry, honey. I called Mac and he will meet us there. My car is parked out front." He'd moved it from the garage and left the heater running before he came back for her. Now he helped her get her arms in the sleeves of the coat. Then he picked her up with the comforter still wrapped around her legs.

"I can walk," she protested, but his strong arms and broad chest made a secure place to rest, and she didn't protest too emphatically.

"I know, I know," he murmured soothingly. He carried her out to the sidewalk and held her in one arm, with her bottom supported by his knee while he opened the car. As he'd hoped, it was warm. He deposited her on the seat, folded the comforter in around her, closed the door and returned to lock the apartment.

"I really hate hospitals," she said when he joined her in the car.

He knew why. He turned toward her, his left forearm draped over the steering wheel, his right arm along the back of the seat. She stared straight ahead; her chin was hidden in the folds of the comforter. He brushed a strand of hair off her cheek and tucked it behind her ear. "They aren't my favorite places, either," he said seriously.

During the hours they'd spent at the hospital with Joseph, he, too, had grown sick of the smell, the whispered sounds, the macabre humor. "Mac wants to check you over, Natalie," he told her gently. "And I want to make sure for myself, too. Okay?"

Natalie sighed heavily and rolled her eyes. He was feeling responsible again. "All right," she said, though she was fully aware that she was going to the hospital whether she wanted to or not. In his present take-charge mood, Jake wasn't flexible.

She rested her head on the headrest and watched from the corner of her eye as he drove, his competent hands easy on the wheel. He was competent at every thing he did. Even in holding her head while she heaved. She would have thought she'd be embarrassed at anyone's having seen her throw up, but she wasn't. Her lips curved in a humorless grin. Instead she'd been grateful—grateful for his support and grateful that she hadn't been alone.

Dr. MacGregor was waiting for them in the emergency room. "Natalie, Jake," he greeted them shortly, while his gaze took in her pale face.

A nurse with a wheelchair waited to take her to the examining room. "I can walk," she objected, just as she had to Jake. But this time she meant it.

"Hospital rules," the nurse said shortly. "Besides, you don't have shoes on."

Natalie looked over her shoulder to stare at Jake. Her eyes were large and dark in her white face. "I forgot my shoes," she said, as though forgetting her shoes was the worst thing that had happened to her tonight.

"Please sit down," said the nurse. It wasn't a request; it was an order.

Jake steeled himself not to cringe at the expression in Natalie's blue eyes. Her look appealed to him for support. He forced himself to smile encouragingly when what he wanted to do was run like hell. "Go with the nurse," he said. "I'll wait here for you."

He returned to the waiting area and slumped down in a molded plastic chair. The noise and bustle of the emergency room surged around him while he sat oblivious to movement or sound.

That look of appeal, of entreaty, had shaken him badly. Especially after the way he'd reacted to her touch earlier. And the hell of it was, he'd brought it on himself.

Jake muffled a groan and leaned forward in the chair, his hands dangling between his knees. On the linoleum floor at his feet was a red-and-white chewing gum wrapper. He picked it up and tossed it into a trash can. A white-clad nurse strode by, on her way into the room where Natalie and Mac had gone. He watched, waited, but no one came out.

He sat back in the uncomfortable molded plastic chair, crossed his arms over his chest and stared somewhere into the middle distance.

When Lisa died he'd thought he'd wanted to untangle himself, to free himself from the complications that surrounded this woman and this baby. He'd had no serious reservations about Natalie's staying in the apartment because he knew that she was very independent, that she would assume responsibility for herself, would not expect more of him than he was prepared—or able—to give.

But he had known for weeks now that he was getting involved more deeply than he'd intended. That was the reason why he had tried to back off a bit, to put some space between them.

This, tonight...this was more than simply being involved in her life, in her health. Tonight, when he'd seen her sick and weak, her body sustaining his child, he'd been scared out of his wits.

He shook himself free of the reverie. He looked around, spotted a soft-drink machine. Getting to his feet, he dug into his pants pockets for quarters. The drink was cold going down; it tasted good. Instead of returning to the uncomfortable chair, he paced the hall, dodging wheelchairs and guerneys, and a lot of people.

As he walked, he forced himself to face a fact he'd been avoiding. No matter how much he wanted to deny it, he was still bound and committed to this pregnancy. For the present, at least.

After the baby was born, after Natalie returned to Charleston, or wherever she decided to live, then maybe he would be free. But that couldn't happen, not now. Not until it was all over.

One thing he *must* not do was to let himself grow attached to the baby.

He wasn't sure how much time had passed when he heard his name called. A grim-faced Mac motioned him into the examining room.

Natalie lay on a white-draped table covered by a light blanket, her head elevated by two pillows. She gave him a weak smile. Her color seemed better, but her skin was not yet the normal peach color he was accustomed to seeing. The nurse was fiddling with something in the corner.

Jake stood, legs apart, and worked his hands, palms out, into the back pockets of his pants and waited.

Dr. MacGregor ran his finger down a clipboard. Finally he said, "Her blood pressure is slightly elevated. I don't think it's serious. She'll be all right, but I want to keep her here overnight for observation."

Jake nodded. "Whatever you think is best."

"She should be gaining weight steadily at this point, but she's lost a pound since her last visit to my office. She has less than two months to make up for the loss. At this point it is premature to predict a low-birthweight baby, but we must see that it doesn't happen."

"I'll make sure she eats three meals a day."

Natalie lay there, hands linked over her stomach. She felt much better now, able to speak for herself. Her expression grew dark as she glared at the two men who were talking across her as though she were an inanimate object.

"Eating is only part of it. There's more, Jake." Dr. MacGregor chuckled, but Jake could tell that the humor was forced. "This is one stubborn woman. She wants to continue working. I've told her I don't think it's a good idea. Standing on her feet—"

At last Natalie could bear this conversation no longer. She didn't care how felicitous their friendship was. "Would you two please stop it?" she interrupted. "I don't like to be talked about as though I weren't here," she snapped as she struggled to sit up. She was frustrated because of her clumsiness, but immediately Jake was there to help and she finally made it. "Dr. MacGregor, you don't understand—"

Jake put a restraining hand on her arm and looked at her defiant expression. "Mac, would you leave us alone for a minute?" he said.

The older man looked from one of them to the other. Finally he nodded. "I'll get started on the paperwork for admissions."

"Jake, I want—" Natalie began as soon as they were alone.

He interrupted her with a dismissive hand motion. "Look, Natalie. Surely you realize that you can't ignore the doctor's advice. What you want, or think you want, isn't what's important here. What we have to concentrate on right now is what's best for the baby."

She was electrified by his suggestion that she was behaving selfishly. Her emotions had been sitting on the surface all night. She felt angry blotches of color stain her cheeks. "We? Did you say *we?*" she barked. "Since when has the baby's welfare been important to you?"

Jake became very still; the color receded from his face. "I suppose I deserve that."

"You suppose right," Natalie said. Her voice shook under the force of her anger. "You didn't even want me to *have* the baby. If it had been up to you there wouldn't *be* one.''

Her eyes narrowed to slits; she squeezed her hands into fists, her nails digging sharply into her palms. All the uncertainties she'd lived with, the foreboding feelings that she'd kept bottled up inside for months, erupted all at once, like a furious volcano. ''I have had it with you trying to dictate my life when you don't care a fig about me or this baby. I'll make the decisions from now on. Do you hear? I'll decide.''

Her hands trembled as she gestured, her eyes darted wildly, her voice rose and quivered like an arrow plunged into its target. And then she began to cry.

She fought it.

She feared it.

But the tears, held in far too long, would not be denied. They welled up in her eyes, blinding her, spilled over and ran down her cheeks. Her breath caught on a huge, harsh sob.

Instinctively Jake reached out for her. His hand was shaking, but she couldn't see. He stroked her back soothingly in big sweeping circles. ''Natalie,'' he said, his tone quiet and reassuring. ''Please, baby, please be still.'' He pulled her into his arms, held her there, against him, as frightened as he'd ever been in his life. He had never heard anyone cry with such despair.

And he had never felt so helpless, so unequipped. He kept rubbing her back, kept talking, barely aware of his words, only aware of the shudders that rocked through her slight body. ''Listen, if it's what you want, I'll stay out of your decisions,'' he went on. ''But you're going to make yourself ill. I do care about you. And about the baby. Please.''

But she didn't hear him.

In the end, all he could do for her was to hold her securely, as he had held her once before, until the tears and sobs and shudders worked themselves out. He laid his cheek on top of her head and waited.

Finally the tempest began to diminish. Her sobs ceased. She gave a last shiver, a last quavering sigh and shifted slightly. The room became quiet except for the sound of her breathing. She whispered something he couldn't understand.

He moved his hands to her shoulders and half bent his knees so he could look at her face-to-face. Her long lashes were spiked, her lips were swollen and red. "What?" His voice cracked.

"I need a handkerchief," she whispered.

He checked in his pocket, but he didn't have one. He looked around. There was a box of tissues on the counter. Keeping one arm around her he reached out and gathered a handful. He handed them to her.

She blew her nose.

"Better now?" he asked gently.

"Yes. Thank you," she said.

One corner of his mouth lifted. "You're welcome."

"Jake, I didn't mean all those things I said." Her voice was still very subdued. "I'm sorry I fell apart like that."

"No apology necessary."

"You needed the release of tears. Your doctor advised that months ago," Mac spoke from the door.

Jake hadn't heard his friend come in. What was he talking about? He looked at him over Natalie's head, lifting a brow in inquiry.

Mac shook his head at Jake, one quick movement. When he spoke it was to Natalie. "The nurse is here to take you to your room, Natalie. You try to get some rest. I'll check on you before I leave.''

Natalie smiled weakly at the nurse. No argument this time. "All right," she said. She felt completely drained and physically defenseless, as though her bones had melted during the onslaught.

Jake helped her off the table and held onto her firmly until she was settled in the wheelchair. He put both hands on the armrests, holding the chair steady. She looked up into his gray eyes, then away. She dragged her fingers through her hair. Then suddenly she realized what she must look like.

"What's the matter?" he asked, a slight smile tugging at his lips.

She looked at him again. "I'm embarrassed."

"For crying?"

When she nodded, he chuckled and leaned forward to kiss the top of her head. It was a casual salute, but she felt the warmth all the way to her toes.

"That's okay," he said, a teasing glimmer in his eyes. "I'd already held your head while you threw up. After that, crying is nothing to be embarrassed about."

Her groan of laughter was a relief. "You're heartless to remind me."

He touched her nose with a finger and his lips curved in a full, genuine smile that activated the dimples in his cheeks. His eyes crinkled when he smiled, too. She wondered why she'd never noticed.

"That's better," he said when she smiled back. "I'd rather see you laugh than cry," he told her, straightening as the nurse moved the chair away. "If Mac says you're okay, I'll be here to pick you up in the morning."

The two men stepped into the hall to watch her being wheeled away. When the elevator doors had closed behind them, Jake turned to Mac, all amusement gone from his face. "Is she going to be all right, Mac?" he asked.

"I think she'll be better than she was before." He paused.

Jake spoke into the silence. "What did you mean about doctor's advice?"

Mac plunged his hands into the pockets of his white jacket. "You know, Jake," he said almost conversationally. "As close as they were all their lives, Natalie had not cried since Lisa's death. The tension and pressure have been building in her for months. I think that's one of the reasons she hasn't gained as much weight as I would like. She wasn't prepared to go through this pregnancy without the support of her best friend. And she wasn't planning to be responsible for a child."

"And it's my fault?" Jake asked, keeping his expression noncommittal.

"Hell, no, Jake. You know that wasn't what I meant. It's no one's fault. Unless you want to blame fate, and that's a useless exercise. It's just that...well, you're my friend, but she's my patient. I have to concentrate on what's best for her. And you're concerned for her, too. Don't try to pretend otherwise. I've seen the way you watch her."

After the physical reaction he'd felt earlier tonight, Jake was on the defensive. He was aware of it, but he couldn't help himself. He crossed his arms as he glowered at his friend, using his own superior size to his advantage. "Mac, you're getting close to dangerous ground here. Lisa—"

Jake's voice held an unmistakable warning, but Mac chose to ignore it. "Hell, man, Lisa would want you to care about Natalie. Natalie was like her sister. She's a beautiful woman, and she's carrying your child."

He couldn't accept that. "You're mistaken, Mac. She is carrying *her* child," said Jake stonily.

Mac gave a sigh, heavy with regret, and made a note on the chart. "Have it your way. Just make certain that she doesn't suffer. I'll see you tomorrow." He looked up suddenly. "Did Natalie tell you that I suggested outside adoption?"

Jake, who had started to turn away, froze. "You did?" he asked softly. He wondered why there was suddenly a lump in his throat. "When? What did she say?"

"It was a while ago, last September, I believe. I told her I could put her in touch with an agency." Mac shrugged. "She told me that she didn't believe either of you would go for it."

Jake looked at Mac for a long time, not really seeing him. At last he left.

When Natalie was settled in her room, dressed in a wrinkled, faded hospital gown and propped up in the bed, she finally focused on the problems before her. Strangely she found she could face them with equanimity. Perhaps the doctor had been right; perhaps the catharsis of tears was something she needed. She didn't know. All she knew was that she was more at peace than she'd been since Lisa died.

Dr. MacGregor had also decreed that she could not spend eight hours on her feet every day if she hoped to carry this child to term and deliver it healthy.

He'd been brusque and blunt. If his intention was to shock her, he'd succeeded. Of course she would do as he advised; there had never been any question about that. But it wasn't in her nature to let someone make her decisions without even the benefit of discussion.

She could still write. And if worse came to worse, she would have to use the money from the trust in the bank. Jake was right about it being there whether she wanted it or not. But she'd had some idea of returning it to him someday. Or, if that were not possible, of putting it aside in an education fund for the baby.

Right now, however, her health and the health of this child were more important than money or pride.

Dr. MacGregor entered the room, cutting into her thoughts. He was followed by a tall, lanky nurse with a toothy smile and a huge, shiny needle. "We need a little blood," the nurse said cheerfully.

Natalie groaned.

Back at home, as Jake wandered through the rooms of his house, he was more aware than ever of the emptiness of the place since Lisa's death. He rarely heard sounds from the apartment below, but knowing Natalie was there had been satisfying. Now, oddly, he found himself feeling abandoned and lonely.

Hell! He stripped his sweater off over his head and threw it onto the bed. Having her here during these first months was a delay of what he would experience when she was gone for good. And he'd better get used to it. He took off the rest of his clothes and got in the shower.

He would probably put the house on the market, he thought later as he lay in the king-size bed, his hands behind his head. It was too much house for a man alone. There was that word again—*alone*.

He made himself face another truth, the matter of Natalie herself, and the attraction he was beginning to feel. No matter how he tried to deny it, she was acting on him like a magnet, pulling him toward something unknown. At first he'd called it simple affection for his brother's widow. But now he was forced to face the implications of her sensual appeal.

He had *loved* his wife. And he felt like the worst kind of traitor.

Because tonight wasn't the first time he'd felt desire for this woman.

He surrendered at last to the memory that he'd denied for so long, letting his thoughts return to another night, another hospital, another occasion when he'd held her while she wept.

Three years ago, both he and Natalie had been exhausted by their vigil. But over the time they'd spent together, he had come to know her well and had grown to admire her tremendously.

Each morning she had dressed in her brightest colors, made up her face with care and fixed a smile on her lips for his brother. Weeks spent in hospital waiting rooms, weeks of watching Joseph wasting away in spite of tests and treatments, painkillers and prayers, had taken their toll, but she was determined not to let Joseph see.

Jake, however, was there when the smile faded. He knew that she had almost reached the breaking point.

One afternoon Joseph's condition had seemed to be slightly improved, giving them hope. They'd had dinner in the hospital cafeteria; Natalie had been animated and talkative.

But there is nothing so merciless as hope given, then snatched away. When they got back upstairs to Joseph's room, they found that there had been another setback, this one more serious than all the others. Joseph had been moved once again into intensive care. Natalie could not hold her tears inside any longer. She'd put both hands over her face.

He'd seen the tears seep through her fingers; he'd seen the determination leak out of her shoulders and backbone. He had gone to her, taken her in his arms and held her while they cried together for the man they both loved.

She had wrapped her arms around his waist, hooked her thumbs into his belt, holding on as though for dear life. Her sobs had quieted at last, but her body was slack with despair. And so he continued to hold her, moving his hand up and down her slender back in a comforting caress, murmuring into her hair.

He had no idea how long they had stood there. He would never know. But suddenly, unexpectedly, he was aroused by her woman's soft curves. And before he could draw away, she had made a soft kittenish sound and moved against him. For just a moment, a split second, his arms had tightened. He'd bent to her, and she had arched to him.

Instantly they'd sprung apart, as though they'd been cleaved with a ax, and stared at each other, horrified. "Oh, God," she'd whispered, her blue eyes desperate.

There was no blame to be attached. They'd been equally moved to reach out for warmth and life in an emotionally devastating moment; they were equally embarrassed. They loved their respective spouses deeply, with total commitment. Nothing would ever come of it.

It was nothing, they told themselves and each other. But why had he never forgotten it?

Chapter 6

The night was long.

The following morning Jake rose early. Sunlight streamed in through the window as he dressed in jeans, shirt and sweater. He hesitated before he left the bedroom. Then he went back to his closet to take out a leather duffel bag.

He might feel uncomfortable invading Natalie's personal space, but, hell, he'd been married. He knew that Lisa would have been grateful to anyone who provided a change of clothes, a hairbrush, her makeup case. He just hoped Natalie would appreciate it.

He unlocked the back door of the apartment and entered the kitchen. On the living room sofa one pillow still bore the imprint of her head; the other, her feet.

In the bedroom he paused over the sight of the white wicker bassinet, its body at waist height on sturdy reinforced legs. A rigid canopy shaped like a deep shell covered half the oval basket. A few items of very small clothing were stacked neatly on the mattress. He touched the rim of the small bed; it rolled slightly. He turned away and went directly to the closet.

He stood there for a minute and stared at the few things that were centered on the rod. He thought the collection looked rather sparse, and it brought home to him how very important having this child was to Natalie. She obviously was very aware that she would never have another. He took out a pink-and-black outfit and folded it. Then he packed it, along with a pair of flat-heeled shoes, in the duffel bag.

In the bathroom he found her makeup and toiletries. He hesitated over the bottle of multivitamins and minerals on the shelf. Then he tossed it into the bag, too. Anything else? he asked himself.

Oh, yeah. Underwear. He opened a drawer.

Like everything in the apartment, like Natalie herself, the drawer was exceptionally neat. A whiff of her scent reached his nostrils, and he identified a bag of sachet. Folded on the right side were the practical items. He unfolded a pair of cotton panties. Roomy. Those, he presumed, were for pregnancy wear. But on the other side was a colorful spill of seductive silk and lace. He couldn't resist lifting a delicate ivory teddy by its thin straps. Sexy, very sexy.

He replaced the teddy as he found it and knew a poignant moment's pang for the loss of soft, silken things in his life.

Natalie was sitting on the side of the bed, staring dolefully at the breakfast tray that had just been delivered by a nurse's aide, when Jake walked in. The smell of citrus after-shave and cool outdoors arrived with him.

"Good morning," he said. He dropped the leather duffel bag he was carrying on the floor at the foot of the bed and grasped the high rail with both hands. "I saw Mac in the hall outside. He'll be here in a minute to dismiss you."

His smile was bright against his dark mustache. His hair was still damp but neatly combed, and his jeans were pressed. The collar of a yellow oxford shirt lay neatly over the neck of his green wool sweater. He slid his hands into the pockets of the jeans, tightening the fabric across his flat stomach. No matter how unsuitable it was for her to notice, he did look wonderful.

"Fine."

His smile faded under a frown of concern. "Don't you feel better today?" he asked.

She had dressed, too. But in contrast, her dress, the same one she'd arrived in last night, was a mass of wrinkles, her hair was flat on one side and tangled on the other. She wrinkled her nose and turned away. "Yes," she said, cross more with herself than with him. "I'm fine. Back to normal."

His smile faded; he leaned forward slightly. "No one would ever know it from your expression. Why are you so grumpy this morning?" he asked.

"I'm always grumpy in the mornings, especially when I look like I spent the night in a toxic waste dump and you're so—" she waved her hand in his general direction "—so neat."

He laughed then, a deep rich laugh. "I can take care of that," he said, the smile lingering on his face. He picked up the duffel bag and laid it on her lap. Then he removed the plastic cover from a plate of limp toast and cold, dry eggs. "Good God," he said.

She agreed; she'd already decided that she couldn't stomach the hospital food. "What's in here?" she asked, eyeing the bag. It wasn't hers.

"A change of clothes."

"For me?"

"Sure."

A change of clothes meant he'd rambled around in her drawers, and she did not like that. She tightened her lips, ready to tell him that he should leave her things alone, when Dr. MacGregor walked in, clipboard in hand.

"You slept well, Natalie," he informed her, perusing the papers on her chart. He lifted her foot in its disposable paper slipper that the nurse had provided and probed her ankle with his thumb. "Your blood pressure is down and the edema seems to be gone." He raised his eyes. "How do you feel this morning."

She made her voice sound chipper. "I feel much better, Dr. MacGregor. I'm certain now that I was just overly tired."

"Exactly," he answered. "And we can't have any more of that. Don't let yourself get run down like that again, Natalie. You're a strong woman and a smart one. You know what you have to do."

"Yes, I know." There was no hesitation, no reluctance in her when she answered.

Jake straightened from the position he'd taken against the wall. "I called John Barnard before I came over this morning to explain why she wouldn't be able to return to work," he told them.

Dr. MacGregor nodded his approval.

"John said for you not to worry. He understood."

The fact that he'd called her employer didn't endear him to Natalie, but she bit back an automatic protest. She'd already made up her mind to put this baby first, even if she had to sit on her pride. Still, she would have preferred to have called John herself. "I could have taken care of that."

He lifted a dark brow. "I thought it would be considerate to give him as much time as possible to find a replacement."

Once again she found herself in the position of having no choice in the matter of her own affairs. And she hated it. "You were right. Thank you. I'll call him when I get back to the apartment."

The doctor shuffled the papers, made a note and looked up with a smile. "Well, Natalie, I guess there's no reason for you to hang around here. I want you to take it easy for a couple of days. You don't have to be in bed, but try to stay off your feet as much as possible. As soon as you're dressed you can leave." He noticed the tray and its unappetizing contents for the first time. He shuddered. "If you're feeling chivalrous, you might even take her out to breakfast," he told Jake.

"I'll get something to eat at home," she said firmly. "But I would like to change my clothes. Thank you for everything, Dr. MacGregor." They shook hands. "I'll be ready in a minute," she told Jake. She carried the duffel bag to the bathroom and closed the door.

Jake had packed everything she needed. Everything. The idea of his rambling around in her underwear drawer still rankled, but she was grateful for the clean clothes. He'd brought black knit slacks and a rose-pink maternity top, banded on the sleeves and hem with black grosgrain ribbon. The color added some life to her complexion. Her black flats were in the bag, and she put them on.

She brushed her teeth, washed her face and applied a touch of blush from her makeup kit. There wasn't much she could do about her hair but brush the tangles out and pull it back with the large barrette he had also packed. Her hair still looked dull and lifeless. When she got back to the apartment she was going to shower and shampoo and give herself a lemon rinse. That should make her feel human again.

Her efforts earned her a smile from both men as she stepped out of the bathroom. Jake's smile was particularly warm. A nurse appeared with the hated chair.

At the main entrance Jake helped her on with her coat. They said goodbye to Dr. MacGregor and left the hospital.

During the first part of the drive Natalie remained silent. Jake, however, talked freely about the very thing she didn't want to talk about—her job and how it had eaten into her writing time. She caught her lower lip between her teeth.

"Jake," she said at last, cutting him off with a slicing motion of her hand. "I know that I had to give up the job, okay? But I enjoyed it. I enjoyed the work, and I enjoyed meeting the people who came into the shop. I enjoyed feeling useful and productive."

He made a sound, drawing her gaze. "What are you laughing about?" she demanded.

He shook his head, smiling absently. "I'm not laughing, but I am amazed that anyone in your condition would worry about being productive."

"That's a very different type of productivity," she said wryly.

He was quiet for a minute. Then he sighed. "Look at it this way, Natalie," he said finally. "Lisa believed in your talent. She wanted you to have time to write."

His statement cut off all further argument, but she did have something else to say, something that couldn't be put off. "Jake, I want to apologize again for the things I said last night and to thank you for taking care of me."

"Taking care of you? I'm shocked. Ms. Independent, is that you?"

Her lips twitched in response to his teasing. "Yes, it's me. I've discovered that, under certain conditions, it is comforting to be able to depend on someone else."

He laughed and reached over to squeeze her hand briefly. His expression was sober, however, when he replied, "And I've found that, under certain conditions, it is nice to be needed."

He offered to stop for breakfast, as Dr. MacGregor had suggested, but she declined. "Before I do anything else, I want to take a shower."

He drove slowly back to the house, avoiding potholes and speed bumpers. He was gentle as he helped her out of the car; indeed, his anger at himself and the world seemed to have faded overnight.

The night Natalie spent in the hospital marked a significant change in her relationship with Jake. They were back to the easy camaraderie they'd shared before Thanksgiving. If she had thought he was solicitous about her health before she became ill, during the week that followed he hovered over her like a Victorian nanny. There was no better word for it.

She suspected that much of Jake's attention was rooted in guilt over her accusations that night in the hospital. Though she had been in an emotional upheaval herself when she'd lashed out at him, she had not missed his anguished reaction. She regretted the outburst and had apologized for it, but she had an idea that her apology wasn't enough to ease his burden.

One evening she sat before the fireplace with a cup of hot chocolate and, with mixed feelings, reviewed her and Jake's relationship since her release from the hospital.

It was funny in a way—here was a man who could probably take on a group of toughs in a midnight back-alley brawl and come away with nary a wrinkle in the crease of his trousers. And yet here he was, counting *her* calories, asking if she'd taken her vitamins, wanting to know if she had walked or exercised that day.

She was gratified by his interest but cautious against becoming too close to him or, despite their teasing, too dependent on him. She was also wary that he might change his mind about the adoption. Setting aside the shock and grief and loneliness that had accompanied the pregnancy, she already felt bonded to this baby in the most intimate way. Mischief was already a part of her.

She rubbed her belly and the baby responded with a movement. She had read that what she drank, the baby also drank, and so she had eliminated all alcohol; she didn't even have a glass of wine. But now she smiled, wondering if Mischief was enjoying the hot chocolate.

Jake's solicitous attention had returned the morning he'd come to the hospital bearing a duffel bag with her clothes. He had begun a fire earlier, and when they entered the apartment it was warm and toasty. While she showered and washed her hair, he went to the coffee shop a few blocks away and came back with breakfast. Since then he had carried logs and stacked them in the fireplace every morning and every evening.

If he saw her light burning as she worked into the night, he would ring her doorbell and direct her to go to bed. He did it with such good humor that it was impossible to be annoyed. If she returned with a load of groceries while he was at home, he would take them from her and scold her for attempting to carry them in the first place. She began to schedule her shopping trips for times when she knew he would be working.

Doubly odd was her reaction. She had always cherished her independence; she disliked being beholden to anyone. And now she was surprised to realize that not only was she not annoyed or irritated when Jake mollycoddled her, she had actually thanked him. She was sure this uncharacteristically submissive behavior was a result of hormonal changes in her body. But if she were not careful, she might get used to it.

She had been made vividly aware of just how far he had gone toward overseeing her life when she had stopped at the gift shop one morning. John was both pleased and horrified to see her. He hugged her, then pushed her away to arm's length. "Jake will kill me if he finds out you came by here," he said in his melodramatic fashion, the French accent thicker than she had ever heard it. "He made me promise."

Instead of being angry, she had laughed. "I'm feeling much better, and I promise I won't stay long. Have you found a replacement?"

He hadn't, and she tried to apologize, but he wouldn't have it. "It is most important for you and the little one—what is it that you call your stomach?"

"Mischief," she told him with a grin.

"Strange name," said John. "Anyway, you must stay healthy."

She had visited for a short time and then returned to the house, more tired than she would admit to herself or Jake.

Each evening when Jake arrived home he would knock on her door and make her recite what she'd eaten that day. His questions were playful and teasing, but his manner was determined.

Tonight she sat before the fire with a fine-tuned sense of expectation that she attributed to the emotional roller coaster that went along with having a baby. Over and over she tried to tell herself she was *not* waiting, but her ears were attuned to the sound of his car. It was all so domestic, she thought wryly—pregnant woman waiting at home by the fire.

Off and on all day long, cold northeast winds from the ocean had blown a driving rain across Savannah. The faint warmth of the sun had struggled to be felt through heavy cloud cover, but had lost out completely at nightfall. With darkness came bitter cold.

She was dressed in her warmest and softest slacks, made of violet wool. Over them she wore a maternity sweater with geometric patterns in amethyst and jade. Her red-and-white striped athletic socks ruined the effect of the outfit, but they were warm.

She heard his car in the alley, and her heart climbed to her throat. In a few moments, Jake arrived at her door, stomping his feet, chafing his hands together.

"God, it's freezing," he said. He blew into his fist. "I hope you didn't go out today."

"No, I didn't." He was dressed in dark cords, blue shirt and tie, a white sweater under his chestnut-brown leather jacket. But he had no hat or gloves. His shoulders were hunched against the wind, his nose was red and his hair stood on end. She swung back the door. "Come in and warm up," she invited.

With the door shut, he straightened. "Today has to be a record breaker."

She held up a mug. "I made hot chocolate. Would you like some?"

"Hot chocolate? That would be great." He grinned. "I haven't had hot chocolate in years."

"Go in by the fire," she told him. "I'll bring it to you."

When she entered the living room a few minutes later, he had shed his leather coat, had added logs to the blaze and was stirring the coals with the brass-handled poker. He stood and replaced the fireplace screen before accepting the napkin-wrapped earthenware mug she handed him. Marshmallows floated on top of the rich chocolate drink. "Thanks."

"Be careful. It's hot." They sat on the sofa and she sipped tentatively from her mug, which she had refilled when she poured his. "Too hot to drink. How was your day?" she asked.

He drew his brows together and shook his head. "Construction has ground to a screeching halt. You can't pour concrete in this kind of weather, but meanwhile the interest keeps growing." He flattened his hair with his free hand. "God, sometimes I wonder why I ever went into business for myself."

Despite his words, his voice held no self-doubt. She smiled to herself. When she first met Jake, she had thought he was *too* self-assured, *too* smart, *too* strong.

Granted, she had heard from Joseph about what a terrific person Jake was until, by the time they met, she was sick of his name.

They had managed to get along fairly well after her marriage to Joseph, and when Jake married Lisa they actually became friendly. But not until the bleak days, weeks, months of Joseph's illness did she come to appreciate him for his remarkable strength and compassion. Since this pregnancy, and his concern for her, she was seeing another side of this multifaceted man, a gentle, humorous side. And a strong, dependable side that tempted her to lean. That could be dangerous, too.

"How did you first get into this business, Jake?" she asked, attempting to change the direction of her thoughts. "I don't think I ever heard Joseph say."

When he relaxed against the back of the sofa, his broad shoulders covered a third of the cushions. He rested his mug on the sofa arm, crossed one ankle over the other knee and looked thoughtfully into the flames. "I got a job on the docks in Charleston when I was eighteen. A young man can make good money loading freight. All it takes is a strong back, and the ability to follow orders.

"I was a cocky son-of-a-gun in those days. After I got whipped in a couple of fights I found out that cocky didn't cut it with the men. I learned early on to do my damnedest to sidestep trouble, but if that wasn't possible I'd better be able to take care of myself."

He spoke slowly, musingly, his deep voice almost mesmerizing her. He continued to stare into the fire, as though, with the leaping flames as a backdrop, he was transported back to that time, seeing things that were invisible to her. She wondered if he even remembered she was sitting beside him and stayed very still so as not to distract him. She knew the general points of the story, but she'd never heard the details.

"I also learned that I didn't want to work for somebody else all my life," he went on. "Joseph was still living with our foster parents, and I was determined to get him out of there. Not that the Petersons mistreated us, but he was my brother, my only family. I felt strongly that as family we had to stick together."

She gave a start of surprise, but he didn't notice her reaction. This was the man who was going to give up his child? She knew a moment's dread. But then she reminded herself that he'd given his word.

He inhaled deeply and let all his breath escape in a heavy sigh before he continued. "To make a long story short, not long after Joseph finished school, the man who started Burns Shipping here in Savannah died without leaving any heirs. He was related, distantly, to the man I was working for in Charleston, who knew that I wanted to go out on my own someday. He told me that the business was for sale. I didn't think I was ready but he encouraged me, vouched for me with the banks. He even came down to work with me for the first month, helped me over the rough spots. I owe him a debt that I can never repay." His voice had grown quieter; he looked down into his mug. "I've been incredibly lucky." He paused and a spasm of pain crossed his face. "Lucky in business, anyway," he added.

Natalie looked away. The only sound in the room was an occasional crackle as the fire reached a bit of sap in the wood, or the thump of a log settling on the grate. "Luck doesn't mean a thing except to those who are prepared for it," she told him finally. Her voice was quiet, too, but adamant.

Lazily he turned his head against the cushions to look at her. The fireplace reflected the amusement in his eyes. "And where did that bit of philosophy come from?" he asked.

"I don't remember, but it's true. If you hadn't been preparing for the responsibility of owning your own business all your adult life, someone else would have bought the company."

He nodded. "You could be right."

"Why didn't you ever change the name?"

"I don't know. Lisa wanted me to change it to Armstrong Shipping. But the organization had thrived for years under Mr. Burns. The people who had dealings with the company knew the name and trusted it. It just never seemed to matter." He shrugged his broad shoulders, dismissing things that weren't essential.

And you didn't need the ego trip. Natalie studied him. How extraordinary, she thought.

After a minute, he laughed under his breath and the moments of introspection were over. "I don't mind responsibility, but I never thought I'd end up in a position where I had to wear a tie to work. I was going to leave that to Joseph." As he spoke he grinned, loosened the burgundy tie and opened the top button of his blue shirt. Still slouched in the other corner of the sofa, he looked comfortable and at home.

She smiled. "You don't have to wear a tie, do you?" she asked lightly. "I mean, you're the boss. I would think you could wear whatever you want to wear."

He appeared to think about that. "It's odd, but I don't really mind it. When I bought the company, I worked beside the men all day long. But later, after we completed our first expansion, I had to spend more time in the office. Andrew came to work for me about that time. He always wore a jacket and tie." One corner of his mouth lifted in a reminiscent smile. "Lisa thought I should dress at least as well as my employees. I'm used to it now." He lifted the earthenware mug in a quick toast to her and drank. "Say, this is really good."

"Don't sound so surprised," she chided. "I may not like to cook, but I do know my way around a kitchen."

He laughed. He raised the mug to drink again, and when he lowered it a small dab of marshmallow was left clinging to his dark mustache.

In the silence of the cozy room, the fire spat loudly, sending a shower of sparks up the chimney.

Suddenly Natalie's heart picked up speed as she gaped at the white spot. "You have—" All at once it was hard to speak. She pointed to her own lip. "Marshmallow." Her breath forced the word from her throat.

"Umm?" He licked his lip. "Did I get it?"

She was restlessly mindful of his moist tongue as it stroked across his lips. "N-no." She gripped her own mug tightly in both hands. She couldn't seem to tear her eyes away from his mouth. An unexpected hunger to feel those lips on hers shocked her. Good Lord, what was happening to her?

Jake licked his upper lip again and glanced over at Natalie for approval. He stopped breathing when he became alert to her fixed gaze. At the same instant he became alert to other things—the way the fire warmed her smooth golden skin and lent light to the curling tendrils of hair that had escaped her barrette, the feminine scent of jasmine mingling with the smell of wood smoke, her pouty bottom lip, moist where she had wet it with her tongue.

His lungs began to burn from lack of oxygen, and he tore his gaze free. He unwrapped the napkin from his mug and wiped his mustache vigorously.

"There, you got it," she said with obvious relief. She met his eyes; their gazes meshed and held. The expression in hers jolted him. The clear, sky-blue color had turned smoky, dark with emotion.

The tension sang in the air between them. "Natalie?" His voice was husky; his throat was dry. "Do you realize that something is happening between us?"

"No." She tore her gaze from his and shook her head helplessly. "No, Jake, I can't accept that."

That was what she said aloud, but silently, inside, she was dazed by the sudden realization of the truth. Inside, somewhere deep and hidden, her feelings for him had been growing, intensifying, without her knowing it. Her head jerked back around. She stared at him.

He must have read some of her turbulent thoughts. "You see?" He raked his fingers through his thick hair, his face twisted, a sign of his torment. Then he relaxed—all of a sudden—against the cushions. "God, why do I feel like I'm cheating? I wish—"

At that moment the baby kicked Natalie, hard, as though to remind her of its presence. She winced and put her hand to the spot.

Jake's eyes dropped to her distended stomach. His expression closed instantly, like the slamming of a door between them.

The interval was over. The baby's movement and her reaction had very effectively removed all traces of titillation from the atmosphere between them. She was unsure as to whether she was relieved or disappointed that the moment had passed. Though it would have been awkward and disturbing, it might have been healthier for them to thrash it out.

She realized that it was the first time they had ever discussed anything as personal as this. If Jake had not said something, she would have been asking herself right now if she had imagined the whole thing, if the heated communication had occurred at all. But then she would also be wondering about her own unexpected feelings.

Jake cleared his throat and dropped another bombshell. "By the way, I'm going to the childbirth classes with you from now on. Aren't they on Sunday afternoons?"

"Jake, no," she said instantly, shaking her head. Last week she'd begun the six-week course offered by the hospital, and she preferred to finish alone. "There's no reason for you to go. Besides, you've already missed the opening session," she argued lamely.

His expression became stubborn and his jaw firmed. She went rushing on. "I wish you'd get over this feeling of obligation, Jake. The nurse that teaches the course has agreed to be my partner. It was my choice to have this child, and I need to learn to manage on my own."

His eyes took on an odd gleam at her protest and his rugged features softened. "Natalie, listen," he said. He paused, evidently to gather his thoughts. He set the mug on a table beside him and leaned forward to gaze once again into the fire. His elbows rested on his knees; he laced his fingers together loosely. "I've thought about this a lot. I owe you a really big apology. When Lisa died, I wanted to deny—"

She leaned forward to touch his arm. "Jake, this isn't necessary."

He covered her fingers with his big hand. "It is for me. I want—no, that isn't emphatic enough—I *need* to be concerned and involved with you through this. Not only because of my first reaction, and because of Lisa, but because of Joseph, too. He's been on my mind a lot. He was my brother, and I loved him. I think this is what he would want."

Her mouth curved upward slightly. "Joseph," she said softly as she withdrew her hand and relaxed against the cushions, linking her fingers over her stomach. She lifted her sock-clad feet to the coffee table. "I've been thinking about him, too. You remind me so much of him. The two of you were very much alike."

"Joseph? Like me?" Jake's head jerked around, and he stared at her over his shoulder. He was truly dumbfounded by her observation. "Joseph and I were entirely different." He frowned. "Successful or not, I'll never be more than a glorified dockhand. Joseph was educated. He had..." Jake searched for a word. "Class."

Natalie dismissed his arguments with a careless wave that astounded him further. "I know that you were proud of him, Jake, but did you ever stop to think how proud he was of you? You're self-educated, and that may be a more complete education in many ways than what he learned in books. And class? I agree Joseph had class, but what does that mean, really? To me, class is compassion, understanding, kindness, intelligence. It certainly isn't status or prestige."

"You're having delusions." His gaze sharpened. "And I suspect you're trying to get me off the subject of the childbirthing course."

She laughed lightly and crossed one ankle over the other. Then she reversed them. Finally she handed him a throw pillow. "Would you...?" He raised her feet and slid the pillow under them. "Thanks," she said with some relief. "You can't blame me for trying."

"It didn't work," he grumbled, but he grinned. "God, you're sneaky."

She hesitated, then said, "Joseph was strong-minded, too, you know."

"Stubborn, you mean."

She shrugged offhandedly. "You said it, I didn't. But I still don't think it is necessary for you to go to the childbirth course."

He folded his arms over his chest. "Too bad."

Sunday afternoon Jake was waiting in the garden when she came out of the apartment. Natalie's footsteps faltered when she saw him, then she resumed her brisk pace.

He joined her on the path, reaching for the two pillows she carried. She held on to them for a second in a small tug-of-war. "You aren't going to like this at all," she warned.

"Let me be the judge of that," he answered. He was dressed comfortably, as she was, in a warm-up suit and sneakers. Hers was aquamarine and as big as a tent; his was black and red and was zipped over his trim belly. Red and black, the devil's colors, she thought sourly as she finally surrendered the pillows and walked beside him to the garage.

She dreaded this. At the opening session last Sunday, they had been shown a video, a very explicit video, of a birth. Such graphic detail had been unsettling for her—and *she* was the one who was pregnant.

She didn't know what to expect from the class over the next five weeks, but there was going to be a certain amount of intimacy. Touching, stroking and massage were employed to help the expectant mother relax. After his observation yesterday that something was happening between them, relaxation was going to be the furthest thing from her mind when he touched her.

Even so, she was relieved that at least she didn't have to watch the video with him.

He opened the door to the garage and motioned for her to precede him. "I can't change your mind?" she asked one more time.

"No," he answered. She looked at him for a minute, then shrugged and unlocked her car.

"Do you want me to drive?" he asked.

"No. I can still drive."

"Okay," he agreed pleasantly.

"You're very determined," she told him when they were on the road to the hospital.

"Yes."

"One might almost say enthusiastic."

He sighed and turned in his seat so he was half facing her. She was aware of his hand resting on the seat behind her head. "Look, Natalie, I know what you're worried about. Nothing has changed, particularly not my mind. You're still going to be the baby's adopted mother. When the time comes I'll cooperate fully with you on the legalities."

That wasn't the point, but she let it slide. She drove the rest of the way with her eyes on the road, but her mind was on the man beside her.

When they arrived at the hospital's classroom, Jake was greeted with a few curious stares. There were only six couples, besides herself, in the class. Last week they had introduced themselves and talked, getting to know one another. He was the stranger here, and she watched to see how he would react.

She introduced him by name, with no addendum. If he wanted to explain their relationship, he was welcome to try. She would prefer to avoid the subject herself.

The nurse-instructor who taught the course, and who had planned to act as Natalie's partner, greeted him pleasantly. To Natalie's surprise, Jake fit in well with all the others. The first half of the two-hour session was devoted to discussion of the different phases of labor. She watched him, waiting for a sign of restlessness, but she saw none.

He paid careful attention and asked questions. He was serious when the discussion turned serious; he laughed with the others when laughter relieved the tension.

Then they took a welcome break. The women all headed for the bathroom, while the men helped the instructor set up a table for refreshments.

Natalie returned, pausing in the doorway to the room for a moment to observe Jake. He was talking easily with another mother-to-be and the instructor. A man turned from the table with a cookie in his hand, said something to them and grinned at Jake's response.

No one asked him where he was last week. She joined the group and noticed, as she sipped her tea, that there was something about him that precluded questions but, nonetheless, commanded respect. People took him as he was. Unfortunately the instructor and the other couples in the group assumed he was her husband. He did nothing to contradict their impression.

Clearly he was leaving the explanations up to her. Irritated, she started to say something, to straighten them out about this relationship, but just then the instructor resumed the class.

"Okay, let's get back to work," said the woman. "Out of your chairs and onto the mats. Today we're going to begin to learn the special relaxation and breathing techniques you will need when the process of birth begins. Did all of you bring your pillows?"

Natalie gave Jake a self-conscious grimace as he grasped her hand and eased her down to the mat. The instructor came over and demonstrated the position she wanted them to assume. Jake was behind Natalie's back with one of the pillows, supporting her firmly. The other pillow was under her spread knees.

With her newfound knowledge of her own feelings, she found it impossible to concentrate. As they practiced the exercises, his breath was warm in her hair. The strength and support of his hard chest against her back, his arms around her, caused her a terrific amount of confusion.

Later, Natalie was panting with relief as she accepted his hand and came to her feet in a quick surge. The intimacy of the exercises, including back massage, had been exquisite torture. But Jake's hands were large and clever, and, she had to admit, the massage was wonderful. She felt as if the class had gone on forever, but at last the two hours were over. She and Jake said goodbye to the others and left the building.

As they walked toward the parking lot, she admitted to herself that during the class she'd also felt envy. Envy for the other couples, the small secret smiles they exchanged, the soft laughter. None of them were embarrassed. She wouldn't have been embarrassed or confused, either, if it had been her husband at her back, if someone she loved had been touching her. As it was, she was much too affected.

Good Lord. What was happening to her? She had tried to convince herself that the incident with the hot chocolate had been an aberration. But it hadn't worked. Her best friend had been dead for only five months, and she was having lascivious thoughts about the friend's husband. Besides which, she had a belly a whale would envy, and it was only going to get bigger.

Mentally she shook herself. The explanation had to lie in her celibacy. She had not had a relationship since Joseph—three years and six months without sex must have finally shattered her rationality.

"Would you mind driving home, Jake?" she asked when they reached the car. "I'm tired."

"Sure." Jake took the keys from her. She did indeed look tired—the shadows under her eyes were like bruises. He closed the car door and circled the hood to climb in beside her. He glanced over, but she was staring straight ahead. "I really enjoyed the class," he said.

"Good," she answered shortly.

"I'm looking forward to next week. I learned a lot of things I didn't know."

She shot him a look that spoke volumes. "Me, too."

"Did it bother you to have my hands on your body?" He wondered why the hell he'd asked such a question.

She laid her head against the seat back and deliberately closed her eyes. "No, the massage felt good," she answered smoothly.

He smiled to himself when he saw a tiny muscle throb at her temple.

In spite of the shadows, she was looking much better than she had the day he brought her home from the hospital. Much better. She was eating better, too, and she'd gained some weight. Her cheeks were fuller, and her color was particularly high today. He adjusted the seat to accommodate his long legs, focused the rearview mirror. Her eyes remained closed. He started the car, pulled into the street and headed for home.

His feelings for Natalie had always been extremely contradictory. The first time he'd met her, at Joseph's and her wedding rehearsal, he'd thought she was perfectly put together, almost intimidatingly so. He'd thought of her as Natalie the placid, the serene, from whom all the warmer emotions were washed at birth.

Lisa had told him he was dead wrong in his evaluation of her friend. Joseph had told him he was crazy.

She and Joseph made a striking pair. Though she had been married to his brother for five years, Jake never felt that he knew her well. After he and Lisa were married, he'd repeated his judgment that Natalie seemed cold. Lisa had been angry—he remembered vividly because she was so rarely angry—at his criticism of her friend.

But that was how he saw her, until Joseph's illness and death. Then he'd had his eyes opened with a vengeance. They had spent many hours together during those endless days, and he had learned just how wrong he was. He'd come to know her warmth and capacity for loving, and to admire her courage and appreciate her depth.

After Joseph's death, Natalie had demonstrated the independence he still teased her about. Despite the intensity of her grief, she'd refused any offer of financial assistance while the insurance was being processed. She wouldn't even accept help on a temporary basis. She hadn't changed one iota in that respect, he thought wryly. She still didn't like to take money from anyone. He was fully aware that the sum in the trust account was growing substantially. It was only because of the circumstances that she had allowed him to help in other ways.

Lisa had explained to him that Natalie's parents had been older when she was born and very set in their ways. Throughout her childhood, they had repeatedly reminded her of the extra expense she generated. When she was in high school, she had worked in the afternoons and on weekends, and she turned all her money over to them.

Lisa had not liked Natalie's parents at all; she'd had a number of choice things to say about them.

Natalie shifted in the seat, and he looked over at her again. Her finely sculpted profile was lit by the late-afternoon sun streaming through the window. Her hair was shiny.

Pregnancy had added a depth to her beauty. He was coming to know her better than he ever had, and he enjoyed her, enjoyed spending time with her. The people in the childbirth class obviously liked her. He had noticed several of the women initiating conversations, laughing with her over their common aches and the sizes of their bellies.

But still there were times when he could hardly bear to look at her, knowing that she carried Lisa's baby.

Chapter 7

Toward the end of January the days seemed to drag. But finally it was February 1. Natalie was actually in the last month of pregnancy. The very idea buoyed her spirits immeasurably, and she decided to go shopping.

She had bought a few things for the baby, but not all they would need. It was time to get everything ready. She left the house and headed for the mall, more enthusiastic about this shopping trip than she'd been about anything for days.

The parking lot was crowded, but she searched for a spot close to the entrance. She was certain to have a lot of packages to carry. Eventually she spotted a car pulling out.

The space was a tight squeeze. Luckily her car was a compact. She pulled in, turned off the motor and removed the keys. She dropped them in her purse, hooked the strap over her shoulder and opened the door, careful not to bang against the car parked next to her.

With one foot on the tarmac and one shoulder out of the car, she stopped. Her stomach was wedged into the angle between the door and the car.

She opened the door a bit wider and twisted around, trying to back out. Then she opened her window and tried again. Panting heavily now, she pulled herself back inside. This was ridiculous.

Surely she wasn't trapped in her own car. Maybe she could get out from the other side. She scooted across the seat and opened the passenger door. This angle of opening was slightly wider.

But not wide enough. At last she gave up, defeated. She sat there for a minute, blinking back the tears. "Pull yourself together, Natalie," she said out loud. "You are not going to cry over something so silly."

"Ma'am?"

An elderly man had bent down to look in at her.

"Did you say something to me?" he asked.

"No, I, uh, was talking to myself." She gave him a weak smile, which he returned. He said something indecipherable to his companion before climbing into the car next to hers.

As soon as they pulled away, she hurriedly opened her door to its limit and got out. She couldn't enjoy the shopping trip, however, for worrying whether she would be able to get back into the car later.

By evening, Natalie was able to view the incident with some amusement. She couldn't decide whether or not to tell Jake. He would get a good laugh out of it. But she wasn't certain she wanted to be the subject of his laughter. Not now. She had managed to rationalize her attraction to him by blaming it all on hormones and celibacy. But she still didn't want him to laugh.

She was dressed in the aquamarine warm-up suit and had her socks and sneakers in her hand when she heard his knock. She went to the door. "Hi. I was just going to walk."

"Want some company?" he asked, tugging at his tie. His suit jacket was slung over his arm. His smile was weary. "I could use the exercise."

"Sure."

He ran a tired hand around the back of his neck. "Let me change my clothes, and I'll be right back."

He headed for the steps. His white shirt, which looked so neat from the front, was creased across the back as though he had sat in a chair all day. She knew how tiring that was.

She stood in the doorway, her eyes fixed on his broad shoulders, envying his effortless movements, until he disappeared through the door to his kitchen. It made her feel depressed to watch. If she were climbing those stairs, she would have to pull her chunky body up hand over hand, holding on to the railing all the way. She sighed and went back inside to put on her socks and shoes. From her perspective, this day, which had started out so well, had deteriorated further.

A few minutes later Jake was back at her door, comfortably dressed in a gray sweatshirt and sweatpants. He raised his hand to knock, but a movement caught his attention. Through the window, he could see straight into the living room to where Natalie sat on the sofa. One sneaker dangled from her fingers. He grinned and tapped the glass with a knuckle.

She looked up, and to his astonishment she burst into tears. The sneaker hit the floor, and she covered her face with her hands.

"What the hell?" The door wasn't locked, and he strode through to where she was sitting. He laid his hand on her rounded shoulder and felt the tremors beneath his fingers. But these weren't the anguished, tormented sobs he'd heard in the hospital; these were the tears of a frustrated child, pitiful, sniffling sounds.

"Sorry," she gasped between sniffles. She fumbled in her pocket for a tissue.

Then he saw what the trouble was. One shoe was half on and the heel had collapsed. He kneeled down at her feet. With deft movements he straightened the heel, slipped the other sneaker on her foot and tied the laces of both of them. "There. Is that better?" he asked her tenderly. With gentle fingers he brushed a strand of hair off her face.

She blew her nose. "Don't be nice to me," she said gruffly, looking at him. Her nose was red and her eyes were swollen. "I might start crying all over again."

He grinned and got to his feet. He took both her hands and hauled her up beside him. "Let's walk."

He kept one hand in his.

The bite of cool air felt good on Natalie's heated face. They had walked only half a block when she inhaled deeply and apologized again. "I don't know what got into me."

"There's nothing to apologize for," Jake told her. "Your emotions are volatile right now. And you're frustrated because you can't move around as easily as you're used to. It's perfectly natural. Remember what the instructor told us last week? Your abdominal size may seem grotesque, and you may feel that you're awkward and unattractive."

She looked heavenward. "Jake, please!" He had read every publication the hospital had on childbirth and took an active part of each session. He knew more than she did. "I'm sorry I ever let you go to that class."

"You didn't let me," he reminded.

"Oh. Yes."

"I meant to ask you—have you had leg cramps?"

Natalie groaned and socked his arm as hard as she could. "Will you please shut up?" He thought that was funny.

They had walked half a mile when they turned back. "Jake, I want to thank you again. This will all be over soon. I know it has been painful, but you're very patient with me and I appreciate it."

He stopped in his tracks. She continued on for a step or two. When she realized he wasn't beside her she turned. There was a curious expression in his smoky eyes as he looked at her. She cocked her head to one side and looked at him with a smile. "What?"

"I think I'm the one who should be thanking you," he said slowly.

She laughed lightly. "What on earth for?"

He shoved his hands in the pockets of his jacket and drew even with her. "You know, Natalie, you've helped me a lot. In dealing with Lisa's death, I mean." He still spoke slowly, as though not completely sure of what he wanted to say. "You've helped me begin to heal." He seemed surprised.

She resumed her walk with him beside her. "I'm so very glad," she said in a soft voice. And in a few minutes she added, "You don't know what it means to me to hear you say that."

"Why?"

She turned her head and looked at him with a small smile on her lips. "The day Lisa was buried, I vowed to myself that I would be there for you when you needed me, as you were there for me when Joseph died."

He pulled her in under his arm for a quick hug.

Natalie had been listening with one ear for the mailman. She was expecting a check from *Southern Life.* When she heard his step on the sidewalk outside, she shut off the computer and went into the living room.

The mail was dropped through a brass slot in the front door. As she had learned to do, she scooted the envelopes across the floor with her toe and sat in the low rocking chair to pick it up. Damn, she would be glad to be able to bend over again, she thought as she struggled to her feet with the mail clutched in her fist.

She returned to her temporary office, sorting through the junk. She tossed a handful of advertising flyers into the wastebasket and concentrated on the two envelopes that were left. One was the expected check. The other was addressed to her but bore no return address. She ripped into it and glanced at the calendar.

And laughed out loud. She had forgotten what day it was, but this was a valentine. Of sorts. No frilly ruffles, no ribbons or lace or shiny red hearts, simply a plain white card on which was printed:

Greetings,

This is a politically correct Valentine, printed on recycled paper, without bias, bigotry, sexism, intolerance, chauvinism, favoritism, nepotism or partiality. However, this card does also include affectionate feelings.

It was signed with a bold black scrawl. "Jake."

She decided that it was time for her to do something for him. So she called the office and invited him to go out to dinner. Her treat.

That night Tibernio's was packed. But as promised, a reservation wasn't necessary. Morris found a table for them near the back.

"I'm glad you suggested this," said Jake when Morris had left.

"Taking you out to dinner seemed the proper way to repay you for a politically correct valentine," she told him with a grin. "Besides, I got a check for an article today. You can have anything you want," she elaborated, waving the menu grandly.

"Well, now," he said, rubbing his hands together with relish. He raised a dark eyebrow at her. "Anything?" he asked, suggestively.

"Almost anything," she said primly. Then she looked down at herself, jammed in between the chair and table, and gave a dry laugh. "Yeah, anything."

He chuckled. "Don't underestimate yourself," he warned. "Even with the stomach, you're a very sexy woman."

"Don't say things like that." But she wasn't angry with him for the remark. She, too, had read the literature from the classes. "Reassure the mother-to-be about her desirability," one brochure had advised.

"It's true. You still have beautiful legs."

"I haven't seen them in weeks. You mean they aren't bowed yet?"

He laughed, and she was saved from more compliments when the waiter appeared to take their order.

The evening moved along comfortably with the atmosphere between them easy and light. At one point, Natalie sighed. "I didn't know how much I needed a night out."

Jake sat back in his chair. He studied her carefully. "It won't be long now," he said.

She hesitated and touched her napkin to her mouth.

During her last appointment, she had talked to Dr. MacGregor about how soon she could plan to return to Charleston. He had said that he would like for her to stay in Savannah for six weeks or so after the baby was born. "It's customary for your attending physician to perform your post-delivery checkup," he said.

She hadn't mentioned the doctor's advice to Jake, so she told him now. "In just about two months I'll be free to leave," she said, her smile a fixture of satisfaction and poignance. "And I know you'll be glad to be rid of me, too."

An enigmatic expression crossed Jake's face, then was lost to his grin. "Oh, I don't know. You're tolerable to have around."

"Wait till there are two of us."

The grin faded; he became strangely subdued. "Yeah, well, I'll manage."

Natalie regretted her flippant tone and searched for something to say that would restore the pleasant atmosphere. Dessert had been served. She had taken one bite when she remembered the scene in the parking lot two weeks ago. "Do you remember the day I couldn't bend down to tie my shoes?" she asked, laying her fork down.

Some of the tension ebbed from him. "How could I forget it?"

"Well, that wasn't all that happened that day," she said. By the time she reached the description of the elderly man who thought she'd been speaking to him, Jake was shaking with laughter and she was chuckling herself, enjoying his response.

Her hand was resting on the white linen tablecloth. He covered it with his own. "I'm glad you can laugh about it. This entire experience has been very difficult for you, hasn't it?" The amusement faded from his eyes.

"It hasn't been easy for either of us. But before long we both can start to get on with our lives. You can concentrate on becoming the largest shipper on the East Coast. And I'll move back to Charleston and learn how to be a mommy."

He linked their fingers and held her hand tightly. "And you'll be a good one."

"Jake? I thought that was you hiding back here in the corner," said a woman's voice.

Jake released her hand and looked around. A couple was approaching the table. Their faces seemed familiar to Natalie, but she couldn't place them exactly.

Jake got to his feet politely, holding his napkin. He shook hands with the man and nodded to the woman. "Carl, Linda, how are you?" They were both short and rotund, and he towered over them.

"We're fine," said Linda, patting his arm. "I've been meaning to ask you to dinner."

"But you seem to be thriving," put in Carl. He looked pointedly at Natalie.

"Do you remember my sister-in-law, Natalie Armstrong?" asked Jake. "Natalie, Carl and Linda Dillon."

"I don't believe we actually met," said Linda. "But I saw you at Lisa's funeral." She was the kind of woman Natalie instinctively distrusted, all sweet and gushy, but her smile never reached her eyes.

"Yes, I was there," answered Natalie. "How do you do?"

"I didn't realize you were Jake's sister-in-law. Someone mentioned that you've been a widow for some time, haven't you?"

The sweetness had evaporated. Natalie felt as though she were under interrogation. She maintained a polite smile. "Yes."

"And I understand you've moved in with Jake," Linda said, her voice taking on a hard note.

Stunned both by the innuendo and by the sudden hostility radiating both from the woman and the man, Natalie put her hands in her lap and said evenly, "Actually I live downstairs in the apartment." She couldn't believe the nerve of the woman. In fact, it had never occurred to her that people would speculate about their relationship. But it was clear that these two had.

"It looks as though you are expecting any day." Linda was demanding information, not making a comment. Clearly these people were not close friends of Lisa and Jake's, or they would certainly have learned the circumstances of this pregnancy by now.

Natalie didn't know what else to do but answer the woman's rude questions as calmly as possible. "At the end of the month."

"So soon?" said Linda.

Natalie expected the next question to pertain to the identity of the father, but instead Linda turned to Jake. "You must be pleased. It's good to see that you were able to recover so quickly from Lisa's death. And with such a pretty companion, too."

It was one of those moments when all sound ceased around them.

Natalie looked up at Jake for the first time.

He was furious. A muscle jumped in his jaw, his eyes narrowed and his napkin was gripped in his tight fist. He maintained a fairly calm demeanor, but it was easy to see that it took an extraordinary effort. "Yes, we are pleased about the baby. Thank you for being concerned," he said very slowly, very deliberately. His voice was low and unmistakably dangerous. His broad shoulders loomed over the couple in a menacing stance they couldn't fail to miss. "But if you're going to interrupt our meal solely to be malicious, Linda, I recommend that you at least get your facts straight. There are any number of my *good* friends who could enlighten you. In the meantime, you are offending not only Natalie and myself, but you're also insulting the memory of my wife. Now our food is getting cold. If you'll excuse us—"

Deliberately he turned his back, sat down and picked up his fork, leaving the couple standing there slack-jawed.

Carl recovered first. He took his wife's arm and led her away, but Natalie heard the woman's parting shot. "I always thought a lot of Lisa. It doesn't look good."

Natalie kept her hands in her lap. She had completely lost her appetite. So had Jake evidently. After a moment, he threw his napkin down on the table. "Are you finished?" he asked.

She nodded, unable to answer for the obstruction in her throat.

"Let's go, then."

He got their coats while she paid the bill. When they were outside he held the coat for her, then shrugged into his jacket before taking her arm. They stepped away from the building. It was cold but not windy. She turned up the collar of her coat and slid her hands into her pockets to hold the coat together over her girth. She'd abandoned the belt a long time ago.

They had almost reached the town house before Jake finally commented on the scene. "It makes me mad as hell that anyone would speculate about our relationship."

She glanced at him. He was walking with his head bent, his hands shoved deeply into his pockets, still frowning ferociously. She wanted to say something, but she wasn't sure what it should be. "Some people are born malicious, Jake. Our friends at the birthing classes have never said anything out of line."

He shot her a look. "That's because they think we're married."

"Not all of them. The instructor, for one, knows we're not." Natalie was growing irritated; she thought he was overreacting to spiteful remarks from a couple of catty people. And he was walking too fast for her. "Besides, who left them with that impression?"

"I didn't want to go into a lot of explanations," he snarled. "The odd thing is that something like this happening never occurred to me," he went on, reflecting her earlier thoughts.

"Nor to me," she admitted. She really didn't want to argue with him. She quickened her steps to keep up with his long strides. "Maybe we should take out an ad in the newspaper to explain the situation," she suggested lightly, hoping to minimize the tension in the atmosphere.

His head zipped around; he pinned her with a steely gaze. "This isn't a joke, Natalie. Lisa was well liked, and gossips like that could tarnish her name."

There was nothing to add to that, she thought, her irritation returning. When they reached her door Natalie had the key ready. "Good night, Jake," she said.

Suddenly he became aware of her own anger. He caught her wrist. "Natalie, are you all right?"

"I'm fine."

He didn't release her. "Thanks for dinner," he said. His thumb stroked her skin absently. He was looking at her with an inscrutable expression.

"Please let go of me, Jake."

He drew her around until she was facing him and grasped her chin. "You *are* upset. Damn them."

"It's not them, it's you," she snapped. Then she bowed her head. "Oh, God, I wish I had gone back to Charleston. I don't know why I let you talk me into staying here." There was a catch in her voice.

His hands tightened and her stomach brushed against him, but for once he didn't seem to notice. "Because it was the practical thing to do."

She gritted her teeth. "Practical for me, maybe. Miserable for you. How do you think that makes me feel? Do you think I haven't noticed that you cannot bear to look below my neck?''

The accusation startled him. He didn't know she'd realized...well, what the hell did she expect? "That's only because—"

She closed her eyes and turned her head away. *Dear God, I never thought I would envy my dearest friend after she was dead.* "This isn't something that can be glossed over for the neighbors. You'd like to forget there's even a baby in here.'' She rested her hand on top of her stomach and felt comforting movement. "Well, it's a little hard for mc to forget, Jake. You can barely stand to look at me, because this will always be Lisa's baby, not mine.''

They looked at each other. They both saw the same thing. The suppressed feelings that each of them had experienced at different times. The guilt that accompanied those feelings.

Jake ran his hands through his hair. "What the *hell* do you want me to say, Natalie?'' he nearly shouted. "Let's get married and give the baby a mother and a father? Then we can be a nice, cozy family group?''

Her answer was automatic. "No!'' She stepped back, away from the force that gripped him. Her anger receded. She saw the bleak emptiness in his eyes and knew that hers held the same expression.

He dropped his hands and stood there looking at her. "Good, because I could never say that. I will never have another family. Ever.'' He spoke with finality.

Natalie took in a jerky breath. Horrified, she realized all of a sudden that her subconscious *had* been working on that very idea. Without her having been aware of it she'd been assembling mental pictures of the three of them as a family, together, warmed by memories of Joseph and Lisa.

Jake had put his feelings into stark, unabashed, emphatic words, shattering those pictures for all eternity. A family was one thing that they would never be. The barriers were too many and too high.

"No," she repeated the lie, averse to his seeing the effect of those words, to his being witness to her splintered dreams.

She shook her head, suddenly defeated. "But the Dillons were right, you know," she went on in a shaky voice. "It doesn't look good for me to be living here." Her small bark of laughter held a note of hysteria. "They were dying to ask if you were the father. There was bound to be speculation among people who don't know us."

"I don't give a damn what people like that think," said Jake angrily.

Natalie looked at him archly. She didn't have to say a word. He had already denied the truth of that statement with his actions in the restaurant. But his defense was for Lisa, not for him. Or her. And that was right; his loyalty should be to Lisa's memory. She felt guilty wanting even a small part for herself.

She was so mixed up! *Lis, I really need to talk to you. I need to know if you hate me.*

He'd once said that they were both adults, that they could work through any problems that arose by her staying here to have the baby. But this was a different matter. She hadn't anticipated this problem, and she knew instinctively that this was something they couldn't work through.

* * *

Natalie had no idea how long she'd been asleep when suddenly she sat straight up in bed, rubbing a band of tightness that had formed just beneath her breasts. She felt flushed; her breathing was short and quick. These contractions had been happening for a week or so; the doctor said they were a dress rehearsal for the main event. At least Mischief had decided to forego the nightly stretching exercises.

After a minute the tightness eased and she sighed, grateful that the episode was over. Pregnancy was such an assortment of aches and pains, urges and appetites. You never knew what was going to happen next.

She made a quick trip to the bathroom. She had made this same trip so many times that she didn't even have to turn on the light. She returned to bed, fell back on the pillows and closed her eyes in relief. In seconds she was asleep again, this time even more deeply.

The second time the tightness seized her, she gave a groggy moan and licked her dry lips. Her nightgown had bunched up around her hips, and she tugged and squirmed until it was smooth beneath her.

The third time, she awakened fully, aware of what was going on. Unless she was badly mistaken this *was* the main event. She stared wide-eyed into the darkness, suddenly afraid. Though the baby was not due for another ten days, it was clearly time to start counting the minutes. She rolled onto her side and reached for the lamp switch. In the subdued illumination, the first thing her gaze lit upon was the bassinet. Oh, God.

She wasn't ready. Her heart pounded with anxiety.

Don't be ridiculous, she chided herself. Hundreds, thousands, of women went through this every day. It was no big deal. She would survive as they had survived.

But it *was* a big deal. Suddenly she felt as if she had a direct line to those other women, a warm kinship with the ones who were experiencing the first pangs of birth at this very minute all over the world.

Nat, you're getting philosophical, she could almost hear Lisa's amused accusation.

She looked at the clock with some surprise. It was not midnight yet. She'd been asleep for less than two hours, yet she felt strangely refreshed. She got out of bed and made her way to the bathroom to splash cold water on her face. Maybe she should take a shower, shave her legs.

Another hour passed before she decided to call Dr. MacGregor. Even then she wasn't certain she was doing the right thing. She reminded him that it was ten days too early. She had expected more discomfort and told him that, too. "All I have is a slight backache," she added with a nervous laugh.

He chuckled at her comment. "Ten days is not uncommon. And don't worry, Natalie. I promise you'll have some discomfort before this is over. Now how long has it been since the last contraction?"

She told him.

"Then there's no hurry and it could be a false alarm, but I would prefer to be on the scene. If the contractions don't stop within the next hour, I want you to come to the hospital."

Natalie hung up the telephone and sat looking around the apartment, dark except for the soft pool of light from the lamp beside her. The silence of the night was absolute; even the normal creaking sounds of an old house were absent. It wasn't a false alarm; somehow she was certain of that.

She glanced toward the ceiling, reluctant to wake Jake. Closing her eyes, she allowed herself to replay last night's unpleasantness with Carl and Linda Dillon.

Even though she'd been hurt by the scene, his concern had all been for Lisa's reputation. Natalie could sympathize, but she decided she couldn't bear to face him. Not right this minute, anyway.

She'd wait. There was plenty of time, she reminded herself.

She showered and dressed in the red dress with the black bow that she had liked so much. Now she hated it. She made up the bed, placed her small bag beside the front door and looked at her watch again. Another contraction began, tightening the band of muscle beneath her breasts. She eased her body into the rocking chair and rested her head against the back. With this episode, the ache in her back became slightly more acute, though it was still tolerable.

At last she went to the phone. With a cowardliness she despised, she telephoned for a taxi. While she waited for the cab to arrive, she walked through the apartment once more.

When she returned in some two or three days, when she saw these rooms again, she would not be alone. Another tiny person would be sharing her space, her life. The idea both exhilarated her and scared her to death.

She paused at the door to the office. Her computer on the desk was black. The double bed was neatly made. The long box containing the parts of the crib along with the mattress were propped against the wall.

The bassinet would serve for now, but eventually someone would have to put the crib together. Maybe that could wait until she was back in Charleston.

All this furniture would now have a purpose, not just be something to avoid stubbing her toe on. The bathing table—the idea of holding and washing a wet, squirming baby left her knees weak. She thought of the clothes in the chest, the things she'd bought. Tiny little tucks and ruffles, tiny little buttons. Were those little buttons actually supposed to be fitted into the little buttonholes?

By what elfin hands?

No, I'm not ready! she thought again, her panic very real. She wasn't capable of caring for a helpless human being.

Suddenly her eyes flooded with tears. Again she felt fear, a tight, unrelenting fear. The precious independence that she'd always cherished seemed to be a burden. If she only had someone to be with, someone who cared deeply about her, about the baby...

She straightened and swept the tears away with her fingers. This was going to be a long night. There were mountains of things—new things, scary things—to be endured. She couldn't fall apart now.

She was on the sidewalk before the taxi could blow his horn. The driver's eyes widened as she opened the back door of the cab, tossed her small bag on the seat and clumsily climbed in after it.

"Oh, my God," he said, frozen into immobility as he stared at her stomach.

"Don't worry, we have plenty of time," she said, smiling reassuringly. She gave the man the name of the hospital and settled back on the seat.

"Are you sure?" he said shakily. He made no move to leave the curb.

She lifted a brow. "Unless you plan to sit here all night."

He recovered himself, put the car into gear and his foot on the gas. The tires spun, then caught, squealing as the cab moved with a jerk. He immediately slammed on the brakes.

Natalie caught herself by digging her heels into the floor mat.

"Sorry," said the driver.

She smiled weakly. "It's okay."

Jake reached the window in time to see Natalie climb into the taxi. She had to be going to the hospital. Dammit, why the hell hadn't she called him? He knew the answer to that.

The thought of her going to the hospital alone sent a pang of humiliation through him. He was a blockhead; he should have dismissed the incident at the restaurant last night as unimportant, which it was. But his reaction to the Dillons' insinuation was in direct proportion to his guilt.

He couldn't admit to himself or to Natalie that he was attracted to her—not a matter of months after his wife's death. And he couldn't, wouldn't, ever make promises again.

The scene at her door was as much his fault as hers, no matter what he'd said. When he thought of the despair in her eyes . . .

All at once he realized his hands were shaking. He brought his fist down hard on the sill, rattling the window. His curses were prolonged and extravagant as he raced back to his bedroom and dressed hurriedly.

Had the tension provoked by the quarrel brought on early labor? Would she be all right? Oh, hell.

He was almost to the car before he remembered his keys and had to go back for them.

A drizzle had wet the streets by the time the taxi got to the hospital. The driver pulled up to the entrance. "Let me get someone to help you."

"Nonsense. I can walk." Natalie opened the door, got out and reached back for her bag.

By then the driver was beside her. He took her arm. "Please, ma'am," he pleaded nervously. "I'll come back for that. Let's just get you inside first."

Finally she gave up and did as he'd asked. But she was smiling to herself as she went through the process of admissions. Poor man had been scared to death that he'd have to deliver the baby in the back seat of the cab.

Dr. MacGregor was waiting for her. He looked past her shoulder with a frown. "Where's Jake?"

"You said there was no hurry, so I decided to wait and call him when the pains are closer together. There's no reason for both of us to lose sleep if it isn't necessary," she told him lightly.

"Get her settled," he instructed the nurse who was standing by. "I have to make a telephone call."

She touched his arm. "No, please. Not right now." She smiled appealingly—she hoped. "We can make the call later, okay?"

"If you're talking about me, it won't be necessary to call," said a voice from behind them.

Natalie spun around. Her hand flew to her breast to still the thunder of her heart.

Dr. MacGregor turned more slowly. "I'm glad you're here, Jake."

"Yeah, me, too," said Jake, not taking his eyes off of Natalie. "Why didn't you wake me?" he asked.

She maintained eye contact and her chin came up. "I wasn't sure it was necessary. Dr. MacGregor said that it might be a false alarm."

Jake looked at her without comment for a long moment, but she knew what he was saying with his eyes, would say if they were alone. He was sorry for the scene last night. He had no intentions of denying that he'd meant what he said, but he was sorry to have hurt her.

She felt the dark, complex communication like a weight upon her shoulders. No one moved.

It was almost a relief when the next contraction interrupted the tension between them. She couldn't control an involuntary wince.

Instantly the scene, which seemed to have frozen in time, was moving again. Jake turned white and reached out to support her with an arm around her shoulders.

Dr. MacGregor gestured and the nurse hustled Natalie off down the hallway.

Although she couldn't understand the doctor's words when he said something to Jake, she heard the impatience in his voice. She resisted the temptation to look over her shoulder.

Jake wiped the perspiration from Natalie's brow during a brief respite, while she breathed deeply and gathered her strength for the next onslaught. The pains were coming almost constantly.

"Let go of that contraction, Natalie," Jake said in a soothing voice. "It's gone, history. Just concentrate on relaxing."

The damp terry cloth was pleasantly coarse against her lips when he moistened them. She felt like every nerve, every muscle in her body had been stretched to the limit. And it wasn't over yet.

Jake had been wonderful, she thought fleetingly. When the hospital admitting routine had been completed and they were established in the labor room, the strain between them had faded immediately under the realization of what was about to happen.

She wondered how she'd ever thought she could get through this without him. He'd told her over and over how brave she was, how strong, until she'd begun, at last, to believe him.

Dr. MacGregor sounded as if he was at the end of a tunnel. "It won't be long now," he said. She wanted to ask him how long, but she was seized by another spasm. The pain spread over her vision like a red haze.

Jake's hand was waiting and Natalie's fingers gripped hard. "Hang on to me, honey. Squeeze as hard as you want to. I'll be right here." He mopped at her brow with his other hand.

He felt her vigorous grip with something akin to relief. The physical effort demanded by labor had gradually grown more arduous as the hours had passed. During the last contraction, he realized that her strength was beginning to ebb. And no wonder, he thought as he glanced at his watch. They'd been at the hospital for almost ten hours.

Most of that time had been spent walking up and down the halls, until he and Natalie knew every crack in the floor, walls and ceiling of this place.

He glanced at Mac, wanting to voice his concern at the length of time that had passed, but he couldn't, not when she could hear. All he could do was give her his comfort and support.

And it wasn't enough, not by a hell of a long shot. A soft sound began deep down within her, crowded past her attempts to curb the sound and emerged from her lips as an extended groan.

Oh, God. The audacity of asking a woman to go through something like this. He knew it was supposed to be beautiful and natural and fulfilling. The sound of violins came in over the speakers—that was supposed to be soothing. Like hell.

Mac spoke. "Okay, Natalie. I can see the head now. We're ready to have a baby. It's time to push, honey. Give it all you've got."

Her hysterical laugh was choked off by a silent scream. Her shoulders came up off the bed as she clamped her lips together, squeezed her eyes shut and pushed. No sooner had he wiped her brow than perspiration popped out again.

A short time later, the room suddenly came alive. The waiting was over; one nurse rolled a cart containing some unrecognizable equipment toward the doctor. Another moved to a monitor. The doctor was issuing orders.

And Natalie, when she could breathe at all, bore down hard, panting through pursed lips as she'd been instructed.

Finally, under his arm, Jake felt her tension give way; she collapsed against him.

"Good, Natalie. Wonderful. It's a girl," crowed Dr. MacGregor. "A beautiful little girl."

"A girl?" said Natalie with a weak, wobbly smile. Her sky-blue eyes, wide with wonder, sought those of the man beside her. "Oh, Jake, a girl."

He suddenly felt taller and knew that a grin was spreading across his own face. Their gazes locked for a wondrous moment, held.

And he knew that from this time he would never see Natalie in the same way again. "You are one terrific lady," he murmured, shaking his head. Then he leaned forward and covered her lips with his. He didn't close his eyes and neither did she. He could see flecks of gold and emerald and sapphire within her irises. Finally he raised his head, but continued to stare at her.

They both became aware of the silence at the same time. Dr. MacGregor and two of the nurses were bent over the small form, their movements busy but undecipherable.

"Jake?" she whispered fearfully and gripped his hand with more force than before.

The baby hadn't cried! How long had it been? How long?

The arm around her shoulders caught her to him; he brought their entwined fingers to his chest. Her body was stiff in his arm. Over her head he, like she, watched the activity, holding his breath, his dread like a gigantic fist squeezing his heart.

Suddenly he heard a lusty cry. Natalie slumped against him. And he breathed again.

"Lazy little lass," said Dr. MacGregor.

"Is she all right?" they asked almost in unison. Natalie's voice was shaky and barely audible over the cries of the child.

In answer, a nurse placed the baby, loosely wrapped in a soft blanket and naked except for a tiny knitted cap, in Jake's arms.

Jake turned immediately to give her to Natalie. He remained bent, his shoulders hunched protectively over both of them. The nurse moved away.

He was hypnotized by the sight of his child. Natalie chuckled softly under her breath. She looked up at him and gave him a blinding smile before she returned her attention to the baby, whispering in a universal language of praise as she examined every inch of the diminutive body, while Jake watched. She counted the tiny toes, the surprisingly long fingers, traced the tiny ears.

The baby, soothed and quiet for the moment, stared at her through slitted, sleepy eyes. The violins played on, their music unbearably sweet.

Jake couldn't make himself look away. Slowly, tentatively, he touched a tiny hand. The skin was so soft, like nothing he'd ever touched. Not the satiny underside of a new kitten, not the sleek petal of a rose, not the silk of a woman's breast, nothing was as perfectly smooth as this new human being's skin. He traced the circle made by the tiny thumb and forefinger.

Suddenly the baby grasped his finger with a grip that was surprisingly strong. When he looked at her, she seemed to be staring directly at him. With Lisa's eyes. From Lisa's face.

Jake was seized with a terrible, overwhelming fear. He pulled his finger free of the hold and straightened. He felt the urge to run—as he had run the day of Lisa's funeral—and keep running until Natalie, the child and all memories associated with them were out of his life. Forever.

Mac appeared at the other side of the table. "She weighs seven pounds, eight ounces, and she is twenty inches long." He grinned at Natalie. "I hope you realize you can't keep calling this beauty Mischief. What are you planning to name her?" The last question was directed at Jake.

"Ask Natalie," he said, his tone raw. "This is her child."

The nurse's head turned slowly. She looked from Natalie, who was absorbed with the baby, to Jake, who met her curious gaze with indifference, to Dr. MacGregor, who studiously avoided meeting her eyes. She was too well-disciplined to actually voice her curiosity—and probably her outrage.

"Her name is Annabelle Lisa Armstrong," Natalie answered easily, smiling up at Dr. MacGregor.

Apparently she had not noticed Jake's sudden withdrawal, nor the severity of his reply.

Chapter 8

When Natalie was finally brought into her room, the sight of a huge vase of magnificent yellow roses took her breath away. They were from Jake.

He had left the hospital soon after the baby was born. She knew that when the excitement had worn off he would be faced with a succession of sad emotions. One of them would be guilt. For his kiss at the moment at Annabelle's birth had not been the kiss of a brother-in-law, and her response hadn't been casual, either, no matter how much either of them might deny it.

His lips had moved over hers with a taste of hunger that had astonished her. His pride in her, in the baby, in his own fatherhood, had shone in his beautiful gray eyes. For that one glorious moment, he had put aside the sorrow and lived for the moment, happily. Natalie could hardly believe it. But the sorrow would return.

Perhaps it already had.

Natalie hadn't missed his reaction when Annabelle had clamped her hand around his finger as though to say, "I know you, you're my daddy." He had pulled away so quickly she'd felt the tug on the baby she held. And when the doctor had asked about the name, he'd immediately turned cool.

She understood Jake's automatic retreat. He didn't want to bond with this baby. Hadn't wanted to from the first. Here was this wonderful child, who was supposed to be his and Lisa's. The baby would always be a reminder of his loss.

She understood, and she would try to make the parting as easy for him as possible. She didn't want to compound his grief. But—oh, God—she couldn't help imagining what it would be like if they could *both* be a part of the baby's life. He had so much to give to a child—his strength, his character, his vigor and integrity. He had so much to teach a child.

They brought Annabelle to her room then and, as she held the child to her breast, all thoughts fled except the overwhelming love she felt for this small creature.

Annabelle was a beautiful baby, thought Natalie. *And not just because she's mine.* Her skin was smooth and pink. Her brows were light, almost invisible. Her eyes, when she deigned to open them, were deep dark blue, the lids fringed with delicate lashes of a darker color than her brows. Her tiny mouth was shaped like a bow, her little nose was slightly tilted up. The hair on her scalp—what hair she had—was dark and silky textured like Lisa's. Too soon to tell if it would curl like Jake's.

* * *

Jake pushed through the hospital door. Ignoring the lot where he had parked his car, he headed off down the street, his long strides eating up the pavement.

He urgently needed physical action, rigorous activity. His head was bent, his shoulders bowed under a great intangible weight. His hands were tight fists, thrust into the pockets of his windbreaker. What the *hell* was he going to do?

He moved quickly, desperately, as though he could outrace his churning emotions.

Jake didn't return to the hospital until the day Natalie and the baby were released, but he called several times, giving her excuses she hadn't asked for.

She knew he had been on the telephone with other people, too, because John Barnard arrived that evening, bringing a selection of current magazines, a stuffed koala bear that played ''Waltzing Matilda'' and a Scarlett O'Hara doll.

Nancy Hightower came the next day, bringing flowers and an exquisitely embroidered dress. She had been to the nursery first and said all the right things about the baby. ''Did Jake tell you that I am buying Lisa's decorating business?'' she asked.

Natalie was pleased. ''No, he didn't. Nancy, that's wonderful. Lisa always said you were the one friend who would never need her services.''

''I'm excited about it. Now if I could just corner Jake long enough to get him to sign the final papers.''

''I thought he was anxious to sell.''

''I did, too. Ah, well, I know he's been working hard.''

''Yes,'' said Natalie, but she wondered.

Flowers arrived from Andrew and his wife. There were even flowers from the Reeds. When she read their names on the card, she couldn't help weeping a little bit. Someday, after she had moved back to Charleston, she hoped they would want to see their daughter's child.

On her last day in the hospital, the phone rang at 8:00 a.m. It was Jake. As usual his deep baritone struck a chord on her tightly strung nerves.

"Is that safe?" he asked, when she told him that Dr. MacGregor was dismissing them later that morning. "It's only been two days."

"I'm sure the hospital wouldn't release us if it wasn't safe."

He was quiet for a second. "What time will you be ready to leave?"

"Around ten o'clock."

"I'll be there."

Natalie wasn't going to protest this time. "Thank you."

Unsure what size she would be, she had packed a pair of gray wool slacks and an oversized sweater the color of ripe Georgia peaches. She pulled on the slacks. Even though they were generously cut, they wouldn't button. She pulled her stomach in as far as it would go, she held her breath, but they still gapped.

The clothes were prepregnancy so she had also packed her blue exercise suit. Now she held up the suit and looked at it with distaste. The elastic was stretched beyond belief. She tossed it into the suitcase and pulled the peach sweater over her head. It covered her hips— and the gaping zipper.

If she ever got her waistline back she was planning to burn a few things, and the exercise suit was one of them.

The nurse helped her dress the baby in a diaper and undershirt before she was called out of the room, leaving Natalie on her own. She managed to maneuver Annabelle's arms into the sleeves of a white batiste gown. It had impossibly tiny tucks down the front and miniscule embroidery around the collar. She'd been right about the buttons, too, but finally she managed to fit them into the buttonholes. White socks and booties came next, then a soft yellow sweater and cap.

Jake arrived as she was tying slippery yellow ribbons under the baby's chin. "Having trouble?" he asked, amusement strong in his tone.

Natalie glanced over her shoulder. "Oh, hi. We're almost ready."

By the time the baby was finally, completely dressed she had become fretful. And no wonder, thought Natalie sympathetically. She herself was rattled and nervous. Her fingers lingered on Annabelle's body when she straightened and turned to smile at Jake.

And became very still.

Jake himself couldn't move, couldn't breathe. Her beautiful hair was loose and the shining mass settled around her shoulders, a few flyaway strands caught on the weave of the sweater. Her smile was gently apologetic for not being ready; her face was becomingly flushed with the effort of dressing the baby. But the element that had brought his senses to a grinding halt was her silhouette—her slim legs, her high breasts and the vacant place where her stomach had been.

His eyes climbed back to meet hers. He opened his mouth, unsure of what he would say. "You look wonderful," he murmured. It was inadequate, but it was all he could manage.

"Thank you," she answered huskily.

Her features softened as she looked at him. He was unhinged by his reaction and wondered if she felt as much at a loss. "Natalie, I—" He crossed the room to stand face-to-face with her. He lifted one hand.

The nurse came back into the room. "All ready to go?" she asked cheerfully.

"Yes." Natalie gripped the footboard of the bed to support herself. Gratified as she was by the warmly appreciative look in Jake's eyes, her sudden, keen response to his eyes on her body had left her shaken.

The nurse checked the drawers, and visually scanned the room to make sure Natalie hadn't forgotten anything. Natalie seemed to be making all the proper responses when the woman questioned her, but she felt as though she were moving in a mist. Now and then her eyes would collide with Jake's heated gaze, unsettling her all over again.

At last they were ready to leave. The flowers would go to the children's ward, except for two of the yellow roses Jake had sent. Natalie had carefully pressed those between the pages of the current issue of *Vogue*, one of the magazines John had brought. Trust John to know what a new mother needed.

Jake carried the bear, the doll and Natalie's suitcase. She said goodbye to the hospital personnel as the nurse wheeled her, and Annabelle in her arms, to the elevator.

"I'll bring the car around," said Jake when they reached the entrance. They were the first words he'd spoken since the nurse had entered her room. His tone was guarded.

Natalie waited at the glass doors, holding the baby, and watched Jake head off through the parking lot. His strides were long and determined.

Her optimism had faded along with his smile. *Well, what did you expect?* she asked herself. Despite his heated appraisal, he was clearly not thrilled.

He pulled into the circular driveway and left the engine running. He came around the car and opened both doors, front and back.

The nurse set the brake on the wheelchair and held Natalie's magazines and her purse, while Jake showed Natalie how to buckle Annabelle into the new car seat in the back.

Natalie got in the back seat beside the baby, and Jake stowed her suitcase in the trunk. She took in a deep breath. The scent of his after-shave lingered in the car, mingling with the smell of fine leather and effectively wiping away the smell of hospital disinfectant.

Jake started the car and moved into traffic. She waved goodbye to the nurse. Then she turned to check on the baby, almost lost in cap and sweater and blankets. Annabelle had closed her eyes. "Thank you for getting a car seat, Jake. I'm ashamed to admit I'd forgotten the law. She looks so small in it."

"At the store they assured me that she will soon outgrow it."

"Really? I can't imagine." She settled back and sighed. "I'm so glad to be out of there."

He smiled at her slightly in the rearview mirror. "Neither of us will ever be comfortable in hospitals."

"You're so right." She smiled back, hopefully. But that was the end of the conversation. What else was there to say? thought Natalie. In light of the circumstances.

When they reached the apartment, he parked in front, at the sidewalk, because the distance was less for her to walk. Before she was out of the car she got her first surprise.

A woman opened the front door of the apartment.

Natalie tapped Jake, who already had his door ajar, on the shoulder. "Who is that?" she asked.

He turned around. Keeping his voice low, he answered, "Her name is Mrs. Mary Davenport. She's a nurse-companion I hired to help you with the baby until you're strong again."

"A nurse? Jake, I can't afford a nurse."

"I said I hired her. I'll pay. She lives in the next block, but she'll stay overnight until you can manage on your own. Then she'll come in during the day."

Natalie looked at the woman skeptically. She didn't have the ordinary look of a baby nurse. Tall and lean, with a severe bun on the back of her neck and an unsmiling demeanor, she came toward the car. "I can manage on my own right now."

He hesitated. "She cooks," he said blandly.

She shot him a look from the corner of her eye. A muscle twitched slightly at the corner of his mouth. He didn't really smile but he was teasing her, a promising sign.

The woman had reached her side of the car and stood waiting a few feet away while they discussed her. Natalie was glad her window was closed. "Well, maybe for a few days," she conceded. "Since she cooks."

He did chuckle then. He got out of the car and came around to introduce them.

"How do you do, Mrs. Davenport?" Natalie held out her hand.

"Call me Mary," she told Natalie, briskly returning the handshake. "Now let's get you both inside. It's cold out here."

Natalie realized almost immediately that she was mistaken in her assessment of Mary Davenport. When the woman headed toward the baby in the back seat, Natalie moved instinctively to stop her, but Jake touched her arm, and she soon knew why.

The moment Mary saw Annabelle, her face changed completely. She murmured to the baby, and when she unfastened the seat buckle and lifted the blanket-wrapped bundle, her capable hands were as gentle as if she were handling delicate crystal. "What a sweet miss you are," she crooned, cuddling Annabelle. "Did you sleep all the way home?"

Her warm smile and soft exclamation melted Natalie's heart. She looked wryly at Jake and smiled her thanks. They both followed Mary inside.

Natalie immediately became aware of the aroma of roasting meat . . . and something with pineapple.

"I hope you don't mind, Mrs. Armstrong. I took the liberty of moving the bassinet into the second bedroom," said Mary, moving through the living room. "If the baby is restless during the night, I can see to her without disturbing you."

Natalie smiled and followed her. "Thank you, Mary. But I don't know how you could fit another piece of furniture in there."

"I rearranged a few things," said Mary as she disappeared into the room.

Natalie stopped in her tracks, alarmed.

Mary stuck her head back out the door. "I didn't touch the computer," she reassured Natalie with a smile.

The next few minutes they were occupied with getting the baby settled. Mary had unpacked the box of linens that she'd found in the closet and dressed the bassinet in the white organdy ruffles and eyelet and blue and pink ribbons. The pretty skirts fell to the floor in cascades. The bed was fit for a princess, and she told Mary so.

"I set it up for her homecoming, but of course we won't keep it decorated this way."

"We won't?"

"Heavens, no. It would be dusty inside a week, not at all healthy for the little one."

"Oh." Natalie shrugged. She could see she had a lot to learn.

Annabelle Lisa Armstrong fit nicely in the bassinet, but it seemed to take a minute for her to feel comfortable. Her tiny hands flailed in the air fearfully when Mary laid her down. Natalie moved forward to remove the baby's sweater and cap and she could feel the little body tremble under her hands. She smoothed down the baby's hair.

"Poor dear," said Mary. "So many strange people and places." She tucked a receiving blanket securely and comfortably around the baby and the panicked movements ceased. Annabelle fell asleep almost immediately.

When Natalie returned to the living room, a cheerful fire was crackling in the fireplace. "Would you like to rest in bed or here in front of the fire?" asked Jake.

"I've been in bed too long," said Natalie, kicking off her shoes and sitting on the sofa. Though she couldn't imagine why, she found that she was a bit tired. She hadn't noticed until now. She laid her head against the cushions and turned to smile at him. Her eyes closed.

Jake looked down at the sleeping woman, free for the moment to let his gaze roam leisurely over her body. From the top of her shining head, lingering on the thrust of her breasts beneath the peach sweater, down her long legs to her nylon-clad toes, she was gorgeous.

The picture was superimposed, however, over his vivid memory of her in the delivery room. She was not only gorgeous, she was vital, strong, courageous and—he recalled the taste of her lips under his—potent.

His eyes returned to her mouth. Her lips were soft, full, slightly moist. The kiss had begun as a celebration. It had ended as something quite different. Now that he knew her taste, would he be able to resist savoring her again?

He muttered a curse under his breath and diverted his gaze. She was tired, not ready to go where his thoughts were taking him. Good Lord, she'd just had a baby two days ago.

She didn't even know when he left.

The first few days at home were much more of an adjustment than Natalie had expected. She knew the arrival of the baby would mean major changes in her life, but what she hadn't foreseen was how an entire household could revolve entirely around a person as small as Annabelle. Sleep, meals, laundry, everything seemed to be adjusting to her, rather than vice versa.

Natalie's characteristic neatness flew out the window.

For the most part, Annabelle was a good baby, but a baby was a baby. She had to be fed regularly; she had to be changed; she had to have clean clothes. And the bath— Good God, thought Natalie one morning as she watched in awe of Mary's deft manipulation of the wet, squirming body. How would she ever be able to bathe the baby alone? The water had to be the right temperature, the soap and towel at hand because you couldn't leave her unattended in the water while you searched for something you'd forgotten.

Mary took responsibility for the baby's care, but Natalie soon realized that she should learn as much as possible from the woman. She asked questions that must have sounded really dumb to Mary.

"I've never been around small children," she explained, having earned another of those incredulous looks. "I had no brothers or sisters. I didn't even have cousins that were close enough to visit."

"You poor thing," said Mary.

Natalie was rather startled by the sympathy; she had never considered herself deprived because she wasn't around babies.

After that admission, Mary began to explain without her having to ask.

March came in like a lamb. The air was fresh and warm and winter washed. Annabelle was two weeks old when Natalie decided that she should have her first botany lesson.

She took the baby into the garden and began to name the flowers, holding her up so she could see the bright colors. The bulbs were in full bloom. Lemon-yellow jonquils and scarlet tulips lined the borders, providing the backdrop for blue and white hyacinths. A few pansies were left, their purple and gold faces low against the ground. That morning Annabelle smiled for the first time.

Mary explained that it was probably gas, but Natalie didn't believe that for a minute.

The most peaceful time for everyone—aside from when Annabelle was sleeping—was when Annabelle was nursing. Natalie loved the intervals, even when they came in the middle of the night. This baby, at her breast, depending on her for sustenance—it was a breathtaking experience.

One sunny morning Natalie was sitting in the antique rocker, the baby in her arms sucking greedily, when there was a knock at the back door. Mary answered and Natalie heard Jake's voice.

"She's in the living room," Mary told him.

Natalie looked around anxiously, unwilling for him to see her with her blouse open, but there was nothing she could do.

He stopped on the threshold, staring at the picture she made. He seemed mesmerized. At last he cleared his throat and came over. He looked down and met her eyes. "Everything okay?" he asked.

She swallowed, then smiled. "Everything's fine," she answered.

He allowed his gaze to drop to the full curve of her breast, the baby's rosebud mouth on her nipple. Sated now, Annabelle closed her eyes. In sleep, she sighed;

her lips trembled, then relaxed. A dribble of milk escaped. Natalie felt it run down into her blouse.

She sat immobile, unable even to breathe, while she watched the expressions that crossed his face. The air seemed to vibrate with the electricity that arced between them.

Jake raised his hand—she thought he was going to touch her. Then he let it drop and turned away.

Natalie felt her spirits and her hope hit bottom.

They didn't see much of Jake after that. He dropped in occasionally after work, but if Annabelle was in the room or started to cry while he was there, he left immediately.

It hurt, but Natalie told herself that it was what she should have expected.

They had been home for three weeks when Mary suggested that she return to her writing. "Our schedule is fairly well established," she told Natalie. "And I've seen the looks you give that contraption when you're in the room with it."

Natalie grinned and kissed the older woman soundly on the cheek. "Thanks, Mary."

She plunged into her work with an energy that she wished she enjoyed at other times. It seemed that she was always tired. Until she sat down at the computer. Then the characters, their movements and emotions, became more real to her than her own. Her plot took on a vitality that rivaled her own life for realism. It was often hard to tear herself away.

One morning, secluded in the bedroom-office, she became aware of a far-off sound. But she was deep into a scene and disregarded the noise.

"Lunch, Natalie," said Mary through the closed door.

Natalie paused, her fingers resting lightly on the keyboard, disoriented for a moment. "Be there in a minute," she called.

The door opened and Mary stuck her head inside. "Not yours, honey. Annabelle's. And I don't think she'll wait a minute."

Natalie heard the baby's cries through the open door and felt guilty. "Oh, Mary, I'm sorry." She quickly pushed the save button and turned off the machine.

She swiveled in her chair and stood, lifting her arms over her head to stretch her muscles. Then she realized that the cries were growing more shrill. She hurried through the living room into the kitchen.

Annabelle's infant seat was in the middle of the kitchen table. A mobile of bright butterflies hung from the light fixture above.

But Annabelle was not amused; her feet and arms were milling wildly as she screamed.

Natalie plucked the baby out of the seat and cradled her in one arm. "Goodness gracious, we are hungry, aren't we?" she asked as she sat down and prepared to nurse the baby.

After a few unsuccessful attempts to get Annabelle to eat, Natalie looked up at the older woman worriedly. "Is she all right, Mary?"

Annabelle would suckle for a minute and scream for a minute. Then she would nuzzle around and try again. The cycle was nerve shattering for Natalie.

Mary folded her arms over her own bony chest. "You're not going to like this, Natalie," she warned gently. She took a breath. "But I don't think Annabelle is getting enough to eat. I believe she needs formula."

Natalie felt her heart squeeze as the baby cried out again, then nuzzled with frustration. She looked down, but she didn't see her daughter's beautiful face. All she could grasp was that she'd failed.

Mary read her mind. "You are not a failure, Natalie," she said firmly. "Many women are not able to nurse at all. You've fed Annabelle for almost a month."

Finally Natalie nodded. "We'll do whatever you think is best," she said softly. But her disappointment was still intense.

"I'll give the doctor a call to check it out with him, right now."

Natalie continued to feed Annabelle, but she now used a rich formula, a plastic bottle and a nipple made of rubber. She often sat in the garden for this task. Annabelle liked to watch the movement of the leaves overhead.

This afternoon she had spread a quilt on the grass. She was feeling particularly melancholy as she fed the baby and burped her. Then she laid Annabelle on her stomach and sat beside her, watching her kick her strong little legs.

Natalie felt she had lost something precious when she could no longer satisfy the baby. It made her think of all the losses she would have to adjust to in the years to come. Annabelle would go off to school and Natalie would no longer be the sole influence in her life. She would grow up, date, leave home for college—now *that* was a frightening concept. She would meet a man, marry, have children—

"What are you thinking?" asked a quiet voice.

Natalie twisted around to see Jake. His coat was slung over the fence and he stood hip-shot, his chin resting on his forearms on top of the gate, watching her. He looked as if he might have been watching for some time.

She had been so absorbed in her thoughts she hadn't heard the car, hadn't known he was there. She thought she laughed, but instead a sad little sound emerged from her lips. "You wouldn't believe it if I told you," she said.

He straightened, took his coat off the fence and came over to where she was sitting. "Try me."

Annabelle turned her head at the sound of another, different voice. Her legs were flaying the air. She kicked off a sock.

Natalie smiled briefly at her antics, then she tilted her head as far back as it would go to look up at him. "I was thinking about grandchildren."

"Good God," he said. He laughed and shook his head. "That settles it. You've got to get out of this house. We're going somewhere for dinner."

"Really?" she said, a smile spreading over her face.

"Really. Where would you like to go?" He sat down beside Natalie. Annabelle kicked harder. He ignored her, but Natalie could see the signs of the baby's growing annoyance. She picked up Annabelle and patted her absently on the back. "Anywhere?"

He grinned. His teeth were white against his mustache. "Anywhere," he agreed.

"To the beach, to one of those loud honky-tonk places where they play hard rock and drink beer and dance until dawn."

"You're kidding," he said.

"Nope."

But it began to rain, so he didn't take her there. They went to Tibernio's instead. And all the unpleasant memories of their last evening there went with them.

"This wasn't a good idea," said Jake.

"Probably not," agreed Natalie.

They were back at the town house by nine o'clock.

"We'll go to the beach another time," he said as he said good-night at her door.

"Yes, another time." But time was running out, and they both knew it.

Chapter 9

Natalie stood at the open front door, her eyes on the park across the street. The azaleas were bursting with color—magenta, flame, coral, white—and overhead, like flowering umbrellas, were the dogwoods, their buds just beginning to open. In another week or so the city would be ablaze in color.

It was such a beautiful day Natalie suddenly decided she couldn't bear to be indoors. She called to Mary, and in a few minutes they were outside. Annabelle was about to experience her first real excursion into the world.

The weather was perfect for indulging in spring fever. The sun was shining in a cloudless sky.

Natalie's heart seemed buoyant, and her mood matched her outfit—the yellow slacks and top she wore for the first time since last spring. Her clothes fit her again, albeit a little tightly. She wanted to dance, to whirl around and around, until she was dizzy. Others seemed to be under the influence of the same frivolous fever. As Natalie, Mary and Annabelle passed through the more commercial areas of the historic district, the streets were crowded with people, and they all seemed to be smiling.

Even Mary was affected by the day. The stolid demeanor that she exhibited most often was washed away by the brilliant sunlight. She talked about herself, something she rarely did. They stopped by her house so she could pick up her mail, and she showed Natalie around. Her home was a much smaller version of Jake's, but it was also a restoration house and had a lovely charm.

"Pshew. It smells musty in here," said Mary. "I'll need to air it out when I come back."

"If you need to—" Natalie began.

But Mary interrupted. "I'll stay with you until you leave," she said in her no-nonsense tone.

"I would like you to continue to be there during the day, but if you want to be at home at night, I'll be fine with the baby." She almost always got up to feed Annabelle, anyway. "I don't know what would have happened if you hadn't been here to teach me what to do, Mary. You saw how incompetent I was."

Mary's look was keen. "You weren't incompetent. You were inexperienced. But you would have learned. You're that kind of person. You do what has to be done." Then she added what was, of course, the most important commendation of all. "Annabelle would not have suffered."

Natalie was awed by the compliment. Mary so rarely handed them out. "Thank you, Mary."

Suddenly Mary nodded decisively. "After your checkup next week, I'll go home at night. If you get into trouble you can call me. I'm close enough to run over."

Natalie laughed. "You'd better take your phone off the hook."

Pushing Annabelle's stroller, they walked over to Bull Street and Madison Square. One of the most charming aspects of Savannah were the squares—two dozen small parks, green oases in the middle of the city bustle.

They passed a nursery and Natalie decided the urns on each side of the front door needed some color, too. She bought geraniums to replace those that had died over the winter and arranged to pick them up the next day. The color was coral pink, a new hybrid that, Mary agreed, would look lovely beside the warm pinkish color of the brick house.

They walked for miles. When they returned to the apartment, tired but still cheerful, they found Jake waiting, a formidable expression on his face.

His brief glance at the baby, dressed in a pink sweater and cap and buckled into her stroller, was indifferent. He said hello to Mary first. Then he turned to Natalie. "I need to talk to you. Will you come upstairs?"

Suddenly the beautiful day was obscured by the seriousness of his mood.

"I'll take Annabelle inside," said Mary quickly. "I imagine the little dear could use a dry diaper by now." She wheeled the collapsible stroller through the door, which Jake held open for her.

Natalie climbed the steps with Jake right behind her. Inadvertently her eyes were drawn to the spot above the mantel where Lisa's portrait had hung. The empty spot had been filled with a seascape. Natalie took a seat in one corner of the sofa at a right angle to the painting and looked around.

She hadn't been in this room, hadn't been any farther than the kitchen, since the day she and Nancy had helped Andrew pack Lisa's clothes and personal belongings. There were a few changes.

In a corner to the left of the fireplace, two delicate Louis XVI chairs had been replaced by utilitarian bookshelves and a small television set.

Lisa had hated a TV in the living room.

A beautiful china tea set had been removed from the low table in front of the sofa. In its place were a bundle of well-thumbed blueprints, a couple of file folders, a newspaper and the remote-control device for the TV, all aligned rigidly with the edges of the table. The desk section of the beautiful antique secretary was folded closed, hiding the carved pigeonholes, the tooled-leather-and-gilt writing area.

Lisa had always left it open, not for any practical purpose but as a display surface for an exquisite brass-and-crystal inkwell.

Except for those alterations everything else remained the same. The sofa on which she sat was a camelback Chippendale, upholstered in white damask. The draperies and swags at the windows were silk taffeta and puddled stylishly on the hardwood floor. Another chair was covered in burgundy moiré, reflecting the predominent color in the oriental carpet.

Jake obviously spent a lot of time in this room, and as a consequence, it had taken on a subtle masculine air despite the elegance of its furnishings. Or maybe it was that his presence dominated the room so completely. Actually it was quite nice. More lived-in, not so very formal, yet still lovely.

He stood looking down at her, his expression unreadable. He had jammed his hands into the back pockets of his jeans.

Natalie was the first to look away. "I just remembered. You lost your home office as well as your den when I moved in," she said, indicating the paperwork.

He shrugged off her unspoken apology and sat on the other corner of the sofa. "This works fine." He crossed one ankle over his knee. "Would you like something? Coffee? A soft drink?"

"No, thank you."

"I signed the papers selling Lisa's business yesterday."

Natalie nodded. "Nancy came to the hospital after I gave birth. She told me that you were negotiating."

They were silent for a moment. She opened her mouth to ask him what this was all about. But before she could speak, he said, "It's a nice day for a walk."

She blinked. "Yes. I think I had a touch of spring fever today." She waited, wary of his mood. He asked her where they went. She told him. They talked about the city's commitment to maintaining the parks.

Suddenly he looked away. "I was holding on, Natalie," he said in a low voice. He propped his elbow on the high arm of the sofa and worried his jaw with a knuckle.

She was confused by the remark. "Holding on?"

"Yes. To Lisa's business and consequently to Lisa. I finally realized that nothing is going to bring her back."

All at once she understood. "No, nothing will bring her back," she said gently. "But it's hard to let go of every contact."

"It's hard to let go, *period*. It's hard to move on." He surged to his feet, made a quick, restless circle of the room, then came back to sit down again. "But I have to. I *have* to."

"Why did you want to see me, Jake?" she asked at last, though she had an idea by now that she probably knew.

"Mary told me that you'd called your old boss in Charleston about a job."

She sighed. Of course. She'd seen him talking to Mary yesterday. "Yes, I have begun thinking about it. Dr. MacGregor wanted me to stay in town until after my checkup. But that's only a week away. By then I hope to have something lined up."

He stretched his arm along the back of the sofa, bringing his fingers to within inches of her shoulder. "I have an idea I'd like you to think about."

Whatever it was, he didn't look completely comfortable. He pulled at a stray thread on the hem of his jeans. She smiled encouragingly. "What is it?"

Instead of answering directly he asked, "How is the work going on your manuscript?"

He knew she had written in December to the agent who had agreed to look at the book, explaining the delay. "I received a letter from the agent a few weeks ago, saying that he was still interested. He suggested that I send the chapters I had completed. So I did." Two-thirds of the manuscript had gone in the mail last week. "Why?"

"How much time will it take to finish?"

"Since this is my first attempt at fiction, I'm not exactly sure how long. Probably another four months, or maybe I can finish in three."

"I think you should continue to live in the apartment until then."

Her eyes widened. "What? I thought you couldn't wait to get rid of me."

He looked at her, meeting her eyes directly. His own were smoky with some sort of emotion that she couldn't interpret. His voice, when he spoke, was low. "I never said that. You did."

"But you said—"

"I said I had no intention of having a family. I didn't say I wanted to get rid of you."

Natalie remained motionless for a minute, searching her memory. She remembered the first statement, vividly. She wasn't sure about the second. "Do you mean under the same conditions?" she asked guardedly. "Me living on your largesse?"

"How many times do I have to repeat myself?" he said, suddenly impatient. "It's your money."

"Jake, you know how this whole subject bothers me," she responded sharply.

He shook his head. "I should know. You've reminded me of it enough times," he snapped. "I don't know where you got this hang-up."

Her own irritation heightened. "Only people who don't have to worry about money can treat the subject so cavalierly. Maybe you don't remember..." She bit off the end of the sentence.

"I do remember how you and Joseph struggled, how his illness swallowed your savings." He paused before he spoke again. "Actually, you have plenty of money. The remaining funds in the trust were deposited in a new account as soon as the baby was born." He picked up a folder from the table. "Here is your passbook. I received my own accounting a few days ago.''

She looked at him speculatively, but she didn't take the passbook. ''You did?''

He tossed it back on the table where it skittered across the smooth surface to come up against a stack of papers. ''Did you even read the stipulations in our original contract?''

''I glanced through them,'' she said defensively. Jake and Lisa were like family; she had simply skimmed the papers. She had no reason not to trust them. But both the medical staff and the attorneys had insisted on dotting all the *i*'s and crossing all the *t*'s. It seemed that Jake and Lisa had paid as little attention as she had. She sighed, resigned. ''Okay. How much is there?''

He named a figure that surprised her. Then he went on to explain. ''You didn't take anything out during the time you worked for John. And even after you quit, you still had additional income from your magazine articles. If you remain in the apartment it should be enough to last for a while.''

''Even to pay Mary's salary,'' she mused. She wasn't convinced this was the right thing to do, but she was tempted. The apartment had become like home to her. It was certainly more comfortable than anything she'd be able to afford in Charleston. She wanted to stay, she admitted, but she didn't think it would work.

And she wondered about his reasons for offering.

She'd barely seen him since the baby was born. The one dinner at Tibernio's had not turned out well. The atmosphere between them had been tense. Then she had another thought. ''Is this another case of your not wanting to let go of something, Jake?''

She expected him to deny it, but, instead, he hesitated. "I don't think so."

"The adoption..."

"The adoption will go through. I've given you my word." He turned so that his broad shoulders backed against the arm of the sofa and faced her directly. "The truth is, I don't want you to go." There was no doubt that his answer was sincere, but his expression was unreadable. She didn't know what to say.

With a fidgety movement, Jake rubbed the fabric of the sofa behind her head, wanting to touch her, wanting to slide his hand under her hair, to stroke the back of her neck. He'd barely seen anything of her since the child was born. No, that wasn't true. He'd seen her; she hadn't seen him. He felt like some kind of voyeur, but every night he'd been at the window. He knew of her habit of walking in the garden, so he'd watched.

Her magnetism was stronger than ever. *Was* he trying to hold on to her because of Lisa?

Though the two were lifelong friends they were very different women. Lisa had been like bright sunlight—energetic, gregarious, sociable, loving. Natalie was moonlight—serene, gracious, gentle, feminine.

His feelings were the consummate paradox. Though his heart was still heavy with sorrow, he often ached with desire for this woman. He was going crazy trying to reconcile the two feelings.

At last she turned to him, tucking her foot under her. "Jake, I don't think it would be a good idea for me to stay."

"What do you mean?"

"You were disturbed by my being pregnant. You would be more disturbed having Annabelle around," she told him. "She isn't exactly quiet." Natalie was genuinely concerned about that factor; she didn't want Jake to ever resent the baby for any reason.

He smiled and finally succumbed to temptation, sliding his hand under her hair; his thumb stroked the side of her neck. It was the first overt signal of sensual awareness he'd sent since the kiss he gave her when Annabelle was born. "You should be worrying if *you* will disturb me. I am."

The last time they had this conversation, she'd been hurt by the outcome. She didn't intend to be hurt again. "Once before, you said something was happening between us." She spoke slowly, but her thoughts tumbled in her mind at a speed that made her dizzy. "You said then that you felt like you were cheating. If I stay, what do you think will happen?"

His thumb slid from her neck around to touch her lips. His eyes followed the motion. "I know damn well what I want to happen."

She was taken aback by his bluntness and aroused by his touch. His thumb moved to trace the curve of her ear. "And if it does, are you going to feel guilty?" she asked, her voice thick. She didn't want to be having this conversation. But she had to know. "Do you think Lisa would approve?"

His eyes met hers. "I don't think Lisa's approval is relevant one way or another. This is between us. And, no, I won't feel guilty."

"But, Jake—"

He withdrew his hand but checked her protest by placing a finger over her lips. His lingering touch was warm and silenced her as effectively as a kiss would have. "No 'buts.' I won't push you. Think about staying here until your book is finished."

He removed his finger. She nodded, but she had to moisten her lips before she could speak. "All right, I'll think it over."

"So are you going to stay?" asked Mary when she got back downstairs.

Natalie cut her eyes to the older woman. "You knew what the subject of the conversation was to be before I did. I'm surprised you don't know what my answer is."

"You *are* going to stay," said Mary with a satisfied smirk.

"I haven't decided yet."

It was a week later; she and Mary were having breakfast. "Don't forget that you and Annabelle both have doctors' appointments this afternoon. I'm going along to help you manage."

"Thanks, Mary." She knew that sometime soon she would have to take the baby out alone with diapers and blankets and bottles and toys, but the very thought scared her to death.

She worked until three o'clock, then gave a regretful look at the computer. She had no idea how long the checkups would last, but she probably wouldn't be back for hours. Mentally she said farewell to the characters and went to dress.

"Have you packed?" she asked Mary when she saw her in the living room with the baby.

"All packed," Mary told her as she tied Annabelle's hat under her chin. They were going to drop off Mary's suitcase before they went to the doctor. From now on, for as long as Natalie and the baby were here, Mary would go to her home at night.

Natalie crossed to lift Annabelle from her infant seat and cuddled her close for a moment. She cradled her head and crooned to the sweet-smelling baby. "Don't you look pretty today, all dressed up, little precious?" She nuzzled her tummy.

Mary had dressed her in a pair of pink corduroy overalls with bright pink flamingos on the bib and a white turtleneck with flamingos on the sleeves. She wore little lacy pink socks.

Annabelle smiled.

Annabelle's smiles were something to see. Even Mary admitted that it was no longer gas.

It was after six when the three of them returned from the doctors' appointments.

Jake was waiting in the garden. He held the gate. "Everyone healthy?" he asked.

Natalie felt the color rise in her cheeks. Dr. Mac-Gregor had pronounced her fit for anything. She knew from the childbirth classes—and so did Jake—that the six-week checkup was usually when husbands and wives were told they could resume their sex lives. "We're both very healthy, thank you."

He fell into step beside her. "Have you decided to stay here until you finish your book?"

"Yes, I'm going to stay," said Natalie, surprising herself with the positive answer.

Mary smiled and disappeared inside with the baby, whispering to Annabelle as she went.

Natalie watched them go, wondering what it was she said when she whispered like that. She turned to Jake. "I need to help her get Annabelle ready for bed. This time of day is rather hectic. Mary is going home tonight, and we're running behind."

"Sure." He stood there, hands in his pockets, looking down at her. If he had been different, if he'd shown any interest at all in Annabelle, she would have asked him to come in. She would have given him a glass of wine. After the baby was settled, after Mary left, they could have ordered in supper. "Well—" She turned to go inside.

"Natalie?"

She paused with one hand on the doorjamb. "Yes?"

"I'm glad you thought it over. I'm glad you're staying."

"Me, too." She smiled and closed the door.

It hadn't been an easy decision; she had thought of little else since he made the offer last week. She had been torn. One minute she would decide that she must return to Charleston. She would be too uncomfortable here. Besides, if Jake wanted to see her, Charleston was only forty-five minutes away.

The next minute she would decide to stay. The apartment was comfortable. Mary was wonderful with Annabelle; she could work without worrying that she might be neglecting the baby.

But there were other arguments, less well defined. She was halfway in love with that extraordinary man upstairs. He was funny, and kind, and sexy. He had been deeply wounded, and he had vowed he would never commit himself again. Knowing that nothing permanent would come of this, should she settle for having as much of him as he would part with before they both moved on?

She wouldn't make any attempt to remove Annabelle from his presence, but she wouldn't try to encourage or push him into taking part in the baby's life, either. If a relationship were to develop between father and daughter, it would grow naturally, or it would not grow at all.

She didn't know which of those reasons had prompted her decision to stay, but now that it was made she wouldn't look back. She would stay here, work on the book and see what happened next. If the decision turned out to be the wrong one, if she got hurt, well, it would be her own fault.

The next morning Mary arrived early. Natalie had a sneaking suspicion that she thought the apartment would be in an uproar, with Natalie pulling her hair out and Annabelle screaming. But the baby had behaved like an angel.

"Good morning," she said cheerfully when Mary let herself in. Annabelle was watching the mobile from her infant seat, and Natalie was dressed and finishing her second cup of coffee.

"Good morning," answered Mary. "Has Jake left for work yet?"

"I haven't heard him."

Just at that moment the door upstairs slammed and they heard his heavy footsteps. Mary opened the door and called him.

He came to the door, stuck his head in. "Hi," he said to Natalie.

"Hi," she answered.

"What's up?" he asked Mary.

"We have a crib that needs to be assembled. Will you help us with it?"

"Wait, Mary." Natalie got to her feet and joined them at the door. "Where are we going to put it? That room is so crowded already that you can hardly walk in there."

"We're going to do some rearranging," said Mary. "If you are going to stay here for several more months, we have to get that baby a comfortable place to sleep."

"I have to meet the inspectors at the building site on Saturday. What about Sunday afternoon?" Jake said.

"That's fine. I'm taking the weekend off. Natalie, can you—"

"I'm not going anywhere," Natalie agreed.

On Saturday night, by the time she finally put Annabelle to bed, Natalie was worn out. She collapsed on the sofa, sliding down until she sat on the end of her spine. Her white slacks were a wrinkled mess. She pulled at the hem of her blue knit shirt to catalog the damage. Two big blobs were obviously formula. There were a few other stains she didn't particularly want to identify. With a sigh, she let the shirt fall.

A knock roused her from her stupor. She rolled her head and peered through the kitchen to the back door. Jake. She couldn't even summon any enthusiasm for him. She motioned him to come in, and then her hand fell heavily to the cushion.

"What's up?" he said, planting his hands at his waist. He looked terrific. He'd worn jeans to the docks today. She tried to remember why, then dismissed it as unimportant. What was important was the way they looked on him, tight and worn and faded at strategic places. The sleeves of his blue work shirt were rolled back over his muscular forearms to the elbow. He looked good.

"Natalie?" He sounded as though he were choking.

"What? Oh." She dragged her gaze up to meet his. She smiled weakly. "This was my first day totally on my own. From dawn to dusk, from beginning to end. Without Mary."

He grinned. "Tough, huh?"

"That word doesn't *begin* to describe this day," she said with a wide gesture. She giggled. "I think I'm punch-drunk."

He sat down beside her and took her hand. "You want to order in some Chinese food?"

She closed her eyes. "Yes."

"I'll run you a bubble bath and while we wait for the food you can relax."

"Ohh," she breathed. "That would be heavenly."

"I've got a great bottle of wine upstairs."

"Yes."

"Then we could get naked and—"

Her eyes popped open. "What?"

He grinned unrepentantly. "I just wanted to see if you were paying attention." He patted her thigh and rose.

Natalie closed her eyes again. She heard him turn on the taps, heard the clink of bottles in the bathroom. She knew she should get up, but she was unable to move.

She felt herself being lifted, one arm under her knees, the other across her back. She smiled and looped her arms around his neck, but she kept her eyes closed. "This feels familiar," she said.

He laughed, a low sexy sound. "It doesn't feel at all familiar to me." He moved his fingers, and she realized they were brushing the sides of her breast. "There is a lot less of you."

She opened her eyes, and he set her on her bare feet. Her hands were on his forearms. The warm skin there was setting up edgy little feelings along her nerve ends. He was looking down at her with a small half smile on his face. His hands lingered at her waist.

Her heart accelerated as he lowered his head, angling his lips to hers. Her eyes drifted shut, savoring the sensations of his nearness. His body radiated heat that seemed to surround her, wrapping her in a warm cocoon, and his scent . . . his scent was virile and masculine and uniquely him.

The kiss was casual, nothing heavy and demanding. His mouth was warm and mobile, his tongue probing lightly past her parted lips.

But when she looked at him, she saw that his eyes were dark, almost black, and burned with emotion, and his breathing had grown shallow.

She held her own breath, unable to look away. He wanted her; the realization was heady.

"Do you need some help getting your clothes off?" he murmured against her lips.

She very nearly said yes. Her hunger for him was intense. But then she backed off. If this happened, it happened. But it would be better if it happened slowly.

She dropped her eyes to the second button on his shirt. "No, I can do it. I'll be out in a minute."

He waited for a minute, then he dropped his hands. "Take your time. I'll go upstairs and get the wine."

"All right. Oh!"

He was about to close the door behind him. He stopped.

"Would you leave the door open so I can listen for the baby?"

"Sure."

He had been heavy-handed with her bubble bath, she noted with a smile. She twisted her hair on top of her head and secured it with pins. Then she eased into the water. It was just the right temperature to soothe her tight muscles, and she sighed aloud with pleasure as she sank in up to her neck and relaxed.

In a few minutes she began to feel the knots loosen. She cupped her palms and lifted handfuls of bubbles, letting them slide down her arms. She piled mountains of suds on top of her bent knees and blew them off, made herself a beard and mustache as she had done when she was a child. She laughed softly.

And heard an answering laugh. "The mustache is fine, but don't you think the beard is a bit much?"

"Jake?" Embarrassed, spitting, she sank down again until the water reached her neck, although with all the bubbles he couldn't have seen anything.

He was leaning against the doorjamb, watching her make an idiot of herself. He held two glasses of wine, one of which he placed on the edge of the tub, and a rose from the garden, which he placed beside the glass.

"How charming," she said with a gentle smile. She picked up the pink rose and held it to her nose. The scent was sweet, the petals like velvet against her cheek. "Thank you, Jake."

Lifting his glass, he toasted her. "Have fun," he said and left, grinning.

Natalie sipped the wine and lay back again in the tub, but her eyes kept returning to the open door. At last she got out and dried herself off. She massaged jasmine-scented lotion into her skin, all over, and dusted herself lightly with powder.

She went to her drawer and took out a teal gown and matching peignoir, which she put on.

She looked at herself in the mirror, then took off the set and put on jeans and a big shirt. When she heard the doorbell she hurriedly pulled on a pair of socks, rejected the idea of shoes, brushed on some lips gloss and went to join Jake.

He was fishing money out of his pocket. He handed the delivery boy a wad of bills. "Here, thanks." He took the two white sacks.

"Thank you, sir."

"That smells great," said Natalie as she followed him to the kitchen. She buzzed around, clearing the infant seat off the table, gathering plates and napkins from the cabinets. "I'm starving."

"I figured you might be after your strenuous day," said Jake. "I ordered dinner for three. Did you bring your wineglass?"

"No, I'll get it. Where's yours?"

"Next to the sofa."

"This is delicious," said Natalie a short while later. The edge was off her appetite, but she was still eating. She wrinkled her brow. "You know, I'm not sure I ate any lunch."

Jake smiled and took a bite of pepper beef, wielding the chopsticks with dexterity. A bit of sauce escaped, and he caught it with his tongue.

Natalie watched, fascinated, remembering the night she had made hot chocolate.

Jake was well aware that she was watching. He was also well aware that she had scented herself with something very sexy. Obviously, though, she'd chickened out when it came to getting dressed.

However, he'd always found jeans very sexy. Particularly faded, well-worn, soft-from-washing jeans that fit as well as hers did. And that big man-tailored shirt probably didn't touch her anyplace below her shoulders. He wondered if she had on a bra. He wondered what color her nipples were—pink or rose or brown. He could imagine tracing a circle around her with his tongue . . .

"Want some more?"

His head jerked up. "What?"

She pointed with her chopsticks. "There's more sweet and sour."

He put a hand to his stomach, patted and rubbed it. "I'm full."

"I think I'll have some more, then. Sweet and sour is my favorite."

"Mmm," said Jake. He leaned back in his chair and picked up the glass of wine, studying her through the golden liquid.

The silence stretched as Natalie ate, and he looked on. She began to grow uncomfortable. She pushed back her plate, and dabbed at her mouth with her napkin. "That's enough for me, too." He had refilled her wineglass, and she picked it up to sip from it.

At last she sighed. "I feel human again. Thank you, Jake." She got to her feet, taking her glass with her. "I'll just straighten up in here. Why don't you go in the living room?"

He smiled, letting his lashes come down to hood his eyes. He looked completely relaxed and at ease; he looked at home. "We'll do the dishes together. Later." He set down his glass and reached out for her hand.

He took her glass from her suddenly nerveless fingers and set it down, too. With this thumb he drew rings in her palm, stimulating nerves far beyond her hand—nerves in her spine, in the nape of her neck, her thighs. "Come here," he said. His voice was deep and husky. "I've been dreaming of this for weeks."

She didn't withdraw her hand and he pulled her between his spread knees. When he covered her stomach with his big hand, she sighed. One broad hand splayed across her back, holding her in place, and the other moved around and around on the big shirt.

The crinkling sound of starchy fabric was not one which she would ever have associated with sensuality—the whisper of silk or the hum of satin were more provocative. But under his warm palm, the sound of cotton was as titillating as the rasp of a zipper. She let her forearms droop over his shoulders, and her head fall back. She sighed aloud as he reached up to scatter the pins in her hair and let it tumble down around her shoulders.

The soft sound was like a signal to him. He suddenly burrowed under the shirt with both hands. "Ahh," he said when he discovered only her soft skin beneath.

She inhaled sharply as his big hands closed around her breasts and began an ardent massage, shaping and reshaping. His fingers brushed lightly over her nipples, arousing them into buds of delight.

"I want to see you," he growled. He withdrew his hands and worked impatiently on the shirt buttons. Then he drew the sides wide apart, holding the fabric in his fists at the small of her back. "God, you're beautiful," he breathed as he drew her closer.

The first touch of his hungry mouth on her breasts provoked a small moan.

He lifted his head abruptly. "Did I hurt you?"

"No. Oh, no. It felt..." He pulled her forward again, and she couldn't go on. The sensation made her delirious. She tunneled her fingers into his dark, crisp hair, whether for support or to hold his head more firmly against her she didn't know. Probably some of each; her knees were certainly weak.

"How does it feel?" he murmured. "Tell me." His head dipped, and the brush of his mustache across her skin sent shivers across the round fullness of her breasts to her midriff.

"It—it tickles!" The word exploded on a burst of air.

At first he looked nonplussed, then he began to smile. The smile grew into a wicked, devilish, suggestive grin. "It tickles, huh?"

He dropped the tails of her shirt and reached for the snap of her jeans. The sliding zipper was cold against her bare skin. He kissed her belly, dipping his hot tongue into her navel. His mouth moved lower. She felt his breath on her acutely sensitive skin. He tugged her jeans from the back until they slid down to expose her bare bottom.

His head came up; he fixed her with a disbelieving stare. "Good God. You're not—"

"Wearing any underwear?" she answered softly.

He surged to his feet, his arms pinning her to his hard body, while his mouth came down to cover hers. The kiss was ravenous, and she clung to him, her head swimming in a misty pool of desire. "Oh, Jake," she murmured.

Jake swept her into his strong arms, leaving her jeans where they lay on the floor. With purposeful strides, he headed for her bedroom.

The light spilling from the hall was enough to illuminate his dark eyes when he set her on her feet and began removing his clothes. His hot gaze never left her, roaming restlessly from her face to her hair, to her breasts, to her thighs, to the soft brown curls at the juncture of her legs.

For a moment she felt shy and hesitant under the force of so much concentrated passion. The shirttails swung free as she sat on the edge of the bed to remove her socks. Then she folded back the spread and the blanket and the sheet, taking her time, fully aware of his eyes on her, watching every move. She finally let go of the sheet and gave him a faltering smile.

He had shed his shoes, socks and shirt. Now he paused with his hands on the waist of his open jeans and came to her beside the bed. "Natalie? Are you afraid?"

She shook her head. His face was in shadow, but she could feel his concern. "No, not afraid, just bashful. It's—it's been a long time for me."

He reached out to hold her shoulders; she looked up at him. "You haven't made love since—in over three years?" he asked gently.

"Three years and a pregnancy," she reminded him as a stain crept up her neck.

He wrapped his arms around her, and she laid her cheek on his broad chest, cherishing the feel of hard muscles beneath warm skin. She touched the black hair that swirled across the expanse, surprised that it was so soft and springy.

"We'll take it very, very slowly," Jake promised, stepping back. His lungs were burning, his arousal throbbed, he thought if he wasn't inside her soon he would explode. He struggled, fought and finally mastered his desire—and he was shaking with the effort.

He nudged the collar of the shirt she wore aside with one finger. He smiled encouragingly and she dropped the shirt off her shoulders, leaving her beautiful body bare to his gaze. He realized that she had seen his shaking hand, and he smiled, tenderly. "Although taking it slowly may kill me," he said ruefully.

She reached up to cradle his jaw. "I'm a little self-conscious, Jake, but I'm a woman, too. You don't have to handle me like a piece of crystal." She lifted herself on tiptoe and kissed him.

"Very much a woman, a warm, sensationally sexy woman." His voice resonated from deep within his chest. He took off his jeans and together they lay down on the fresh cool sheets, facing each other. His hand traced her arm from shoulder to elbow, then moved to her side where her waist dipped and rose to the flare of her hip.

Natalie gave a soft moan and moved closer, tilting her head, parting her lips in a conscious invitation. Her breasts brushed his chest.

His mouth covered hers, his tongue delving, exploring, while his hands moved slowly over her, finding all the wonderful intimate places to give her pleasure. Her blood was moving slowly, thickly through her veins, like sweet honey. She raked her nails lightly over his back and heard the satisfying growl of reaction.

Suddenly he moved above her, nudging his manhood against the wet, warm center of her yearning.

She felt the passion in the tension of his body, smelled their desire, heard him call her name softly. Her hips came off the bed to meet him and he entered her with one sure thrust.

Jake froze, holding himself motionless until she adjusted to having him inside her. But it took a Herculean effort. He wanted to drive into her, impress himself on her, so that she would always remember this moment. She was tight, oh, God, so tight, so wet and hot.

She moved beneath him, demanding with her body language, her hips rotating hungrily. Here it was, the sensuality that he'd always suspected lay deep within her ladylike facade. But he couldn't— "No, wait— baby!"

He made a fist in her hair, held his breath. And then he felt her muscles seize him, climax around her. God, he'd never felt . . . he threw his head back, ground his teeth, clenched his jaw and broke into a million fragmented pieces. His knees buckled and he collapsed on top of her, gasping for breath.

Natalie was still in the throes of the most passionate climax she'd ever experienced. Her body shuddered, trembled, reveling in the weight of him.

Jake rolled to his side, hauling her on top of him, his hands moving restlessly up and down her back. His chest was like a bellows beneath hers; they both were desperately dragging in air and expelling it in quaking sighs. It was long moments before either of them could speak.

He lifted his head off the mattress and dipped his chin to look at her sprawled on him. He had to clear his throat. "You are something, you know it?"

She propped her chin on her folded hands and smiled at him. Her eyes were drowsy with passion; her lips were swollen and ripe. "How so?"

He let his head fall back, rolled it from side to side. "How? So neat, so feminine, nurturing and womanly. So passionate, so exciting and earthy."

She made a satisfied little sound and rubbed her cheek against him. "Thank you."

He combed through her hair, lifting the gold and silver strands and letting them fall again. Her hands strayed over his chest, memorizing the shape and placement of his muscles. The clock on the bedside table ticked away the minutes.

"Can you reach the covers?" he asked, his voice slow and sleepy.

"Umm." She felt around her feet and yanked the sheet and blanket up over them. They slept like exhausted children.

At 3:00 a.m., Annabelle woke up for her bottle. Natalie got up and put on the shirt she had worn earlier. She changed and fed and burped the baby, yawning all the time. Annabelle went right back to sleep.

When Natalie returned to her bedroom, however, Jake was waiting. With a grin he lifted a corner of the covers so she could climb back in beside him.

Chapter 10

Morning dawned too soon. Annabelle awoke again at seven.

Natalie reluctantly but carefully lifted the warm arm that curved around her waist and rolled silently out of bed. She picked up the shirt she'd discarded earlier. As she slid her arms into the sleeves, she paused for a last longing look at the large masculine form in her bed.

It had been an astonishing night. She'd been married to a man she loved very much, but Joseph had never brought her to the level of arousal she'd encountered with Jake. She hadn't known she could be swept away so completely, so totally, that she could be so eclipsed by passion and sensation.

Jake rolled to his back, twisting the sheet across his hard body. His chin was shadowed with an overnight growth of beard; his hair was rumpled. But the lines of tension on his brow, around his mouth, lines that he'd worn for months, had eased. He was sleeping soundly. And he looked altogether sexy.

She went into the second bedroom and picked up the baby, who quieted for a moment at the sound of her voice. Natalie changed her diaper, gave her another bottle, played with her for a few minutes and finally put her down in the playpen.

She planned to sneak a quick shower while the baby was happy.

She tiptoed back into her room, opened a drawer, withdrew what she needed and closed it silently. She couldn't mute the click of the closet door, though.

At the sound, Jake sat up suddenly in bed, the sheet falling around his hips. "What?" he said, tense and disoriented. When he saw her his body relaxed and he scraped a hand down his face. "God, I haven't slept like that in a long time."

"I didn't mean to wake you. I was going to hop in the shower."

The white shirt dipped in front and back to cover her modestly, but the sides left her beautiful thighs bare. He thought she looked luscious. "Why don't you hop back in here instead?" he asked with a slow smile. He held up the covers invitingly as he'd done at 3:00 a.m.

"I can't, Jake," she answered with a real regret. Her expression was diverting—half pout, half smile. "The baby is awake."

Jake decided it was for the best. He'd lost control last night, and that had scared the hell out of him. He'd never lost control under the force of passion.

And now he was surprised at the frustration he felt when she refused to come back to bed. They'd made love three times. He would have thought the edge would be off his appetite for her. But it wasn't. If anything he was more eager than ever.

"She's in the playpen in the living room," Natalie went on, unaware of his thoughts. "I thought I'd bathe while she's dry and full. Neither condition will last very long."

"Okay." He was still sitting there when she disappeared into the bathroom. In a moment he heard the sound of the shower. At last he flung the covers off and got to his feet. He dressed quickly in his wrinkled clothes.

When he was ready he knocked on the bathroom door. "Natalie? I'm going upstairs to dress," he called out.

He thought he heard a response. As he left, he paused in the living room to look down at the baby. Natalie had stretched something that looked like a miniature gym across the rails and she seemed to be batting at it.

All activity ceased when he came into view. The baby became very still, her wide dark eyes fixed on him. Lisa's eyes, he saw again. She smiled, showing her toothless gums, but he had already left.

He was back in an hour, showered and shaved and dressed in clean jeans and a white cotton sweater. He carried a bag from the doughnut shop. "Breakfast," he said, holding up the bag.

Natalie had been equally fresh after her shower, but her shirt had already been splashed when she gave Annabelle her bath. It had dried but was wrinkled. "Good. I'm hungry," said Natalie, putting out her hand for the bag.

"Me, too." He held the bag out of her reach and curled an arm around her waist. He took his time giving her a long kiss that left her breathless. Then he handed her the bag.

"Is this a reward?" she asked with a wry smile.

"Of course," he said with an unrepentant grin.

They ate sticky buns and drank coffee and shared the Sunday papers while Annabelle had a morning nap. She woke around twelve and had a bottle. Not long after that she was ready for an afternoon nap.

"Is that all she does?" asked Jake when Natalie returned from putting Annabelle down. He had followed her into the kitchen where she assembled the things she would need to prepare formula. "Eat and sleep?"

Natalie caught her breath. It was the first time he had asked a direct question about his daughter, the first sign of interest or curiosity he'd shown. "Yes, pretty much," she answered, striving to keep her attitude light. "She's beginning to stay awake for intervals, but they don't last long."

"During the next interval, I'll assemble the crib Mary wanted put up."

"Oh, drat. I forgot about that. We'll have to move some stuff. I guess my computer will have to be brought into the living room," she said.

Jake came up behind her and put his hands on her hips. "In the meantime, an afternoon nap sounds like a wholesome, healthy thing to do. Why don't you and I have one, too?" His hands slid around to rest warmly on her stomach and he nibbled on her neck.

Natalie felt the shivers begin. She bent her head to give him better access. "Wholesome, huh? Mmm, that feels good," she said huskily. "Are you sure a nap is what you had in mind?"

He chuckled and bit her earlobe. One hand came up to squeeze her breast lightly. "Well, for what I had in mind, you take off your clothes and get into bed. Does that qualify?"

Natalie turned in his arms and raised her arms to wrap them around his neck. "It's close enough."

Natalie struggled to keep from laughing and put her hands over Annabelle's ears. "Jake, such language! And in front of the baby."

"Whoever wrote these instructions was either an idiot or a sadist," he complained.

It was early evening and he'd been working on the crib for an hour. But Jake's discomfiture was a result of more than the length of the job or instruction booklet that had been taped to the long box.

While he had been grappling with the baby bed, Natalie was sitting cross-legged in the middle of the guest room bed with the pajama-clad baby propped against her stomach. Natalie talked to the child nonstop, teasing, baby talk, that grated on his nerves for some reason.

But the thing that bothered him the most were Annabelle's dark eyes. They seemed to follow every move he made.

He returned to his task, reaching for the screwdriver and an oddly shaped piece of metal that had been left over. "This must be the piece I was looking for that raises and lowers the rail." He frowned and glanced at the booklet again. "Although it bears absolutely no resemblance to the picture."

Annabelle began to squirm and whimper. Natalie uncrossed her long legs and got to her feet. "I guess she's ready for her next bottle."

He was relieved when they left the room.

A short time later, Natalie laid the baby in her bed, arranged the crib bumper around the edge of the mattress and tied the small strips to the rails. "There. Isn't that nice, Annabelle? You have lots of room to stretch your legs."

Jake packed his tools away. He picked up the extra screws and brads, the useless booklet and various assorted unidentifiable fragments. He put them all back in the plastic bag they had come in. "What do you want to do with this big box?" He was ready to get out of here.

She turned from where she was leaning over the crib. "The box? Gosh, I don't know. I guess I should save it for when we move."

He looked at the box, then at the closet door. "If I laid it on its side it should fit into the closet."

"That's fine. I don't use that closet, anyway."

He opened the louvered doors.

At the same moment, Natalie remembered what was in that closet. She straightened with a jerk and whirled in time to see his whole body stiffen.

"What the hell—"

"Jake, please. I can explain," she said in a rush.

When he turned, his eyes were filled with the wild, tumultuous pain that she hadn't seen since the funeral. In his hands was the portrait. Lisa's beautiful face smiled at them.

He seemed to have grown taller and menacing in his anger. He spoke in a caustic, grating voice. "What is there to explain? I gave orders that this portrait was to be destroyed. Was this Andrew's idea or yours?"

"It was my idea. Andrew didn't know." She clenched her fingers together at her waist. "It's a beautiful painting. I thought that after you had a chance to think, to heal a bit, you might regret destroying it.''

His broad shoulders rounded slightly as he stared at the smiling woman. Slowly his anger was replaced by a more anguished emotion. "How could you—after—I can't believe you would do this to me, Natalie," he said in a low, broken voice.

When he raised his head she saw a parade of expressions cross his face, the most obvious of which was his pain. She saw the guilt, too. They had spent the last night and day making love to each other. Now he couldn't look at her. She had destroyed more than a blossoming relationship. She had destroyed his trust.

She shook her head. Her vision blurred. Oh, God! Why hadn't she found another place for the portrait? Why hadn't she remembered in time?

He set the frame down carefully, propping it against the wall. Then he shoved the box in the closet and shut the door. "I'll see to it myself," he said.

"Jake, don't do this. If you don't want the portrait let me have it. For Annabelle. Someday she may want to know who her mother was." She was speaking desperately, in a rush.

"*You* are her mother," he said in an awful, dead voice. He picked up the portrait and headed for the back door.

"Jake, please. Please," Natalie cried, going after him.

He had to set the portrait down again to open the door. She grasped his arm but he shook her off and turned, his eyes like icy steel. "No!"

She let her hand fall to her side. Under that gaze, she was as cold as death.

"It was too soon. I knew that. But I couldn't seem to keep my hands off you. Now I have to live with it."

If it hadn't been for Mary, Natalie would have left Savannah immediately. When the older woman arrived on Monday morning, she knew that something was terribly wrong. Patiently she got much, though not all, of the story out of Natalie.

Mary managed to talk some practical sense into her. "You want to run? Okay, run. But I think you're a coward. You're in love with him, aren't you?"

Natalie nodded miserably.

"Then be patient. Give him some more space. He can't forgive you right now. But there will come a time when he'll see that you're right. Besides, the adoption isn't final. You have to stay here. Now you sit yourself down in front of that computer and get to work."

Patience. She wondered.

Chapter 11

Natalie left the French doors ajar so she could hear the baby and walked out into the garden where daylight lingered. A late-afternoon shower had left the air clean and amazingly fresh for August. She ambled along the paths, through the roses with their rich, heady scent. A comforting breeze skimmed her bare shoulders. The off-the-shoulder cotton dress was as cool as its white color. The lightweight fabric of the skirt brushed against her bare legs.

Summer had arrived. The garden had become her favorite place, especially at this time of day. She could relax here, listening to the sounds of the crickets, the birds settling for the night, the rustle of the breeze through the leaves, watching as the darkness slowly sucked the color from the garden.

It was becoming a habit, this waiting for Jake at the end of the day. A habit she was loath to break, no matter how smart it would be to do so.

At first, they had barely spoken, usually just a casual, "Hello, how are you?" At first, he came through the gate and went directly upstairs. But the contact, no matter how small, was a contact with him. He was working long hours; the expansion was in full swing. He was thin and haunted looking.

Then once or twice he hesitated, lingered for a short time. If the weather didn't cooperate, if it was too humid and hot or if it rained, she was anxious and edgy until she saw him again.

Natalie broke off a white peony with a soft pink center and put it behind her ear. Her manuscript was complete; she had mailed it two weeks ago. She longed to talk to him about it, about how proud she was of the finished product, and how she was chewing-her-nails nervous. What if it wasn't as good as she thought? But he wasn't ready for that kind of conversation.

Like the Southern summer, the time they spent together had evolved into a period of relaxed and easy, slow and warm comradeship. It was a time of trying to redevelop trust.

And then one day just a couple of weeks ago, she realized that, like the temperature of a Southern summer, the temperature between them was rising steadily. It was a time of growing awareness, a tense and dangerous time.

She recognized the signs in him, signs of physical awareness, because they so perfectly mirrored her own. The casual touch that lingered a bit too long, the meeting of eyes that made her forget what she was going to say, the sudden sideways glance that caught him focusing on her breasts, her legs. When that happened one or the other of them would usually find an excuse to break off the contact.

She knew she should put an end to this daily tête-à-tête. She should decide to have other plans one evening. Ask Mary to stay late, go to a movie, out to dinner, anything that would send a clear signal. But she kept postponing that.

He had never mentioned the portrait again, of course. And neither had she.

She had to remind herself, constantly it seemed, that they were two very wary people who had hurt each other, living in close quarters for a limited time. There were too many walls, too many hurdles between them. Lisa. Jake's reserve when he was around Annabelle.

As far as Natalie knew he had not touched the baby since the day she was born. That worried her. She'd caught him looking at Annabelle with a curious light in his eyes, but he'd never asked to hold her or shown any affection. Natalie had realized weeks ago that since the adoption was final now, Annabelle was legally her daughter. But Annabelle would someday need this man in her life.

Her feelings scared Natalie for more reasons than the obvious ones. Her agent had called to tell her she'd sent the manuscript to an editor at a publishing house. He'd promised a quick decision. Once Natalie had heard from them, she would have to leave. She would have no excuse for staying longer.

And excuses were what had kept her here, kept her waiting each evening for Jake's arrival, kept her from having other plans. Excuses. And the rise in temperature.

Again Natalie tried to convince herself to be patient.

Suddenly she heard his car. Despite her good intentions she couldn't control the anticipation that engulfed her. She smoothed her skirt, touched her hair, moistened her lips.

He entered through the gate and closed it behind him. "Hi," he said softly when he saw her. As he came down the path, she noticed that his white shirt was wrinkled, his tie was pulled down and his shirt unbuttoned. His jacket was hooked over his shoulder on two fingers. He looked tired and unbearably sexy.

"Rough day?" she asked.

Instead of answering, Jake came to a halt in front of her and studied her for a silent heartbeat. His free hand rested lightly on his hip. His hooded eyes revealed nothing.

Then he smiled, held out his hand. Without a thought, she laid her hand in his and he grasped her fingers firmly. She felt the tingling all the way to her toes. He pulled her to her feet and wrapped his arms around her waist, bringing her softness into alignment with his hard body. She looked at him with raised brows and circled his waist, but loosely, only for balance. Not holding on to him. Not leaning on him. So she told herself.

He rocked them gently from side to side. His coat slapped lightly against her bottom. "Hell of a day," he said huskily. "The construction foreman broke his leg, and the longshoremen are threatening to strike. The steel that's supposed to go out tomorrow is caught on a railroad siding somewhere in Alabama, so it doesn't matter a hell of a lot. How was yours?"

She smiled and attempted a casual shrug, which wasn't easy in this position. Their clothes rustled slightly; she could feel her breasts swell at the contact with his hard chest. "I would have said my day was very busy, until I heard about yours."

Her last word caught, came out on a puff of air as she felt his growing arousal nudge the juncture of her thighs.

His eyes darkened; he tossed the coat away and cupped her bottom in his big hands. "Yes." His voice was rough. "Yes, I want you again. Quite desperately, as you can tell. Seeing you waiting here for me—right or wrong, I want you." He bent his head to her bare shoulder. His lips moved to her neck, while his hands pressed her hips closer, moving their bodies together. "I remember everything about the night we made love. I know your skin is like silk. Sometimes, when I see you in the fading light like this, I'm shocked by my own fantasies. I want to throw you down and rip off your clothes. I want to touch your beautiful breasts, kiss them. I want your gorgeous long legs wrapped around me, your nails digging into my back. I want to bury myself in you again, deeply, and hear you moan."

"Jake!" His name was a stunned whisper on her lips, escaping just before his mouth covered hers. His tongue drove into her mouth, sweeping over her teeth, tasting, exploring.

"Jake." She wrenched her head to the side. "No."

"Isn't this what you want, too?"

She could not deny the obvious. "It wouldn't be right. Not like this. There is still too much—"

"It isn't right that we should please each other? That we should have warmth and understanding and physical satisfaction with each other?"

"No, you said it yourself. It's still too soon. Maybe it always will be."

"Do you know what next week is?" he demanded.

She hesitated, thought for a minute. Then she said, "Yes."

"The anniversary of Lisa's death," he said, just so she would be sure.

Her head fell forward. "Yes," she whispered. "And she always will be here. If it isn't her birthday or your anniversary—"

He interrupted, changing the subject, confusing her. "Do you feel guilty for making love with me?"

"I didn't at first. But...yes. I suppose I do."

"I made you feel that way." He sighed. Suddenly all the tension drained out of him, leaving him weak. "You're still feeling guilty over something else, too, aren't you? The scene in the hospital when Joseph was sick.

"Natalie, we both know that nothing would have come of that, ever. If either of them were alive today we would never have betrayed them. But you know I wanted you that day I held you in my arms. Just as you know right now." His voice took on a wry tone. Despite her good intentions she was listening.

"I felt the guilt, too. Don't think I didn't. And it was hell for a while. I couldn't look Lisa in the eye. And all we'd done was hold each other. We hadn't even come close to being unfaithful."

"We'd thought about it, though."

"Yes, and don't you see? That was our strength. We're grown-ups. Instant gratification is not an imperative need, not if it would hurt someone we loved. We would never have done anything to distress them, either of us. But they're gone now."

"Are they?" All the fight seemed to go out of her at once; she slumped against him. "You're still set against having a family again, aren't you?"

"Don't make me out to be some kind of emotional cripple, Natalie," he cut her off shortly. But he didn't release her. "Yes, it's going to be hell getting past the anniversary of her death. Just as it was rough getting past her birthday and Christmas, and every other day that was special to us." His voice dropped to a low purr. "But I am healing, Natalie. I put pressure on the wound too quickly, and you were caught in the aftermath. But I've begun to want to live again. You knew Lisa for years. You should know that would be the way she'd want it. She wouldn't want me to crawl into the grave with her—" This time he cut himself off.

He turned from her then and picked up his coat from the chair where she'd been sitting. He was almost at the steps when he heard her say his name. Very softly.

He stopped, then retraced his steps. When he reached her side he raised her chin, making her face him so he could look deeply into her eyes. Before they could speak, though, the telephone in the apartment rang.

Natalie uttered silent curses all the way into the house. This was the first time they had talked—really talked—in months. And the telephone had to interrupt.

He followed her, smiling at her frown of annoyance as she grabbed the receiver. Suddenly she put on her business look. It must be the agent from New York. A smile spread across her face, lighting her blue eyes. "He really wants it? Of course, I'll be glad to do revisions. *How* much? My God. I'll wait for his call tomorrow."

She hung up and held on to the phone for a minute as though for support. "Jake," she breathed. "You won't believe this!"

A few days later Jake called. It was nearly 9:00 a.m.; Natalie was sitting at the computer, finishing the last of the revisions the editor had requested.

"Could you take a few hours off?" he asked when she answered the phone. "I thought we might drive out to the docks. You haven't seen the addition and it's almost complete. We could stop somewhere for lunch on the way back."

Her heart soared. She wanted to dance and shout. But she hesitated. "I should be through here in about half an hour." Her attention was drawn to the baby, who sat on the floor in her infant seat, kicking away and making bubbles. "But, Jake, Mary isn't coming today. I'd have to take Annabelle."

"That's okay," he said, surprising her.

Natalie eyed the baby warily. Annabelle was teething. She had been drooling like an open spigot, all over everything, and she was occasionally fussy. Natalie bit at her lower lip. It might not be a good idea. This was the first time Jake had shown any interest in being around his child; she would hate for the day to be a disaster.

Before she could refuse, he'd taken her acceptance for granted. "I'll shower and be down in thirty minutes."

"Make it forty-five."

While Natalie stood under the pulsing spray, she thought to herself that Jake was about to get a dose of all the things entailed in taking a baby anywhere. She just hoped Annabelle wasn't too out of sorts.

She dried herself and reached for the bottle of lotion scented with jasmine. While she dressed in cool white city shorts and a red blouse she talked to Annabelle. "Now I want you to be a very good girl today, precious. This is an important outing. Understand? Do you want some lotion? Okay." She spread a dab on Annabelle's arm. "Mmm, you smell so good."

Annabelle laughed. Maybe it would be all right.

When Jake knocked on the door, Natalie greeted him casually, determined to be matter-of-fact about this. She handed him the diaper bag and her purse. She carried the backpack and the baby. "We'll have to go in my car or switch the car seat."

A couple of hours later, when Natalie dragged in, she was so depressed she could have wept. Jake hadn't complained, but he'd quickly agreed when she suggested having lunch another time. He'd also shown concern, worrying that the baby might be sick. That was a hopeful sign, wasn't it?

Hell, no, thought Natalie. *Quit fooling yourself. Just be grateful that the check for your book is enough for you to live wherever you choose.* When they'd pulled into the garage, he had paused only long enough to help her get the baby's equipment inside. Then he'd taken off in his own car.

Their own relationship was in the dust. Now it seemed there was no hope that he would ever have one with his daughter, either.

The day had been as big a disaster as Natalie had feared. The baby had cried and fussed and gnawed on her fingers and cried again, until Natalie had finally asked him to take them home.

Now Annabelle whimpered as Natalie laid her down for a nap. Then she started to scream. Her poor little gums were flaming red. There was nothing to do but to hold her, rock her and listen to her cries. And wipe the tears away.

After Jake dropped them off he drove to the cemetery. He'd been visiting here regularly. It was peaceful to walk under the towering oak trees with their spotty cloaks of Spanish moss.

When he reached the grave site he stood with his head bent, looking down for a long time. A year ago he had stood at this same spot. He'd thought his life was over. He had waited a long time for a woman like Lisa, a bright happy creature, someone as different from the rest of his life as day was to night.

"Lisa, my love, I think the time has come to say goodbye. To get on with my life. What do you think, sweetheart?"

Suddenly, without warning, he felt a surge of the sun's warmth on his head, pressure on his shoulder, like a message. A revelation, a blessing?

He didn't know. But the weight he'd carried around for more than a year was minimized within the blink of an eye. He straightened his shoulders and breathed deeply. He smiled. "Thanks," he said softly, and then headed back to the car.

He wasn't sure what would happen with Natalie. Perhaps, as she said, they would always be friendly but not intimate. They both had their ghosts to contend with. They were both wary because they had been left alone once too often. Too often to lean on, depend on, or need another person for their own happiness and survival.

Or perhaps they would become more than friends. Oddly, the other day, the day her agent had called, he'd begun to consider alternatives. As soon as she had voiced the misgivings she felt, he began to wonder. But then she'd announced the sum of money she was going to get for her book. And they wanted another as soon as she could write it.

With that much money Natalie could go anywhere. Why should she want to tie herself to someone who had given her nothing but grief?

Chapter 12

"Come to New York? Now?" exclaimed Natalie into the telephone. It had rung while she was heating the baby's bottle. "But I just finished the revisions yesterday. I haven't mailed them yet."

"Within the week. The sooner the better. Bring the revisions with you," answered the agent. "The publisher wants this contract signed and the book in production, Natalie. He wants a big splash next year at the American Booksellers Association's national meeting. This is a substantial amount of money. I think it would be worth the trip."

Natalie put her fingers to her other ear to shut out the sound of Annabelle's fussing. "Look, Alan, let me finish feeding the baby, and I'll call you back."

She went to Annabelle and scooped her up. "Sorry, sweetheart. Are you starving? Mommy's sorry." Balancing the baby on one hip, she took the bottle out of the warmer and tested the temperature.

Damn, now it was too hot. She turned on the cold water and let it splash on the bottle while she jiggled the baby on her hip, trying to calm her. "Just a minute now. You don't want to burn your tongue."

Annabelle's screams had reached a crescendo by the time the bottle cooled down. She popped the nipple into the baby's mouth. The screams ceased with a suddenness that, as always, surprised her. She chuckled, cuddled the baby and reentered the living room. The rocker was piled high with clean clothes so she settled on the sofa with a sigh.

Annabelle's fingers, which had been clenched into angry little fists, began to relax. She flexed them around the bottle, moving it from side to side. She wasn't strong enough yet to take the bottle away from her mother, but it probably wouldn't be long. After a few minutes, the edge was off her hunger and she paused briefly, smiling around the nipple.

Natalie heard the key in the door and smiled down at Annabelle. "Here's Mary," she told the baby, who sucked greedily, her cheeks rosy and tearstained.

Natalie laughed. "Look at this," she said when she heard footsteps approach. She cherished these moments. If she couldn't feed this child herself, at least she could hold her to her breast, close and warm, while she took her bottle. "A few minutes ago Miss Priss was crying as though her world was coming to an end."

Silence greeted her words. She looked up into Jake's gray eyes. He was dressed for work, his dark blue suit perfectly pressed, his tie neatly knotted at the collar of his white shirt. "Oh." The word came out on a soft puff of surprise. "I thought you were Mary."

"She just called me. She'd been trying to reach you, but your line was busy."

"Yes, I had a call. I'm sorry you were disturbed."

"It's okay. I was ready to leave for work. Mary will be a half hour late. She's waiting for the plumber to finish."

"Thank you for taking the message." She couldn't look away. For some reason he looked more rested, more relaxed. Obviously he had recovered from the trip with Annabelle yesterday. She held her breath, waiting for him to mention it.

But he didn't say anything. He simply stood there, watching her.

"The call was from New York. The publisher who is buying the book wants me to fly up there for a day or two."

Jake nodded, thoughtfully. "When are you going?"

"I'm not sure if I can arrange it. I'd have to talk to Mary first."

"She wouldn't mind moving back in for a few days," he assured her with an easy smile. "You know that."

She studied him for a minute. At last she made a decision. "I'm concerned about this flu that's going around. Would you—" She broke off. She was about to take a big chance and it made her nervous.

"Would I, what?"

Unconsciously she had removed the bottle to gesture with her hand. Annabelle squirmed, and when that didn't work, she squawked, immediately reminding her mother of the main objective here.

Natalie replaced the nipple in the baby's mouth and Annabelle relaxed again. "Umm . . . would you consider looking in on them every now and then, just to make sure they're both all right?'' She released the request in a rush.

''Of course, I'll check on them,'' he agreed without hesitation. ''They'll be fine. Don't let that keep you from going.''

Natalie breathed easily again and smiled at him. It was the first time she had asked Jake to take any responsibility for the baby. ''Thank you, Jake.''

''Well, I've got to get to work.'' He didn't move. ''Will you be leaving today?''

''Today?'' The idea surprised her. ''I suppose if I could get a flight out...'' She didn't want to leave, not now. She needed time with him. ''The sooner I go, the sooner I can get—back.'' She almost said, *Get home.*

His eyes narrowed as though he knew what she'd been about to say. ''That's true.'' He rocked on his heels and looked down at the floor between his feet. Then he raised his warm, smoky eyes to hers.

Holding her gaze, he leaned forward, planting his hands on each side of her shoulders. He lowered his head until their lips were inches apart. Though he was careful not to crush the baby in her arms or touch her anywhere else, she could feel the heat of his body. It sent her own temperature climbing.

''Call me at the office before you leave, will you?'' he asked in a husky voice. His breath smelled of mint. Then he closed the gap. His mouth was warm, his tongue was slick as he tasted the inside of her upper lip.

She was suddenly weak and limp. When he broke off the kiss, her pulse thundered in her ears. ''Yes, yes, I will,'' she breathed.

She felt him start, saw his eyes widen as he straightened. She looked down at the baby, whose fists were flailing. Her fine brows were drawn together in a frown of annoyance. "Did she punch you? I'm sorry. She caught me on the jaw the other day."

"Good grief," he said, looking down at the baby for a minute. "Call me," he repeated. Then he left.

The contracts were duly examined and signed and Natalie was given a check. She took a taxi back to the Plaza Hotel. The editor was taking her and her agent out to dinner tonight, and tomorrow morning she would get the earliest return flight. They couldn't believe that she didn't want to stay over an extra day and shop, but she couldn't wait to get back to the peace and quiet of Savannah.

She was amazed how much she missed Jake and Annabelle and Mary. The scene in the garden the other night, and the kiss he'd given her the morning she left, had stirred hope once again in her breast. As she opened the door to her room, she heard the telephone ringing. She dropped her purse and the file containing her copy of the contract on the bed.

"Hello."

A unidentifiably hoarse voice answered. "Natalie, this is Mary."

Natalie's heart skipped painfully. "Annabelle?"

"The baby's fine," Mary reassured her quickly. "Natalie, I hate to do this to you, but I'm afraid I might be coming down with the bug that's going around. I haven't felt well all day."

Natalie glanced at her watch. Four-thirty. "I'll phone the airport and call you right back, Mary."

"Are you finished with your business? I hate this, honey. Wait."

"Mary?" She heard voices on the other end of the line. "Mary?"

"Hi, Natalie." It was Jake.

The sound of his deep voice was enough to make her knees weak, but she was also relieved. She sank down on the edge of the bed and gripped the receiver.

"Oh, Jake, I'm so glad you're there. Mary says she's sick."

"She doesn't look too good," Jake admitted. She could hear Mary remonstrate with him.

"But don't worry," he went on. "You finish your business. I'll take care of things on this end."

"Oh, thank you, Jake," she said in a rush. "I'll be home as soon as I can get a flight. But it probably will be tomorrow."

"Okay." He stopped. "Natalie?"

"Yes, Jake?"

"I miss you."

She squeezed her eyes shut. "I miss you, too," she murmured. "I'll see you as soon as I can." Dear God, she prayed, please, please don't let this mess things up.

The airline couldn't guarantee her a position on the last flight of the day, but they offered to put her on standby, and she decided to take the chance. She called the editor and her agent, explaining the situation. Then she called the desk to have her bill ready. She tossed her things into the suitcase. Twenty minutes after Mary's call, she was on the way to the airport.

Jake made a third trip from the apartment, loaded with necessities. According to Mary. Playpen, high chair, mountains of clothes, towels—babies, it seemed, couldn't be dried with the same towels adults used diapers, toys, vitamins, bottles, food and formula.

Keeping her belly full would be the easy part, he decided. All he had to do was open a can or a jar. Or mix the cereal with a little milk.

The last trip would be to bring the child herself. God, what had he gotten himself into? Taking care of a baby was as alien to him as flying without wings. His ears rang with instructions and warnings.

Hell, he hadn't even been *around* a baby since Joseph had been born.

He called a taxi for Mary and picked up the last of Annabelle's paraphernalia, a fat pink shoulder bag that held extra diapers. Or was it formula? "You get home and into bed," he ordered. "I don't want to catch that bug, either."

He acted more confident than he felt when he slung the strap over his shoulder and plucked Annabelle off the quilt where she'd been playing. He strode to the door with the baby in his arms, pausing only long enough to say, "Call me if you need anything."

Mary didn't come near him, but she didn't have to. She simply stopped him with a look. "Thank you, Jake," she said quietly.

They both knew that there was more to the platitude than mere gratitude. But he looked at her with mock severity. "You'd better not thank me yet." The baby squirmed and looked up at him curiously. "You, either," he told her.

"I'll have the phone right beside my bed. Just call if you have any questions."

Annabelle looked over the big man's shoulder to where Mary stood waving bye-bye. She raised her hand, but the door shut before she could wave back. She thought about crying, then decided against it. She could always cry later if she needed to, but this promised to be an adventure. She'd seen this person around, but he'd never paid much attention to her. He seemed to be a friend of her mommy's, though, so she guessed it was okay.

She sat on his arm and hooked her hand in his collar. He took her outside and up some stairs. A tree hung over the steps, and she stretched out her arm to grab for the leaves, but he was moving too fast. All she got was a touch. She looked at her fingers to see if any color came off on them.

The man took her into a room where she'd never been before. She looked around. Wow. There were a lot of things to play with, bright shiny things she'd never seen before. There was a picture of a pretty lady on the wall. She was smiling.

He put her in the playpen, laying her on her back. His big hands were gentle. "Well, kid, I guess we're going to get to know each other," he said. He picked up a ring of big plastic keys and dangled them in her face.

She'd outgrown keys a long time ago. She snatched them away from him and threw them to the other side of the playpen.

"Okay, you choose," he said.

She looked around the confined space at her toys. But nothing caught her fancy. She'd rather look at him right now. She put two fingers in her mouth.

He had backed away. He sat on a sofa and crossed one leg with his ankle resting on his knee. He spread his arms along the sofa back and continued to stare, studying her as if she were a creature with whom he was unfamiliar.

Why didn't he smile? Everybody smiled at her. "Ooo," said Annabelle through her fingers.

He wiggled his foot. "I didn't plan on this, you know," he said. "But we'll survive."

"Urgh." She rolled over from her back to her stomach and squirmed her way to the mesh barrier. She put her face into the netting until her mouth and nose were pushed grotesquely out of shape.

The sight evidently alarmed him. "Hey, don't do that," he said.

She pulled her face back and laughed. Then she grasped the mesh and, after a few false starts, struggled to her knees.

He looked as if he was impressed. "I didn't know you could do that."

I can do lots of things you don't know about, thought Annabelle. "Arrr," she said. She stretched her arm up until she could reach the rail, planted one foot flat on the floor of the playpen, dragged the other one forward and stood, teetering dangerously. She peered at him from over the top rail and laughed again, so he could see her new tooth.

She knew she was sort of shaky, but he didn't have to watch her with such a nervous eye. "That's very nice," he said.

Very nice? It's actually wonderful, is what it is, man, thought Annabelle. She frowned, though. If she could just figure out how to get down it would be even better. Her mommy or Mary was usually there to help when she got stuck like this. Let's see...

"Why don't you sit back down before you fall?" he suggested.

The words had no sooner left his mouth than she was surprised into losing her grip. She sat down hard on her bottom. He leaned forward, concerned.

She was too well padded to be seriously hurt, but she might as well teach him a lesson. As he watched in dismay, she slowly extended her lower lip beyond her upper; she wrinkled up her eyebrows, looking pitiful. Water welled in her eyes.

And she spread her arms toward him.

Suddenly the man's face took on the strangest look, like he was wounded.

Bad.

It hurt her to see him. She pulled her lip back in. *No, no, don't look like that. I'm sorry.*

Before she could smile again to let him know she wasn't seriously injured, she was plucked from the playpen and wrapped very tightly in his big arms. He held her against his solid chest. His whole body was trembling; she could hear his heart under her ear. It was going very fast.

He rocked her back and forth and whispered several of her names. She wasn't sure yet what her most important name was. Her mommy called her Precious, and Mary called her Sweetheart. Sometimes they called her Annabelle. Now this person, who had first called her Kid, kept saying Annabelle and Ohoney over and over.

It seemed to make him feel better to hold her like this, so she stayed still for a long time. It felt good. His arms were warm and secure; she had the feeling that even a big wind wouldn't budge him.

Finally she just had to squirm.

He pulled back, and she smiled at him. That awful look wasn't gone, but it wasn't as bad as before.

"Ahhh," she cooed. There was water on his face; she tried to slap it away.

He caught her hand and kissed it. The hair that was on his mouth tickled. She giggled and pulled at the hair.

He carefully untangled her fingers and kissed her hand again. "You, Annabelle, are full of mischief," he said with an unsteady chuckle.

There, again, another new name. Mischief. That one sounded familiar, though. She wondered where she'd heard it before.

"Do you know who I am?" he asked after a minute. "Silly question, of course you don't. I'm your daddy. Can you say 'daddy'?"

"Umm," said Annabelle.

"Good try."

She smiled.

"What a pretty smile," he said softly, smiling himself. "You look like Lisa when you smile."

Who is Lisa? Annabelle wondered. She raised her eyebrows and made her mouth into an *O*.

He stood with her in his arms and walked to the fireplace. "This pretty lady is Lisa. She's—" He hesitated. "She isn't here anymore but, thanks to your mommy, we have this picture to remember her by. Someday your mommy and I will tell you all about Lisa."

She stretched out her hand to pat the picture.

Natalie went all through the apartment. Then she looked toward the ceiling. He must have taken her upstairs. *Oh, Lord, Annabelle, I hope you've been a good girl.*

Everything seemed quiet. She had an idea. She went to get her key ring. Then she went to the stairs that led to the main part of the house. The door hadn't been opened since Lisa had locked it a year ago.

She put her head through. And heard his voice coming from the kitchen, growling, "Your mommy must be a lot better at this than I am."

Annabelle gurgled. Something hit the floor.

Oh, no. Natalie stepped through the door and headed for the kitchen where she came to an astonished halt.

Both Jake and Annabelle looked as though they had taken a bath in baby fruit. Plums, evidently. Purple stuff was in her hair and his, all over the tray of the high chair, her face, his shirt. The baby looked healthy enough, but Natalie could have cried.

Jake was bending down to pick up a spoon from the floor when he caught sight of her in his peripheral vision. He swung around. "You're home."

"Yes. Need some help?" she said brightly.

Instead of answering, he rose in one smooth motion, came to her and hauled her up against him. His mouth came crashing down on hers. "Thank you," he said when he lifted his head. His eyes were blazing, his hand shook as he brushed her hair off her cheek. "Oh, God, Natalie, thank you."

Natalie tried to soothe him. "You're welcome. I was lucky to get a flight out. I'm really sorry you were left with this Jake. I'll get her out of here right now."

He looked taken aback. "Annabelle's not going anywhere. And neither are you."

She faltered. "You said—"

His smile would have melted the statue on the waterfront. Her knees were no contest.

"I said, thank you. Thank you for being patient with me when I was so full of bitterness. I was willing to throw away everything important in my life. Thank you for telling Mac that neither of us would consider outside adoption."

"I didn't know you knew about that."

He went on as though she hadn't spoken. "Thank you, my love, for fighting me when I was acting like an ass. Thank you for not giving up on me."

Her heart began to flower under the warmth and love in his eyes, but she was cautious. "Jake, I don't understand."

"Let me see if I can explain it to you without making myself seem any more blind and stupid than I am." He kept Natalie in the circle of his arms, but turned her until her back was against his chest and they both faced the baby.

Annabelle was watching with a pleased expression on her face. She swirled her palm in the goo on the tray. Then she gave her high-powered grin.

"I think Annabelle loves me," said Jake with quiet pleasure. "Though, God knows, I don't deserve it." He tilted her face up. His voice dropped an octave. "And I know I'm in love with you."

She looked at him over her shoulder. Her hand sought his where it lay at her waist. "You are?" she said weakly.

His voice was low and rough; his fingers entwined with hers and held on tight. "I put you through hell, and I will never be able to make that up to you. But I would like to spend the rest of my life trying, if you can forgive me."

"Oh, Jake, you have nothing to make up for. I forgave you a long time ago." Could this really be happening? she wondered as she turned in his arms and cradled his face between her hands. "You've given me Annabelle, you've given me a home and you've helped me tear down my own barriers. I love you, too." She raised herself on tiptoe and wrapped her arms around his neck.

The kiss was long and deep and full of exchanged promises. When he finally released her mouth, he rested his forehead against hers. "Do you think, although you are now rich and about to become famous, you might consider marrying me? Letting me become a legitimate part of this family?" He paused, his eyes dark with an abundance of love. "Let—let me learn to be a father?"

Could they make a life together along with their own ghosts? Natalie smiled at the thought. Yes, because their ghosts weren't the least bit forbidding. Joseph and Lisa must be smiling somewhere. They were both affectionate and warm and loving; this is what they would want, too. She was as sure of that as she was sure of anything.

"Jake—" She broke off, unable to believe that her dreams were going to come true, all of them, at last. She buried her face in his neck so he wouldn't see her tears. "I think we might consider it," she choked against his warm skin.

His arms tightened around her. "Oh, honey, I love you so much." He kissed her again, hungrily. He smelled of baby powder. She tasted plums.

They finished feeding Annabelle—together, amid much laughter. He asked dozens of questions about the baby. It seemed that he wanted to find out about everything he'd missed in fifteen minutes.

At one point during the questioning, Jake suddenly sobered. "There is one other thing we should talk about."

She was occupied in wiping Annabelle's chin and didn't look at him. "What's that?"

"The Reeds."

Her head whipped around; she caught her breath. She had not allowed her thoughts to dwell on them. "They won't approve, will they?"—

"Approve? I don't know. I hadn't thought about it," he said, dismissing her concern.

"Then what—?"

He grasped the back of her neck and gently began to massage her there. "At first, they were as cruel to you as I was, Natalie," he said softly. "But they're nice people. They've asked about you and the baby, and I'm sure they regret the way they acted. If you can forgive them as you're forgiving me, I think we should drive up to Charleston, take Annabelle with us. After all, they're her only grandparents."

Natalie felt the sting in the back of her eyes.

Jake misunderstood the tears that welled there. He caught her in the circle of his arms. "I'll be with you, my darling. I'll never let you down again, I swear it," he said earnestly. "If things get unpleasant, we'll come home."

"It isn't that," she said blinking hurriedly. "I'm not worried about facing the Reeds, certainly not with you there." She smiled. "I was just thinking what a magnificent man you are. I'm very lucky—"

He cut off the words with a hard kiss. "I'm the lucky one," he growled. Then he covered her lips again.

Annabelle banged on the tray and squawked impatiently.

Natalie laughed at the picture the three of them made. She had some plums on her face, but father and daughter were a real mess. "I think we all could use a bath," she suggested with a laugh.

Jake scooped Annabelle out of her high chair and reached for Natalie's hand. Natalie noticed, as they climbed the stairs, that their daughter looked very much at home in her father's arms.

"I've got a better idea. We'll bath Annabelle together. Then when she's in bed we'll have a bath, the two of us." He grinned down at her.

She swallowed a lump in her throat. She had thought never to see such happiness in his eyes again or to feel such happiness in her own heart.

They were on their knees at the edge of the bathtub, watching the baby splash. Natalie had kicked off her shoes and pulled the pins from her hair. Jake was nibbling at her neck, whispering a vivid description of all the decadent things they could to, later, in the tub.

"Jake!" Natalie blushed, which was ridiculous—she hadn't blushed in years.

Though she had loved Joseph, it was becoming quite clear that Jake was the more imaginative brother. She looked up at him with curious relish. "Can we really do all those things?"

"Yep," he said with a chuckle. "We might even invent a few more."

"It's a good thing the baby isn't old enough to understand what you were saying," admonished Natalie primly as she soaped the washcloth and scrubbed Annabelle's hands. "You would have a lot of explaining to do."

Annabelle laughed.

*   *   *   *   *

TAKE A WALK ON THE DARK SIDE OF LOVE

October is the shivery season, when chill winds blow and shadows walk the night. Come along with us into a haunting world where love and danger go hand in hand, where passions will thrill you and dangers will chill you. Come with us to

In this newest short story collection from Sihouette Books, three of your favorite authors tell tales just perfect for a spooky autumn night. Let Anne Stuart introduce you to "The Monster in the Closet," Helen R. Myers bewitch you with "Seawitch," and Heather Graham Pozzessere entice you with "Wilde Imaginings."

Silhouette Shadows™
Haunting a store near you this October.